If It Feels Good

If It Feels Good

Josh Jango

"Try Anything" book 2

CyberActive Media®
www.cyberactivemedia.com

Cover design: Al Teter.
Cover art copyright
©iStockPhoto® or ©Shutterstock.com®
Photos or art used for illustrative purposes only
and any person depicted in the cover art is a model.

Published in the United States by
CyberActive Media, PO Box 5031, Glacier, Washington 98244

ISBN 978-0-9834526-7-6

4 3 2

www.joshjango.com

for
Mark Von Wald

– Spirit Brother –

Special thanks to:
Bill Bramham *for his excellent suggestions for story developments throughout the novel, especially in the Jensen Beach portion, and for his invaluable input as a beta reader.*
Special thanks to:
Rick Bramham *for his perceptive and supportive suggestions regarding story developments, as well as his invaluable input as a beta reader.*

Chapter 1
HITCHHIKER

August 16, 1986 Saturday

THE STEADY RAIN wasn't the greatest for driving, but sunnier weather was on its way. Besides, the two young men were together. That was the important thing. As long as they had each other, everything else was secondary.

Ziggy and Josh had left St. Louis early that morning, heading east on the start of their first-anniversary vacation. They drove for a couple of hours, and then stopped for breakfast.

With their bellies full, and with coffee surging through their blood, they headed back to Interstate 70 to continue on. Through Illinois and Indiana and beyond.

When they turned onto the highway entrance ramp, a young, forlorn-looking hitchhiker was standing by the road. He was holding a wet, crumbling piece of cardboard with one word scrawled on it: "South." Hitchhikers were becoming a rarity these days, but what especially stood out was that he was sopping wet. He was standing out in the rain, totally drenched. And he was shivering, although it wasn't that cold out.

"Jesus," Ziggy said. "Look at that poor kid."

"Nobody's gonna pick him up." Josh looked out at the fellow as they passed him by. "Not looking like that. Who would dare?"

"We should stop." Ziggy pulled out of the way of traffic and slowed down.

"Uh, Zig, I don't know about this. Did you get a good look at him? He's not only a mess; something about him doesn't look . . . right. The guy could be some sort of maniac."

Ziggy stopped the car and looked in the rear-view mirror. "He needs help, Josh. Aw, shit. He doesn't even know we stopped."

"Not only that, we're going east and he wants to go south."

"I know, but we can get him closer to where he needs to be. We'll be going through Indianapolis soon. We could drop him at a highway that actually goes south. Fuck, he'll never get a ride if he stays here." Ziggy honked the horn. "There, he heard that. Do we have room in the back?"

Josh sighed. "Yeah, we have room." He rolled down his window, anticipating the introductions.

The guy ran up to the car and peered in. Water dripped down his long, thick, dark brown hair into his face. "Thanks guys, for stopping." He was smiling. "Lovely weather ain't it?"

Ziggy leaned forward, to see around Josh, and they both looked the guy over. He was a short little guy, appeared to be about fifteen years old. One of his front teeth was so crooked it pointed sideways more than down, but it was right in the middle of his big smile and . . . well, you had to give him credit for not trying to cover it up. Unusual, and yet . . . it looked okay, on him.

He looked like he had spent the night sleeping in the woods. He was totally wet, and dirty. Other than that, he looked like some sort of tough little redneck skateboard punk, ready for anything.

Somehow, at the same time, he looked delicate and fragile. There was something . . . off about his face, but it all seemed to work together. He was cute. Almost handsome.

His road-weary face was only inches away from Josh. For a fleeting moment, Josh wondered what it would be like to kiss that wet face. Not that he necessarily wanted to, but what if? Somewhere, surely, there was someone who loved this young fellow. His mother, if no one else. Someone loved him and would probably cover him with kisses if he were to come back home safely.

Josh imagined making love to the guy out in the woods in the pouring rain – what would that be like? Then it occurred to him, this little guy might not have ever made love to anyone.

"Where y'all headed?" the kid said.

"East," Josh said. "We're going east."

Ziggy said, "Washington D.C., bro. Where are you headed?"

"Macon Georgia. Shit. This ain't gonna work. We're goin' in two different directions. Don't that figure?"

"You need to be thumbing on a road that goes south, dude. We can drop you at one, no problem."

"Sure, that sounds good. But uh, I'm kinda wet here. I'm afraid I'll mess up your nice car. It's a beauty."

"Kinda wet, hell! You're fucking drenched. But it's okay. It's just water. Come on, get in. You need to get the fuck out of the rain."

Josh opened the door and he leaned the seat forward so the fellow could squeeze behind it, into the back of the Mustang. Ziggy checked the side mirror for traffic and pulled out.

"Christ, guys, I'm dripping all over everything back here. You got any towels or anything? I'm gonna ruin your leather seats."

"Nope. Oh wait, there's a hand towel up here we keep for the windshield. Would that help any?" Josh held it up to show him. It wasn't any bigger than a dishtowel, but it was clean.

"Sure." The hitchhiker took it and dried off his face, and then he toweled some of the water out of his hair. "Fuck, I thought I was gonna die out there. Say, uh, you think you could turn up the heat for a while?"

"No problem." Josh turned on the heater and directed the vents toward the back. "How's that?"

"Yeah, thanks. Feels good." He used the towel to sop up the water from the seat around him.

"What's your name, guy? I'm Josh."

And then Josh realized what looked odd about the fellow: his eyes were slightly crossed. *Jeez. Can a person see straight like that?*

What does he see? But again, like the guy's crooked tooth, somehow it seemed to add, rather than detract. He was a cute-looking kid.

"Crumb is my name," he said. "That's my last name. Franklin's my first name, but most people calls me Crumb. Even my stepparents, if you can believe that. When they're not callin' me something worse."

"Franklin it is then," Josh said. "That's a good name. I like it."

"Aw, man, thanks." He was still shivering a little.

"Franklin," Ziggy said, "no offense, but I gotta say you're the sorriest-looking mess I've ever seen. You can't be hitching looking that way, dude. Nobody's gonna pick you up, sopping wet like that."

"Don't I know it. I've been out there for hours. Don't know why *you* stopped, but I ain't complainin'. I'm mighty grateful. Once I get warmed up here in a bit maybe I can make it up to you. Are you sure you ain't got nothin' else I could dry off with?" He looked around the rear of the car. "Guess not, huh?"

"You need some dry clothes, bro. And hell, some sort of raincoat if you're gonna be standing out in the pouring rain."

"That's what I need alright, but I ain't got none. Not no more. And no money to buy 'em with. But I know what you're sayin'. Truth is, I figure my goose is cooked. You guys was nice to stop, but I'm still in a mess of trouble. Shit." He rolled down the back window, held the towel outside, and wrung the water out of it. Then he took his flannel shirt off and wrung it out, too.

Josh turned around when he heard the window open. Ziggy looked briefly, too, and then back to the road. He slowed down a bit so the wind at the window wouldn't be so fierce.

The guy spread his damp shirt across the back of the seat, and then he took off his undershirt and did the same thing with that. Half naked, now, sitting in the back seat.

He had a fit body, and nice skin. Muscles like a farm boy, with no fat. A little hair on his chest, on down to his belly. He was still young, still growing. He was a good-looking kid.

"I ain't even got money for food," he said. "Sucks."

"Dude, why in the hell are you hitching in the rain?"

"Hell, I ain't crazy. Didn't have no choice. Say, there ain't no southern route to where you're going, is there?"

"No," Josh said. He turned further sideways so he could watch the kid. "But a few miles is better than nothing, right? Especially if you end up in a better spot."

"Ain't gonna argue with that."

"Tell you what," Ziggy said, "We'll take one of these next exits and see if we can get you some dry clothes, bro."

"Told you I ain't got no money." The guy slipped his soggy shoes off, and then he unbuttoned his jeans and awkwardly pulled them off. There wasn't much legroom in the back of the Mustang. He had to lift his legs up to the seat to pull them off. He put his feet back on the floor and then wrung his jeans out the window as best he could. All he was wearing now were wet briefs and wet socks. His legs were hairy.

"You're hitching to Georgia with no money and no extra clothes? That's a long way to go."

"I *had* some clothes. I had a sack full of clothes. And a little extra money too." He spread his jeans out on the seat beside him, and then he pulled the wet socks off of his big feet. "Last bastard who gave me a ride, when he let me off, he drove away with all my stuff. Everything. Includin' my daddy's guitar." His voice broke when he said that.

"Dude."

"He might come back looking for you," Josh said. "Maybe he didn't realize what happened."

"He won't be back." He squeezed the water out of his socks and lay them out to dry. "Bastard knew what he was doin'. Anyway, that was hours ago. He'd of been back already if he was comin' back. No, my shit's gone. Don't care so much about the clothes. Long as I get out of this alive that is. But that was my daddy's *guitar*. How can people be so fucking mean?"

"Your dad's gonna be pissed, huh?"

"Most likely. But he's dead. Five years. That's the only thing of his I had left, and now it's gone. Man, I loved that guitar. It was a good one, too." He raised his hips and pushed his wet briefs down to his knees.

"I play good, too," he said. "Daddy taught me everything he knowed. Shit, this underwear's soaked. You mind?" He pulled his briefs the rest of the way off. "I'll put 'em back on when they get dried out a bit. If you want me to."

He wrung them out and then spread them across his jeans. "Startin' to warm up a little now. Feels good to get all this damn wet stuff off. Don't like wearin' clothes anyway, never did."

Ziggy and Josh looked at each other. Ziggy just shrugged his shoulders, but Josh didn't know what to think. Enjoy the show, he guessed, and meanwhile hope they weren't pulled over by a cop. This guy had even more nerve than they did.

"You know these parts, Franklin?" Ziggy said.

"Naw. But I know I-65 up yonder goes south to Nashville, I know that much. From there I can take 24 to Chattanooga, and then 75 to Macon. I got it all figured out."

Maybe it was from all the looks he was getting from Josh and Ziggy, and what they were looking at, but his dick was starting to fill out and rise, already at half-mast. Uncut, with the pink head of it beginning to peek out. Hairy crotch, and hairy balls, but no hair on his cock, just a veiny – and tasty-looking – hefty shaft with a pink head blossoming out from a thick foreskin.

"If you can drop me at 65 I'd be mighty grateful. Shit, look at me, I'm gettin' a boner." He laughed. "Can't help it. Hell, look all you want, though, it don't bother me."

"Uh, no problem."

"We'll be going right by I-65," Josh said. "When we go through Indianapolis."

"But first we're gonna find a second-hand store, dude. Get you something dry to wear."

"I done told you, I ain't got no money."

"We'll cover it, bro. Won't cost that much if we can find a thrift store. Maybe they'll have a raincoat too. And a backpack."

"Your good deed for the day, huh?"

"Sure," Ziggy said, "why not?"

Franklin's dick was fully hard now, standing straight out and up. It was a weighty one, and at least seven inches long. Josh could hardly keep his eyes off it. Ziggy had casually adjusted the rearview mirror so that he could see it, too. But Franklin didn't seem embarrassed.

"Hell, I'll take all the help I can get," he said. "I can't pay you back though. Unless you want blowjobs. That's the only thing I got to offer. Wouldn't be the first time – I done it before." He looked Ziggy and Josh over carefully. "A couple of good-lookin' guys like you," he said, "I wouldn't even mind doin' it."

"You wouldn't?"

"Naw. Not if you was gonna like it. And you would, I'd make sure of that. Shit, it'd be hot for me, too. Sex is sex. And like I said, I've done it before. Most of the time I liked it, too. It ain't as weird as you might think."

Ziggy and Josh were speechless.

"Just so you know, though," Franklin said, "I'll tell you right now, my ass is off limits, so don't get any ideas." He wrapped his hand around his cock and gently started stroking it.

"Really?"

"Damn right. I'm savin' that for somebody special."

Chapter 2

FAMILY

"No dude, I mean you'd suck us off? Both of us?"

"For dry clothes? You bet. Damn, I hope we find a raincoat. I'll be in deep shit otherwise. Fuck, you guys are gonna be savin' my life. It's the least I can do."

"And you'd enjoy doing it, huh?"

"Aw fuck, now don't tell me I've gone and offended your sensibilities or somethin'. You don't look like fag bashers to me."

"We're not. Not at all."

"It ain't that I'm queer exactly. I just like sex, that's all. I don't see why people make a big deal out of it. Girls or guys, who cares? Either way it feels good, so who gives a flying fuck?"

Josh and Ziggy looked at each other.

"Not that it's anybody's business. As long as it don't hurt nobody, why not? Why shouldn't I thrill whoever I want to? And like whoever I like?" He was still erect, and still stroking. "Fuck, I'm so horny. Sorry, I ain't jacked off for days."

"Girls *and* guys, huh?" Ziggy said.

"That's right. Well, if I had to choose, actually what I'd like is one extra-special guy friend. Just him and me. I ain't gonna lie about it either. Might end up gettin' me killed one of these days, but if you can't learn how to be yourself, what's the sense?"

"I couldn't agree with you more," Ziggy said.

"Same here," Josh said. "We both feel that way."

Not a peep in response came from the backseat. Ziggy looked in the rearview mirror to see if the guy was still awake.

Josh was already staring at him. And his dick. Maybe it made the guy feel a little self-conscious, but he seemed to love the attention. He kept on stroking, and now the head of his cock was wet with pre-cum. He looked at both of them and said, "What?"

"I was just checking to make sure you're still there," Ziggy said. "That's the first time you've stopped talking since you got into the car. Was it something we said?" He smiled.

"Yeah, well, what you said, yeah, I wasn't expectin' that. Oh, fuck, I'll tell you what, I might come here in a minute if I keep this up. God knows I need to, bad." He lifted his hips into the air a bit.

Josh and Ziggy glanced at each other, and then back at Franklin. Ziggy adjusted the rear-view mirror again so he could watch and drive at the same time. "Dude," he said, "Go ahead if you want. Shoot your load, bro. We don't mind."

"Yeah," Josh said. "We don't mind at all. As long as you let us watch."

"Oh Jesus, you want to watch? Awesome." He kept stroking. "I won't get any on your car, I promise. You sure it's okay?"

"Hell yes, go right ahead. We want to watch you shoot off."

"Fuck, get ready then." He was breathing heavily and fast. "'Cause there's a big cumload fixin' to launch any second."

He aimed his dick up at his face and moaned quietly, almost silently. "Unghhh." His dickhead got bigger and then suddenly a stream of cum shot out. Most of it landed in his mouth, or close to it. He moaned again; the next spurt was even bigger, and covered half his face. Then came more squirts, landing all up and down his bare chest. After another minute or two he was pretty much finished, although more cum was still oozing out of his cock.

He collapsed back into the seat, his hand still holding his cock.

Nobody said anything at first. Franklin wiped off the head of his dick with his fingers and put the cum in his mouth. Then he looked at Josh and Ziggy.

Josh said, "I do that too, sometimes."

"What, jack off?"

"No, eat my own cum."

"Jesus." Franklin wiped some cum off his face, licked it from his fingers, and then wiped up more from his belly. After he got most of it up, he used the hand towel to clean off his face and chest. "Fuck, that felt good. I needed that."

Ziggy laughed. "I know how that is."

Franklin laid back his head. "You guys really surprise me. Now and then I meet a guy who likes it like I do, but never two at once. And none of them ever outright admitted to it. You guys . . . are some kind of unusual, you know that?"

"No we're not," Josh said. "Just honest."

"Ha! You think honest ain't unusual? Christ. I think I've been rescued by angels. Josh and . . . and you, whatever your name is, that's what you two are. Angels I'll bet."

"My name's Ziggy. But no, it's not like that, Franklin. We're not angels, believe me, dude."

"Ziggy Stardust? Okay, shit, I'm dreamin' then."

"Not Stardust. Just Ziggy. And no, you're not dreaming. There's plenty of guys like us, bro. You just haven't met them yet. That's all it is. Or maybe you have, and you didn't know it."

"Ain't met 'em yet, most likely."

"That was hot, you jerking off. It made us horny."

"If you pull over somewhere I'll take care of you both," Franklin said. "Seriously, I'd be glad to do it."

"Nah, thanks, we'll be okay. Feels good sometimes just to let it stay hard for a while, you know?"

"Franklin, you said you have *two* stepparents?"

"Yeah, ain't I lucky? I ain't had no blood family for years. Not to speak of. My Ma disappeared when I was ten – run off or killed, I don't know which, nobody tells me anything – then Daddy married again later to some damn bitch who never did like me from day one. Her son and I get along great, but not her.

"She flat out hates me, always has. I don't know why. Then my daddy died, too. So much for family. She turned around and married some other guy right off, some guy she already knowed.

He don't like me neither. But I did the chores, so they kept me on. Till one mornin' they caught her son suckin' me off."

"*He* was sucking *you* off?"

"Yeah, that kid taught me everything. Well, not really, but I let him think so. I told him I didn't even know how to jack off, so he showed me how to do it. Yeah, he was suckin' me off, but I was the one got blamed for it. 'Corrupting their child.' They told me to pack my clothes and get the hell out and don't ever come back.

"I grabbed the guitar and walked out the door, told 'em they was cold-hearted bastards, and they just laughed. Then I told 'em they was gonna burn in hell. They told me to get off their property."

"Jesus. That's gotta be illegal. You're not even eighteen yet. Don't they have to support you?"

"I'm eighteen. I'm almost nineteen."

"You look fifteen."

"Hell no. I just look young 'cause I'm short."

"How long ago did you get kicked out?"

"Couple of weeks. Been happier on the road than I was with them, but it gets lonely as hell sometimes. Don't know what happened to her son, either. Nothin', most likely. They all liked him. So did I. He was the closest thing to family I had and now I won't never see him again."

"They kicked you out of your dad's house?"

"It ain't my daddy's no more. Belongs to her now, I guess. And her new Nazi hubby. Fuck it. Ain't life grand? Kicked out of my own house by two sorry sons of bitches I hope I never see again. Question is, what do I do now? Only friends I got are still livin' with their own parents. Had a friend whose family moved to Macon; I'm hopin' he's still there. They'll put me up, if I can find 'em. Said they would at least. If I can just get there."

"Here's an exit coming up," Ziggy said. "Cloverdale. I'll take it. There might be a Goodwill or Value Village or something like that. We'll find out."

They left the interstate and drove slowly through the town, eyes peeled for any store that might sell secondhand clothes.

"Look," Franklin said, "there's a laundromat. Maybe that's all we need."

"Uh, to dry your clothes?"

"Yeah. I guess I'd have to wait in the car, but hell, it'd be cheaper than buyin' clothes."

"But then you'd get wet all over again later, when we drop you off. If you don't have a raincoat."

"Well, maybe the rain'll stop."

"And you'll get cold at night without a jacket. When you're in between rides."

Franklin sighed. "Okay, so, maybe it's not such a great idea."

"We could put your clothes in the dryer, and then pick them up after we find you some new stuff."

"If we can even find a thrift store."

"There's one now, right over there. Look."

"Sure enough."

"Let's do it then."

—

THEY PARKED around the back of the building. Franklin stayed in the car while they put his clothes in a dryer.

When they came back out, Josh pulled some of his own clothes out of the trunk for Franklin to wear, so he could go inside the thrift store and try things on. They didn't want to risk getting him clothes that didn't fit.

It didn't take long to find everything they needed, including underwear, some brand new socks, a second pair of shoes, and a decent backpack for Franklin to carry it all in. Meanwhile Franklin, the whole time, was grinning like a kid on Christmas morning.

When they returned to the laundromat his clothes were dry, so now he had a change of clothes, a raincoat, and an insulated vest he could wear if he was cold. Then they stopped somewhere for lunch, paid for his, and gave him a few dollars for dinner later on.

—

FORTY MILES DOWN the road, they reached what would be their parting place. A highway interchange on I-65, just south of Indianapolis.

"I don't know how to thank you guys enough for all you've done."

"Aw, don't worry about it," Ziggy said. "Someday you'll help somebody else out the same way. That's the way it works."

"Are you sure you don't want me to, you know, get you off? It'd be my honor. And I'm pretty good at it. We can still find a place."

"Nah, that's okay. Thanks for the offer, though."

"I sure wish I had some friends like you guys."

"You will someday, Franklin. Wait and see."

"Not that it's any of my business," Franklin said, "but you guys are more than just friends to each other, ain't you?" He grinned. There was that crooked tooth again. It was beginning to look good on him. It was his warm, honest smile, that's what it was.

"Yeah," Josh said, "you're exactly right. We are."

"You don't need any help from me gettin' yourselves off, then. Now I get it."

"We had most of that figured out the first two weeks we knew each other," Ziggy said. "But who knows? If you'd caught us on another day we might have taken you up on it anyway."

"Save yourself, Franklin, for that special girl or guy you're gonna find."

"Special guy. I like women okay but like I said, what I really want is a special guy friend. Don't know if I'll ever find him though. A buddy I can settle down with. Just him and me, from then on. That don't sound weird does it? Aw, fuck it, weird or not, that's what I want. It ain't too much to ask for, is it? And if he's got a family I can be part of, even better. I miss havin' a family."

"That doesn't sound weird at all," Josh said. "I think it's a great idea. That's how Zig and I are."

Chapter 3
BALLS

"No KIDDING? I was right, then."

"Actually, as far as family goes, Josh and I are pretty much all we have."

"How long have you two been like that?"

"Without our own families? Or do you mean, together?"

"Together."

"A year. We've been together for a year."

"Damn. You guys are lucky."

"Yeah, we are. Dude, you'll find somebody someday. It'll happen. Just don't try *too* hard, because it happens when you're not expecting it. Don't ever give up."

"I won't give up. I want that more than anything. You know what else I want? Friends. I wish I had some friends like you."

"Aw, we're nothing special."

"Yeah you are. You're good guys. That's what I want, is some good guys to be good friends with. It would almost be like havin' family, you know?"

"Yeah, having friends is awesome."

"Sure would be."

They looked at each other. No one said anything. Then Franklin reached for his backpack.

"It looks like the rain is lettin' up. Listen guys, uh, I guess I'd better be gettin' along if I'm ever gonna get to Macon. I need to let you guys git too, so you can get to where you're goin'." He had tears in his eyes. "I won't never forget you two. Thanks for buying me all this stuff. Maybe *you* don't think you're angels, but I do."

"Aw, Franklin, it didn't cost that much."

"Yeah, maybe not, but you didn't have to do any of this. Most people wouldn't have."

"Take care of yourself, Franklin. And don't ever give up, okay?"

"I will. And I won't give up, don't worry about that."

—

"YOU THINK he'll be okay?"

"I don't know, Zig." Josh drove up the entrance ramp to the interstate. "I hope so."

"I feel bad," Ziggy said. "We should have done more."

"More to help him out?"

"Yeah."

"Like what?" Josh merged into the highway traffic.

"I don't know. He's just so . . . all alone. We helped him get dry and warm and then we pushed him out on his own again. He needs friends. Hell, he needs family."

"We should have given him our phone number," Josh said. "Or our address, so he could write to us."

"Yeah. We should have. Hell, everybody needs friends. We could use some ourselves. We've talked about that, remember? We keep to ourselves too much. You and me and Eleanor are basically all we've got, but it doesn't have to be that way. We should reach out more. Good friends could be family for people like us, Josh."

"He seemed to be a really decent guy, too. He's just down on his luck."

"Yeah," Ziggy said. "Damn."

"Oh well."

"Aren't you glad we stopped for him, though? You didn't want to at first."

"Yeah Zig, of course I am. He might have died out there tonight. No one else would've picked him up."

"Well, somebody might have, you never know."

"Who else would have had the balls besides you? God, he was a mess. Or looked like one, at least."

"Those are the ones who need help the most, Josh."

"I know, but sometimes fucked-up people are beyond help."

"Aw, don't say that. Nobody's beyond help."

"What I mean is, sometimes the help they need, is more than what you have to give. More than you're able to give."

"Yeah, true enough. And anyway, you can't help everyone who needs it. And some people don't want your help in the first place. But he was there," Ziggy said, "and we were there, and it seemed right. To give him a ride, at least. And he turned out to be pretty cool."

"Heck yeah, he did. He's also a little fireball. That kid's got guts. And heart. And you saw it right off, Zig. I didn't, but you did. When you first saw him. Don't tell me you didn't."

"Josh, I don't know what I saw. It just felt right to get him out of the rain. That's all I know how to tell you."

"I've learned a lot from you, Zig. I'm still learning. To trust my feelings, and let things happen."

"You've always known how to do that, bro. You wouldn't be here."

"You've still got more balls than I do."

"You've got just as much guts as I do. Maybe more."

"I don't know about that. I'm more cautious than you. And I'm shyer, that's for sure."

"Yeah, okay, so I'm the bold guy, and you're the shy guy. But you're just as brave as I am."

"I'm not as shy as I used to be, am I? After a year with you, how could I be?" Josh smiled.

"You're more sure of yourself now, I'll grant you that. But sweetheart, I think you're always gonna be a little shy. No worry, though." Ziggy grinned. "It's one of the things I love about you."

—

ZIGGY AND JOSH HAD MET a year before, at an after-hours club across the river from St. Louis. Josh was too shy to be the first to speak. In fact, he hardly dared to look at Ziggy; he thought Zig was way out of his league. Ziggy spoke first. From the very beginning, Josh had assumed Ziggy was straight, but besides that, Josh was living in Memphis at the time, and committed to some-one, so he took it for granted any kind of relationship with Ziggy was out of the question.

But one thing led to another, and now, here they were, a year later, closer than any blood brothers.

Some people think love takes time, that it starts slowly, from nothing, and only develops over a lengthy period of time.

Others think love exists from the moment you meet a person. You can pretend it's not there, or you can embrace it and let it grow, letting your heart lead the way. Josh and Ziggy were proof of this.

They liked each other from the moment they saw each other. They were lucky just to have connected, but they did. And then they took a chance and let their feelings bring them closer. That's all they had to do; let things happen. They were cautious, always respecting each other's freedom and individuality. But they were bold in letting their love grow.

—

JOSH WAS DRIVING now, Ziggy riding shotgun. They were back on track, making their way to Washington, D.C. the first leg of their anniversary road trip.

"I used to be terminally shy. You can't imagine, Zig. God it was awful. Especially combined with, you know, being gay. For the longest time I thought I was the only one."

"Don't tell me you never had sex with another guy, though, while you were growing up. Nobody's that shy." Ziggy looked out the window at the fields passing by.

"A few times I did. Not that often. If you could even call it sex. What little I had was unexpected. And it was over way too quickly. And it was never my idea either," Josh added. "I was too hung up about sex to initiate anything myself."

"What's the quickest sex you ever had?"

"What do you mean?"

"Like, how quickly *was* it over with? What's the shortest time it ever took for you to shoot your cum with another guy?"

"Oh, jeez. Let me think about it for a minute. Oh, wait, I know. Yeah. Listen to this: one time I went all the way from not even thinking about sex to it being over and done with in less than a minute."

"No way!"

"It's the truth."

"I don't know if I can believe that. What happened?" Ziggy grinned. "Tell me. I want to hear all about it."

"I was ready to graduate from high school, and so a group of us were touring the University of Maryland, you know, like maybe we would be going to school there in the fall."

"Okay."

"It was actually pretty exciting. All sorts of good-looking guys: jocks, longhairs, nerdy guys, and teachers, too, all kinds of people walking back and forth to classes, strangers who I might meet in the fall, you know, if I really did go there. The whole scene. I knew I wouldn't be living in a dorm, unfortunately, but still there would be all these new people. New friends and stuff. That is if I could get up the nerve to talk to anyone. Anyway, that's when it happened."

"You're telling me you had sex at your college orientation?"

"Well, we were taking a lunch break. It was, like, free time; everyone was on his own. We had to meet back together at a certain time, but until then we could do whatever we felt like."

"And you felt like having sex."

"No, not at all. Well, yeah, I mean, of course, constantly, you know how it is when you're that age. But no, I wasn't actually thinking about it at the time. I just had to pee. We were outdoors somewhere, like, in this big open area in the middle of everything, the Quadrangle I think they called it, and I had to find somewhere to pee."

"So . . ."

"So I went into one of the buildings, looking for a bathroom. There were classrooms, and then I found a bathroom, went inside, stood at the first urinal I came to, and unzipped."

"Was anybody else in there?"

"Nobody. So I stood there, peeing, and then when I was just about finished all of a sudden some guy rushes in and comes right up to the urinal next to mine. There were, like, five or six urinals all in a row, but he picked the one nearest to me. No dividers between any of them, and he chooses the one next to me."

"Hmmm. That's . . . kind of unusual. Guys usually maintain a distance when they can. It's like, you know, etiquette."

"Oh hell, that's nothing – wait'll you hear the rest of it. For a second or two I figured, what the fuck, maybe he had to pee really bad and took the closest one available to where you come in the door. But as soon as he gets beside me he opens his jeans, pulls out a totally hard dick, and starts jacking off."

"Jesus."

"Frantically. And while he's jacking off he's looking at my dick, and then up at my face, and then down at my dick again."

"Christ. What'd you do?"

"It was so crazy. I didn't even have time to think. I got hard too, instantly. I couldn't stop looking at his hard cock and him stroking it. I've never gotten a boner so quick in all my life. It took about three seconds for me to get completely hard. From watching him. Then, while he's still beating off, he reaches over with his other hand and starts jerking me off."

"Jesus. Dude, now you're giving me a boner."

"I looked at his hand pumping my cock, and looked up at him, and he was grinning. He was frantically jacking both of us off. I never came so fast in my life. And I just about fell over, from my legs going weak, shooting the biggest load ever, into the urinal, while he's stroking me. Then he moans and I see him spurting a big load of cum out, too."

"Fuck!"

"As soon as we finished shooting he let loose of me, put his dick away, grinned, and took off out of there. I had gone in there to empty my bladder, and then in less than a minute he came in, got me hard, jacked us both off, and left. I was standing there in a daze, with cum still dripping off my cock, totally blown away."

Chapter 4
ROAD TRIP

"THEN SOMEBODY ELSE came into the bathroom, so I flicked the cum off my dick, zipped up, and went out looking for the guy, but I didn't see him anywhere. I don't know what I would have done if I'd found him, but it didn't matter because he was gone."

"Jesus. That's wild, Josh."

"God, I know. I couldn't get over it. I was getting a hard-on constantly for the next few days every time I thought about it. Hell, for weeks."

"Damn. I wish somebody would do that to me. You know, just once, so I'd know what it was like. So unexpected."

"Just once?"

"Well, no, fuck, how about every time I pee in a public toilet?" He grinned. "Josh, that sounds absolutely awesome."

"It *was* awesome. I went back there a couple of times that summer just to hang out and see if he showed up again, but I never saw him after that one time."

—

JOSH AND ZIG WERE ON another adventure: a two-week vacation to commemorate their first road trip. The first stop was Washington, D.C. Josh had been raised just north of the city, in the Maryland suburbs; Ziggy wanted to see first-hand where Josh had grown up, where his family used to live, and look at his schools, visit his favorite hangouts, everything.

They drove all the way from St. Louis to D.C. that first day. By the time they reached the hotel in Maryland, they were exhausted.

All they wanted to do was snuggle up together and get some sleep. So that's what they did.

Sunday

EARLY THE NEXT MORNING, Josh was the first to wake up. He lay in bed and looked around the room.

Zig was still sleeping soundly, with his arm around Josh. They were curled up together under the covers. Naked of course. Josh never tired of this – cuddling with his favorite guy in all the world.

Their legs were entwined and their smooth, bare feet were nestled together. The way they were sleeping, front to back, Josh's buttocks and Ziggy's groin fit together perfectly.

Zig's dick was hard at the moment, pressed into the crack of Josh's ass. Maybe that's what had woken Josh. His cock stiffened in response and he lay still, waiting to see what developed. If Ziggy woke up aroused like this – well, anything could happen.

Ziggy's breathing was slow and easy, while Josh's was deliberately quiet, cautious, eager.

Eventually, though, Zig started going soft – a good indication that he was still asleep. Josh gently untangled their legs and carefully slipped out from under Ziggy's arm and out of bed.

He quietly circled around to the phone, called the hotel desk, and cancelled their wake-up call. Then he turned toward the bed again to watch Ziggy sleep.

Josh wanted to see all of Zig. He lifted the covers gently and pulled them down all the way, so he could admire Ziggy naked.

Zig was so smooth. Maybe he had some native-American blood in him or something; that could explain it. His facial hair was as sparse now as Josh's was at the age of fourteen; he hardly needed to shave at all. As for the hair on his head, he kept it somewhat short; he liked it that way.

His strong chest had hardly any hair at all. There was just a faint trail between his belly button and his groin, which led to a nice thatch of hair around his dick and his balls.

His muscular legs and arms were hairy enough, but it was thin hair, masculine, not quite as thick as Josh's. Josh was the hairy one, but not overly so; they were a good match in that way. Ziggy liked to run his fingers through what fur Josh had, while Josh enjoyed touching and caressing Ziggy's smooth skin.

As he was doing now. Not enough to wake him, just barely touching Ziggy's skin, feeling the softness, and the curves.

The first time Josh had ever done this to Ziggy – remove all the covers and watch him sleep – Ziggy's body eventually noted the change in temperature and curled up in order to be warmer. Ever since then, however, it was just the opposite: when he moved, instead of curling up, Ziggy turned flat on his back and spread out. As if he felt the air and wanted to expose his naked body to it as much as possible.

Which was great for Josh, because it made it that much easier to climb into bed and suck Ziggy off in his sleep – while Josh jacked himself off, too. Usually, Ziggy's cock was already hard by the time Josh got to it. Josh tried his best not to wake him up. Usually the orgasm did, especially if they came together. Zig would wake up suddenly, with the biggest grin on his face.

Would it happen that way this morning?

When Josh pulled the covers down, Zig lay on his side for a few minutes, facing away from Josh, peacefully snoozing, unaware. Then, as Josh lightly caressed him, he stirred a little and turned over onto his back. His eyelids began to flutter.

He was dreaming.

And as Josh watched, Ziggy's cock began to grow.

Dude. These are some big waves.

No problem. We've faced bigger ones.

Ziggy was sitting in the stern of a rowboat, riding the rapids of the Colorado River, holding on as best as he could.

Sitting in front of him, facing him, rowing, was Ziggy's mentor, fellow orphan, and best buddy from years past: George.

George was rowing so calmly and effortlessly, the boat might have been floating on top of a cloud,

Naturally, George was there. The only thing wrong with the picture was, those were some BIG-ass waves.

Dude, you can't even see where we're going. We could flip.

George was naked. So was Ziggy.

Nah, I got it covered.

You sure?

Piece of cake, Z. It's like a big orgasm. You feel it don't you?

Yeah, of course. We're gonna fuck?

You bet. Cover me li'l bro.

George stood up in the boat. His dick was stiff and hard. And wet.

You know what I mean, George said. *Cover my dick.*

Ziggy stood up, too. And then George's cock was in Ziggy's ass, and Ziggy was getting fucked.

Oh, fuck. Oh, fuck. Yes. Oh yes.

You've got the sweetest ass, Z.

It feels good, G. So good. Make me come.

When we reach Denver.

A wave swept over the boat. Eleanor was there. Ziggy was fucking her. Ziggy was fucking her and getting fucked by George at the same time.

Looks like I taught you well, little bro.

Wait! Don't go, Ziggy said.

Take the oars, Z.

Ziggy took over the job of rowing. They reached an outcrop of rock on the shore, and then George and Eleanor stepped out of the boat.

George said, *Will you be coming back this way?*

Ziggy looked at him, eyes wide. *Hell yeah I'll be back. Of course I'll be back.*

I might not be here.

I'll be back, G, you know I will.

George groaned in ecstasy. *I'm coming.*

Ziggy groaned, too. He felt it coming on. He was getting sucked off now. Someone was sucking him. He looked down. Kneeling on the bottom of the rowboat was Josh.

Josh?

Josh let Ziggy's hard cock slip out of his mouth, looked up, and grinned. Then he licked Ziggy's balls.

You're always there for me, dude. Zig sat down and leaned his head back. *Jesus, Josh. I'm coming!*

Josh let Ziggy's balls slip out of his mouth and he deep-throated Ziggy's cock.

Coming! Ahhh! Zig put his hands behind Josh's head. *Unhh! Unhhhhh!*

He opened his eyes, and he was lying on a bed, pumping his load into Josh's mouth.

"*Ohhhh, fuck! Take it, Josh.*"

Josh drank it down while he jacked his own dick to orgasm. Cum was flying everywhere.

"Unnnnh! Fuck!" Ziggy's hips jerked a few more times, and then he let his head fall back onto the bed, totally spent. The last drops of his cum oozed out onto Josh's tongue.

Josh milked the last of his own load out, while he slid his lips up and down Ziggy's shaft. When Ziggy started to soften, Josh let him go and slipped back into bed next to him.

Ziggy gave him a kiss. "You beat me to it again."

"Only because I woke up first."

"I dreamed about you," Ziggy said. "George was there too. And Eleanor."

"Your three favorite people."

"Fuck yeah. It was so real. George was still alive, and right there next to me in the boat. He was fucking me."

"You were in a boat?"

"Yeah, a rowboat. We were getting swept down the Colorado River in a rowboat. Through the Grand Canyon. I thought we were gonna tip over. And then George was saying good-bye. I think he was leaving me. That's when I really got scared. One minute we were all fucking and then the next minute George was leaving, and Eleanor was going too. And then you showed up."

"You and your dreams."

"Aw, come on, Josh. Your dreams are just as weird. That's the way dreams are."

"I don't mean that part, I'm talking about all the sex you have in your dreams. Not that I mind. I'm just saying." Josh grinned.

"Uh, you don't think it has anything to do with who I'm sleeping with, do you?" Ziggy smiled. "I mean, dude, of course I'm gonna dream about sex if you're sucking me off in my sleep."

"I don't do it unless you're already hard."

"Yeah, well, even so, seems like you'd wanna play fair. You always get the jump on me. I wish you'd let me wake up first sometimes, so I can do you," Ziggy said. "I want to make you happy too, Josh."

"I'm already happy from making you happy. You don't need to do anything, Zig."

"Oh yes I do. It's not fair unless I get to do stuff for you too. I want to."

"Okay."

"I don't think you really understand, Josh. I love making you come. I wish you could see your face! It's awesome knowing how good I'm making you feel. You gotta let me do it more often, bro. That way we get to share the fun. Fair's fair."

"Okay. I'll try. It's so tempting, but . . . sure, I'd love that."

"Cool."

"Yeah."

"I guess it wasn't all that weird a dream, actually. After all, George really did end up leaving me. And Eleanor probably will too, someday. You know, when she gets married."

"George didn't leave you. He was taken from you."

Chapter 5
THE ROCKS

"YEAH, WELL. Same difference."

"No, Zig, it's not the same at all. George never would have left you intentionally. It was completely beyond his control."

"Oh hell, I know. Still, it fucked me up bad. Really bad. Even now I still feel a little lost sometimes without him."

"Do you?"

"Well, yeah, of course. Sometimes when I think of him I can't help feeling that way. That's just the way it is. When you're good buddies with somebody for years, thinking he'll be around forever, and then he gets killed, it's . . . devastating. Same as it would be if I lost you, Josh. It would fuck me up totally. I don't know what I'd do without you."

"Same here, Zig."

"I don't even know how to tell you how much you mean to me. Sometimes I think you're too good for me. You treat me too good, is what I mean. I don't know how to make it up to you. I don't even know if I can."

"You could give me another kiss. That should go a long way toward taking care of it."

Ziggy was happy to oblige. Many times over.

—

SOON ENOUGH, THOUGH, it was time to get up. Ziggy sat up in bed. "So, what's up for today?"

"Well, I'm totally flexible." Josh sat up, too. "But there's a whole lot of cool stuff in downtown D.C. to look at."

"Museums, right? I've been to some of them."

"Yeah, and art galleries, monuments, and plenty of other stuff. It would take us weeks to see it all."

"No use in busting our balls. Let's pick out one or two places and be happy with that. We're still gonna take a look at your old neighborhood, right? And where you went to school?"

"If you really want to, sure. We can do that tomorrow."

—

THE HOTEL WAS in Silver Spring, Maryland, so they stopped at the nearby Woodside Deli for breakfast, and then headed downtown in the Mustang.

Josh was driving. "I'm gonna take the Park down," he said.

"The park?"

"Yeah, Rock Creek Park. It runs all the way from here in Maryland down to the Watergate. It's my favorite way into and out of D.C."

"The Watergate? You're talking about . . ."

"Yeah, *that* Watergate. High-rise condos down on the Potomac. The Kennedy Center for the Performing Arts is there too. And the C&O Canal."

"There's a canal in D.C.?"

"Yeah, in Georgetown, next to the Potomac River. It's pretty cool. Canal boats used to haul coal down from Cumberland. You know, in the old days. Parts of it are still in use, like, as a park mostly."

"Wow."

"We can check it out if you want."

"You're the guide, bro. Whatever you think would be cool."

They drove down 16th Street, turned right onto Kalmia Road, and worked their way down to Rock Creek. They turned south onto Beach Drive and then, with the forest on both sides, they were on their way to downtown D.C.

Josh pointed out a footbridge over the creek as they drove by. "You see the steep hill on the other side of that bridge? My parents used to bring my brothers and me down here so we could play on that hill. We called it 'the Rocks.' It's awesome. We could stop here on the way back and look at it closer if you want to. It's pretty special."

"When you were kids?"

"Yeah. We played games up there. I've never seen any other place quite like it."

"Yeah, sure. Let's stop, on our way back, to check it out."

They drove on, following the slow, winding, peaceful road through the park.

"So, you already went to some of the museums here in D.C., back when you were in 8th grade, right?"

"Yeah," Ziggy said. "We went to the Natural History museum, History and Technology, the Air Museum, and, uh, Arts and Industries. All on the National Mall."

"Wow. Well, they added a new building, they call it the Air and Space Museum now."

"Then we oughta go there, Josh. There's bound to be some cool new stuff I haven't seen yet."

—

THEY DROVE BY the Watergate complex and the Kennedy Center, then parked the car in Georgetown. They walked among some of the oldest historic buildings and houses in all of D.C., and took a good look at the canal.

Ziggy frequently put his arm around Josh's shoulder as they walked. This was typical for Zig, almost from the beginning of their friendship, and it never failed to give Josh a thrill.

From Georgetown, Josh drove east on P Street and parked again, this time in the Dupont Circle district. Once again they set out on foot. Josh only said that it was an area that Ziggy might "find interesting." But as they walked around the neighborhood, Ziggy soon realized they were in one of the few places in D.C. where two men could hold hands in public without attracting attention.

"Dude," Ziggy said, grinning. "This is awesome." He gently took Josh's hand and they spent the next hour exploring the neighborhood, hand in hand. As if it was the most natural thing in the world to do. Which of course it was, for two men who loved each other as they did. Everyone else seemed to think so, too, because very few people even seemed to notice. The few who did, smiled.

After that, they spent a couple of hours on the National Mall, much of it inside the Air and Space Museum and at a nearby art museum, the Hirshhorn Museum and Sculpture Garden. They visited the Lincoln Memorial and, Josh's favorite, the Jefferson Memorial, next to the Tidal Basin and the cherry trees.

When they'd had their fill of downtown sightseeing, they headed back to the Maryland suburbs.

—

OF COURSE, THEY TOOK Josh's favorite route again, through Rock Creek Park. And they didn't forget to stop at the footbridge. They locked up the car and walked across to the other side of the creek.

There was a bridal trail for horseback riders at the end of the bridge, and then the rocks and the hill climb were immediately on the other side of the trail.

"This place looks like it gets a lot of use," Ziggy said.

"Yeah, definitely. I don't know how many people know about it, but plenty of people come here to climb. And play."

"Play?"

"Yeah. Look at this place. Can you imagine all the games kids could think of to play here?"

"I can see why you called it "The Rocks.""

Multiple footpaths, worn smooth, circled around and between a large number of huge rocks on a steep incline. No better place existed for kids to climb just for the fun of it, or to play Capture the Flag or Hide and Go Seek.

"Do you feel like climbing?" Josh said. "We used to go all the way up there, as far as you can see from here. Almost to the top. There's trees and a little meadow up there, too, past that, but you have to scramble over the ridge if you want to see them. I used to love this place."

"Sure, I'm up for it. Lead the way, sweetheart. I'll be right behind you."

They started climbing.

Chapter 6
Above the Rocks

JOSH REACHED THE TOP of the rocks and decided to keep on going. He pulled himself up and over onto the field of grass and stood there, looking around at the lush growth of trees and brush while he caught his breath. *Same as it ever was,* he thought.

Ziggy followed right behind him and stood next to him, also out of breath. "You used to come up here a lot, huh?"

"Not usually this high. Too hard to get over the top. Besides, my brothers and I came here to climb on the rocks, not to look at trees. I was the only one who ever came up this far."

"Josh Smith, the trail blazer. The bravest explorer of all."

"Oh, hell, Zig, you know better than that. Shyest of them all is more like it. Loner by default."

"Still brave. Fuck, dude, it takes balls to be different."

"Anyway, what do you think?" Josh looked around again at the trees. "Complete solitude. No paths or trails, see? Nobody ever comes up here. No one comes down from above, either."

They had climbed past the boulders on the steep hill. Hidden above the rocks was this secluded, woodsy little meadow.

Ziggy grinned. "I'll tell you what I think. Looks to me like a good place to fuck. Or get sucked off." He wrapped his arms around Josh from behind and pulled the two of them together. "Let's make love, you want to?"

Josh felt Ziggy's stiff cock press against his ass. "Three hours and you're already horny again?" Josh began to harden up, too.

"From watching your butt the whole way up the hill, bro. Your fault for putting your ass in front of my face."

Josh laughed. "No problem, I'm horny, too." He pushed his ass back against Ziggy's boner. "You want some of this, huh? Or a suck?"

"Nah. I want you to fuck me, Josh. After we smooch a little. Lick my ass real good, and then fuck me. Will you do that?"

"Actually put my tongue in your ass?" Josh pretended to be shocked.

"Dude, you know you love it as much as I do. Come on. Let's do it. Right here. In the middle of the woods."

Josh turned around and faced Ziggy. "Okay," he said. "You're on."

First, they kissed. And kissed some more. Deep kisses, swirling tongues together, licking each other's faces, smooching. Tickling each other's necks with their mouths, nibbling ears, and more kisses.

Then Josh popped the buttons of Ziggy's jeans open and yanked them down. Down past Ziggy's ass, all the way to his ankles, so his muscular bare legs and his boner-bulging white briefs were exposed to the world. Or at least to the forest trees surrounding them.

Josh licked his way up Ziggy's legs, starting at the top of his socks and continuing upward. When he reached the edge of Ziggy's briefs, Josh pushed his tongue under the fabric, getting closer to Ziggy's cock. Then, for the briefest moment, Ziggy felt the wet touch of Josh's tongue on the head of his dick. He shivered with anticipation.

Josh pulled back and then nuzzled his nose against the soft cotton fabric that held Ziggy's stiff boner inside it. He pushed Zig's t-shirt up above his nipples and then continued on with licks and kisses all the way from Ziggy's belly button to his nips.

Ziggy's moans of pleasure told Josh he was doing well. He moved up further and kissed Ziggy's neck, his ears, and finally his lips. When Josh pressed his mouth to Ziggy's, Zig responded with passion. Their tongues pushed together and around each other. Ziggy was a good kisser. Both of them were.

Josh moved down again to Ziggy's smooth chest. He gently pinched and kissed Ziggy's nipples, then licked his way down to Ziggy's belly button where there was the faintest trail of fur. Ziggy shivered again.

Josh slowly pulled down Ziggy's briefs, inch by inch. Suddenly a stiff, thick, 6-inch cock popped out and stood high and hard, already wet with pre-cum. Josh lapped up all the slippery wet stuff and then he licked the cock all over, from base to head. Ziggy shivered and groaned.

Josh pushed his own jeans and underwear down to his feet and squatted on his heels. He stroked his own hard cock as he put his mouth over the mushroom head of Ziggy's dick. He took it all the way to the back of his throat, working his tongue around the shaft as he went.

"Jesus, Josh." Ziggy gently pulled Josh's head off his dick. "Don't. I don't want to come yet."

"Okay." Josh licked Ziggy's balls, got them good and wet, and took them gently one by one into his mouth and hummed. Then he let them hang free and licked them some more.

"Damn, Josh. That feels good. Hold up a minute, let me get out of these clothes." Zig kicked his shoes off and stepped out of his jeans and underwear. Then he spread his legs wide to give Josh better access.

Josh swirled his tongue all around Ziggy's nut sac, then he turned around and sat down on his butt, backwards, between Ziggy's legs, so he could lick easier behind the balls.

Ziggy reached down and pulled Josh's shoes off, and then his jeans and his briefs. Then he pulled his own t-shirt off. He moaned as Josh continued to work his magic.

Josh licked closer and closer to Zig's asshole; Ziggy pulled his butt cheeks apart to make it more accessible. He gasped when

Josh's tongue finally pressed against the opening. Josh licked it a few times.

Then he got up, brushed off his butt, and kneeled down on all fours behind Ziggy.

He licked Ziggy's crack and pressed his tongue into Zig's hole until it relaxed. The more Josh licked, the more Ziggy relaxed. When Josh put his wet thumb against Ziggy's pucker, it went right inside. Zig sighed with pleasure.

Josh moved his thumb around gently, massaging inside Ziggy and getting the opening to relax more and more. He went back to licking for a while, got everything nice and wet, and then put two fingers in. They went in easily.

"Josh, go ahead. I'm ready to go, bud. Put your cock in there." Ziggy leaned forward and put his hands on his knees, aiming his ass at Josh, eager for the real thing.

Josh kept his fingers inside Zig while he reached for his jeans and took a condom out of the pocket. He tore open the wrapper with his teeth, stood up, and rolled the condom down over his hard seven-inch cock.

He gently moved his fingers around inside Ziggy while he spat on his other hand and spread it over his dick. When his cock was good and slippery, covered with spit, he said, "Ready?"

"Hell yeah. Put it in."

Josh took his two fingers out, held his cock up to Ziggy's hole, and gently pushed forward. There was a little resistance, and then Ziggy relaxed and the head of Josh's cock popped right inside.

In unison they both said, "Aahhhhhh."

Josh held there for a minute, and then he gently pressed forward. He slowly pushed his stiff dick further into Ziggy, deeper and deeper, inch by inch. When he was all the way in, Josh held still and waited.

Ziggy took a deep breath, and then he said, "It feels good. Your dick feel good, Josh. Damn good."

"Same here, Zig."

They held it there for a minute, then Ziggy said, "Okay, dude. Go for it."

Josh gently pulled back and then moved forward again.

"That's it. Like that."

Josh kept it up, slowly and gently, in and out. Finally Ziggy said, "Okay. I'm ready for you now. Fuck me fast and hard. Or however you like. Get off good, bro. Use my ass like you own it."

"Alright. You want it, you got it."

"Damn right. We have all day, too, so take your time."

"You just said fast and hard!"

"Yeah, fuck me as hard as you want."

"Zig, you nut, I can't go fast and slow at the same time."

"I'm talking about when you take it to the edge, Josh, and then back off before you come. Makes it last longer that way."

"Uh, I don't know if I've ever done that before."

"Sure you have. You do it without even thinking. Because the longer we keep it going, the better we get off when we finally shoot."

"I'll try."

"Aw, hell, don't worry about it. Fuck me however you want to. You're a natural at this."

"'If it feels good, do it?'"

"That's right. You know it."

Josh tried the hard-and-fast for a minute, fucking Ziggy's ass as hard as he could. He slammed so hard against Ziggy they almost fell over.

"That's the way." Ziggy laughed. "Damn, bro, you catch on quick."

"Fuck, I'll wear myself out if I keep that up." Josh took off his t-shirt and tossed it.

"Just do whatever feels good. That's the main thing."

Now they were both naked except for their socks. Two lean and fit young men, in perfect health.

Josh tried it again but a little slower this time.

He reached around and felt Ziggy's cock; it was rigid and stiff. Ziggy was obviously enjoying this. Josh fucked Ziggy with passion, easing up at times, switching between slow and easy and fast and hard.

He suddenly stopped in mid-fuck.

Ziggy said, "You okay?"

"I'm great. I almost came. Barely stopped in time."

"See, I knew you could do it."

Josh waited another minute, and then started moving his cock in and out of Ziggy's ass again. "Zig," he said, "I want to make you come just by fucking you. Without you touching your dick. Like I did that first time."

"Yeah, that's the best. But that wasn't the only time you've done it. You know that, right?"

"How do I do it?"

"Don't worry about it, bro. Just do whatever feels good. When you enjoy it, so do I. It happens naturally."

"Well, okay." Josh continued to fuck Ziggy's ass. Faster, now. Then he switched to pushing his cock in fast and hard but holding it there, staying deep inside of Ziggy briefly before pulling out and slamming it in again.

"Fuck, Josh, that's awesome. I love that. You'll make me come for sure, if you keep doing that."

"Excellent," Josh said, "because it feels awesome on this end, too." Josh hammered his dick in deep again and held it there.

He was holding Ziggy tight against his crotch, his cock buried deep in Ziggy's ass, when they heard a women's voice say, "Oh my god!"

Startled, Ziggy and Josh turned their heads in the direction of the voice. Standing there at the top of the rocks was a young woman, watching them.

Chapter 7
Don't Stop

THE GUYS AND THE WOMAN STARED at one another, jaws dropped, mouths wide open.

Josh was speechless.

Ziggy said, "Oh fuck!"

Josh's dick was deep inside Ziggy's ass. They'd been caught fucking naked in public. Both of them knew this was not good. People ended up in jail for less.

The woman said, "Um, gosh, um, sorry, didn't know anybody was up here. Sorry." She quickly turned around to go back down the way she had come.

Her way was blocked, though, as a young man appeared from below, out of breath. He said, "We made it. Come on, let's get naked, babe."

The girl stood in front of him to block his view and motioned to him that they should go back down, but the guy looked around her and saw Josh and Ziggy, bare ass naked, with Josh's cock deep inside of Ziggy's butt, the two stuck together like dragonflies mating in midair. Ziggy's cock was fully hard and standing up and out, stiff, wet at the tip.

The guy said, "Holy shit!"

"Come on," the girl said to him. "We'll go someplace else."

The guy didn't move. He shook his head, stunned by what he was seeing. "I've heard of guys fucking, of course, but this . . . this is . . . oh, my god, Trudi, this is hot!"

"Come *on*, Danny. We don't belong here."

"No, Trudi." The guy couldn't take his eyes off of Josh and Ziggy. "We *do* belong here."

He said, "Sorry, guys. Don't stop. We didn't mean to interrupt you. Don't mind us, we won't bother you, not at all. We're here to fuck, too."

He turned to the woman and said, "Trudi, can't you see? We're all up here for the same reason." He turned back to the guys and grinned. Then he looked at her and said, "Right, baby?" He started unbuttoning her blouse.

She didn't stop him, but she said, "Danny, are you sure . . ."

"Yeah, babe, hell yes, why not? Wouldn't be the first time. Remember Ray's party?" He gently pulled off her blouse and then kissed her as he unfastened her bra.

Meanwhile Josh hadn't moved. Ziggy was still impaled on Josh's cock, grinning. "Dude," he whispered. "This is unbelievable. They're gonna fuck too. This is awesome."

"What should we do?" Josh whispered.

"Keep fucking me. Why stop now? And we can watch them, too. Go ahead, keep on fucking. This is turning you on, isn't it? Dude, your dick is as hard as wood, and so is mine. Go on, Josh, fuck me. Hell, they're not even paying attention, they're doing their own thing."

"Okay." Josh pulled his stiff cock halfway out of Ziggy's ass, and then he pushed it all the way back in.

"That's it. Makes your dick feel good, don't it? Let your dick take over, Josh. Let your dick do the fucking."

Josh continued moving his hard cock in and out of Ziggy's asshole, getting more and more into it, letting the feeling take over, almost too good to stop. Then he looked over at the other couple. "Jeez, they're watching us."

The young man and woman were nearly finished undressing each other. They weren't any older than twenty-two, the same age as Josh and Zig. The woman was completely naked, and she had stripped her boyfriend down all the way to his briefs. But they had paused and were watching Ziggy and Josh. The guy seemed especially fascinated.

He was taller than Ziggy or Josh by at least an inch or two, had mid-length brown hair, a lean body with good muscle tone, and a huge boner filling out his briefs.

When he and his girlfriend realized they'd been caught watching, they turned back to each other again. She pulled his underwear down and his mammoth cock came out, at least nine inches if not more, and it was thick, too. Standing straight out and throbbing.

Ziggy said, "Jesus. Look at that thing. It's huge."

"Fuck," Josh said. "Incredible." He slammed into Ziggy, pulled back out, and slammed in again.

"Oh, yeah. Fuck me, Josh. Fuck me with that beautiful cock of yours."

"Jeez, that thing makes mine look tiny."

"Oh, bullshit. Your cock is perfect. Go on, fuck me till we both shoot our loads. And if they're watching so much the better. They'll see me shoot my cum. Damn, this is kinky."

The woman was down on her knees. She licked her boy-friend's cock and put as much of it inside her mouth as she could, which wasn't much. The guy couldn't take his eyes off of Ziggy and Josh. Then he grimaced, pulled her up, and got down on his knees himself. He went right to her cunt and started licking like crazy.

"Oh, god, look at them, Zig. Look at what he's doing to her."

Ziggy looked and grinned. "He knows what he's doing. Look, it's driving her wild." The woman had her eyes closed and was moaning loudly.

Josh suddenly stopped in mid fuck again.

Ziggy said, "Jesus, don't stop now, dude. I'm getting close, aren't you?"

"Yeah, that's why I stopped. I was gonna come if I kept going."

"Well, go right ahead and fuck me till you come. I'm right on the edge, bro. Don't stop. I'm gonna come, just from you pounding me."

Josh resumed fucking. He went faster now, in and out. He looked over at the other two and said, "Now they're fucking, too."

Ziggy looked over and sure enough, the guy had his big cock halfway inside her, moving in and out while she was obviously in the throes of her orgasm.

Josh, with every thrust, pushed his cock into Ziggy as deep as it would go. Then he pulled almost all the way out and slammed in deep again. Moaning now. "Fucking you, Zig. Ahhhhh! Fucking the hell out of you!"

"Jesus, Josh. I'm gonna shoot! Keep it up, bro, I'm gonna shoot my load."

"You and me both, Zig. I don't think I could stop now if I had to."

"Oh, fuck, I feel it."

"I'm close, too."

"Keep going, dude. Oh, yeah. Oh, fuck, fuck yeah, fuck yes, that's it, I'm coming. Aaaaahhhh! Unnnnh!" Ziggy's first spurt of jizz shot out of his dick, then another even bigger shot, and more, one wad after another. Ropes of cum launched out of Ziggy's hard cock out into the air.

Josh kept fucking Ziggy hard, and then he yelled, "Fuck, I'm coming, too! Aaaaahhh! Aaahhhh!" Josh pistoned his cock into Ziggy's ass a couple more times and then held it deep while his balls emptied inside of Ziggy. "Ooohhhh."

Josh had his arms around Ziggy and held them tightly together as they twitched and moaned and shot their cum. When Josh was finally drained, he rested his head on Ziggy's shoulder, catching his breath.

Ziggy was spent, too, but excited. "You really hit it, bro. You made me come with your cock again. That was awesome." He straightened up, slowly, keeping Josh's dick in his ass. He turned his head and gave Josh a kiss. Josh loved it when they kissed.

Josh looked down at his cock as he slowly pulled it out of Ziggy's butt. Then off with the condom.

"Josh." Ziggy whispered, "We have an audience."

Josh looked. The girl and guy had finished fucking; they were dressing, watching Josh and Zig. Their smiles turned to grins and they started clapping when both guys looked their way.

Josh turned red with embarrassment. Ziggy just laughed.

The young man said, "You guys were awesome. We got totally turned on from watching you."

Ziggy said, "Same here, dude. Watching you." He grinned. Zig was still naked; he even had a strand of cum hanging from his semi-hard cock. "A good time was had by all," he said.

The guy laughed nervously, staring at Ziggy's dick. "Uh, you guys live around here?"

"He used to," Ziggy said, "but I grew up in St. Louis. That's where we both live now." Ziggy looked over at Josh.

Josh was still naked, too. He was bound and determined to stay nude in front of these people as long as Ziggy did, no matter how embarrassed he got.

"How about you," Ziggy said. He walked closer to the couple. "You live here?"

"I was born and raised here," the guy said. "Not in D.C., out in Maryland. Silver Spring. My friend, here, too, right, babe?" She nodded. She was blushing.

"We didn't mean to barge in on you guys," she said. "We didn't think anyone else knew about this place."

"No problem," Ziggy said. "It worked out just fine."

"Good thing it was us and not somebody else," the guy said. "Hell, I've . . . I've always wanted to watch a couple of guys go at it like that. That was hot." He was looking at Josh now, and blushing. "Really, really hot."

Josh said, "You grew up in Silver Spring? So did I."

"You did? I was just telling Trudi that I know you from some-where. Uh, you didn't by any chance go to Takoma Park Junior High, did you?"

Josh, still naked, walked over and stood next to Ziggy. "I sure did. You went there?"

"Yeah. I'll be damned."

"Wait a minute," Josh said. "Jeez, I know you. The basketball team."

"Yeah, that's right, I was on the team. Hey, now I remember. Of course. You were one of our managers. Umm, Joshua, right?"

"Yeah. Josh. Small world."

"I'm Daniel." He stepped over to Josh and shook hands. Now it was Josh's cock he couldn't stop looking at. It hadn't gone down much. It was half-hard and there was wet cum smeared on the head.

"I know your name," Josh said. "Jeez, Danny, you were my favorite out of the whole team." Josh looked down to see what Daniel was staring at and started blushing all over again.

Josh shook his dick to flick the cum off and then used his finger to wipe off what was left. He licked his finger, and then he blushed some more.

Memories flooded back. He couldn't count the number of times he'd wondered just what Daniel's cum tasted like. For the first time since high school, he wondered again. All the sexy things Josh used to fantasize about doing with Daniel flashed back to him. His cock started to tingle.

"Josh, we used to walk home together, remember that? After I got out of the showers? My house was on your way home, so we walked together."

"Yeah, I remember. I used to wait in the locker room for you while you showered."

"I don't know why we never . . . I mean, I don't know why I never asked you . . . over, or something. You seemed like a pretty cool dude, really." Daniel's eyes flicked from Josh's face down to his dick and then back up again.

"Danny, you were on the basketball team. You were first string, everybody's favorite athlete, and I was just a lowly manager."

"Everybody's favorite? No, I don't think so. But what difference would that make? I thought you were a cool dude. We should have hung out."

Josh's dick began to rise. "We were in different, uh, social circles, for one thing." Josh didn't need to look, he could feel it getting hard. How embarrassing. And each time he saw Daniel look at it, it got harder.

"Oh, right. The cliques. But I wasn't like that, Josh. Believe me, I wasn't in any clique. We should have hung out together." He stared at Josh's boner. Then he looked up. "Who cares what snobby people like that think anyway?"

Josh didn't know what to say.

Ziggy said, "Josh was kind of shy back then. Right Josh?"

"Yeah, I sure was."

"So was I," Daniel said. "That was my biggest hang-up."

"What? No way."

"Yeah, Josh. Couldn't you tell? Fuck, I still am. I'm sorry I never asked you over. God only knows what we missed out on."

"Aw, no problem."

"You live in St. Louis now?"

"Yeah. With Ziggy. Ziggy, this is Daniel. Daniel, Ziggy." As he shook hands with Ziggy, Daniel smiled. Then he looked at Ziggy's cock again, still half-hard and dripping cum.

Daniel started blushing again. He held onto Ziggy's hand. He looked into Ziggy's eyes, and then to Josh, and he seemed as though he was about to say something. But he didn't, or couldn't. He took a good look at Josh's dick again, which was fully hard and throbbing, much to Josh's embarrassment.

After a few more awkward moments, Daniel let go of Ziggy's hand.

Trudi looked as if she was ready to leave.

Daniel said, "I guess we ought to get going, guys. Listen, Josh, I still live in the same house. Drop on by before you go back to St. Louis." He shook Josh's hand. "Ziggy, you come, too. We'll eat some pizza, watch some flicks, drink some beer, and catch up on old times." He grinned. "You know, talk about whatever comes up."

Josh said, "I'd like to, Daniel, but I don't know if we can. We're only here for a couple of days."

"Make time, Josh. I'll . . . I'll stay home all day tomorrow. Come on by. It would mean a lot to me. Seriously, we need to, well, uh . . . hell. I want to see you guys again." He looked into Ziggy's eyes, and then to Josh's. Pleading.

Josh looked at Ziggy; Ziggy shrugged his shoulders.

Josh didn't know what else to say.

"Well, think about it. Because I really want you guys to come. And thanks for letting us join you up here. It was hot."

They said their goodbyes, and then Daniel and Trudi began their climb down. After they disappeared behind the hill, Ziggy picked up his underwear.

"You wanna get going too, Josh? Or do you want to go another round? You look like you're ready to go again." Ziggy grinned.

"God, no. That wore me out."

"Let's go back to the hotel and sit in the hot tub for a while, you want to?"

"Sounds good, Zig."

"And after that I'll give you a massage. If you want one."

"Now you're talking. Hell yes."

—

ZIGGY AND JOSH MADE THEIR WAY down the hillside. They crossed the footbridge over the creek and got back inside their car, a yellow '72 Mustang. It was Josh's car, actually. Ziggy rode shotgun as Josh drove north toward their hotel.

"I'm starving," Ziggy said. "How about you?"

"Yeah, me too. Let's stop somewhere for dinner. Want to?"

"Definitely, bro."

"I'm thinking seafood, but anything'll work for me. What are you up for?"

"They have fresh-caught crabs around here, right? And oysters? Seafood sounds perfect, Josh. I've never had it fresh before."

"Oysters aren't in season, but the crabs should be excellent. Fresh off the boat."

So they ended up at Crisfield's on Georgia Avenue, just south of the heart of Silver Spring.

They ordered their food and waited.

"This reminds me of the very first meal we had together," Ziggy said. "You remember?"

"Bacon and eggs and pancakes at Denny's," Josh said.

"You got it. A year ago." Ziggy grinned.

"August 25, '85. Seems like just yesterday, but in a way it seems like ancient history. I feel like I've known you forever, Zig."

"Same here, but you know what? I still thank my lucky stars, every night, for letting me meet you. No telling where I'd be right now, otherwise. Not a very happy place, I'm sure of that."

"Oh, hell, you'd have found someone in any case."

"Nobody like you. Not even close. And I wouldn't have settled for less."

"I'm the one who's lucky, for meeting you. There's probably no one else on earth like you, Zig. Anyway, if it weren't for you I'd probably be dead by now. Or still cleaning house for the Beastmaster."

"Well, we're both lucky then."

"We are."

"Damn right," Ziggy said.

"You sure had me fooled at first, though. I thought I was gonna have to give up sex to be your friend."

"You fooled yourself, Josh. I never claimed to be straight."

"Yeah, I know, I know. It was probably for the best anyway. It really helped clarify what I really wanted."

"You wanted a friend."

"Yeah."

"Me too, Josh. That's what I saw in you when we first met. Somebody who could maybe be my true friend. My best buddy."

"That's what I saw in you too, Zig, except I thought it was impossible. You know, to even get to know you."

"Yeah, I remember."

"Then, two days later, I was in love with you."

Ziggy grinned. "That fast, huh?"

"Yeah, looking back on it. Yeah. That fast. Sunday night."

"It took me a little longer."

"Well, that figures, I guess, since you're not, you know, strictly gay. How long did it take you?"

"Looking back on it?"

"Yeah."

"Honestly?"

"Yeah."

"For me, it was more like three days."

"What? Aw, go on. No way."

"Dude, you turned my whole world around. By the time we went to bed that Monday night, yeah, Josh, I was in love with you. Maybe I wouldn't have called it that at the time, but I was. I was silly in love. Goofy in love. It was all I could do not to tell you. Not that I would have known what to say. But I was."

"Oh my god. You're blowing my mind."

"We did the right thing, though. That was a good thing, keeping it to ourselves. We let it grow naturally. We let it simmer. To perfection. If we'd talked about it too soon we might have spoiled it, somehow."

"I think I understand, Zig. But jeez, that's so cool. To know you felt the same way. I feel tingly all over, thinking about it."

Ziggy laughed. Then he lowered his voice. "Josh," he said, "do you have a hard on?"

"God yes," Josh whispered. "How'd you know?"

"'Cause I do, too."
"Really?"
"Fucking hurts, it's so hard."
"I have an idea, Zig."

Chapter 8
AS IN MOTION

ZIGGY DIDN'T HAVE TO ASK what the idea was.

"You think we have time?" he said.

"Hell yes."

Ziggy looked around the restaurant and saw where the bathroom was. "Okay," he said. "Fuck, they can't help but notice our boners if anyone sees us walk by, but I don't care, let 'em look. I'll go first. Wait half a minute and then follow me in."

"Okay."

—

BY THE TIME THEY RETURNED, the waitress was setting the food down on their table.

"There you boys are. I was beginning to wonder if you were coming back."

"Sorry," Ziggy said, as they sat down. "Nature called. You know how that is."

"Oh yes, I do. Not a problem. I knew you'd be back eventually. I saw the two of you get up. I hope you feel better now. Both of you." She winked at Josh. Josh turned beet red.

Ziggy just laughed. "Yes, ma'am, we feel much better now. Ready to eat some of your famous seafood."

"Well, it's ready for you. Enjoy your meal. Let me know if you need anything." She smiled and walked away.

"Zig," Josh whispered, "I think she knows we sucked each other off in there."

"Yeah," he said, "I think so too. But she didn't seem to mind. Whatever. Let's eat."

—

WHEN THEY RETURNED to the hotel, they changed into swim trunks, walked to the pool area, and submerged themselves into the swirling, soothing water of the hot tub. Ziggy lay his head back and relaxed.

"Feels good, don't it, Josh?"

"Feels great."

They were silent for a while, moving up and down in the hot water, shifting their bodies to let the water jets hit them in different places, relaxing.

After ten minutes or so, Ziggy spoke up. "So," he said, "I actually got to meet one of your lust objects from the basketball team, how cool is that?"

"Yeah," Josh said. "Amazing. And did you hear how he was talking? Was I only imagining it or was he saying we could have been fooling around back then?"

"It did kinda sound that way. Or it could be he was just lonely back then and wanted a friend. After all, he was shy. You know how that can be. Maybe he didn't have any close friends. Maybe he still doesn't. Maybe he needs some."

"Jeez, Zig, either way I would have been in paradise. If I'd only known."

"Known what?"

"That he wanted somebody. That he didn't already have somebody. I don't know. Hell, I just wish I'd known he was shy."

"What would you have done?"

"Um, ask myself over, I guess."

"Yeah, that would have worked."

"You think so?"

"Sometimes that's all it takes."

"Really? That easy."

"And if not, it's a first step. Can't take the second step till you've taken the first."

"The first step is the hardest."

"That's exactly right, Josh. It is. Once you get that far, things get easier."

They sat in the hot tub for another few minutes, and then jumped into the pool to cool off.

"Dude looked strong."

"Daniel? Yeah, I know. I used to think he had the perfect body. Basketball and swimming kept him in shape, and judging from the way he looks now, he's still at it."

"He must be doing something right, that's for sure."

"Zig, were you serious about giving me a massage?"

"Yeah, definitely. I want to make you feel good, bro." He grinned. "Why, are you ready for it?"

"I am *so* ready."

Ziggy laughed. "Let's go, then."

—

ZIGGY WAS GOOD at massages. It always started with a shower together. Then, with both of them still naked, Josh would lay face down on the bed. Ziggy kneeled over him, one knee on each side of Josh's back, and then he sat down on Josh's ass.

Ass to ass, Ziggy worked on Josh's shoulder muscles. That's how he started. He didn't stop until he'd massaged every part of Josh's entire body and, most of the time, both of them had come at least once.

When the massage was over, they lay side by side and stared at the ceiling for a while.

"Zig, I get to massage you next time."

"I'm ready whenever you are, bro. Just say the word."

"Cool."

They lay on their backs for a few more minutes, then Ziggy turned on his side toward Josh and said, "You the bear?"

"Yeah, I'll be the teddy bear tonight." Josh turned on his side facing away from Ziggy, and Ziggy pulled him close. They fit together like spoons. Ziggy had his arm wrapped around Josh, and Josh held Ziggy's hand to his chest.

"Does that guy Daniel know how to get in touch with you?"

"No," Josh said. "I've moved at least four times since those days. Actually, he probably never did know where I lived."

"Oh yeah? Why is that?"

Josh was silent for a minute. Then he said, "Well, I guess because I never asked him over,"

"Do you know where he lives?"

"Yeah, I know where he lives."

"Then it's your move, dude."

"What?"

"Your move."

"I'm supposed to make a move?"

"Not like in a game. Your move like, as in, motion. As in, do something. Because the way he was talking, it's not too late for a little of whatever you missed out on back then. *He* can't take the next step because he doesn't know how to find you. It's on you, bro. Your move, or else it won't happen."

"It still sounds a little like playing checkers. My move."

"Well, think of it as strip poker then, not checkers. But it's not a game. I'm talking about real life. People always have a little back-and-forth interaction when they're getting to know each other. It's how you find out if you're on the same wavelength." Ziggy turned onto his back and put his hands behind his head.

"Look," he said, "your cock used to get hard just from walking home with him. You've told me that. Now *he's* talking about what you guys should have been doing together. About what you didn't do because you were both shy. I'll bet his dick got hard sometimes too, back then, thinking about you. And now he's not as shy as he used to be, and you're not, either."

"Are you saying I should go over there and see if he wants to fuck? Or suck?"

"Or you could at least be buddies for a day, which is just as good. Why not? You liked each other. I don't mean ask him outright about sex – just hang out together for half an hour and you'll know. You won't even need to ask. If he's horny, you'll know it."

"But why would he want me?"

"Josh, we've talked about this sort of thing before. Why *wouldn't* he want you?"

Josh turned onto his back and looked at Zig beside him on the bed. "But you and I are only here for a couple of days, Zig. Then we go to Florida. This is our vacation, our anniversary. I want to be with *you*, not away from you. I'd be thinking of you the whole time. And besides, things have changed since those school days."

"How so?"

"I know what love is, now. Don't laugh. I mean it."

"I'm not laughing. I'm with you all the way, Josh. I love you, too."

"So why . . ."

"Because you still know what lust is, too. You lusted for him big time, back then. You told me you did. If that's changed, if he doesn't turn you on anymore, then fine. But you could have been buddies, and here's your chance finally. You wanted him, he wanted you, at least in some way or another, but it didn't happen, and that's the way you parted. This is your chance to bring an old friendship to a better finish. Or reconnect. And in the process, if he still makes your dick get hard, why not find out if he wants you, too? You could finish that situation with a smile. What have you got to lose?"

"You. That's what."

"Josh. You know better than that. You and me are buddies for life, man. Or as long as you can stand me, whichever's longer."

"I'll never get tired of hearing you say that, Zig. Same here. Buddies forever."

"As for Daniel, well, the way I figure it, the more friends, the better. The more real friends, at least. That goes for all of us. Look, we already missed out on making friends with an awesome dude, Franklin, just yesterday. Now you have another chance with Daniel. He seems like a decent guy. I'm not talking about sex necessarily, I'm talking about friendship."

"Okay. Alright, Zig, I'll go. But only if you come with me."

"Dude. If it turns out he does want to have sex with you, how are you gonna get naked with him with me around? Think about it."

"Zig, *you* think about it."

"Uh . . . you mean, the three of us?"

"Why not?"

Chapter 9
ALWAYS WANTED TO

"I DON'T KNOW IF HE'D GO for that, Josh. I don't even know if *I'd* go for it. I've never been with two guys at once. How does that work?"

"Zig, come on, you gotta be kidding. The same way it does for you and me and a girl, you goofball."

"I guess that figures. Well," Ziggy said, "he did look pretty hot fucking Trudi with that huge dick. I guess I could do something with him if you were there, Josh. But no way is that monster dick of his gonna go up my ass. And if you want my advice, you won't let it go up yours either. That thing's huge."

"Aw, it isn't *that* big. I've seen porn stars just as big. Or bigger, and they don't have trouble finding guys who can handle it. Anyway, there's plenty of other stuff we can do. Maybe he doesn't want to fuck anyway. Maybe he only wants to *get* fucked. Or suck and be sucked."

"I could fuck him, Josh, but then I'd probably have to let him fuck me. With that cock? Jesus, no. That thing looked like the thick end of a baseball bat. You saw it. It must weigh at least five pounds."

"No way. You're exaggerating."

Ziggy turned on his side toward Josh. "Well, maybe so, but that's the way I remember it."

"Aw, this is nuts." Josh rolled over facing Ziggy. "We don't even know if he's interested. He's probably completely straight."

"Yeah, like you used to think I was."

"Zig, I'm serious."

"He asked you over, plain as day."

"Yeah, well, for old time's sake. Hell, he has Trudi, why would he want me?"

"Josh, remember how hard you got from watching them fuck? Your dick was so stiff it felt like wood. They got off on watching us, too. He even said so. Didn't you see him stare at our dicks?"

With all the talk about sex, Josh's cock was totally hard now. Ziggy's dick was growing, too.

"Really," Ziggy said, "we've had sex together once already, basically, and I think he wants to again. Why not? Only this time, with all four of us *really* together. Sucking cocks, fucking each other, getting fucked . . ."

"Aw, jeez, stop, Zig." Josh lay flat on his back again, and his hard cock stood up, throbbing. "You talk anymore like that, I'll have to jack off just from thinking about it."

"You're ready to go again? Fuck, you are, aren't you."

"Yeah, if you keep talking that way. Danny's hot."

"All four of us, sucking, fucking, getting sucked . . ."

"Alright, that's it," Josh said. "You're sucking me off."

Ziggy laughed.

"If you want to, that is."

"Josh, I definitely want to."

Ziggy put his hand on Josh's hard cock. "You know, I like the way that Daniel guy thinks. Not too many dudes would have stayed right there and fucked alongside of us the way he did." Ziggy moved down lower on the bed for better access.

"I only know of two people like that in the whole world," Josh said. "Ahh, Zig, that feels good."

"Who's that?"

"Daniel, and you."

Monday

JOSH AND ZIGGY ENDED UP GOING to Daniel's house the following day. Josh pointed out the house and drove around the block twice. But then he surprised them both by driving away.

"Jesus, Josh! Park the car. We'll knock on his door. What's the worst that could happen?"

"I don't know. Maybe he was just being nice. Maybe he doesn't really want us to come over?"

"Josh. We both know he meant it. So what is it?"

"I don't know. Being shy, I guess. Okay, hell, I'll do it." Josh turned at the next corner to head back. "But his parents might be there. I've never met them."

"So? If his parents are home, we'll go up to his room or something. Ask him out for a ride. And Trudi, too, of course, if she's there. Problem solved."

"And then what? Take them to our hotel room?"

"Well, god knows our bed's big enough. Get coffee or drinks somewhere, and then, yeah, that's probably where we'd end up. Unless you'd rather go to the woods again." Ziggy smiled. "At the hotel we could get them stoned and lie on the bed and watch the Playboy Channel. That might stir things up a little."

"Oh, jeez, Zig. Playboy Channel doesn't even show soft dicks, let alone hard dicks or sex. I don't know why people watch it."

"No way."

"Swear to god. We'd be better off renting a fuck flick."

"Okay, let's go rent a movie, then. A bisexual flick, with a woman and at least two guys who fuck her and fuck each other, too, and they suck each other's dicks and eat pussy and stuff. Regular-looking guys like us, not porn stars."

"Amateurs, you're talking about. I like those too. Okay, well, there's a video store not too far from here. Hell, let's do it."

"And then we go back and knock on his door, right?"

"Scout's honor. Remember, though, he's probably straight."

"Maybe he is, Josh. We'll find out. Don't worry, I'm not gonna assume anything. We'll just see how it goes."

—

DANIEL ANSWERED THE DOOR. He started blushing right off, but he was happy to see them.

"I was afraid you guys wouldn't come by," he said.

By the time they were done shaking hands he had a huge boner. It was reaching down the leg of his jeans, pointed toward his knee, and it was thick. His jeans didn't do much to hide it.

He led them inside and caught both of them looking at his huge erection. He turned even redder in the face and said, "Fuck, guys, that was so hot yesterday, I can't stop thinking about it." He took them into the living room.

The TV was on. "Make yourselves at home," he said. "Uh, I was watching baseball. We can turn it off if you want. It's just us here, by the way."

"Your parents aren't home?"

"They both passed away, Josh. My dad when I was young, and then my mother, last year. Go ahead, sit down, guys." He turned down the TV volume.

Josh sat at the end of the couch. "Sorry to hear that."

"Trudi's not here? I thought maybe you two were, you know, together." Ziggy sat at the other end of the couch, leaving a spot in the middle for Daniel.

"Nah. We tried that. Didn't work out, so now we're just good buddies. We fuck around sometimes when we're horny, you know? Anyway, she, uh, stayed away today on purpose. She thought it would go better if it was just us guys. You're not bummed out, are you?" He smiled, nervously.

"Yeah," Ziggy said, grinning. "I wanted to see you two fuck again."

Daniel started blushing again, but he laughed. "Sorry to disappoint you." He sat on the couch, between his two visitors.

"She wouldn't want to do that again anyway. I probably would, but she usually likes to keep stuff like that pretty private."

"She wasn't very private yesterday."

"That's the only time we've ever done it in front of other people like that. Except once at a party where everybody ended up stoned, or drunk, naked, fucking all over the place. She's not into having sex in front of other people."

"Are you?"

"Uhh." His face started turning red as he stared at Ziggy. "Do you really want to know?"

"Yeah, sure."

"Well, uh, actually, I love it. Isn't that perverted? But I do. At least I did the few times it's happened. I've always liked showing off my hard dick, but having sex in front of other people . . . god."

Ziggy laughed.

Josh looked surprised. "I wish I had known that."

All three of them took a good look at Daniel's huge boner, perfectly outlined inside his jeans.

Then Danny looked up and smiled. "So, uh, Josh. You used to wait for me in the locker room, after basketball practice?"

"Yeah, you know I did, Danny."

"I figured you were cleaning up or something, putting the balls away, doing Manager stuff while we were showering."

"Well, that stuff took all of about five minutes. No, I was mostly just sitting on a bench, listening to you guys chatter while you took your showers. And I watched you come back to your lockers, one by one, naked."

"That must have been hot, huh?"

"Yeah, it was. Kind of a forbidden thrill. But the best part was walking home with you, that's what I liked best."

"Yeah, I liked that, too," Daniel said. "I wish I'd known you were gay back then."

"What would you have done?"

"I don't know. I really don't know, Josh. Hell, it was all I could do not to get a hard on in the showers, looking at all those cocks and asses. It would have been nice to know that you and I had, uh, you know, kind of a mutual interest."

"A mutual interest?"

"You know, like, 'Show me yours and I'll show you mine.'"

"Well, that would have been awesome. But I could hardly admit to myself, feeling that way, in those days. You would have had to make the first move."

"Some of the guys on the team were hoping you were gay."

"What? No way!"

"Yeah. Vernon, and Jack, and, uh, Mike, at least. I heard them talking once. They thought you might be. Wishful thinking, that's what I figured. I mean, as far as I know those guys were straight, but they didn't have steady girlfriends, so yeah, they would have gladly let you give them blowjobs."

"*Let* me?"

"That's how straight guys talk about it, Josh. Of course, they wouldn't have kept their mouths shut about it afterwards; they weren't very smart that way. But I figured they were dreaming. You? Gay? Shy, yeah, but not gay. It just didn't seem likely to me."

"God, what jerks. Maybe that explains . . . I don't know if you knew it, Danny, but at the beginning of the season, Vernon took his sweaty shirt off one time, out on the court, when he and I were the last ones in, and he tossed it to me. He said, 'Carry my shirt in for me, *Manager*.' I threw the smelly thing right back at him and said, 'Carry it yourself.' He looked kind of surprised. Disappointed. I always wondered what that was all about."

"He was testing you. Seeing how far you'd go."

"That's kind of what I thought. *You* never would have done something like that, but I guess he didn't mind pushing it. Actually, if you had thrown me your shirt I would have gladly carried it. But you had a girlfriend. You *always* had a girlfriend. Linda, in seventh grade, and then from eighth grade on you were going with Deana. I never had a chance."

"Josh, it wasn't like I was fucking either one of them. Hell, how old were we, fourteen years old? Fifteen? You definitely had a chance. We just didn't know. We didn't know that about each other."

"At least you let me be friends with you. That meant a lot to me, Danny."

"Of course I did."

"Some of those guys really thought they were hotshots. But you weren't like that."

"Fuck no. Yeah, some of those guys could be real assholes. The girls saw right through it, though – there was a reason those guys didn't have steady girlfriends. They could be real dicks sometimes. You couldn't have told them that, though. They thought it was their right."

"You treated everyone with respect."

"I didn't have any reason not to. That 'Better than thou' attitude was bullshit. Every little thing was competition to them. Did you know those guys used to make fun of how big my cock is?"

"Aw, that's crazy. Really? They were just jealous, Danny."

"I know. I figured that out pretty fast. The few times I got boned up in the showers, they couldn't keep their eyes off it. A couple of them even asked if they could feel it, can you believe it?"

"They probably all wanted to."

"Maybe. When it was hard, they all got boners from looking at it, every one of them. Then they wanted to see me jerk off. You must have heard them talking."

"God, no. I don't remember that."

"I did it, too."

"You jacked off in front of them?"

"Yeah! That one time I did. And they did, too. Watching me. It was horny as hell."

"The whole basketball team jacked off in there?"

"Yeah, that one time, every one of them did. Watching me. I loved it. It was trippy. God, there was cum everywhere."

"Incredible."

"I told you I like to show off. I like to watch, too," Daniel said. "Fucking in the woods yesterday was totally awesome. I got to show off and watch you guys at the same time. I'd never seen a guy fuck another guy before." Daniel lowered his voice. "I always wanted to, though."

"Always wanted to what," Ziggy said, "fuck another guy?"

"Christ, that's not what I meant. But, uh, well, I *have* tried to imagine what it would be like. I'll probably try it if I ever get the chance. But until yesterday I had never actually seen it. Seeing you two fucking right in front of me – that was awesome."

Daniel's big hard-on hadn't gone down at all. He had been sneaking looks at Josh and Ziggy since they got there. He knew guys usually got boned up when they saw him hard, and he was totally okay with that. Josh, definitely, was full-on hard now, and Ziggy looked well on his way.

"You guys were hot yesterday," Daniel said. His face started turning red again. He leaned back in the couch and closed his eyes. "I get horny thinking about it. Imagining." The hard dick inside his jeans was proof of that.

"You liked that, huh?"

"Fuck yeah." Daniel opened his eyes and grinned. "I'd love to watch you two fuck again."

Ziggy grinned, too. "You never know. Anything's possible."

"You should try it yourself," Josh said. "You might like it."

Daniel laughed nervously. "I might have to, if it's as hot as it looks." He shook his head. "But seriously, I didn't know it could be that good for both guys. Doesn't it hurt?"

"Nope," Ziggy said, "not if the guy doing the fucking knows what he's doing, and takes his time. It can be really awesome."

Daniel grinned. "Josh must be an expert, then."

"Oh, you could tell, huh?"

"Hell, Ziggy, it was obvious. Your cock stayed stiff and hard the whole time he was fucking your hot ass. He had to be doing something right."

Ziggy smiled. "He *is* good. He's just naturally good at it. If you ever want somebody to fuck you, Daniel, choose Josh. I promise you won't regret it."

"Whoa, wait a minute, I never said I want to be fucked. I'm not . . ." Daniel blushed again. "Scratch that, what I mean is, I never . . . I've never done anything like that before. I've . . . okay, I've thought about it, but hell, I wouldn't know how to go about doing it."

"Aw, that's no problem. We could show you."

"Oh god."

"Ziggy showed me how to enjoy it," Josh said. "He was really gentle. It was the first time I ever actually liked it. And I learned how to be good at fucking him, too. I wasn't expecting that."

"Well, I'll say this much: after yesterday," Daniel said, "I've thought about it a lot. I mean, more than ever. Oh, hell, I can't stop thinking about it. I've been trying to imagine what it must feel like. It sure as hell must have felt good for you, Ziggy. You got off without even touching your cock, didn't you? That was so horny to watch. It must have been pure ecstasy."

"It was. And Josh is right, you should try it. It's awesome."

"Oh, man. Having a dick up my ass? I mean, thinking about it is one thing. I've fantasized about it. But actually doing it? Jesus. I don't know."

"Well, keep thinking about it at least. Even straight guys like it sometimes. You'd be surprised."

"Yeah, that's what Trudi said."

"What?"

"But another thing I've been thinking about is how good it must have felt for Josh yesterday. Fucking your hot ass, Ziggy. The look on his face while he was fucking you. God, I get a boner every time I think about it. His eyes were glazed and everything.

Fucking your beautiful ass. Now *that,* Ziggy, is something I *would* love to try. If you're up for it."

Chapter 10
Too Much

FOR ONCE Ziggy was surprised. "Listen to you, Daniel. Jesus, for a shy guy you sure do get right to the point." He smiled. "I like that."

Once again, Daniel was blushing. "Well, we fucked right in front of each other yesterday. It's not like we haven't seen each other naked before. Naked and hard and shooting our cum. We got off on doing it, too. If we'd been any closer we'd have been fucking each other. So there's no use in being shy about it now."

Ziggy, totally hard now, looked at the huge boner lurking in Daniel's jeans. "Dan," he said, "I do love getting fucked by Josh. I'd be lying if I said I don't. We love each other, and that's a big part of it. Another big part is that it feels so good. Somehow he knows exactly what to do. His cock is big, but I can handle it. Hell, it's a perfect fit. Yours – fuck, I don't know."

"Yeah, I know. It's too big."

"I don't know about that, but it's definitely bigger than anything I'm used to. Fuck, dude. Watching you and your awesome cock yesterday was definitely hot, but honestly, I'm not sure I could take that monster."

"Aw, come on, please don't call it that. Yeah, it's big, but it's not that big. Nine inches, max. It's just . . . extra large. Not a monster. It makes me feel like a freak when people call it that."

"Okay, well, um, what I mean to say is, theoretically, I wouldn't be opposed to trying it. After watching each other yesterday, we're basically fuck buddies already. And you and Josh go way back. So, uh, sure. But Dan . . . I've only had two dicks up my ass, ever, and neither one of them comes close to the size of yours."

"Well, I'd love to fuck somebody's ass, for sure, but I didn't mean to presume . . . I just thought . . . you enjoyed it so much yesterday . . . you might . . . I don't know." Daniel sighed. "Fuck, that was so horny. Watching him fuck your sexy hot ass. But Josh, don't get me wrong, buddy, I'd be up for fucking you too."

"Oh god, no, Danny. I'm not ready for that. I mean, yeah, really, I'd love to get you off one way or another, but—"

"Oh hell, I know. No need to explain. I know. My cock is too fucking big, that's what everybody says. I hardly ever get to fuck anybody. Girls won't let me. They talk as if they want to, but as soon as they see how big the fucking thing is they say, no way." He sighed. "I'm used to it. No problem."

"Well, hold on now," Ziggy said. "Yeah, it's pretty damn big, but other guys have dicks that big, and they find asses to fuck."

"I wish somebody would tell me how, then."

"It's not impossible, not by a long shot. Fuck, you can't give up like that. Hell, I'll bet most people would love to have a dick like that up their ass, if they knew it wasn't gonna hurt. You just have to make sure you get the person's asshole completely relaxed before you think about putting it in."

"Completely relaxed? Okay, how do I do that?"

"It's pretty simple, but it requires some work, and patience. If you do it right, most of the time they'll *ask* you to fuck them."

"You can't be in a hurry," Josh said. "Also, with a dick that big, it would help to find somebody who's already used to getting fucked. Ziggy's right, it could feel good for both of you if you do it right."

"Well, I'd love to learn how. Girl or guy. People take one look at this cursed thing I have and you can almost hear their assholes and pussies slam shut. You don't know how lucky you guys are to have normal size dicks. I'd trade mine for either one of your guys' cocks. Gladly."

"Aw, Danny, you don't really mean that," Josh said.

"Oh yes I do. Sure, people like to *look* at my cock; they want to hold it, feel it – but that's as far as it goes. Fuck, I'm tired of being treated like a freak. And not getting laid."

"I'd love to try and get it in my mouth," Josh said. Then he started blushing.

"That doesn't work either, Josh. I can't even get good head. It's not only too long, it's too thick. All the guys talk about how fantastic it is to get a good blowjob, but Trudi can't even get the head of my cock in her mouth without scraping it with her teeth."

"Ouch."

"Just like every other girl who's tried. If I can even get them to try. Usually they won't. Hell, I'm lucky that Trudi lets me fuck her at all. She can't take the whole thing. I always have to be careful not to go in all the way. It leaves me feeling horny, constantly."

"Jeez, Danny, couldn't she just lick it? That's enough to get me off sometimes."

"Josh, she doesn't *want* to lick it *or* suck it. Truth is, she thinks cocks and cum are nasty. That's the other problem. Fuck it, guys, let's not even talk about it anymore. It gets me depressed."

Ziggy looked at Josh, and Josh looked at Ziggy.

"Daniel," Ziggy said, "we brought some good weed, bro. That might make you feel better. You get high, don't you?"

"Hell yes. Break it out. You want me to get my bong?"

"Yeah, a bong would be great."

Daniel went into his bedroom and brought out a nice water pipe made out of decorative glass. He handed it to Ziggy. "You guys want a beer? Or a Coke?"

Josh said, "I'll take a Coke."

"I'll take whatever you're having," Ziggy said.

"Two beers and a Coke, coming up." Daniel walked into the kitchen.

Ziggy whispered to Josh, "Let's find out how horny he is, want to?"

Josh grinned. "Definitely."

Chapter 11
CONFUSION

THE THREE OF THEM spread out on the couch, watching the baseball game and taking turns on the bong.

Daniel's boner still hadn't gone down at all, and Josh and Ziggy couldn't help noticing. Seeing the outline and shape of it was keeping their cocks hard, too, which didn't go unnoticed by Daniel.

After they had a good buzz going he said, "Fuck, I can't watch baseball when I'm stoned. Let's do something else. You mind?"

"Not at all," Ziggy said. "Any good movies on?"

Daniel flipped through the channels. "There's not much to choose from. I only get basic cable. But I have a VCR, we could watch a fuck flick."

"You have porn videos?"

"Well, only a couple."

"What kind?"

"I don't know if you'd like them. They're straight flicks. Um, gangbang flicks. A bunch of guys with one girl. Like, one after the other, they fuck her. Or get sucked off by her. Sometimes two at once. Hell, sometimes three at once."

"You like those?"

"Yeah, actually I think they're pretty hot. I know, I know. Some people think that sort of thing is demeaning to the woman, but that's not why I like them. I like looking at the horny guys and all their hot, hard dicks and, god, the constant cumshots. Christ, I've watched those tapes so much I've just about worn them out."

Josh and Ziggy didn't know what to say. They looked at each other, and then back at Daniel.

"I don't know," he said, "on second thought, maybe you guys *would* like them. All those horny guys stroking their hard cocks, fucking and getting sucked off, shooting their loads. One cumload after another. It's hot."

"Jeez, Danny."

"Do you think it sounds gay? I mean, for me to like dicks so much? Trudi says she thinks I'm bisexual. And lately I've been thinking maybe . . . maybe she's right. Maybe I am."

"She does?"

"Yeah. Oh, she's okay with it. She knows me better than anyone else. Better than I know myself, sometimes. We grew up together. Anyway, so, yeah, she thinks I want to be with a guy. And the more I think about it, the more I think she might be right. Especially after watching you guys yesterday."

"You think so?"

"Yeah." Daniel's eyes started to fill with tears. "So, like, I don't really know what to say or what to ask, but I was hoping maybe you guys could help me figure it out. Somehow." Daniel was trembling. "It's kind of been driving me crazy."

—

JOSH WAS THERE for him. "Oh my god, Danny. Of course we can help. You're blowing my mind, though," he said. "I wasn't expecting this. I always figured you were straight."

"I always thought so, too, but the last couple of years it's been confusing. I mean, I've always liked looking at guys' dicks, but I never put much meaning to it. Because I do like women. But lately I've been thinking about it more and more. Trudi picked up on it, and said something about it, and she's really been . . . supportive, I guess is the word for it. Supportive of whatever it is that's going on with me. But yesterday, seeing you guys made everything a hell of a lot clearer to me."

"Watching us made it clearer?"

"Yes! Because I didn't just want to watch you guys, I wanted be part of it. I did. I wanted to join in. I wanted to be the one fucking Ziggy, or the one getting fucked by Josh. Or even hotter, be in the middle, between you guys. Getting it both ways. Or even if I could have just sucked Ziggy's awesome hard cock. I've never done anything like that before. But yesterday I think I would have. I wanted to."

"Wow, Danny. Yeah, that's . . . that's clearly . . . something."

"Not only for the sex, either; for the . . . intimacy. That's what I've been missing. I want that. I want a buddy I can do stuff like that with. Hug each other – you know, put our arms around each other and, hell, just generally touch each other anytime we feel like it. Any place we want to. But I don't want to give up girls, either. I don't have to choose, do I? Fuck, I'm so confused."

"Danny, it's always confusing. Figuring out this kind of stuff about yourself. Don't worry, it'll . . . work out. And sure, we'll help you," Josh said. "Let's talk about it."

Ziggy said, "Well, it seems to me the first thing you should understand is, however you are, or want to be, it's completely okay. And natural. To be that way. It's what you are, Dan – the way you were made. What would be unnatural would be to deny it or fight it. Don't think you need to hide it, whatever it is. You sure don't need to hide it from us, at least. Believe me, no matter how it turns out we're still gonna be your friends."

"I've been worrying about this so much, I think I'm already there, Zig. Hell, at this point I pretty much don't care. Bring it on. Fuck. If I'm gay, fine. If I'm bisexual, fine. I just want to figure it out. What I am, who I am, and then learn how to deal with it. Learn how to accept it. It's driving me crazy, not knowing. I don't know how to act, half the time."

"Well, let's take one part at a time. Do women still turn you on?"

"Oh sure, definitely. That hasn't changed. The only thing is, like, sometimes I wonder if I'm misrepresenting myself to women.

I mean, are they assuming I'm completely straight? Should I tell them I like guys too? But I'll figure that out eventually I guess. That's a minor detail."

"If you still like women," Josh said, "if they still turn you on, then as far as labels go, that leaves out being gay. You're either straight or you're bisexual."

"But if I'm bisexual doesn't that mean I'm partly gay?"

"That's one way to look at it," Ziggy said. "I mean, that's what I am. Partly gay and partly straight. But what took me a while to understand is, I'm both, at the same time. I guess that's why they invented the word bisexual, although I'm not completely happy about that label either."

"But you're okay with that? Being partly gay? And partly straight?"

"I'd rather look at it in a different way, Dan. I'm attracted to both sexes. I'm not partly anything. My affection for people potentially covers everybody. The people who are restricted to liking only one gender – those are the people who are only 'partly' something."

"Oh. Wow. That's awesome. I like that."

"But this whole label business is pretty lame if you ask me. I'd be a lot happier if people didn't worry about it. Worrying about all that stuff seems like a big waste of time to me. Worrying about it, that's not gonna change who you are. People should like who they like, love who they love, and have sex with whoever they choose, as long as it's consensual and doesn't hurt anyone. Period. People should let people be. Everybody's different, and that's a good thing."

"You make it sound so easy, Zig."

"Well, it is easy. But that doesn't mean it can't be confusing. I'm gonna go out on a limb here, Daniel, and say that a lot of your confusion might simply be from not having tried *doing* the stuff you want to do."

"Yeah. That's probably true. I've been afraid to, I guess."

"Well, maybe so," Josh said, "but you can't try it without having someone to try it with."

"Tell me about it. There's never been any guys I could even talk to about it, let alone try something with."

"Until now, at least," Josh said.

"Yeah," Daniel said. "Thank god I have some guys I can talk to now."

"Not only talk to," Ziggy said. "You've got guys you can try something with now, too."

"Jesus! Sure, if you're willing. Fuck, I'd love to. But I don't even know where to start. It's all a little scary."

"Zig," Josh said, "We have those movies we rented. We could watch one of those for starters. I mean if Danny wants to. They might be more appropriate than, uh, the ones he has."

"You rented some movies?"

"Yeah, a couple of skin flicks," Ziggy said, grinning. "But dude, all this is your call. I think Josh is right, though. It might be a good place to start."

"Fuck yeah, let's take a look. Might be just the thing to lighten things up."

"They're right outside in the car," Josh said. "I'll go get 'em."

Chapter 12
DEMONSTRATION

JOSH WENT OUT THE DOOR, and Daniel said, "Listen, Ziggy, I want to apologize for assuming too much."

"About what?"

"That you'd let me fuck you."

"No problem, bro. You never know unless you ask."

"It's just that . . . you clearly enjoyed it so much yesterday, I thought maybe, well . . . you know. Look, are you and Josh, um, in a monogamous relationship? I don't want to interfere with something like that, either."

"No, we can fuck around with other people if we want to. So far we haven't, or at least I haven't, except for when we do it together, but it's . . . allowed. We're free spirits, Dan. We're also partners. Nothing's gonna change that. We love each other too much for anything to fuck that up."

"That's cool. Wish I had someone like that."

"Well, most likely you will, someday."

"So, you guys do threesomes?"

"Yeah." Ziggy grinned. "We have a woman friend we like to get with on a regular basis. It's a blast."

"Both of you are bisexual? I guess I shouldn't be surprised."

"Well, I'm bi. But like I've said, I'm beginning to think everyone is."

Josh came back in carrying a couple of video tapes. He sat down next to Daniel again and handed him the videos. "Take a look and see what you think," Josh said. "They're bisexual flicks, not gay, but maybe that's a good thing, huh?"

Daniel looked at both of the boxes, front and back, and then looked again. He adjusted himself. His boner was bigger than ever. "Fuck," he said. "These look hot. Look at those guys. They're fucking her and each other, too. And everybody's sucking cocks. Jesus. Let's put one on, Josh."

"Which one?"

"Either one. They both look hot. I'm ready to see some hard cocks fuck some wet holes and shoot some cum." Daniel rubbed the big cock inside his jeans and squeezed. Ziggy and Josh looked at each other.

Ziggy said, "Damn, Daniel, you're horny as hell, dude."

"Aren't you? Fuck, I get this way all the time. But this is the first time I've had guys I could talk to about some of this stuff." He got up and turned on the VCR, put one of the movies in, and brought the remote back to the couch.

—

THE WAY THE MOVIE STARTED out, two guys are sitting around bored, and then they start talking about women they've fucked. Pretty soon they're both horny with obvious boners. Then one asks the other to call a girl he knows and see if she wants to come over.

He calls her, and she says, Sure, I'll be right over.

Josh interjected, "This looks good so far. They're both fit, good-looking guys, you know? They'll look good naked I'll bet."

"And they don't have that porn-star look either," Daniel said. "I like that."

"Me, too," Ziggy said. "Makes it more believable."

Then, in the movie, there's a knock at the door. It's the young woman. They welcome her in, and they all sit down, one of them on the couch with the girl, and the other guy in the armchair.

"Oh boy, this is gonna be good," Daniel said. "She's hot, don't you think? I'm glad she doesn't look like some dance-hall whore."

Then the girl and the guy sitting next to her start kissing. Daniel squeezed his cock in anticipation.

While the girl and the one guy kiss, the second guy comes over and sits on the other side of the girl. He strokes her back, her shoulders, and then he kisses the side of her neck.

One thing leads to another. Both guys start removing her clothing, and once they have her breasts free and available, they each lick and suck and nibble on one. Occasionally the men's faces meet and touch.

One guy stops briefly to remove his shirt, and the other guy does the same. Then they continue licking and nibbling at her breasts. Eventually the men's tongues touch together and then it's suddenly an all-way three-way. The two men have discovered something new: kissing each other.

"Oh, god," Daniel said. "Look at that! That's hot." Then, embarrassed, he looked at Ziggy, then at Josh, but they were both watching the movie, both of them just as boned up as Daniel. If they heard what he said about the men kissing, it didn't seem to faze them. "Uh, by the way," Daniel said, "I was wondering, do you guys do that, much?"

"Do what?"

"You know, uh, kiss each other. I saw you do it yesterday after you finished fucking. That was hot. But, I'm just, uh, you know, curious. How much you like doing it."

They turned and looked at Daniel. Then at each other. Then at Daniel again.

"Dude. Do you like kissing girls?"

"Yeah, sure."

"A lot?"

"Well, basically, yeah. But it depends on the girl. The more I like her, or the more I want her, then the better I like it. If it's a girl who I like a lot, it's fucking awesome. And it makes me horny as hell. But I wouldn't, you know, kiss any old girl. Has to be someone I'm pretty close to, usually. Or someone I *want* to get close to. And if that's the case, then hell, the more we kiss the better."

"Same here," Ziggy said. "Kissing is awesome. But not only with girls. With guys, too. That's the way I feel about kissing Josh, at least. We kiss all the time. Not in public usually, but when it's just us, we do. I guess mostly because I love him so much, but it makes me horny too. Nothing wrong with that, right?" Ziggy smiled.

"No, of course not. But what about other guys?" Daniel said. "Do you ever want to kiss other guys?"

"Yeah; George, my best buddy at the orphanage, we used to kiss all the time. Well, not *all* the time, but sometimes when we were alone somewhere he would kiss me. I loved it. It's sexy. And, you know, special. And if we were fucking we always kissed a lot. Before, and during. And after. Same with Josh. Even more with Josh, because Josh loves it. Gotta make my buddy happy."

"Okay, how about other guys, any other guys you ever wanted to kiss?"

"No, not that I can recall. Well, actually, I've never been that close to any other guys, so I don't know – maybe I'd want to, in the right situation. See, I've never had sex with any other guys besides Josh and George."

"You haven't? Oh, wow. I figured you were, uh, the more experienced one."

"Not with guys. But I would kiss another guy. Why not? What I mean is, if I wanted to. I just haven't wanted to yet."

Daniel turned and looked at Josh. "What about you?"

"How much do I like kissing?"

"Yeah."

"A lot. Ziggy knows how much I like it. But it's just like you said: it has to be someone I'm close to, or want to be close to."

"Okay. Makes sense."

"So, it sounds like we all like kissing," Josh said. "No surprise there. It's sexy, and it really is special. Like shaking hands, or hugging, but way better. Girl or guy."

"Way better," Daniel said, grinning. "I guess."

"You guess?"

"Well, I've never kissed a guy before. It's gotta be different somehow, right?"

No one said anything.

Josh reached for the remote to rewind the movie so they could watch what they missed.

"I mean, I've wanted to," Daniel said. "There's been a few guys I would have tried it with, if I thought they wanted to."

"Is that right?" Ziggy said.

Daniel let out a big sigh. "Yeah, but I was never sure."

Josh stopped the video from rewinding and started it playing again, where the guys were both kissing the woman's breasts – and each other. Putting their tongues in each other's mouths, and enjoying it.

"Oh, Jesus," Daniel said. "Look at those guys."

Josh said, "You want to try it?"

Daniel looked at Josh with surprise. "You mean . . . like, right now? Like those guys are doing?"

"Yeah, sure," Josh said. "I mean, if you want to. Do you?"

"Oh my god, are you serious?"

"Yeah, I'm serious. I've wanted to ever since we were in school together."

"Can I kiss both of you?"

Josh looked at Ziggy.

Ziggy said, "Sure thing. Um, Josh first, okay? I want to watch." He smiled. "Then it's my turn."

Josh paused the video tape, and turned to Daniel.

"Danny," Josh said, "Danny, come here." Josh took hold of Daniel and held him close. Josh gently touched his lips to Daniel's. Daniel wrapped his arms around Josh and closed his eyes. They licked each other's lips, and then pushed their tongues into each other's mouths. It was a soul kiss, heartfelt by both of them.

After half a minute or so, they came up for air. Daniel had tears in his eyes and a big grin on his face.

"Hey," Ziggy said, smiling, "don't I get any?"

Daniel turned to him. "Oh yes. Please."

Daniel and Ziggy gently put their lips together and it became a passionate kiss. Their tongues touched and then pushed deeper, around and against each other. They sucked each other's lips and tasted each other. Finally, they broke apart.

"Wow," Daniel said. "You guys kiss good."

"Lots of practice," Ziggy said, grinning. Josh laughed.

Everyone leaned back and resumed their positions on the couch.

"Wow," Daniel said. "That's all I've got to say, is wow."

"You liked it?"

"It's even better than kissing a girl. With you guys, anyway. God, that was awesome. Thanks."

"You're a good kisser," Ziggy said.

"Yeah he is. That was hot." Josh pushed play on the remote and started the video going again.

In the movie, one of the men removes his jeans, and then resumes kissing and caressing the woman, going from her neck to her breast to her belly and back again. Meanwhile the other fellow takes off his jeans as well. Now both of them are stripped down to nothing but their briefs, with their hard cocks barely hidden.

"Look how hard their cocks are, " Josh said.

"Yeah," Daniel said, "Damn, they need to get that underwear off."

Together they unbutton her blue jeans and pull them off of her, but they don't stop there; they want her naked. Her panties are the next thing to come off. One of the men gets on his knees on the floor and licks her cunt. She moans with pleasure.

"Oh Jesus," Daniel said. "Look at him go down on her. This is so hot." He squeezed his boner.

"Yeah," Ziggy said, "go for it, dude. Make her feel good."

The other man stands up, and when he removes his briefs, his stiff cock pops up. He gets down and joins the other man, the two of them licking her cunt together, and licking each other while they're at it.

"God, look at them." Daniel said. "And that one guy's cock is wet. Do you see that? He's already got pre-cum."

The other man gets up and takes his underwear off, too. His cock stands up stiff, almost vertical. He gets down on the floor next to his buddy, lowers his head, and licks the pre-cum off the other guy's cock.

"Oh shit, look!" Daniel said. "He's licking his buddy's cock! Jesus, I gotta get my dick out, guys, I hope you don't mind. Fuck!" Without waiting for a reply Danny unzipped his jeans and pulled them off.

Chapter 13

LICKED

ZIGGY GRINNED and said, "Hell yeah, let's get these clothes off." He and Josh followed Daniel's lead.

They watched each other strip, especially when the underwear came off and their hard dicks popped out into view. They dropped their clothes on the floor and the three of them sat on the couch again, naked, stroking their hard cocks as the movie played on.

"This is so horny, guys." Daniel looked at Josh on one side and Ziggy on the other. He stared at their hard dicks. "Watching a hot movie and jacking off with some buds. This is so hot."

"Let's see how long we can go," Ziggy said, "before we shoot our loads, okay? It's better that way."

"Jesus," Daniel said. "Okay, I'm game. But I can come more than once. Three times, at least."

Josh could hardly keep his eyes off Daniel's big cock. Ziggy was fascinated with it, too. Meanwhile Daniel slowly stroked his cock and watched the movie.

Then he realized he was being watched. He looked at Ziggy, then at Josh. "Guys," he said, "if you want to touch it, go ahead. Everyone else does. I don't mind."

"You sure?" Josh said.

"Yeah, go ahead. I kind of like the attention." Daniel took his hand off his cock and let it stand out free.

Josh reached over and gently put his hand around the base of it. Daniel quietly moaned.

Josh said, "My god Danny, it's . . . huge."

"You got that right," Ziggy said. He put his hand around the other half of Daniel's cock, above Josh's hand, and Daniel groaned.

"Fucking unbelievable. Jesus, Dan, it's twice as long as mine. And thicker too."

Daniel looked at Ziggy's stiff dick. "Not by a long shot, Zig. You have a nice cock. Sexy as hell, and it's a big one. Be proud of it."

"Well, almost twice as long."

"Trade you."

Ziggy laughed.

Josh said, "Um, can I try sucking it?"

Daniel looked at him. "Are you serious? I've never . . ."

"I've been wanting to since ninth grade, Danny. Please?" Josh's dick was hard and throbbing in anticipation.

"Damn. I wish you could. I'm horny enough, that's for sure. But I don't think it'll work, Josh."

"Let me try, okay? I'll keep my teeth off it, I promise. And if it won't fit in my mouth then I'll lick it. I'll lick it until you come, okay? I want to make you come."

"Jesus!" Daniel looked over at Ziggy and said, "Uh, are you okay with this?"

"Hell yeah," Ziggy said, grinning. "We gotta get you cheered up anyway we can. Besides, I wanna watch. It'll be hot."

"God, you guys are something else. Okay, what the hell. Go for it, Josh."

Josh got down on his knees and held Daniel's monster cock up vertical. "You have nice balls, too." He licked Daniel's ball sac. Daniel groaned.

Josh gently slipped one of the egg-shaped testicles into his mouth and hummed.

"Oh, god!"

While Josh was holding Daniel's cock high and slurping his balls, Ziggy rubbed his knuckles against the underside of it and gently caressed the velvety skin.

Daniel moaned. "Fuck, you two sure know how to make a guy feel good."

"We're guys, Dan. Of course we know how to make a guy feel good."

Josh pushed Daniel's cock up against Ziggy's hand and Ziggy took hold of it. He held it up high to allow Josh plenty of ball-licking room. Ziggy had already been stroking his own cock. Now, as he continued doing that, he spat into his other hand and moved it slowly up and down the length of Daniel's shaft, stroking both cocks at once.

Josh switched balls, putting Danny's other one in his mouth.

"Fuck," Daniel groaned, "why can't any girls make me feel this good?" He slid forward on the couch so Josh would have unrestricted access to his ball sac.

"You just haven't found the right girls," Ziggy said. "Or else you did and you didn't know it. Some of them love dicks. And balls, too. They just don't know how to make them feel good. All they need is for you to tell them what to do. And what not to do, if it comes to that."

"I don't think I could do that, Zig."

"What are you talking about?"

"I can't tell a girl what to do."

"Of course you can."

"No, it's too much like . . . like ordering them around. I don't want a . . . a slave, I want an equal. I don't want a girl to do anything unless she wants to do it. Jesus, Josh!" Now Josh was holding Daniel's balls up and licking behind them, while Ziggy continued to stroke Daniel's cock.

"You wouldn't be ordering them around, you'd only be letting them know what makes you feel good. They want to know, Dan, believe me. Fuck, it's for everybody's benefit. Go ahead and try it now, Dan. Tell Josh what you want him to do."

"Uh, Josh, um, lick my balls."

"There you go." Ziggy spat in his hand again to keep it slippery on Daniel's cock. "But dude, he's already licking your balls."

"Yeah, I know. I've never felt so good in all my life. One guy on my balls and one on my dick. What more could I want?"

"Well, I know there's one thing you haven't ever had done right," Ziggy said. "And Josh can do it if anyone can."

"Oh, right. Josh, um, you were talking about sucking me. You still want to try?"

Josh had one of Daniel's balls in his mouth again. He said, "Ummm hmmm," but kept moving his tongue around the big nut in his mouth.

Ziggy laughed again. "You didn't tell Josh what you want, bro. You asked him what *he* wants. Tell him what *you* want. He'd like to hear it."

Daniel was breathing heavy. Pre-cum flowed out of his cock now. He could come at anytime if he received the right kind of attention. "Yeah, um . . . well . . ."

Josh let loose of Dan's balls and said, "What do you want me to do?" Josh stroked his own dick in the meantime, keeping it happy and hard, waiting for an answer.

Daniel moaned. "Oh god. Josh . . . Josh . . ."

"Yeeeess?"

"Josh . . . oh, god . . . Please. Suck my cock!"

Immediately Josh pressed his whole tongue against the base of Daniel's shaft, and slowly licked upward, the whole nine inches, all the way from the base to the head. Daniel moaned, almost wailed. He jumped when Josh licked the pre-cum off the sensitive cockhead.

Daniel had already been on the edge too long. Josh gave a couple of repeat slurps to the frenulum area, below the crown of Daniel's mushroom-shaped dickhead, and that was all it took. Before Josh could even get it in his mouth, Daniel gasped.

"Unnnnh!" A big rope of cum shot out of his dick and splattered against Josh's forehead. "Aahhhh!" Then another big spurt hit Josh below his nose, on his lips.

"Yeah, Dan," Ziggy said. "Shoot your load." He grinned and stroked his own cock. "Shoot your cum."

Daniel groaned and his body jerked with each spurt. His next shot hit Josh's neck, but then Josh got his lips wrapped around Daniel's cockhead to catch the rest of the cum in his mouth. He swallowed at least five more healthy shots of jizz before Daniel started winding down.

Josh kept his mouth on the head, licking underneath it to help keep it pumping, and then when Daniel started getting sensitive there, Josh moved his tongue lower again and licked along the bottom of the shaft.

Finally, Daniel was finished and collapsed against the back of the couch. Josh gently let go and wiped the cum off his face. He licked it off his hand and ate it. Then he got up off his knees and sat on the couch again, next to Daniel.

"Josh, I am so sorry," Daniel said. "I couldn't help it. It just happened so fast."

"Sorry for what?"

"For shooting my cum on your face."

"Don't be sorry. That's what I wanted you to do."

"But on your face? I didn't even give you any warning. That was so rude."

"No, that's completely okay. It was a little unexpected, but that's okay. It made it better, actually. The surprise of it. I almost shot *my* load when I tasted your cum on my lips."

"You *wanted* my cum on your face?"

"Yeah. Or in my mouth. Your cum tastes good by the way."

Daniel just looked at Josh.

"He likes cum," Ziggy said, smiling. "He likes mine, at least, and I guess he likes yours too. His cum tastes just as good, if you ever get a chance. Did he make you feel good?"

"Did he? Christ, I haven't come that good in ages. Josh, could we do that again? I mean if you want to. You guys! Fuck, what are you doing to me?"

"Making you feel good," Josh said.

"Yeah, and we're not done yet, either." Ziggy's cock was still stiff and hard. Josh's was, too. "You said you can come more than once, right?"

"Oh, god, let me rest for a minute or two. It won't take long. You guys go ahead. You haven't come yet. I want to watch you make each other come."

"But I didn't get a chance to suck your dick," Josh said.

"You still can, Josh. Just give me a couple minutes. And next time I won't come so fast, I promise. But hell, who needs a blowjob when you can make me come like that? That was incredible. Thanks. Both of you. Thanks."

"Thank *you*, Danny. We're just starting, though." Josh grinned. "Unless there's somewhere you have to go."

"Fuck, no. I'm staying right here until you guys are done with me."

"Careful what you wish for," Ziggy said, smiling.

Chapter 14
SHOW ME

IT WAS TIME FOR A SECOND ROUND of drinks, and a piss break. Daniel rewound the video back so they could see what they missed. They settled back into the couch, still naked as ever, and watched.

The guys and the woman in the movie were fucking in a daisy chain. One man was in the middle, fucking the woman and getting fucked by his buddy at the same time.

The guys watched the movie silently for a few minutes, sitting next to each other. stroking their cocks, and then Daniel spoke up.

"You know what I want to do?" he said. "Learn how to get someone relaxed. You know, so I can fuck their ass. You said I could do it. Can you guys teach me how?"

"Sure, no problem bro. It's sexy, it's fun, and it works. And it feels good, of course."

"Feels good for the other person you mean?"

"Yeah, definitely. But it can be exciting for you too."

"Anything that's gonna lead to me fucking somebody is definitely gonna get me excited." Daniel grinned.

"Well, that's part of it, naturally. But just knowing how good you're making the other person feel, even if it doesn't lead to anything else, is awesome."

"I can relate to that," Daniel said. "I know it turns me on to lick a girl's pussy, even if I can't fuck her. Because I've seen what it does to her. How good she feels. They just about go crazy."

"Exactly."

"So, you're saying, this thing I can do with someone's ass is like that?"

"Pretty close to it."

"Yeah, then I definitely want to know how to do that. Whatever it is, I can promise you nobody's ever done it to me before, or I'd remember."

Josh laughed. "Yes, you would."

"All this is new to me. I mean, I didn't even know getting fucked in the ass could feel good, not until yesterday, when I saw how much Ziggy enjoyed it. So, what's the secret? How do you get somebody ready? Must be with your fingers somehow, right?"

"With your tongue, dude."

"What?"

"Yeah."

"And your fingers, too," Josh said, "but especially your tongue."

"Oh my god."

"You eat pussy, so basically you already know how to eat ass. Same principal. And it feels almost as good, I promise you."

"You guys do this to each other?"

"Every time we fuck."

"Oh, Jesus. I mean, no offense, but isn't that . . ."

"We shower beforehand. We wouldn't do it otherwise. We're clean as a whistle, inside and out. An asshole is dirty only if it's unwashed, Dan. Sit on the can and do your business, and then take a shower. While you're under the shower, put a soapy finger in your ass. Move it around good, use plenty of soap until you're relaxed, and bingo. Usually that's all it takes. Asshole's clean. Problem solved."

"Yeah, but . . . still."

"Josh, you hear him?"

"Maybe his mother was like mine."

"Another mother against sex."

"My mother wasn't against sex," Daniel said.

"How about touching your asshole, did she think that was okay?"

"Hell no. Neither did my father. I got beat one time for sticking my finger up my ass. I was four years old. It's one of my earliest memories. They said . . . it was dirty."

"Yeah, and their parents probably beat them too, for doing the same thing. It would have been a hell of a lot easier on everybody if they had taught you, instead, how to clean your asshole while you're in the shower, now wouldn't it? They teach you to clean behind your ears, why not your ass?"

"Because they're prudes," Josh said. "My parents were, at least. They couldn't talk about *any* of that bodily stuff. And forget about sex. I don't know how they ever expected us to learn about any of it. Through osmosis, I guess. What we did learn, though, is that you don't talk about things like that. Not with them, anyway, and who else is there, when you're a little kid? And of course, anything you can't talk about ends up falling under the category of 'naughty.' Including taking a shit. Or being naked. And if it's something you *have* to do, for god's sake, don't let anybody see you doing it. Fuck, don't get me started."

"My parents weren't *that* fucked up," Daniel said, "but I guess they were at least a little prudish. They definitely never taught me to stick my finger up my butt in the shower. Makes perfect sense, though. Just out of general cleanliness. Even if you're not planning on somebody licking it."

"Sure."

"Still, I never would have considered doing such a thing. Licking someone's asshole."

"Help me out here, Dan. You're totally willing to fuck someone in the ass, right?"

"Definitely. As long as we both enjoy it."

"So, were you planning on fucking something dirty? Or what?"

"No, of course not. I'd want you to be clean, first."

"But you're saying, something can be clean enough to fuck, but not to lick?"

"It does sound kind of stupid when you put it that way. God knows I've licked my share of pussies, and that never bothered me."

"And let me ask you this: isn't that the way some girls feel about cocks? Even if you're fresh out of the shower?"

"Jesus, tell me about it. They might be fine with you fucking them, but don't let that nasty thing get anywhere near their mouth. It's not . . . rational, for them to think that way. Seriously, there's no earthly reason not to put a clean dick in your mouth."

—

"Okay," he said, "Okay. If I'm gonna fuck an asshole, of course I'd want it to be a clean one. I wouldn't want to fuck anything else. And . . . and if it was that clean, then . . . I guess . . . licking it would be okay, too." Daniel thought about it. "Kinky." He thought about it some more. "Fuck, why not?"

"We're making progress. Daniel, I gotta tell you, I have a lot of respect for you, bro. I wish there were more people like you. Open-minded, willing to give new ideas a chance."

"Well, thinking about it's one thing. But actually doing it, fuck. I don't know if I'm ready for that."

"I was the same way," Josh said. "But after you do it the first time, it's no big deal. A piece of cake. Figuratively speaking."

"Um, I don't suppose you guys would be willing to demonstrate for me, would you?"

Ziggy laughed. "On you? Is that what you want?"

"Oh, god. If you want to, sure. But I was talking about one of you doing it to the other. That way I can watch."

"Josh, would you be up for that?"

"Uh, sure." He grinned. "Why not?"

"Okay, Dan. So. We'll give you a demonstration."

"Awesome! Oh, man. This is gonna rock."

Josh stood up. His dick was harder than ever now. "You wanna lick me, Zig, or should I lick you?"

"How about you do me?"

"Okay. So . . . where are we gonna do this?" Josh's dick was leaking pre-cum.

"You can use my bed if you want. Come on guys, the bedroom's at the end of the hall." Daniel led the way. His dick was hard again. "This is gonna be kinky."

Daniel pointed them to the bed, then he sat in a chair where he could watch. Ziggy lay flat on his stomach, ass end up, with the pillows spread around under his chest and face so he could relax and still breathe comfortably.

Josh climbed on top and kneeled there for a minute, looking at Ziggy's naked body. He said, "Ziggy has a nice ass, don't you think?"

"Ziggy has an incredible ass," Daniel said. "A beautiful ass." Daniel's cock was stiff and trying its best to get horizontal, all nine inches of it.

"Yeah. So inviting."

Josh leaned down and licked Ziggy's balls, and continued up the crack all the way to the top of Ziggy's ass. Ziggy moaned.

"Feel good, Zig?"

"Fantastic."

Josh smiled. He looked at Daniel. "What do you think, Danny? Could you do that? To someone who, say, you just took a shower with?"

"Yeah, I could do that." He gently stroked his stiff cock.

"How about going a little deeper? You think you could do this?" Josh pulled the cheeks of Ziggy's ass apart and gave his asshole a direct lick. Ziggy moaned.

"Oh, god," Daniel said. "Ziggy, what does that feel like? Tell me what it feels like to be licked like that!"

"Absolutely wonderful."

"It feels fantastic," Josh said. "I know, because Ziggy licks me the same way. It's a little like being tickled, only ten times better. And in the most sensitive part of your body. That's what makes it fun to do to somebody else, because you know how good you're making them feel. Plus it'll make his asshole relax if I do it long enough."

"And you guys just took showers."

"That's right. Just before we came over here. My tongue is playing with clean, sweet skin and nothing else. You think you could do it?"

Daniel didn't say anything.

Josh continued licking Ziggy's ass crack, making sure that each lick, whether it was high or low, included his pucker. Ziggy softly moaned.

Daniel was silent for two or three minutes while he watched Josh eagerly tongue Ziggy's ass. Ziggy enjoyed it so much he could hardly stop moaning. Suddenly Daniel spoke up.

"Yeah, I could do it," he said.

"You could?"

"Yeah. If he . . . if he licked mine first, I would do it."

Josh's cock was erect, stiff as wood, leaking pre-cum. He went back to licking Ziggy's butt.

For five long minutes, Daniel watched Josh lick Ziggy's ass. The longer he watched, the sexier it looked. They both enjoyed it so much. For Ziggy, of course, it was an awesome experience, but Josh enjoyed it just as much; he was giving Ziggy an ecstatic feeling and he knew it. Obviously he loved making Ziggy feel good.

Daniel wanted to make Ziggy feel good, too. Daniel imagined his own face up in that beautiful ass, and it made his dick get even harder.

Daniel's long meaty cock was throbbing and leaking pre-cum, an impressive sight if there ever was one, but no one besides him could actually see it at the moment. Ziggy was face down in the comfy bed, and Josh had his face pressed up into a beautiful ass. Daniel could watch what was going on, close up, without being watched himself. Somewhat of a rarity. And he did watch. It was hot, what he was seeing. He could do this, he knew he could.

After a few minutes at that level of horniness, Daniel realized he'd have to find some relief soon. Otherwise his balls would be hurting. Josh had said he still wanted to suck him, and Daniel wanted to take a turn on Ziggy . . . oh, what an idea.

After several minutes of no one talking, suddenly Ziggy and Daniel spoke at once.

Daniel said, "Josh, you still wanna suck—"

And Ziggy said, "Dan, you want to try it?"

. . . and it took a minute of silence for minds to decipher who said what, and the implications.

Then Ziggy said, "Sorry, Daniel. I interrupted you."

Josh paused his ass licking and spoke up, too. "You didn't get to finish, Danny. Were you gonna ask me something?"

Chapter 15
PREPARATION

DANIEL WAS READY. Ready to do more than watch. He said, "Yeah Josh, I was gonna ask . . . But Ziggy, did you ask me if I . . . if I want to try licking you?"

"Yeah. Do you want to try licking my asshole? Just once? Just to see what you're missing? Josh won't mind, bro. He'll move over and let you give it a try. But you have to be the adventuresome type. Only adventurers allowed." Ziggy smiled.

"Jesus. And Josh, you said you wanted to suck my cock. Fuck, guys. I know exactly what I want to do. I want to do both."

Daniel drew up his courage. Talking fast, as if he was afraid he'd lose his nerve if he didn't get it out in a hurry, he said, "I want you to suck my cock, Josh, if you still want to. I want your lips around my dick again, even if you can't get any further than the head. Don't make me come too soon, okay? I want it to last. And this time I want to shoot my whole load inside your mouth. While you're sucking. Do you think we could do that? Do you want to?"

Josh said, "Hell yes. I'll show you how good a blowjob can be. Come on, get up here on the bed." Daniel grinned and stood up. Josh moved over and made room for him.

"But also," Daniel said, "I want to do what Ziggy said. I want to lick his hot ass. Put my face up in it, like you were doing, Josh. Guys, do you think we could do both at once?"

It took a minute to sink in. Daniel wanted to lick Ziggy's ass, and apparently not just one lick. He planned on doing it for the duration of the blowjob from Josh.

Ziggy said, "Hell yes, we can do both. Daniel, get over here and put your tongue in my ass. I'd be honored, bro."

"But you have to lick my asshole first, okay? I'll . . . I'll feel better about it that way. Otherwise I . . . I might feel—"

"No problem. I'd love to. Um, have you showered lately?"

"Oh crap. Listen guys, I'll go shower right now. It won't take long. Don't shoot any loads while I'm gone, okay?"

"Don't worry," Josh said. "Hey, while you're in there, clip your fingernails short, okay?"

"Huh?" He looked at his fingers. "Uh, sure, okay. Listen guys, go ahead, play around, keep your dicks hard, but please, wait for me, okay? I'll be quick, I promise."

Ziggy laughed. "Take as long as you want. As long as it isn't more than ten minutes. After that we're gonna send a search party in looking for you. And if you're still in the shower, the search party might have to get in there with you and teach you a lesson."

"Oh, is that right?"

"Consider it a promise."

"Wow. Okay, I'll be back, guys."

Daniel left the bedroom and, half a minute later, they heard the shower running.

Josh stuck his head out the door and looked down the hall. "He left the bathroom door open a crack."

"Only a crack?"

"Like, about an inch."

"Damn. Well that's better than being closed. You think he'll take more than ten minutes?"

"Who knows." Josh grinned. "But a promise is a promise. Let's watch the clock."

"I'll watch the clock if you keep licking my ass, Josh. Unless you want to spend some time on my balls, that'd be cool, too."

"Okay Zig, deal."

"I hope he stays in there longer than ten. Shower sex is fun."

Josh thought so, too, but he didn't say anything, because his mouth was busy.

Chapter 16
FIRST LICK

EIGHT MINUTES LATER the shower stopped, and Daniel was at the bedroom door, wet and naked, harder than ever, toweling himself off. "You didn't come yet, did you? Neither one of you?"

"No," Josh said. "We were waiting for you, pal."

"'Pal.' I like that, Josh. That's what you and I should have been in junior high school."

"You really think so?"

"Sure, why not? I had a bunch of friends, but nobody I could call my best buddy. Nobody I could do this kind of stuff with. Somebody I could trust and confide in."

"Same here," Josh said.

"And good lord, I was so horny back then I could hardly stand it. Still am, as far as that goes. We could have beat off together. After basketball practice. Maybe even tried some of this other stuff. I would have loved to have a jack-off buddy."

"Well, you have one now." Ziggy grinned. "Two of them."

"Yes, I do." Daniel laughed. "Horny ones, like me."

"Yeah. So, Dan. You're gonna lick my asshole, but only if I lick yours first, that's the deal, right?"

"That's right. And I'm squeaky clean now, inside and out. You don't mind, do you?"

"Come over here and put your ass in my face, bro."

Daniel walked over to the edge of the bed where Ziggy was, and then he turned around and faced away from Zig.

Ziggy was right there, behind him. Daniel was so excited he was trembling. Everything he did from here on out would be a first.

"I'm gonna do this," he said. He could hardly believe it. "I'm actually gonna do this."

"Yeah, bro. You'll like it, too," Ziggy said.

Then Daniel felt Ziggy's hand, gently caressing the cheeks of his ass. Daniel sighed. Ziggy's fingers gently followed Daniel's ass crack up and down, feeling the skin, feeling the curves and where they came together.

And then Ziggy did it again, this time a little more firmly. He was feeling Daniel's flesh, not just his skin. Ziggy's fingers massaged the deepest part of Daniel's ass crack. Daniel sighed again.

Ziggy moved lower and gently stroked the sensitive skin between Daniel's ass and his balls. Daniel moaned. Then Ziggy caressed the ball sac, and gently cupped Daniel's balls in his hand. Then he moved back to Daniel's ass. This time he used both hands, one on each side, and gently spread the globes apart.

Daniel gasped as he felt the wet touch of a tongue. Exploring, licking up and down. Gradually pushing deeper.

"Aw, you're doing it," Daniel said. "You're licking my ass."

Ziggy kept going. He spread Daniel's ass cheeks open a little more, and now his tongue touched bottom. He started at Daniel's balls and brought his tongue upward again, slowly, this time deeper, with more pressure. Daniel felt the tongue move firmly across his asshole.

Daniel groaned. "You did it. Oh god, you did it."

But Ziggy wasn't finished. He kept Daniel's ass spread, moved his tongue to the hole, and licked it again. And again.

Daniel shivered and groaned. "Ahhhhh, Zig, that feels incredible."

Ziggy pressed his tongue harder against Daniel's hole and wiggled his tongue against it until it finally started to relax.

"Unhhhhhh. Oh god, this is too much." Daniel said. "I'll shoot another load if we don't stop." He straightened up and turned around, his cock standing up stiff, the head wet with pre-cum.

Ziggy moved his mouth closer, as if he might lick Daniel's cock, but Daniel jumped backward. "No Zig, I don't want to come yet."

Ziggy grinned. "That was your first ass-lick, right? You liked it, huh?"

"It was incredible. I almost shot my load when your tongue went inside. But now I want to do it to you."

"I'm ready," Ziggy said. "My asshole's been yearning for a tongue on it for the last fifteen minutes."

"Josh didn't keep licking you while I was gone?"

"He was working on my balls," Ziggy said.

"Oh."

"But the lesson today is assholes, and how to relax them."

"And I'm ready to learn," Daniel said. "So, uh, can I lick your ass now?"

"Yeah." Ziggy lay down flat on his belly. "Lick away, Dan. And Josh, tell us again, what are you gonna be doing?"

"I'm gonna suck Danny off while he's licking your ass, Zig. I'm gonna give him the best blowjob I know how."

Daniel grinned at both of them. "You guys. This is the horniest fun I've ever had with anybody. I love your attitude about sex."

"Daniel, my asshole is waiting for you."

"I'm on it." Daniel lowered his head and took his first lick of Ziggy's butt crack. He did it slowly, starting at Ziggy's ball sac, and licked all the way up to Ziggy's back. He raised his head, grinning, and said, "I did it."

"You're not stopping already, are you?"

"Hell no, just getting started." Daniel licked Ziggy again. Meanwhile Josh positioned himself below and started licking the head of Daniel's big, stiff cock.

"Ummmph! Fuck, Josh, you're gonna make me cum too fast again if you keep that up. I want it to last a while. I'm already near the edge."

"Okay."

"God, I'm so turned on. This is hot."

Josh kept his tongue away from the head of Daniel's cock, for the time being, and licked the shaft and the balls. Meanwhile, Daniel spread Ziggy's cheeks and pushed his tongue deeper into Ziggy's ass crack. His tongue finally touched the opening.

"Aaaahhhh," Ziggy said. "You got it, bro. That's the spot. Keep that up until you feel my hole relax."

Daniel stopped for a moment so he could talk. "I like this," he said. "A lot. It's so sexy and . . . kinky. You have a sweet ass, Zig." Daniel stuck his tongue out again and licked some more.

"Remember, you have to get me relaxed before you put your cock in. Otherwise it's not gonna feel good for me to get fucked."

Daniel pushed his tongue into the center of Ziggy's pucker, wiggled it around, and lapped at it. Then he paused again. "Uh, Zig, do you mean, like, theoretically speaking, or are we really gonna try it?"

Chapter 17
NO PROMISES

"DEPENDS," ZIGGY SAID. "First you have to loosen me up enough. Yeah, we can try it, but only if you do your part."

"Damn. You're serious? You might let me fuck you?"

"I'm not making any promises. Depends on how good you are at this, Dan. And then if you're willing to take it slow."

"I'll go as slow as you want, Zig. We have all day. God, I'd do anything to fuck you. Anything. You and your beautiful ass."

Ziggy laughed. "Well, in that case you better cancel that blowjob Josh is working on. Unless you can come three times in one afternoon."

"I can." Daniel said. "At least three times. I do it all the time. Please. I'm just getting started. Josh can suck me off and I'll still have plenty left to fuck you with. I can do both. I want to do both. Fuck, sometimes it seems like I can never get enough."

"Alright, well, in that case, go for it Josh. We have a sex maniac here. Go ahead and suck him off, he'll just be getting warmed up."

They didn't talk much after that. But there was plenty of moaning. By Ziggy, for one. Daniel was doing an inspired job on Ziggy's asshole. His tongue work was more than enthusiastic, and without even being told, Daniel eventually started trading off with his spit-slicked thumb.

Daniel was moaning, too, from Josh licking the shaft of his cock and his balls.

Josh held off as long as possible, but finally he couldn't wait any longer. He had to see if he could get his mouth around the head of Daniel's cock. He'd never seen a cock this big before, not this close up. Josh opened wide and carefully slid the entire head inside his mouth. He pressed his lips around the shaft, just below the flair of Daniel's head, and then moved his tongue full circle around the head.

Daniel, for the first time in his life, had his cockhead totally inside a soft, smooth, warm, wet mouth. The sensation of that alone would have been enough to make him come, but when Josh's tongue licked the underside of his cock, he totally lost it.

Daniel had his tongue in Ziggy's asshole, and then Josh licked underneath the crown of Daniel's dick, and Daniel just lost it.

"Mmmmmmph! Josh! Aaaahhh, fuck! Unnnnnnh! Can't . . ." That's all he was able to say before the first shot of cum suddenly spurt out of his cock into Josh's mouth. "Unnnnnh!"

Josh knew it was coming. He felt Daniel's cock swell up to that extra fullness and he was ready and eager for it. The amount of cum surprised him, though. And the rapid-fire spurts shooting so quickly, one after another. With Daniel moaning the whole time. But Josh managed to swallow it all. He went on tickling under the cockhead with his tongue, coaxing out all the cum he could get, until finally he'd gotten all of Daniel's salty-sweet nectar. Or at least all there was to this load.

Daniel stopped licking Ziggy for a minute to catch his breath. He rested his forehead on the globes of Ziggy's ass. "Jesus, Josh. Holy fuck, you did it pal. My first blowjob. That was fantastic."

"Yeah, I thought so too. And you came as much as you did the first time."

"I still have at least one more load in me. For when I'm up in Ziggy's butt. You wait and see." And with that, Daniel put his face into Ziggy's ass again and resumed licking.

"Danny," Josh said, "you have any condoms? I have some but I don't think they're big enough for you."

"Yeah, in the top drawer of my dresser. Always ready for a good fuck, just in case. I got lube in there, too."

"You have lube? What do you use that for?"

"Duh."

"Jacking off?"

"Three or four times a day. I can't help it."

Josh looked in the drawer. "Extra large. Good." He put a couple of condoms on the end table next to the bed, and handed the lube to Daniel.

"Josh, I don't think we're anywhere near ready for lube yet."

"Yeah you are. Your tongue has him relaxed, right?"

"Yeah, but not nearly enough. I've been using my thumb, too, but he's not ready for my cock yet."

"I know. That's where your fingers come in. And the lube."

"I'm supposed to put my fingers up his ass, too?"

"Yeah, that's why you clipped your fingernails. Your thumb is a good start, but like you said, it's not enough. He's probably ready for two of your fingers. But that's not enough for your cock. You have to get him more relaxed than that. Enough to take three fingers, and then four. You gotta work your way up. Hell, Danny, you would have figured all this out anyway, I'm just helping you along."

Daniel held his hand up with four fingers together, to see what it looked like, and then he looked at Ziggy's asshole. "Uh, Ziggy," he said, "are you hearing all this?"

"Yeah. You have to take your time. Josh is right. The only way I'm gonna let you fuck me is if you get me ready for it first. Keep on using your tongue, but use your fingers, too. This is gonna be good if you can do it, dude. Your first ass fuck." Ziggy smiled.

"I don't want to do it if it's gonna hurt you."

"Don't worry," Ziggy said, "I wouldn't let you. Believe me, I'm not into pain."

"I'm not into pain, either." Daniel said. "Otherwise you could probably talk me into getting fucked, too." He laughed nervously. "You know, just to find out what I'm missing."

"Dan, I'm telling you, Josh is your man. If anybody can get a dick inside you and make you love it, it's Josh. He's a natural."

"Danny, he's exaggerating. Jeez."

"No I'm not, Josh. You know how much I like what you do."

"Well, don't ask me how I do it, because I couldn't tell you. But Danny, if you want me to, I'm up for it. I never dreamed I'd get to fuck you, but if you want me to, hell yeah. I'd love to."

"I don't know, Josh. The way you fucked Ziggy yesterday? I don't think I'm ready for that. God, you were pounding the hell out of him."

"Only because he wanted me to. I can be gentle, too. I'd be gentle with you."

"Really? You know, as horny as I am right now I . . . I think I'd be up for that."

"Alright! You'll like it, I promise."

"But right now I've got some work to do on Ziggy's ass here." Daniel grinned. "This turns me on, guys, getting up in Ziggy's ass like this. Who'd have ever thought?"

Daniel put his face in between the cheeks of Ziggy's butt and pushed his tongue again into Ziggy's wet, relaxed hole. He licked for a while and then he gently stuck his thumb in again.

"You have a gentle touch, Dan. Try some lube on your thumb and see how that works."

"Okay." So that's what he did, and his thumb went right inside Ziggy without any resistance at all. "Jesus, Zig. That feels so sexy. How does it feel to you?"

"Feels good."

Ziggy turned around, onto his back, and put his legs up in the air to give Daniel better access.

"Now try a couple of slick fingers in there."

"My god, Zig. Just a little pressure and your asshole opened right up for them."

"That's because you've got me more relaxed now."

"I'm feeling inside of you. This is so kinky."

"Move your fingers around and stuff. You think it's relaxed now, just wait."

Meanwhile Josh moved around on the bed behind Daniel and ran his tongue up Daniel's ass crack.

"Jesus, Josh. What are you doing?"

"Licking your ass. You liked it when Ziggy did it."

"Oh my god, yes. That's awesome."

"You're getting into the mood more." Josh licked him again. "Now you know how good you're making Ziggy feel."

"Don't stop, Josh. I love it."

"Can you keep going with Ziggy while I do this?"

"Yeah, sure. Too bad I can't lick him and finger him at the same time."

"Sure you can. There are other things you can lick besides his asshole, you know."

Daniel stared at Josh, wide-eyed.

Josh said, "What?"

"What you said."

"Yeah?"

They stared at each other for a minute, neither one saying a word.

Chapter 18
IT'S A GOOD THING

FINALLY DANIEL SAID, "Oh, fuck." He was red with embarrassment. "Yeah, I want to. Lick other things. My god, look at you guys. Stark naked right here in front of me, so fucking sexy. Hard dicks, beautiful asses, legs, feet, fingers, armpits – I want to lick you all over. Both of you. Is that perverted or what?"

Josh smiled. "It's not perverted at all. Jeez, join the club." Josh held his arm in the air and moved up closer to Daniel. "You wanna lick my armpit, go right ahead."

Daniel, fingers still inside Ziggy's ass, stared at Josh for a minute. Then he moved his head forward and lapped at Josh's pit as if it was covered with honey. Josh laughed and giggled from it tickling so much. Daniel was blushing like crazy, but laughing. "I did it, Josh. Oh my god, I did it!"

"And you're still the same ol' Danny you've always been."

"Oh no I'm not. I'm a new Danny. Fuck, I feel like I'm turned inside out. But it feels right, damn it." He turned around and looked at Ziggy. Ziggy grinned right back at him.

"Help yourself, Dan," Ziggy said. "Anything you want. Go for it."

Daniel reached down with his free hand and caressed Ziggy's ball sac. Then he ducked his head down and licked. Licked every inch of Ziggy's balls, and then raised his head again, defiantly. "There. That's for starters, anyway."

"Daniel, the ball-licker," Ziggy said. "I'm proud of you, man."

"Me, too," Daniel said. "You guys, fuck, I'm in love with you. Thank you. Thank you so much for helping me do this."

—

JOSH LICKED Daniel's butt, and Daniel fingered and licked Ziggy's asshole. And now, when he licked the crack of Ziggy's ass, Daniel wholeheartedly included Ziggy's ball sac in each lick.

Danny had one of Ziggy's balls in his mouth when Josh replaced his tongue in Daniel's asshole with a slippery finger.

"Ummngh!" Daniel let loose of Ziggy's nuts. "Josh, what the hell are you doing?"

"What you're doing to Zig. You want me to stop?"

"No, uh, hell, it feels good. Is that your finger?"

"Yeah."

"My god, guys. I've fingering a guy's ass, licking his balls, and another guy has his finger in my butt, and I love it. I fucking love it. Am I gay, or what?"

"You don't have to put labels on it," Ziggy said. "If it feels good, do it. That's what Josh and I say. Try more fingers now, Dan. Gently, okay? This'll be a first for me, a dick your size. And keep licking my balls, too. Your tongue feels great."

Daniel put more lube on his fingers, put three together, and slipped them into Ziggy's ass. He held them there, to give Ziggy time to get used to it.

Then Daniel felt two of Josh's fingers go into his own ass. "Oh, Jesus, Josh! Two fingers now?"

"Yep."

"I can handle it, I guess, as long as you're gentle. Fuck, are you playing with my prostate? I don't wanna come yet, Josh, please don't make me come."

"Okay. Your next load is for Ziggy's butt. I think we all agree on that."

"I love this, though," Daniel said. "Playing with each other's asses. But nobody's playing with yours. I hope you don't feel left out."

"Oh, don't worry. I'm having plenty of fun. This is horny."

"Dan," Ziggy said, "Your doing everything right, bro. Keep doing what you're doing. You mind if I rest my legs on you? It'll be easier for me to relax."

Ziggy lowered his feet down onto the bare flesh of Daniel's shoulders. Then he scooted his ass a little closer. "Ah, yeah, much better."

Daniel sheepishly grinned. "Zig, I like it. I love it. Your feet on my shoulders. It's . . . intimate. It feels good. God, I'm tingling all over. I love this. You guys are making this so . . . easy for me. So right. You're like a rescue team on a mission, sent here to save me. I gotta thank you. I needed this so bad. You don't know how much I needed it. *I* didn't know."

"Well, we thought maybe you needed a friend," Josh said. "And we hoped you'd be up for sex."

Daniel laughed. "I needed both." He looked down at his fingers disappearing into Ziggy's ass. "Fuck, Ziggy, it's not gonna be easy to lick your balls now."

"Well, whatever. Lick something else, Dan. You're doing great. My dick's staying hard, dude. Stiff and hard."

"Yeah, I noticed. You have the sexiest hard dick I've ever seen. The way it curves up, and your skin's pulled all the way back, and the big head – the whole thing's beautiful." Daniel started blushing. "Listen to me talk."

"Hey, you can talk about my dick anytime you want, bud." Ziggy grinned. "Glad you like it."

"I think it's beautiful, too," Josh said.

"Josh, you have a hot cock too," Daniel said. "They're both beautiful. Fuck, listen to me, I'm a cock connoisseur now. But it's true, guys. You both have really lickable dicks. Uh, *likeable*, I mean. Daniel turned beet red, he was so embarrassed. "Ah, fuck," he said. "It's true, though. I *do* want to lick your cocks."

Chapter 19
GETTING INTO IT

DANIEL KEPT HIS FINGERS inside of Ziggy's butt. With his other hand he caressed Ziggy's balls, but what he really wanted right now was Ziggy's cock. He wrapped his hand around the stiff shaft. Ziggy moaned in pleasure.

Daniel blushed, but he was smiling. "It's the first dick I ever held, besides my own." Then he bent down and licked it. Licked it and then put the head of it inside his mouth and sucked on it.

"Jesus!" Ziggy threw back his head in pleasure.

Daniel took it out and said, "I did it!"

"Dude, you didn't have to do that."

"I wanted to. Had to. To find out what it was like."

"So now you know," Ziggy said.

"Yeah." Daniel grinned. "I . . . I liked it."

Ziggy's asshole was getting more and more relaxed. Daniel's cock was so stiff and hard it was throbbing. He continued to hold Ziggy's dick. Ziggy gently put his hand around Daniel's dick, too.

Daniel moaned. "No, Zig," he said, "you better not. I'll come."

"Okay. Josh, how about putting one of those super-size condoms on him? I think we're ready to try this."

Josh reached for a condom and carefully tore open the package.

"Oh god," Daniel said, "we're really gonna do this? Hot damn. I'm gonna fuck you, Zig?"

Ziggy smiled. "We're gonna try. But it's not in till it's in."

"I understand," Daniel said. "Slow and easy, and if it hurts just tell me. I'll stop."

Josh held the condom at the head of Daniel's cock and started unrolling it down the shaft.

"Oh Jesus. You better let me do that or I'll shoot right now." Danny took his hand off Ziggy's cock and took over the job of unrolling the condom.

Meanwhile Josh grabbed Ziggy's cock and stroked it a couple of times, and then he put his mouth over it and took it balls-deep down his throat for a few seconds. Ziggy groaned.

Daniel was covered now, and he looked for the lube. Josh found it and opened the cap. He held it upside down and dribbled slippery stuff all over Daniel's big cock.

"Spread it around, Danny. Get every inch of your cock covered with this stuff."

Daniel said, "Uh, Ziggy, are you ready?"

"Yeah. Go slow. Stop when I tell you to, okay?"

Daniel took his fingers out of Ziggy's ass and aimed his cock straight at Ziggy's relaxed hole. He slowly moved forward until his cock pressed against Ziggy's opening.

Ziggy said, "Wait till you feel me relax, and then try to push it in. Just the head to start off with."

It took a minute or two for Ziggy to relax; when he did, Daniel pushed forward. The slippery head of his big cock popped inside. Then Ziggy's ass clenched again.

"Whoa, hold it right there, Dan. Wait until I get used to this. Jesus! How'd I ever let you talk me into this?"

"Ah, Zig, don't say that, please don't say that."

"Just kidding. I want you to do this. But hold it there until I tell you. And don't let it pop out, either. Keep it in there."

Another two or three minutes went by until Daniel finally felt Ziggy relax again.

"Okay, Dan, go slow, bud, but go ahead. Push it in slow and steady, unless I tell you to stop."

Daniel pushed gently and his big dick slowly disappeared into Ziggy's ass, inch by inch, until more than half of it was inside.

"Hold it there for a minute. Jesus. We're entering unexplored territory now," Ziggy said. "Fuck, I could come right now, but we want you to get all the way in. I gotta do a little meditating here or something. I can do this, I know I can, I just gotta get in the right frame of mind."

"I'll wait as long as you want, Zig."

Josh moved behind Daniel and started to lick his ass again.

"Oh fuck, Josh. God, you don't know how good that feels."

"Yes I do. I know exactly how good it feels."

"I don't see how it could get any better than this," Daniel said. "This is ecstasy."

Josh kept on licking.

Finally, Ziggy gave Daniel the go-ahead. "Slowly, Dan. I think I might be ready for it, but go slow."

Daniel pushed forward gently. More and more of his cock disappeared into Ziggy's ass. "I'm almost there. Just another inch or two." Daniel kept going until his thighs pressed against the globes of Ziggy's ass. "Oh, god. That's it! I'm all the way in."

Chapter 20
IGNITION

"UNH. UNBELIEVABLE. I never thought I'd even *see* a cock as big as yours, Dan. Now I've got it inside me. Jesus."

"Look at your dick. Stiff and hard. And it's wet, too. Pre-cum."

"Fuck, don't touch it or I'll shoot. I'm close, Dan. I don't want to come yet. Hell, you haven't even started fucking me yet."

Meanwhile Josh took his tongue out of Daniel's ass and put two fingers in again. Daniel jumped a little and pressed harder into Ziggy's ass.

"Unnnnh!"

"Oh fuck, sorry, Zig. Josh put his fingers back up my ass."

"Ahhhh, that's okay. Fuck, I'm so close. Your cock has me on the edge of shooting a load, Dan, and you're not even moving it yet. Leave it right where it is until I tell you, okay? I want to get used to this."

"Okay. God, I've never had my dick this deep into anything before." Daniel and Ziggy both were breathing hard and heavy. Meanwhile Josh moved his slippery fingers in and out of Daniel's asshole.

"Danny," Josh said, "how's this feel? You're really relaxed now."

"It feels amazing, Josh. I . . . I like it."

"Do you think you're ready for three?"

"Oh, fuck. I guess. You seem to know what you're doing."

"Thanks to Ziggy. He taught me everything I know."

"You guys. Christ. You're unbelievable."

Daniel wasn't expecting it so soon, but Josh didn't wait. He went ahead and put three slippery fingers deep into Daniel's ass. "Jesus!" Daniel jumped and suddenly thrust hard into Ziggy.

Ziggy gasped. "Oh, fuck. Unnnnnh! FUCK! I'm coming! I'm coming!"

A thick spurt of cum shot out of Ziggy's cock onto his face. "Unnnh!" More spurts. "Unnnnnnh!" Sperm landed on his neck and his chest and just about everywhere else. His body jerked with each spurt of cum. "Unnngh!"

Daniel groaned. "I can feel it, Zig. I can feel you coming. Jesus, you're gonna make *me* come, squeezing my dick like that."

Ziggy kept spurting, gasping, squirming, moaning, and then, finally, he was winding down. He twitched a few times, and then he relaxed. "Fuck," he said, "That was good."

"Sorry, man. I didn't want to make you come so soon."

"Oh, hell no, Dan, that was excellent. I'm fine with it. You didn't come, did you?"

"Nope. Almost."

"Because you haven't even started fucking me yet." Ziggy rested his head back on the bed, recovering. But he was ready for more. "Try pulling out a couple inches and pushing in again. Yeah. Oh, yeah. That's it. Yeah, Dan. Keep doing that."

"Oh my god, I'm actually fucking your ass now."

"Yeah you are. It feels good, too. Try pulling out a little farther now before you go in again. Yeah, that's it. Oh, fuck yeah."

Meanwhile Josh used his free hand to put one of his own condoms on. He slicked it up with lube, pulled his three fingers out of Daniel, and gently pushed his cock against Daniel's hole. He waited until he felt Daniel relax, and then pushed inside an inch or two.

"Jesus, Josh! Is that your dick? Oh fuck, I've got a dick in my ass. Oh my god. Oh fuck." Daniel closed his eyes. "It . . . it feels good."

Very gently, carefully, Josh moved slowly forward, inching his way in, slowly, until finally he was balls-deep inside of Daniel. "I'm in, Daniel. All the way in. You okay?"

"Yeah." Daniel was taking short, deep breaths. "Fucking sandwich is what this is, and I'm the filling." He had stopped momentarily, but now he resumed moving his cock gently in and out of Zig.

Ziggy said, "Try pulling out farther. You can go faster if you want to."

"Alright." Now Daniel was fucking Zig faster, with more force, and at the same time fucking himself on Josh's cock.

Ziggy's cock was as hard as ever. Stiff, sticking straight up and curved toward his head like a rhinoceros horn. A fresh drop of pre-cum appeared, and then another. He groaned, with his head thrown back and his eyes closed. "Unnnhh, I think I'm gonna come again if we keep this up." He grunted each time Daniel pushed his cock in deep.

Daniel seemed to be in a daze. He moaned constantly, thrusting his cock forward into Ziggy, then moving backward onto Josh's cock, forward and back, experiencing pleasures he had never known until now.

Josh did everything he could to be gentle, which for the most part consisted of not moving. He let Daniel set the pace and the depth of the fucking he was getting from Josh. But soon it evolved into something more pleasurable for both of them.

Josh started thrusting forward gently each time. The room was filled with the moans and groans of all three men, and the sound of slapping ass each time Daniel thrust forward into Ziggy and each time he bucked backward into Josh's thrust.

"Are . . . are you guys close?" Josh asked. The only answers were the moans and grunts of ecstasy from Ziggy, and from Daniel, who was getting louder and louder, almost wailing. "Because I am," Josh said. He was breathing heavily. "Unnh. Fuck, guys, I can't hold back much longer. Should I pull out?"

Daniel said, "Keep going, Josh. I'm right there, too. Fuck. Ohhhhhhh! Fuck! I'm coming! Unnnnh! Coming inside Ziggy." Daniel pushed forward and held his cock deep inside Ziggy as his balls emptied. "Unnngh! Unngh! Ahhh!" While he still had Josh's dick up his ass.

Ziggy, meanwhile, was completely filled with Daniel's cock. "Oh, fuck," he said, "I really think I'm gonna come again."

Josh slapped against Daniel's ass with thrust after thrust until finally he said, "Unnnnh! Coming! I'm coming." Josh slammed into Daniel's ass one more time and then he held it deep while he unloaded.

"Unnnh!" Ziggy said. "Jesus, I'm so close."

Josh hugged Daniel tight, his own cock as deep as it would go inside Daniel's ass while his balls emptied and his orgasm went all the way to its last throes. "Unnnnnnnngh!"

Daniel's pelvis jerked in spasms a couple more times as his orgasm leveled off.

When Josh was finally done, he rested his head on Daniel's shoulders.

Meanwhile Ziggy was stroking his cock.

"Fuck." Daniel said. "That was awesome."

Josh's cock softened a bit and he slowly pulled out of Daniel.

Daniel waited a few moments, and then he slowly started pulling his big dick out of Ziggy.

"Aw, don't pull out yet," Ziggy said. "Leave it in, Dan. I haven't come yet." He was jacking his cock frantically.

"Fuck, I'm sorry, too late," Daniel said. His cock had started softening and it slipped out of Ziggy's ass.

"I'm really close, though," Ziggy said. "Hang on. Unggh!"

Daniel watched Ziggy stroke a couple times and then said, "Let me do it, Zig."

"Fuck, I'm almost there. Unghhh!" Ziggy kept stroking, with pre-cum flying out of his dick in every direction. "That's it. Yeah. I'm coming again. Ahhhhh! Unnnngh!"

Daniel, without a moment's thought, leaned down and put his mouth over the head of Ziggy's cock.

"Fuck!" Ziggy said. He was way past the point of no return, and with Daniel's mouth firmly on his dickhead, he let loose of his cock and let it shoot. "Ungghhh! Unghhh! Unnghh!"

Daniel closed his lips tighter around Zig's cock and let it slide deeper into his mouth. He was taking Ziggy's load.

"Unnnnh. Unnnh. Oh, fuck," Ziggy moaned, as his cum spurt out into Daniel's warm, wet mouth. Daniel stayed on it until Zig was totally spent.

"Jesus." Ziggy collapsed against the head of the bed, drained.

Daniel kept licking Ziggy's cock until Ziggy laughed and said, "Dan, stop. You got it all, bro. Stop."

Daniel took his mouth off Ziggy's cock and licked his lips. "I could get used to that," he said. "Your cum is sweet."

Ziggy let his feet slide off of Daniel's shoulders, and then Daniel collapsed on top of Zig. Josh, in turn, fell on top of Daniel.

The three of them lay in a pile like that, catching their breath and letting their heartbeats return to normal.

Ziggy used the sheet to wipe the cum off his face from his earlier explosion. They looked at each other and grinned.

Daniel was beaming. "That was incredible, guys. Fuck, I've come three times already. God, I'm beat."

"You're not the only one," Josh said. They lay there for a few minutes, exhausted.

Nobody said anything. Five minutes later they were almost asleep when Ziggy said, "Come on guys. Let's get in the shower. Dan, can we all fit in your shower together?"

Daniel said, "Let's find out."

Chapter 21
BARELY ENOUGH

THEY SMILED as they climbed off the bed. All three of them were slippery with sweat and cum. "Follow me, guys," Daniel said. He led the trio into the bathroom and turned on the shower.

He got the temperature right and said, "Go ahead, get in. I know at least two of us can fit." Josh and Ziggy stepped in.

Ziggy said, "Come on, Dan. There's room."

"You sure?"

"We should all be in here together."

Daniel cautiously stepped into the crowded tub. There was no way to avoid rubbing against each other, but that just added to the pleasure. It was intimate.

"That was the best fun I've ever had," Daniel said. "Thanks."

"Thank *you*," Ziggy said. They started soaping each other up. "Hell, we had to show you what it's all about."

"Now you know," Josh said, "how to fuck somebody with that big ol' cock. How to get somebody to *want* to be fucked by it."

"Yeah, that's one lesson I'll never forget. God, I can't believe it. My first balls-deep fuck."

"Won't be your last, though."

"God, I hope not." Daniel laughed. "You guys are super, you know that?"

"Remember," Josh said, "wait till they *ask* you for it. They will, if you get them ready first." They switched places to rinse off.

"Guys," Daniel said, "I'd love to do this again tomorrow. I could call in sick again. Are you gonna be around?"

"We're leaving in the morning," Ziggy said. "Gonna spend some time in Florida, and then it's back to St. Louis."

"Aw fuck, no. I wanted to try some other stuff with you guys. Couldn't you stick around for another day?"

"Jeez, what did we miss?" Josh said. "You got a pretty good sample of just about everything."

"No, not everything. There's other stuff we could try." He started blushing. "Kinky stuff. And I liked sucking Ziggy's dick. I want to suck you off too, Josh. I want to suck both of you."

"You liked that, huh?"

"Yeah. And we could role-play. You guys could tie me up and spank me and make me suck your cocks until you both come in my mouth."

"Jeez, Danny. Uh, actually, that does sound hot."

"Dan," Ziggy said. "I wish we could. I like that idea. It sounds like a lot of fun. Hell, it sounds hot. But dude, we gotta get on the road early. We're gonna drive to Orlando."

"In one day?"

"Maybe. I doubt it. But we're gonna get an early start and see how far we can get."

"Fuck. See how you are. Turn me queer and then abandon me."

"Aw, fuck. Now you're gonna make us feel bad."

"I'm just teasing. You didn't turn me into anything I wasn't already. Seriously, I appreciate all you've done for me. But you guys are the only ones I know, for crissakes. The only ones I can do this gay stuff with. I don't even know of anybody else I can *talk* to about it. I'm gonna be lost without you."

"Aw, Danny, it won't be like that," Josh said. "Hell, I'll bet you already know some guys who'd be up for it. You just don't know it."

"I don't think so."

They were finished showering, so Ziggy turned the water off. They stepped out of the tub. Daniel handed out towels.

"You can always call us if you want to talk, Danny."

"And you can come visit us in St. Louis, bro. Right, Josh?"

"Definitely."

"Really? You really mean it?"

"Yeah, of course. You're our buddy now, Dan. You gotta come visit us."

"Hell, I'd love to. How soon will you guys be back home?"

"Uh, depends on when the money runs out," Ziggy said. "But we both have to be back to work the day after Labor Day."

They put up their towels and walked naked from the bathroom into the living room.

"I've never been to Florida," Daniel said. "I wish I could go with you."

"Dude, any other time that would probably be a great idea. But . . . not this time, bro."

"This is a special vacation for us, Danny. It's our anniversary. We'd love having a friend like you along, but . . ."

"That's okay," Daniel said. "I get it. I understand." He stared down at the living room floor. "Hell, I probably couldn't get off work anyway. And I don't know when I can go to St. Louis, either. I'll have to run that one by the boss." Then he brightened up. "But I know I could get some time off at Christmas."

"Christmas? Don't you have family around here? Aunts or uncles? Grandparents?"

"No. No family, here or anywhere else."

"Well, you got family now," Ziggy said. "Tell you what: come stay with us for Christmas. We won't have anybody either, except for each other."

"I . . . I'd really like that," Daniel said.

"This has all been such a surprise," Josh said. "Running into you in the woods, first of all, and then, you know, all the fun we had today. Especially."

"Not anymore than I surprised myself," Danny said. "But it's about time. I'm gonna stop worrying about what people think. I want to try everything, guys. If I can do it with you, that is.

Nobody else, just you." He looked at Josh and Ziggy, all of them still naked, and his dick started filling out again.

"Aw, Dan, one of these days," Ziggy said, "when you're least expecting it, you'll meet a cool guy right here in D.C. Sooner or later, you will. A great guy who you can fuck and be friends with too. He'll seem like some regular guy at first, but when you get to know him, you'll realize – that he's like us. Like you. And then you'll figure out a way to let him know *you* are, too. Dude, wait and see if you don't. That's the way it happens."

"I guess."

"And we'll still be your friends too. We're bros now."

"I . . . I love you guys, you know that? You don't judge me, and you want me to be happy. I've never met any guys like you before."

"You're a rare one yourself," Josh said. Still naked, he wrapped his arms around Daniel from behind and hugged him close. "Good friends are hard to find. I'm glad we found each other."

Daniel didn't answer.

"Danny? You okay?"

"He can't talk right now," Ziggy said. "He's okay, though, Josh. A-ok."

Daniel was crying. He covered his face with his hands. "S-s-sorry, guys. I can't believe I'm crying in front of you."

Ziggy moved in and wrapped his arms around Daniel and Josh. All three of them held each other close.

Daniel smiled through his tears. "You guys," he said. "How'd you ever get to be so fucking sweet?"

"It's all an act," Josh said. "We're actually the meanest guys you'll ever meet."

"Oh, bullshit." Daniel laughed. They let loose of each other and Daniel tried to wipe the tears from his face.

Josh picked up his t-shirt. "Here, Dan, use this." Daniel took it and wiped his face dry, smiling all the while.

"Thanks, guys."

—

THEY RELUCTANTLY BEGAN putting on their clothes again. Their dicks were starting to fill out again, and in any case, it felt more natural to be naked – naked was how Josh and Ziggy preferred to be, whenever they could get away with it – but it was time to go.

They stood at the door, saying their goodbyes. Daniel looked more scared than sad.

"Jeez," Josh said, "we forgot to give you our address. Do you have something to write on?"

Daniel brightened up a bit. "Hell yes! Hold on a sec." He ran into the kitchen and came back with a notepad and a pen. "And your phone number too, okay?"

"Of course." Josh started writing. "And you gotta give us yours, too."

"Okay." Daniel looked a little relieved now. "I'm gonna be lonely, but that's nothing new I guess."

"Dude, anytime you start feeling lonely, you give us a call, you hear?"

"Uh, guys, can I get another hug?"

"Oh, hell yeah." Ziggy put his arms around Daniel and the two of them held each other close. Then it was Josh's turn.

"Listen, guys, I really appreciate everything."

"You'd better come visit us," Josh said, smiling. "We'll be pissed if you don't. Don't piss us off, Danny, you'll regret it."

Daniel laughed. "That's right, I forgot how mean you can be."

"That's us," Josh said. "Just call us the Mean Brothers."

"The Sweet and Sexy Brothers is more like it," Daniel said. "I'm gonna come out and visit you guys as soon as I can. Gosh, I could even move to St. Louis. Wouldn't that be cool?"

Josh and Zig looked at each other.

Ziggy said, "Uh, Dan, that might not be such a good idea."

"Why?"

"Think about it. You own a house here, the house you grew up in, and you have a good job. Everything that Washington D.C. has to offer is right at your doorstep. You'd want to think long and hard before you give all that up."

"I know," Daniel said. "But friends are more important. That's what I think. I was already thinking about moving away from D.C. anyway. Some place new where nobody knows me yet." He sighed. "In any case, I'm gonna miss you guys."

"Christmas at our place," Josh said. "You can hold out that long."

—

JOSH AND ZIGGY HEADED BACK to their hotel. Neither one of them said anything for a few minutes.

Finally Ziggy said, "Why so quiet?"

"I was just gonna ask you the same thing."

"Oh, just thinking."

"About Danny? Because that's what I've been thinking about."

"Yeah," Ziggy said. "About Daniel."

"You know the cliché about creating a monster?"

"Yeah. That's what we just did, isn't it?"

"Well, I don't know," Josh said. "I hope not."

"Dude was cruising along fine until we popped up and rocked his boat," Ziggy said.

"Well, we don't know if he was fine. He might have been miserable for all we know."

"Maybe he was. I was doing my best to cheer him up, I know that much."

"Yeah you were," Josh said. "You went further then I probably would have."

"Josh, you put as much into it as I did. He needed us. And we were both up to it, I think. We gave him some help because we wanted to."

"Now we're responsible for him. You know, like when you save someone's life? We're gonna be there for him, right?"

"Sure. Fine with me. You're right, Josh. We want to look out for him. I don't mind. He's a good person. He'll be a good friend."

"That's how I feel."

"I hope he's not expecting to fuck me again, though."

"Did it hurt?"

"Nah. It was awesome. But my ass is for you, Josh. That's how I want it to be. We taught Daniel how to find his own piece of ass, so let him."

"He certainly was horny," Josh said. "That's for sure."

"Yeah, Jesus, that was so crazy. I had a good time, but still, we got carried away. Jesus, we went over there for closure. Remember? Instead of closure, we started something new. A new friendship I hope, but god only knows."

"He sure was . . . hyper. I don't think I've ever seen anyone so horny in all my life."

"I don't think we changed that, either. He's probably hornier now than ever."

"But at least now he knows how to deal with it better."

"Yes, he does. We accomplished that much. The dude can do it if he has the balls to get out and meet people. You think he will?"

"I don't know," Josh said. "He's still shy. Or so he says."

"So are you, sweetheart."

"I know. I really got lucky, meeting you."

"Both of us were lucky, Josh. But it wouldn't have happened if you hadn't got yourself out where you could meet people."

"Well, maybe he'll get out too."

"Maybe. I hope so. Or maybe he'll just move to St. Louis. To be with us."

"You think?"

"Dude might decide to rock our boat."
"Zig, I don't want our boat rocked."
"Me neither."
They rode the rest of the way to the hotel in silence. Thinking.

Chapter 22
EARLY RISE

Tuesday

JOSH WOKE UP EARLY, before their call from the hotel desk. He cancelled the wake-up call, walked back to the bed, and pulled the covers down, so he could look at Ziggy.

After a few minutes Zig usually turned flat on his back, while his dick filled out and rose up into the air. Sometimes, though, Ziggy rolled over onto his side, close to the edge of the bed, with his hard cock facing outward. In that case, Josh got down on his knees on the floor and sucked Ziggy from there. When it happened that way, Ziggy usually woke up halfway through the blowjob and gently pumped his cock into Josh's mouth until they both came.

Sometimes, instead of turning flat on his back, Ziggy rolled over the other way, onto his belly, with his sexy ass just begging for attention. Josh's favorite thing to do was suck Ziggy's cock, but if Zig offered his butt instead, Josh enjoyed that just as much. What Josh liked most was giving Ziggy a joyful experience, whatever way he wanted it. ·

It was almost a ritual, this waking sex of theirs. It had its variations, and sometimes a reversal of roles, but one way or another they usually started the morning out this way. More often than not, Josh was the first one to wake up, but not always.

After a good fucking or sucking, with orgasms for both of them, they'd lie down next to each other again. Ziggy would pull Josh up close and they'd kiss. Then they'd cuddle some more, and maybe go back to sleep.

No going back to sleep this morning, though. They wanted to get on the road early. Orlando was waiting.

They had packed the night before, so they were ready. They ate a good breakfast and then they were on their way.

—

THE FASTEST WAY TO GO was I-95, which would take them through Virginia, then North Carolina, South Carolina, and Georgia. And then finally into Florida – Jacksonville and Daytona Beach, and then the turnoff, west, to Orlando.

On their trip from St. Louis to D.C. they had driven straight through in one day, and they didn't want to put themselves through that again. The drive to Florida was even longer, about 850 miles from D.C. By the time they reached Savannah they were looking for a hotel for the night.

And after they settled in at the hotel, and had a few bong hits, it was time to relax.

"I forgot to tell you, I got a letter from Tony a few days ago," Josh said. "Just before we left home."

"Your buddy in Memphis?"

"Yeah. He wants to come up and visit us in St. Louis. I haven't seen him since I moved in with you, Zig. He said he misses me." Josh smiled. "And he's really curious about you."

"What's he curious about? I'm just a regular dude, not much different from anybody else."

"Oh hell, Zig, you're one of a kind. I've told him all about you and he's really . . . intrigued."

"Oh shit." Ziggy grinned. "What did you tell him? No, never mind, don't tell me. It doesn't matter. Bring him on. I don't know what he's expecting but I'll probably disappoint him."

"Naw, it's not like that, Zig. He's not expecting anything. He just knows you're, well, you know, an independent thinker. He knows how much you mean to me, so he wants to meet you. You'll like him, I know you will."

"He's gotta be a good bro if he's the best friend you have there. Good lookin' dude, right? I think I remember what he looks like. That night I saw you at the club, at first I thought he was your partner."

"Yeah. You told me you watched us that night. Remember when we talked about that? You thought he was my boyfriend because he was the only one who could make me smile."

"Yeah, I remember. A year ago. Well, tell him to come on up. Our bed's a little bit bigger now, so, we should be able to fit the three of us on there, no problem."

"He asked if Labor Day week would work. He has that week off. He knows we won't be home until Sunday night, but he's okay with that. What do you think? Is that too soon?"

"Uh, shit, you're talking about the week after next. The first day we're back home? Uh, yeah, I guess it's okay. Sure, why not? The apartment's kind of a mess, but I don't care if he doesn't."

"Cool. I'll tell him, then."

"Is he gonna drive up?"

"No, he'll take the bus. He doesn't have a car."

—

THEY ATE DINNER at a nearby restaurant – Southern-style cooking, naturally. Then they spent a quiet evening at the hotel. There was a swimming pool, so they went for a dip, horsed around a little there, sat in the hot tub for a while, and then they went to bed early.

Wednesday

THEN THE NEXT MORNING, onward to Florida. After a hearty breakfast, they hit the road. Josh was driving.

Ziggy looked at the map. "Josh," he said, "have you planned out our route back home yet?"

"Yeah, pretty much. From Fort Lauderdale we'll head back north to Orlando. Then up through Atlanta, Nashville, Paducah, and across the Mississippi to I-55 and St. Louis."

"There's another route we could take. After Nashville, I mean."

"What route is that?"

"Well, it's the long way around, and it would probably mean a three-day drive instead of two. But it has one advantage." Ziggy smiled.

"Oh, jeez, Zig. Isn't nineteen or twenty hours on the road enough?" Josh grinned. "Okay, knowing you, you have some kind of adventure in mind. Go ahead, tell me. What is it?"

"I was thinking, we'll be so close to Memphis, why not go around that way?"

"Memphis? Jeez, why in the hell would we ever want to go back to Memphis? Even if it wasn't at least three hours out of our way?"

"So we can pick Tony up. He could ride up to St. Louis with us, instead of taking a bus."

"Oh."

Josh watched the road, driving, while he thought about it. Ziggy smiled, watching Josh, waiting.

For a couple of minutes they drove in silence. Josh occasionally looked at Ziggy, then back at the road. Thinking.

Finally Josh said, "By the time we get to Memphis we'll be totally beat. But that's no problem; Tony can put us up overnight. Fuck, he'd love to ride up with us, I know he would. I'd like it, too. And it'd be a great way for you two to get to know each other."

Ziggy grinned. "I figured you might like the idea."

"But you're right; it would mean a three-day drive instead of two."

"We wouldn't have to leave Florida any sooner," Ziggy said. "We could still head back Saturday morning. We'll just get home Monday instead of Sunday, that's all. Time would go by fast with your buddy along. Wouldn't it?"

"Damn right. Let's do it." Josh put his palm up, and Ziggy slapped it. High-five! "I'll call Tony at the next rest stop and tell him."

"Tell him not to tell anybody. Otherwise your asshole beast-master ex-boyfriend might show up."

"Yeah, you read my mind. We don't need that."

"Are they still friends?"

"I don't think they ever were. They know each other because of Jerome, that guy who had the Lincoln. He plans trips and the bunch of them end up going together."

"Oh."

"But Tony's not gonna tell Fred or anyone else where he's going. Not until after he comes back, at least. He still feels bad about leaving me behind in St. Louis last year."

"But . . . doesn't he know that's what brought you and me together?"

"Yeah, he knows. Believe me, he knows."

"Well, then why would he feel bad . . ."

Josh sighed. "I think it's because *he* wanted to be my boyfriend. I'm pretty sure I'm right about this; if Fred and I ever broke up, I think he was planning to . . . step in. But you got to me first."

"Oh, fuck. Way too much information. Sorry, I shouldn't have asked. Hell, I want to like the dude."

"Naw, it's not gonna be like that. I'm sure he's gotten over it by now. He knows damn well how good you are for me, Zig. It's just . . . one of those twists in life. Regrets over something that can't be changed. You can't live your life dwelling on what you coulda, shoulda, woulda. He knows that. At least I think he does."

"So," Ziggy said, "he's not gonna have any hard feelings?"

"I don't know. I wouldn't think so. Not if he wants me to be happy."

"Well, from what I've seen, it's not easy for people to give up deep feelings like that."

"Tony's not the type to hold a grudge."

"That's not what I'm talking about."

"What do you mean?"

"If he wanted to be your boyfriend, then he probably had some kind of crush on you. Maybe more than a crush. Maybe he was really in love with you."

"Oh, jeez."

"Why else would he want to be your boyfriend?"

"Yeah, good point."

"And if he was in love with you, well, that's difficult to part with. Even when somebody wants to, it's not easy. When you feel that way about someone, you can't just shut it off. It takes people years to get over stuff like that."

"Oh, Jesus."

"But who knows, maybe it's not like that with him. I really should have kept my mouth shut. Hell, he's one of your best buddies. Sorry."

"No, you're right. I've seen it myself. People don't give up love easily. But I know he wants me to be happy."

"Of course he does."

"He's a caring guy. A nice guy. Don't worry, you two will get along fine. We're gonna have fun."

"Cool."

"So, sounds like a plan. We spend the night at his place that Sunday night, and take him back to St. Louis with us in the morning. He's gonna be excited."

"What's he like? Anything like Daniel?"

Josh laughed. "No one is like Daniel. Daniel is a trip."

"You got that right," Ziggy said. "But Tony, um, you know, what sort of stuff does he like? Does he like to walk? Does he go to the bar every weekend, or does he chill out with friends at home? Does he like to read, or is he a TV addict, or what?"

"Wow, lots of questions."

"Well, I'm curious. We're gonna be one happy family for a week, in our little one-room apartment. And we'll be sleeping together. He's not gonna have a problem with that, is he?"

"I seriously doubt it. He and I have slept together, no problem. He likes to cuddle. Once he gets a look at you, Zig, I guarantee he won't want it any other way." Josh smiled.

"Josh, how could you know that? Not everybody likes my looks. Some people think I'm . . . well, you know."

"What?"

"Goofy-looking."

"As far as I'm concerned, nobody looks hotter or more handsome than you, Zig. Nobody. Anyway, I know Tony, and I know the kinds of guys he goes for."

"Oh, Jesus, are you saying he'll want to fuck me?"

"Um, more likely he'll want you to fuck him." Josh smiled. "But he's adaptable. With the right guy, he's usually up for anything. So he says."

"You gay guys! Seems like you're always ready for sex."

"You're not any different, Zig. You know you aren't."

"Okay, okay. You're right. Hell, even my straightest and narrowest friends are always horny. Frustrated and horny."

"Aren't you glad you're not one of them?"

Ziggy laughed. "I get horny all the time, but I can't remember the last time I was frustrated. Had to be at least a year ago."

"That's when we met, is a year ago."

"That's what I'm talking about."

Josh laughed. "Well, the same goes for me."

"Um, how's that gonna work, by the way, while Tony's there? I mean, the three of us *are* gonna sleep together. You think we'll actually have sex with him?"

"I'm sure he'd be in favor of it. Knowing him."

"Fuck." Ziggy grinned. "How about you?"

"Well, um, what I figure is, why not?"

"Oh shit." Ziggy laughed. "First Daniel, and then Tony."

"Well, we don't really know."

"You seemed pretty sure a minute ago, dude."

"Tony's unpredictable. Hell, he might want to sleep on the floor."

"I can't see that."

"Me neither."

"You know what, though? I'm not so sure I want to be having sex with other people on a repeat basis. The only one I want like that is you, Josh."

"Me, and Eleanor."

"Well, yeah. I was talking about guys."

"Yeah, I know."

"But hey, about you and me and Eleanor, I think you already know, if I ever had to choose, I wouldn't even need to think about it. I go where you go, Josh."

"Same here, Zig. With you. Fuck, I'm getting a hard on."

"So, uh, if you and I want to do something while Tony's staying with us . . . ."

"What, just the two of us? It won't be a problem. We always figure something out, you know that."

"Yup."

"Tony doesn't know he's gonna be sleeping with us."

"What?"

"I'm not gonna tell him yet. But when he finds out, and he sees how small the bed is, he's gonna freak. In a good way, I mean." Josh grinned. "Watch, he'll take me aside and beg me to let him sleep next to you, I promise."

"Oh, Jesus. Maybe he's not so different from Daniel after all. He definitely sounds horny."

"Isn't every guy?"

Ziggy grinned. "Yeah, pretty much."

"As for the questions you were asking, yeah, he does like to walk. He walks just about everywhere. TV, uh, he has a few favorite shows, for sure. Goes to the bar sometimes, when he's lonely, or horny, or gets invited out by his friends. But so did I. So did you."

"Well, whatever. Hell, we'll probably hit it off great. But I'll be happy if we just get along with each other, period."

They drove on for a few minutes in silence.

Then Josh said, "Fuck. I've still have a hard-on from talking about all that stuff."

"I'm horny, too," Ziggy said. "Want to take care of it at the next rest stop?"

"You're on."

Chapter 23
FLORIDA

THE FIRST ORDER of business when they reached the rest stop was to empty their bladders. Ziggy and Josh stood side by side at two urinals and tried their best to pee, but, as happened so often, it wasn't easy with the stiff boners they were sporting. They watched each other's hard dicks, smiling about the minor problem they'd long ago become accustomed to. Finally they managed it.

Empty of piss, the next goal was to shoot their loads, preferably with each other's help. But the restroom was a little too busy for that. They stood at the porcelain, stroking their hard cocks, waiting for the moment when no one was in the restroom with them, but they kept getting interrupted.

"Fuck this," Ziggy said. "Let's go back out to the car."

"Jeez, Zig, I gotta do something with this hard-on or I'm gonna have blue balls."

"Same here. Like I said, let's go back to the car. I think I know what we can do."

With some difficulty, they stuffed their boners into their jeans, and Josh followed Ziggy out to the Mustang. Zig started the engine.

"I'm gonna drive down to the end of the lot," he said. "We can do it in the car, Josh."

"Do what, jack off?"

"Fuck no. Let's suck each other off, want to?" Ziggy grinned. "You do me first, Josh. I'll keep an eye out and let you know if anyone's coming. After you get me off I'll do the same for you."

Josh smiled. Then it turned into a grin. "Hell yes. Let's go."

Ziggy parked the car in the last space, near some trees. They weren't in the shade, and every vehicle that drove out of that place would pass right by them. But the only people who walked that area were the occasional people with dogs.

Ziggy unzipped his jeans and pulled his stiff cock out from his underwear. "Put your head in my lap, Josh, and keep it there. Nobody'll even know you're in the car unless they walk up close, and I'll warn you if someone's coming."

Josh looked around to make sure nobody was close by; then he leaned over, rested his head on Ziggy's thighs, and put his mouth around Zig's cock.

"Oh, fuck yeah. Lick it, Josh. Suck on it and lick it, bro. Ahhhh!"

Josh used some suction, and wrapped his tongue around it.

"That's it Josh. Fuck, keep doing that. I'm gonna give you a good load, dude."

Josh kept it up, and then he gently licked right underneath the head with a slow, steady motion.

"Ooohhhhhh, fuck, yeah Josh, fuck, I'm gonna give it to you right now, are you ready?"

Josh nodded his head slightly and gave out a muffled "ummm hmmmm."

"Ahhhhh! God, I love it when you hum like that. Oh, fuck! Coming, Josh! Drink it down, bro. Fuck! Ooohhhhhhh! Fuck! Fuck! Ahhh! Unhhh!"

Josh kept on licking the underside of Ziggy's cock while wad after wad of cum spurt out into Josh's mouth. Ziggy's sweet, sweet cum. At least a half-dozen healthy spurts, and then Ziggy was winding down.

Then he straightened up. "Somebody's coming this way. You better sit up, Josh."

While Ziggy put his dick away, Josh casually sat up, as if he'd been napping and just woke up.

"Fuck, that was good," Ziggy said. "Jesus, sweetheart. You're the best, you know that? Nobody but you can make me feel that good."

Josh licked his lips, still savoring the flavor. "Nobody else has ever sucked your cock."

"Yes, they have. Some girls have tried it. Eleanor tries sometimes."

"Girls don't count, Zig. Only a guy can really know how to make a guy feel good."

"Daniel did it too, remember?"

"Right, I forgot about that. But you were already coming by then. How was that? He definitely swallowed your cum, that's for sure."

"It was alright. You know, it's always good to come in a mouth, but it wasn't as good as you." Ziggy looked around for people. "Coast is clear, dude. Take your dick out."

Josh opened his jeans, pulled his briefs down, and maneuvered his stiff boner out into the open.

"Jesus, look at the pre-cum. You really are horny."

"I'm horny as fuck. Jeez, what do you expect? Especially after sucking you off."

"Never fear, relief is on its way." Ziggy lay down horizontal with his head on Josh's lap. He grasped Josh's hard cock and put it inside his mouth. "Mmmmm."

Josh moaned.

Ziggy licked it, pressed his lips around it, and gave it a little suction.

"Ahhhhh. Zig, keep that up and I'll come. Oh fuck."

Ziggy took it out of his mouth and said, "Come whenever you're ready, Josh. Give me a good load." Then he put Josh's cock back in his mouth and sucked.

"You'll get a good load, Zig, count on it. Ahhhh! Fuck! Jeez, where'd you learn to suck so good?" Josh moaned again.

"From you, bro. Who else?"

"Fuck, you better get your mouth back on it, I swear I could come any second."

Zig put the cockhead and the stiff shaft back in his mouth, wrapped his tongue around it, and sucked.

"Ahhhhh! Oh, that's it Zig, coming. Coming!" Josh groaned. The head of his dick got bigger, and a shot of cum suddenly spurt into the back of Ziggy's mouth. "Unhhhh! Unhh!"

Ziggy kept licking. He held his lips tight around Josh's cock so that he wouldn't miss any cum. Josh moaned and convulsed. Several thick ropes of jizz spurt out onto Ziggy's tongue. Zig gulped it down and got every drop.

Finally Josh said, "You got it, Zig. Fuck, I needed that."

Ziggy let loose and sat up just as an elderly woman and her dog passed by. She didn't seem to be paying any attention to them, though. "Jesus, Josh, you were supposed to keep an eye out."

"Sorry. I forgot."

"Oh well." Ziggy smiled. "Maybe it gave her a thrill."

"Oh, man." Josh leaned back in the seat. "That was good."

"Hey," Ziggy said, "we take care of each other, don't we?"

"You got that right."

They sat there for a few minutes in silence, relaxed in an after-glow state of mind.

"Don't forget," Ziggy said, "about calling Tony."

"Oh, right. Yeah. I'll do it right now. I'll be right back. Unless you want to come with me."

"Nah, I'll stay here and relax."

—

THEN THEY WERE BACK on the highway heading south.

"Tony was excited. He's really looking forward to it."

"So, he's gonna put us up overnight?"

"Yeah. He has a fold-out couch-bed in the living room, that's where he usually puts his guests."

"Not in his own bed with him, huh?" Ziggy smiled.

"Well, it wouldn't be the first time. But he won't be expecting anything like that. He still doesn't have a clue that we'll all be sleeping together in St. Louis. I want it to be a surprise." Josh grinned. "He's excited enough already, just to be staying with us."

"Like Daniel wants to do."

"Danny can visit us, too. He's gonna spend Christmas with us, right?"

"Yeah, if he can wait that long. He'd be with us now if he could have swung it."

"Not on this trip. Not him or Tony, either one. This is our anniversary."

"For sure. This trip is for us." Ziggy sighed. "But you know who I *do* wish could have been with us?"

"Uh, yeah. Of course. I wish he could be with us, too, Zig."

"I still have dreams about him. Sometimes I wish George and I could have stayed at that orphanage forever. But then I wouldn't have met you. And that wouldn't do, would it? I wouldn't give you up for anything, Josh."

"Who knows," Josh said. "Maybe somewhere out in all those alternative universes, there's one where the three of us are together."

"That's a nice thought. The three of us. Three-way partners. What a trip that would be."

"But you never know, he might be with us right now. Anyway, I figure all three of us will be together in our next lives. How much you want to bet?"

"Oh god I hope so. That would be perfect."

"When you dream about him, what are you guys doing, fucking?" Josh grinned.

Ziggy laughed. "Nah. When I dream about sex, it's with you. With George, we're usually sitting down by the river, or walking somewhere, just talking about stuff. Maybe with our arms around each other. The sex with him was excellent, but what I really miss is just being with him. Talking to him."

"Yeah, I know you do. You guys really loved each other."

"Yeah." Ziggy's eyes got glassy with tears. "We did."

They drove on in silence for a while.

"Ah, well," Ziggy said. "Like you told me, at least we had those years together. Precious memories."

"Yep."

"The sex we had was part of it, of course. Every day we gave each other the gift of ecstasy. Fuck, how much more intimate can you get with somebody? If we didn't love each other to begin with, we sure did soon enough. He took care of me, Josh. Not just sex-wise – others ways, too. And I took care of him too, the best I could."

"Those punk friends of his who you guys hung out with, did they know you two were fucking?"

"I don't know. I don't remember anyone mentioning it, but I always assumed they knew. We were always together, him and me. We didn't try to keep it a secret. But we didn't talk about it with anybody, either. We just did it."

"When you and those guys had those jack-off sessions together, did any of them ever, uh, you know, do each other?"

"Oh, sure. Not at first, but it wasn't a big deal. Eventually they all paired off with regular stroke buddies. Jacking yourself feels good, but you can do that anytime. It feels better when you have somebody else's hand doing it for you." Ziggy smiled.

"But you two didn't?"

"Nah. We watched each other, of course, but that's all."

"The other guys jacked each other off, but you and George didn't?"

"No, we didn't. Does that seem weird?"

"Well yeah, kind of."

"Josh, remember, George was fucking me on a daily basis. Sometimes more than once a day. So while our friends jacked each other off, George and I got a kick out of just watching each other.

Thinking about what we'd be doing later, or about what we'd done that morning together."

"I guess it would have been too tame, anyway, compared to what you did in private."

"Uh, maybe. Yeah, I guess it would have been. But no, I don't think that was it. I think it was more like when we touched each other, it meant a lot more to us then what those guys were feeling for each other. I think they were only helping each other out, you know, because it got them off better."

He looked at Josh as if that explained it.

"Well," Josh said, "that sounds . . . reasonable, but why would that stop you?"

"Because if George and I had jerked each other off, we would have done it different from those guys. We would have been more . . . intimate. Fuck, we'd have had our hands all over each other. And in places those guys probably never thought of touching. Chances are we'd have been kissing, too. I guess we didn't want to do special stuff like that in front of other people. Just watching each other jerk off, knowing what we knew – that was hot enough."

"Wow." Josh thought about it. "I wonder if any of my friends were fuck buddies like you and George, and I just didn't know it."

"I wouldn't doubt it, Josh. As horny as teenagers are? Half the guys in your school were probably doing circle jerks, at the very least. More than half. Ninety percent. That would be pretty typical. But put two of them together, alone, when they're both horny? Most of them probably fucked or sucked a buddy at least once. And if they liked it once, then they did it again. Count on it."

"Incredible."

"Not at all."

"What I mean is, I didn't know. I thought I was the only one who wanted to do stuff like that."

"Hell no."

ZIG AND JOSH were in Florida now. Onward they drove, through Jacksonville and Daytona. They talked about stopping in Daytona Beach to take a look at the ocean, but there was plenty of time for that later. They drove straight through to Orlando, where they had a hotel reservation and a comfy bed waiting for them. Whenever they were tired of Orlando, they would drive farther south and stay at one of the ocean beaches.

Thursday

AS IT TURNED OUT, one day in Orlando was more than enough. They spent the day at Disney World and quickly got their fill of being herded around with the other tourists.

Friday

FIRST THING the next morning, they fled eastward on Florida's Turnpike, a toll road that would take them back to the coast. The goal was to find a place to swim and lay out on the beach for a few days.

It was Ziggy's turn to drive.

"Jesus," he said. "What were we thinking? The rides at that place were fun, but we spent ninety percent of our time waiting in lines."

"And it wasn't cheap, either," Josh said. "But the rides were cool, and I've been wanting to go since I was a kid."

"Yeah, me too, Josh. I'm glad I got that out of my system. Now we've been there and done that, like they say."

"Onward to Fort Lauderdale."

"Yeah! Dude, I can't wait. What's it like? The ocean? You grew up in Maryland, you've probably been there more times than you can count."

"I forgot you've never seen it. Yeah, I have, dozens of times, but it was up north, not in Florida."

"Yeah, but still. The ocean, dude. I can't wait to see it. To be there and see it with my own eyes. I know it's gonna be way better than any pictures or movies. Too bad it's not Spring Break, though, huh?"

Josh looked at Ziggy as if he was crazy. Then he realized he was joking. "Aw, you had me there for a minute, Zig. Thought you'd gone frat boy on me or something."

Ziggy laughed. "Actually, I'm thinking even off-season Fort Lauderdale might be too much. We might be better off at someplace less famous. Someplace smaller."

"Yeah, maybe. I wanted to see what all the hype is about, though. I've been hearing about Fort Lauderdale since I was little."

"Yeah. Like Orlando."

"Oh shit, it can't be that bad. Can it?"

"We'll find out, bro."

Chapter 24
ROUTE A1A

THE FIRST LEG of the turnpike took them east toward the ocean. Then it would turn south, follow the coast, and take them close to Fort Lauderdale. Josh was looking at the map of Florida.

"Zig, believe it or not, there's another highway we could take that runs along the coast, like, basically, out in the ocean. On islands."

"No kidding?"

"It comes all the way down from Jacksonville. Route A1A. If we get off at Fort Pierce, we can hook up with it there."

"Dude."

"It looks pretty amazing. It runs across offshore islands, and when there aren't any islands, it runs along the shore. All the way down to Fort Lauderdale and Miami. Talk about a good look at the ocean."

"Sounds excellent to me. I'll bet it goes through all the little beach towns along the way."

"Yeah. It does. It'll slow us down, but we're not in any hurry, right?"

"Nah. We have all day."

"This is fun, going wherever we want to go. In search of sand and sea. I can see how a trip like this would be fun for a whole carload of friends."

"Oh, yeah, definitely."

"When we were leaving Danny's place I thought about inviting him along. But then I thought about the trip you and I took last year, just the two of us, and I thought, no way. This vacation is just for us. You and me. It's our anniversary. I always enjoy remembering that trip, Zig."

"Me too, bro. The beginning of something big. We were just getting to know each other then."

"Yeah."

"And the more I learned about you, the more I liked. It was the same for you, Josh, I know it was. The two of us together was like . . . magic."

"It still is, Zig."

"Yes. It still is. I think it always will be. I don't see how it could stop."

"Remember when we shook hands on it? On our friendship?"

"God yes. We ought to do that again. You want to?"

"Oh, hell yes."

"Okay. You remember what we were shaking on?"

"By heart."

"Same here. Okay then. Same thing goes." Ziggy held his hand out, and Josh grasped it with his. It was gentler, more intimate than a handshake. A transfer of energy, a sharing of spirit. They held hands for a minute or two. When they finally let loose, they were grinning.

—

"I'VE BEEN THINKING some more about Danny," Josh said.

"Yeah? What'd you come up with?"

"Well, he needs some friends. Friends like us. He seems pretty harmless. And I like him – I've always liked him. It'll be fun to have him come stay with us for a week or two. I don't think he'll be any problem. Hell, he's a nice guy."

"Yeah, I think so too," Ziggy said. "Fuck, the guy's almost as sweet as we are."

Josh laughed. "Are we really sweet, like he says?"

"Naw, we're just honest. And we care about people. Maybe we're a little less selfish than most folks, but hell, life's too short not to be. Maybe that's what he's talking about."

"He's the same way, though."

"I know. That's why I like him. I think you're right, Josh. He's harmless. He's . . . needy right now, but that's understandable. I want him to visit. But I don't think he should give up everything he has in D.C. and move to St. Louis just because we're there. That's when I would start worrying."

"Yeah, that would be kind of over the top. If he brings that up again, Zig, we might have to spell it out to him."

"Spell what out? We can't tell him where to live. He can move wherever he wants to."

"Yeah, I know, but what if he plans on spending all his time with us? I mean, I like the guy, but . . . well, you know. I want us to have some time of our own together. Just us."

"He's smart, Josh. He'll take a hint if it comes down to that. And if not, then we'll just be straight up about it with him. For everybody's benefit. Hell, it'll work out. I'm not worried about it."

—

THEY WERE GETTING CLOSE to the Fort Pierce exit.

"I think I can smell it, Zig. You smell that? We're close to the ocean. It's this next turnoff. All we have to do is drive through this little town and then we'll be on route A1A going south. There'll be signs for it, there always are."

"Okay."

Ziggy slowed down and steered into the exit ramp. Suddenly he shouted, "Jesus Christ Almighty!" He started pumping the brake pedal like a lunatic. "Fucking pedal went to the floor."

"No brakes? Shit!"

"Hang on, Josh. I think we'll be okay. I can stop it."

It was tense. Ziggy's pumping allowed the brakes to slow down the vehicle. At the end of the ramp he pulled off and stopped, turned the engine off, and dropped back in his seat.

"Holy shit, dude. I was freaking out. Josh, sweetheart, your brakes are fucked."

"Pumping the pedal like that helps?"

"Yeah. I'm thinking it's your master cylinder. Air gets in the line. If the brake pedal goes to the floor and still isn't stopping you, pump it. It'll bring up the pressure when it first fades out like that. But it's a dangerous situation. It'll get worse, too."

"Jeez, of course it's dangerous. We can't drive it like that. Can we?"

"Maybe enough to get it to a mechanic, but it's chancy. Pumping the brake usually works, but 'usually' isn't good enough when it comes to brakes. Pumping takes time to get the pressure up. If you need to stop fast, you don't have time. Somebody could get killed."

"Oh, great. So what should we do?"

Ziggy shrugged his shoulders. "Find a mechanic or a garage. We gotta get it fixed, bro."

"Uh, what kind of money are we talking about?"

"It won't be cheap, Josh, but we can handle it. Between the two of us we'll have enough."

"No Zig, I should pay for it. It's my car."

"Yeah, but I use it as much as you do. We'll split it, okay? I want to pay half."

"Well, whatever."

"Fair's fair."

"Okay, if you want to. Anyway, now we have to find a garage. Maybe there's one here in Fort Pierce."

"Well, if you see one, holler. But all I see is truck stops. I think we should go ahead and drive along the route you were talking about. We'll look for a garage along the way. It shouldn't take too long – every town's got one. Look, I'll drive really careful, and keep extra far behind other cars. That ought to work for now. I hope."

"You know more about this stuff than I do, Zig. That sounds scary to me, though. Maybe we should just get it towed somewhere."

"It pisses me off. If we were in St. Louis I could fix it at work, myself. But I don't have the tools here, even if I had the parts for it."

"Well, let's not just sit here. We need to do something."

"I see a sign for route A1A. You up for giving it a try?"

"Yeah. Sure."

They drove onward.

Every traffic light, stop sign, and pedestrian they approached seemed like a disaster waiting to happen, but they managed to stop when they needed to. They were both too nervous to take their eyes off the road for more than a few seconds at a time, but one thing was for sure: there weren't any car repair shops.

Finally they came to a convenience store and Ziggy said, "Fuck, I'm gonna pull over and park. I haven't even gotten a good look at the ocean yet. Driving like this is stressing me out. Every muscle in my body is tense."

"Yeah, same here. And I'm not even the one driving."

"We ought to trade massages tonight if you're up to it, Josh. Wherever the fuck it is we finally end up."

"Hell yes, Zig, I'm up for that." Josh grinned.

"In the meantime, we need to rethink this brake situation. We're not gonna find a garage on this road. This Quickie-Mart here, or whatever the fuck it is, is the best we're gonna do. Hell, I'd be surprised if they even sell engine oil, let alone brake fluid."

"Are we gonna call for a tow truck?"

"We might have to. But I'm gonna go inside and talk to these people and see what I can find out. It'll only take me a minute."

Five minutes later Ziggy came back out. "Good news, bro. They gave me the address of a garage on the mainland, in Jensen Beach."

"Jensen Beach? Where's that?"

"We're already in it. Or at the edge of it. The shop is maybe three miles from here. They even wrote down directions for us. It's not far. I think we can make it."

Ziggy slipped behind the wheel again and carefully, slowly, drove south on A1A. In less than a mile, they came to the road that would take them off the island, onto the mainland, and into the town of Jensen Beach, Florida.

—

"YOU'RE THE NAVIGATOR, Josh. Read the directions and tell me where to turn."

"Uh, as soon as this causeway thing reaches the mainland, we're supposed to turn left onto Indian River Drive, going south. Or it might be called County Road 707."

"Well, we're coming up on the mainland now. Oh shit, is that it right there?"

"Yeah, that's the road."

"Fuck, look at this crazy intersection. We'll never make it. I'm gonna put it in low gear."

They made it through without a hitch.

"Then we look for Jensen Beach Boulevard on the right," Josh said. "It's about four or five blocks down. We're gonna turn right, to the west."

"Alright. Fuck, what's that asshole behind us honking at?"

"Uh, us, I guess. We're going, like, two miles an hour."

"Fuck him! Fuck the bastard if he can't take a joke! Fuckin' asshole. Jesus."

"What do you mean? What's the joke?"

"Oh, I don't know, it's just something George used to say all the time."

"Look at that sign. Mango Terrace. What a name for a street."

They drove onward, slowly.

"Is that it right there, Josh? Is that it?"

"Uh, no. Ricou Terrace. What's a ricou?"

"Fuck if I know." They drove on. "Okay," Ziggy, said, "this has to be it. Yes!"

"Yeah, that's it. Jensen Beach Boulevard. We're making progress, Zig."

They made the turn and Josh said, "Now we're on the road the garage is on. It's on the left, two or three blocks up. The address is 1650. Skyline Garage."

"Fuck, another crazy intersection. We're gonna run into somebody for sure."

"Just take it slow, Zig."

"I am, I am. Fucker behind me is right on my tail."

"Fuck him."

"I'll bet he'd like me to. But that little privilege is reserved for you, sweetheart."

Josh laughed.

Ziggy smiled. "And that's no joke."

"Yeah, me, Eleanor, and the occasional Daniel dude."

"Well, yeah, I'd fuck him. He fucked me, after all. I'd be glad to return the favor. I'd like to see if I could get that monster cock of his to stay hard the whole time I'm doing it, too."

"I know you could. You do that and more to me. Look! That's the place, Zig. It's gotta be."

"Hell yes! Hallelujah."

Ziggy maneuvered the car into the lot and turned off the engine before he could hit anything. "Ahhhh. We made it, Josh. Un-fucking-believable. Thank god."

Chapter 25
AND EVERYTHING

THEY SAT THERE a few minutes, winding down now that the stress was over.

"I don't think I could have done it. I'm glad it was you driving, Zig. You done good."

"Aw, you could have done it. Come on, let's go see if they can help us."

Josh followed Ziggy into the office, but there was only one person in there, apparently a customer; waiting. Reading.

Ziggy asked him, "Are you getting your car worked on?"

"Yes."

"Where is everybody?"

"In the garage there. Are you here to get your oil changed? They'll be done with mine in ten or fifteen minutes, maybe less."

"No, we got a bigger problem. Our brakes went out."

"Oh. Yes, I would call that a *big* problem."

"Yeah. We're lucky we didn't seriously fuck ourselves up. Uh, sorry. Excuse my language."

"That's quite alright. I imagine right now you're feeling very frustrated."

"Frustrated and pissed off. I could have fixed it myself if this happened at home, but no, it had to wait until we were on vacation in Florida to fucking go to hell. Aw, shit. Sorry."

"Oh, curse all you want. I've heard it all before. I do it myself, now and then."

Ziggy laughed. "Somehow I can't picture you using language like that."

The man smiled. "Now, why would that be?"

"I don't know. It's just that you look, uh, like a more refined dude. More mature. Uh, I mean that in a good way. More mature than me or Josh here, even though you don't look much older. Thirty years old, give or take, am I right? And you're polite. More polite than me, anyway."

The gentleman laughed. "Oh, I'm older than thirty. You'd be surprised."

"Oh, well, age doesn't matter, anyway," Ziggy said. "You're as young as you feel, right? That's what matters." He smiled.

"Well said, young man. I see it the same way."

Ziggy and Josh stood there in silence for a few minutes, waiting for an employee to come in and help them. The man picked up his reading again, and the boys looked him over.

He seemed out of place there. He could have been a model, or a movie star, or possibly a product of the good breeding typical of family dynasties. He was strikingly handsome. He seemed like someone who would normally have a servant run such errands for him. The fact that he was friendly didn't alter that; sometimes even the rich have humility and a kind word for everyone.

"Zig, I'm gonna go out and see if I can talk to one of the mechanics."

"I'll go with you, Josh." To the man waiting, Ziggy said. "See you in a few."

They cautiously walked through the door into the service bay. Some shops don't allow customers in the work area. But the first mechanic they found was glad to help.

Ziggy explained the problem. The mechanic said they'd be glad to look at it, only it would have to wait for a couple of hours, as they had other work to finish, work that was promised that same day.

Josh and Ziggy came back to the waiting area looking glum. They sat down next to their fellow-customer.

"Any word?" The man asked.

"They can't even look at it for a couple of hours. They gotta finish some other work first. But I think I already know what it is. I work on cars, myself. I just hope they can fix it today so we can move on. Fuck, it's Friday. We could be stuck here all weekend."

"Where are you boys going?"

"Well, Josh here wants to check out Fort Lauderdale, which is okay with me. So long as there's ocean, sand, and a comfy bed for the two of us, I'll be happy."

"You've heard how it gets there during Spring Break, no doubt. Is that what you're hoping for? Some wild parties?"

"No, hell no. Peace and quiet. We figured it might be less crazy right now since it's off season."

"Well, possibly so," the man said. "But if you want my opinion, you're already in one of the nicest beach towns in Florida. All things considered."

"You live here?"

"Yes, I do."

"Did you grow up here?"

"No, I've been here five years or so. I moved here in 1981. I considered many places, when I was making my choice, but Jensen Beach appealed to me the most. It's relatively quiet here, somewhat of a small-town atmosphere, but big enough to keep things interesting. And I simply like the place."

"That's what I like," Ziggy said. "Peace and quiet, but plenty of things to do if you get bored."

"Where are you boys from?"

"St. Louis. Both of us. Right Josh?"

"Yep. That's where I'm from now." Josh smiled. "And Zig's lived there since day one."

"You're good friends, I take it."

"The best," Ziggy said. "Best friends, and more."

"Oh, is that right?"

"Yeah. We sleep together and everything."

"Oh, my goodness. You *are* good friends."

Josh's face was red from embarrassment. "Jeez, Zig!"

"Well, it's true. You're not ashamed of it, are you?"

"No, it's not that," Josh said. "I'm . . . I'm proud of it. But this guy doesn't want to hear our whole life story. He doesn't even know us. He might not *want* to know us, now."

"Oh, just the opposite," the man said. "I'm honored. There's no need for embarrassment, Josh. That is your name, correct? And your partner's name is Zig? My name is Kevin. I'm pleased to meet both of you."

He shook hands with Josh. Then while he shook hands with Ziggy, Josh looked him over again and was surprised to see that Kevin had a big erection now.

Kevin said, "There you go. Now we do know each other. And I would love to hear your life story. We won't have time to share much of it, I'm afraid, but we can certainly make a start."

"I'll tell you about Josh and me," Ziggy said. "We met one year ago, Kevin. It didn't take more than a couple days for us to be best buddies, and from there it's only gotten better. Now I wouldn't give him up for anything. This is our one-year anniversary vacation trip. To celebrate when we met."

Josh said, "The day I met Ziggy was my luckiest day ever. He changed my whole life, Kevin. Meeting him was . . . a miracle."

"I'm so glad you two have each other," Kevin said. "That you found each other. Very glad. You might be surprised to hear that I, too, had a best-friend partner. He and I slept together, also. 'And everything.' For years. So. The three of us may have a bit more in common than we originally thought." He smiled.

"Kevin," Josh said, wide-eyed. "You – are you saying that you're . . ."

"Gay? Yes, Josh." He chuckled. "I'm careful, of course, about whom I share that with, but yes, I am. Are you surprised?"

"Yeah, I am. I always am. God, my gaydar is terrible. I didn't have a clue."

Ziggy laughed. "It's kind of a joke between us, Kevin. I have better gaydar than Josh does, and I'm not even gay. Well, not completely gay. Oh, hell, I guess I'm more gay than I am straight. As long as I have Josh, at least. Which is forever, I hope."

"Kevin," Josh said, "he makes me have sex with women. Can you believe it?"

Kevin burst out laughing. "You two are quite a pair."

"We were made for each other, Kev," Ziggy said. "It's the only explanation for how well we get along. But listen to me, talking on and on. What about you? We'd like to know more about you." Ziggy lowered his voice. "And your partner, too, if you care to talk about him. But if you don't, that's okay too – Josh and me both can relate to that."

"Well, I'll tell you what," Kevin said. "I have a suggestion. My car is almost ready, and you boys have a two hour wait. I'd be honored if you would allow me to take you to lunch while you're waiting. We can have a chat while we eat, and afterward, of course, I'll bring you back here to pick up your car."

"Oh gosh, Kevin, lunch definitely sounds good," Josh said, "but you don't have to buy."

"Yeah," Ziggy said, "We wouldn't impose on you like that. We can pay our own way. Lunch would be awesome. But Kev, don't you have any plans for the next couple of hours?"

"Nothing whatsoever. It would be my privilege to have your company."

Ziggy looked at Josh, who nodded his head emphatically. "Well, if you're sure we wouldn't be imposing, then hell yeah, dude. Let's do lunch." Ziggy grinned.

Just then a mechanic came in from the service area. "Kevin, your car's ready."

"Thank you, Sam."

"By the way, Kevin," the man said, "I want to thank you for bringing my daughter home from softball the other day. With the wife and I both working, it leaves a little gap sometimes in our being there for her."

"No problem at all, Sam. I'm glad my schedule permits it. Or rather, my lack of a schedule."

"Well, it's much appreciated, believe me."

"Glad to help."

"Looks like you found yourself some new friends."

"That I have. As a matter of fact, we're having lunch together while they wait for your diagnosis."

"I'm sorry to make you fellows wait," Sam said. "But you couldn't ask for better company than Kevin. Give us a couple of hours, we should know something by then."

Kevin paid for his oil change and then Sam went back out to the service bays.

"You must know each other pretty well," Josh said.

"Well, they don't know much about my personal affairs, and that's probably best, but I've been bringing my car here for years, Josh. I wouldn't take it anywhere else. They're the nicest guys you'll ever want to meet, and they're professionals too."

They found Kevin's car waiting for them, sparkling clean and with the top down, the perfect vehicle for a warm sunny day.

"Nice car, dude."

"Oh yes. I've gotten to be quite fond of this car."

"Might be the first BMW convertible I ever remember seeing. Are there many of these around?"

"I don't think so. BMW didn't make it this way. It's an after-market conversion. My partner had it imported from Germany. He said it would be worth the extra cost, and now I must say I agree."

"Um, Kevin, you said you *had* a partner?"

"Yes, I . . . he . . . well, it's a very sad thing. He was killed in an automobile accident. Someone evidently fell asleep at the wheel; the vehicle hit him head on. As it turned out, he ordered this car for me as a gift, but he died before it was delivered. One day it showed up in front of the house. I couldn't have been more surprised. A gift from . . . a spirit."

"Oh, Kevin."

"Dude, that's so sad. How long were you guys together?"

"Almost fifteen years."

"Wow. That's a long time."

"Yes. Though not long enough. Precious years, they were."

"When did it happen?"

"Six years ago. I tried to get on with life, but it was painful. That was my motivation for moving here. I wanted to get away from the sad reminders and focus instead on the happy times we had together."

"I'll bet you have a lot of sweet memories of him."

"Oh, yes. I do. I missed him terribly, for so long. But now I think he . . . well, I know it may seem a stretch, but I think he actually visits on occasion. In any case, whenever I drive this car I imagine him sitting there where you are, Josh, smiling as always. I . . . I believe we'll see each other again someday."

"You will," Ziggy said. "That's gotta be the way it works. Wouldn't make sense any other way."

"Fifteen years," Josh said. "Jeez, were you guys boyfriends in high school?"

Kevin laughed. "Honestly, Josh, I'm quite a bit older than thirty. But thanks for the compliment. I'm flattered."

"I don't even want to know," Ziggy said. "Far as I'm concerned, you're still a spring chicken. You look young, you think young – and I'll bet you have more stamina than either one of us."

"I exercise regularly at the gym," Kevin said. "I'm sure that helps a bit. But I do have to get my fair share of sleep, as well."

"Fuck," Ziggy said, "doesn't everybody?

"Yes, but the young recover easier from lack of sleep. No all-nighters for me; that's a thing of my past. You young men should enjoy your youth while you have it. That's my advice. Do you two enjoy seafood?"

"Oh, uh, most definitely," Ziggy said. "Is that where we're going for lunch? If you know a good place for it then that's my vote."

"Seafood sounds great," Josh said.

"One of my favorite seafood restaurants is right up the road here."

"Cool."

—

IT WAS A LOCAL favorite. A restaurant named Conchy Joe's. Kevin made sure they got a table away from the other customers so they could talk freely.

Each one of them ordered something different, the plan being to divide each order between the three of them.

Josh said he wanted to wash up while they were waiting. Ziggy said, "Yeah, me too. We'll be right back, Kevin."

While they were peeing, Ziggy said, "So, dude, what do you think of Kevin?"

"I like him. He's nice. A friendly guy. And I'm sure he's harmless."

"Yeah, I agree. But you think he's hot, I'll bet."

Josh's face turned red. "How'd you know?"

"Because I think he's hot, too. Sexy as hell. And fuck, the guy could be a movie star, he's so good looking. I saw the way you were looking at him. Checking him out. Looking at his dick." Ziggy grinned.

"God, Zig, did you see it? He got a big boner when you told him we sleep together. It's at least as big as mine. Bigger."

Now Ziggy was blushing.

Josh laughed. "You did see it. You were looking at his hard dick too. Go on, admit it."

"Yeah, I was. What can I say? The guy's hot. Hot and handsome. Jesus Josh, I never used to look at strangers that way. Not guys anyway. Except for you. But since we fucked around with Daniel, sometimes I look at guys. At their crotches, wondering what their dicks are like. I have a pretty good idea of what Kevin's looks like."

"Well, welcome to 'If it feels good, do it.'"

"We better get back to the table or he'll think we're fucking. But listen, I have an idea I think you'll like. Want to hear it?"

"Of course."

"Here's what I was thinking. Sooner or later he's gonna come in here to pee, right? And when he does, we get up and follow him in. We lock the door and we seduce him. Get him off! Right here in this bathroom."

Chapter 26
STUCK

"SEDUCE him?"

"He'll be so surprised, Josh, I bet he'll get hard and shoot his load in a minute. What do you think?"

"Zig, you are so crazy."

"Hey, I'm not the only one. You were the one who was so set on going over to Daniel's and fucking him, remember?"

"Uh, no. I believe that was you you're thinking of."

"Oh, yeah. Come to think of it, I guess you're right. I forgot."

"You're so funny. Funny and crazy. I love you, Zig."

"I love you too, Josh."

"But what did you have in mind, anyway? Jeez, we just met the guy. What do you mean, seduce him?"

"We wait until he's finished peeing, and then grab him."

"Oh jeez Zig, no. We hardly know him. And we sure don't know if he'd appreciate something like that. Hell, he might freak. Some people don't like to be touched, especially by strangers. Or he might feel obligated to his partner still. Maybe he gave up sex. Maybe Kevin's celibate."

"Josh, get serious. Nobody gives up sex."

"With other people, I mean."

"You think?"

"I don't know. That's the problem, we don't know. We just met him, for crissakes."

"Yeah, you might be right. But look, this'll be our only chance. We'll never see him again after he drops us off back at the garage. He's gay, Josh, he won't freak. Most likely he would be flattered. All that other stuff you said, that's not very likely. Fuck, every guy on earth likes to come. It's built in. Part of what we are. We'd be giving him a gift, Josh. Something he would probably always remember. With a smile."

"Zig, if it was somebody else, somebody more . . . like us, I might say what the hell, let's do it. But Kevin – jeez, he's from a whole different world than ours. He's refined, polite, classy; hell, we don't even know him that well. But we know him enough for me to think he wouldn't go for that. He wouldn't necessarily freak, but most likely he'd think it was totally inappropriate. I want to be his friend, Zig. Even if it's just for one day."

"Aw, Josh, don't be a spoilsport. You usually go for my ideas, why not this one?"

"Because it would be a disaster."

Ziggy sighed. "Okay. Hell, you're probably right. You're better at thinking things through than I am."

"I love your crazy ideas, Zig. Don't ever stop dreaming them up. They're usually brilliant."

"I come up with some pretty good ones, don't I?"

"That's for sure. This one was good, too. It's just a little too much . . . over the top."

"They're a lot of fun, you gotta admit."

"Oh, they are. And I end up loving you more than ever, if that's possible."

"That's what it's all about, Josh."

"Come on, we better get back to Kevin."

—

"No food yet, huh?" Ziggy sat down next to Kevin, and Josh across from him.

"Should be here any minute. What were you fellows doing in there, anyway? Or should I ask?" He smiled.

"Just tending to business, Kev. And talking about what we're gonna do. We tend to make it up as we go. You never know what's gonna happen next, with us. Most of the time we don't, either." Ziggy smiled.

Kevin lowered his voice a bit. "So tell me boys, what were you doing before you met each other? What was life like for you?"

Josh said, "I had a so-called partner in Memphis, who I loved at first, but he treated me like I was a live-in maid. I finally had enough of him using me, and left him. The only person he loved was himself."

"The beastmaster, we call him," Ziggy said.

"Yeah. He was the beast. But he's the master no more."

"I know Memphis," Kevin said. "My younger brother lives there. We visit each other quite often."

"I'm glad I'm gone from there, to tell you the truth."

"So when did you meet Zig?"

"About the same time. Ziggy helped me bring my stuff up from Memphis to St. Louis. Zig and I lived together right off, before we even knew each other. It just felt right."

"Love at first sight, huh?"

"Naw," Ziggy said. He lowered his voice, too, even though no one was sitting nearby. "Friends at first sight. That was miracle enough. That we even met, first of all, and then when we did, we already knew each other. I can't explain it any better than that. We were strangers, but we knew each other. We didn't fall in love for at least another couple of days."

Kevin laughed. "That's close enough to love at first sight for me."

"Or maybe we already loved each other. Oh look, here's our food."

A waiter with a huge tray in his hand came up and started putting dishes of food on the table. There were extra plates so they could divvy it up. The waiter left, and the men started eating.

"Ziggy and I think we knew each other in a past life," Josh said.

"You probably did. A lot of people say that relationships carry through from one life to the next."

"I hope so, because I want to be with him in my next life too."

"Amen, Josh."

"What about you, Zig? Or should I call you Ziggy?"

"Ziggy is my real name, but Zig is fine, Kev. That's what Josh calls me."

"What were you doing, Zig, before you met Josh?"

"Oh, same job I have now, an auto mechanic, going out with the ladies when I got lonely or horny, and reading the rest of the time."

"Yeah, we both like to read, Kev."

"I do too, Josh. But Zig, only the ladies? Josh is your first boyfriend?"

"Well, no. More like my second. But my first one, George, we didn't think of ourselves as boyfriends. Partners, best friends, fuck buddies, but not boyfriends. He was like a big brother to me, Kev. He also taught me everything he knew about sex."

"By showing him," Josh said. "And then Ziggy taught me, later. The same way."

"Oh, for goodness sake. It sounds like an explicit novel. And a romance novel, as well. Such a wonderful chain of events. Whatever happened to George?"

Ziggy looked down. "He died."

"Oh, Ziggy. Oh, dear. I'm sorry. Such a shame."

"Yeah."

"It must have broken your heart."

Ziggy's eyes were shiny with tears. "It did. It really did. I still miss him."

Nobody said anything for a few minutes, they just ate.

Josh said, "I told Ziggy all three of us are gonna be together in our next life. I believe it, too."

"I sure hope so, Josh. You and George are my two favorite people in the whole world. I don't think I could stand it if I didn't have at least one of you."

"Zig, remember what George told you?"

"About if something happens?"

"Yeah."

"Yeah, I know."

"Same thing goes for you and me, Zig."

"I hate to think about it, Josh."

"Yeah, me too, but Zig, you gotta promise me. Like you did George."

Ziggy didn't say anything at first. He was obviously thinking, but the longer he thought about it, the more pained he looked. Finally he said, "No, Josh. I can't. I won't. If anything happens to you, I'll just go it alone. *You* promise. You're the one who should promise. You, more than anyone, deserve another partner if something happens to me. Everyone should get at least two."

"Oh jeez, Zig, I'm sorry I brought it up. Sorry."

"No, that's okay, I'm glad you did. Say it, Josh. Say, 'Everybody should get at least two.'"

"Aw, Zig, nothing's gonna happen to you." Now Josh's eyes were glossy with tears.

"Josh, it's only right. Fair's fair. Trust me, your heart's big enough for two. You'll need somebody. You can't do it alone. Not until you have at least two under your belt. That's the rule."

"I never heard of that rule before."

"Well, you have now."

"Zig, I don't think I could stand it if you . . . if you died. Kevin, I'm sorry to make you listen to all this. Zig, we oughta talk about it some other time."

"Oh no, don't worry Josh, it's quite alright. Go ahead and talk this out with Ziggy, I'm okay. Sometimes it doesn't do to put things off."

"Yeah, well, have you ever heard of that rule? I don't think there is such a rule. Zig, you just made that up."

"No I didn't. Kevin, tell him."

Josh and Ziggy watched Kevin, waiting for him to say something.

Kevin thought about it for a minute or two, and then he said, "Josh, I have to side with Ziggy on this one. Yes, there is a rule. People have different ways of saying it, but you can't let your love die. You have to keep on loving, no matter what. Zig is offering you a gift, Josh. You might not ever have to use it, but take it. Just in case."

"I'm passing it on from George to you, Josh."

"Aw, let's talk about it later. I'm gonna have to think about this."

"Okay, that's fair enough. Thanks, Josh. I appreciate it."

"No, thank you, Zig. For looking out for me. Like you always do."

"We look out for each other, bro."

"Yeah, we do, don't we?"

"We do."

"Kevin, you must be dying from boredom."

"Not at all. This is fascinating."

"Really?"

"You have no idea. To hear two young men talk about love this way – oh, it's wonderful. You really do love each other, deeply."

"Yeah. We do."

The food was excellent. No one talked for a few minutes while they continued eating.

"Kevin," Ziggy said, "what about you? Have you found another friend to love? I mean, tell us about yourself. You're a mystery dude, so far."

"No, I haven't found another partner. It's not out of the question, Zig, really, I just . . . well, I still think of Drew quite often. Oh,

I know he would want me to find someone. He wouldn't want me to be alone. And someday perhaps I will. We'll just have to wait and see about that."

"Yeah, you should, Kev. At least keep an eye out. Somebody out there needs a friend like you, remember that."

"All in good time, Zig. If there's someone waiting, he'll just have to wait a little longer."

"What kind of work do you do?" Josh asked.

"I'm an architect. I once had my own firm in Nashville. It was quite successful. Nashville is where I was raised, but after Drew's death I decided to sell the firm and move . . . somewhere else."

"To Florida."

"Yes. I still do freelance architecture, and I do some writing. Articles for professional journals, mostly, but I'm also working on a novel. I have high hopes for it, if I ever finish it."

"Wow. An architect and a writer. That's cool," Josh said, "I write, too. Or try to. I'm still new at it."

"What sort of things do you write?"

"Fiction. My first novel was an x-rated story about two guys in high school. Now I'm working on a more mainstream idea I have."

"Did you get the x-rated one published?"

"Yeah, I did. Didn't get much for it, but I did. It was sort of a practice thing, anyway. Sold it to a company that prints the type of novels you find at adult bookstores."

"No royalties then, I take it."

"No, just a one-shot deal. I was lucky to get that. As it turns out, fuck-books are apparently going out of style. Videos are the big thing now, if you want jerk-off material." Josh started blushing. "Not that you would know about that kind of thing."

"Now, Josh. I'm a man, aren't I?" Kevin leaned forward and whispered, "Of course I masturbate." He leaned back again. "I'm lucky, I suppose. Usually my imagination is all I need. But I know of the books and videos you refer to. Drew was quite the fan of 'pornography.' A ridiculous term for it, though, in my opinion. 'Explicit' is a more appropriate word."

"Gosh, I can't imagine why *anyone* would need, uh, explicit material, if he had you for a partner, Kev. You're so sexy and handsome." Josh started blushing again.

"Josh is right, Kev, you are," Ziggy said. "I was telling him earlier, you could be a movie star, you're so hot."

Kevin laughed. "You boys are so kind."

"Just telling the truth."

"Well, I only have my parents to thank, and certainly not everyone would agree with you, but I'm flattered. Thank you. As for Drew, I assure you, he and I had a very fulfilling sex life together."

"So, Kev, what's the novel you're writing about?"

"Oh, my goodness, it's turning out to be quite the epic. It's a story involving two of my favorite subjects: ancient history and science fiction."

"Wow. Aliens built Stonehenge, something like that?"

"Well, it's a bit more complicated than that, Josh. But you can be one of the first to read it, if I ever finish it."

"Gosh, I'd be honored."

The men continued eating.

After a few minutes Ziggy said, "Uh, Josh, that idea I had . . ."

"Yeah?"

"Well, uh, do you still think it's a bad idea? I mean . . ."

"Definitely, Zig. More than ever."

"You boys planning some sort of mischief?"

"Oh hell, uh, just the usual, Kev. We're always cooking something up."

"Ziggy gets all sorts of ideas, Kevin. It keeps things interesting, that's for sure."

"I have no doubt of that."

When they were finally done eating and the check was paid, Kevin said, "Now if you'll pardon me for a moment, I'm going to wash up." He stood.

Ziggy wistfully watched Kevin make his way to the bathroom.

"Zig, it wouldn't have worked. Not the way you wanted it to."

"I know, I know. It's a shame, though. He's so sexy."

"Tell you what, Zig, maybe we could do some role-play tonight. You close your eyes, and I'll pretend to be Kevin."

Ziggy's eyes lit up. "Cool."

When Kevin came back to the table Josh said, "Me next. I have to wash this seafood stuff off my hands."

"I'll go with you," Ziggy said.

They washed their hands and dried them, then Josh put his arms around Ziggy and gave him a nice long kiss. Ziggy was surprised, but he got into the spirit quickly.

When they finally broke apart, Ziggy grinned and said, "You're such a sweetheart." He licked Josh's ear.

—

"SORRY GUYS," Sam told them when they returned to the shop. "The master cylinder needs to be replaced. Here's the estimate." He handed it to Ziggy.

"That's about what I expected," Ziggy said. "Can you do it today?"

"Not today, no. Monday's the soonest we can get to it. Sorry fellas. If you want us to do it, I'll go ahead and put the order in for the parts."

Ziggy sighed. "That's what I was afraid of. Shit. Okay, yeah, go ahead. Fuck. We don't have any choice."

"They do good work, boys," Kevin said. "And they're honest. They won't overcharge you."

"Well, that's good. But this pushes our plans back a whole fucking weekend. And we'll have to find a hotel. Kevin, are there any decent ones nearby? A hotel near the beach would be awesome, but we have to find some place inexpensive."

"I'll be glad to show you your choices. Put your luggage in the back of my car. I'll give you a ride to wherever you want."

"Oh yeah, our backpacks. We'll need those. We didn't bring much, but we'll need what we've got."

"Traveling light, are you?"

"Uh, swim trunks, a change of clothes. That's all. We don't wear anything if we have a choice." Ziggy grinned.

"Uh oh, look out," Sam said. "I think we have a couple of nudists here."

"Oh, Sam, he's just kidding. These two are always up to mischief. You have to take some things with a grain of salt."

Ziggy and Josh just smiled.

—

WITH THEIR PACKS in the trunk of Kevin's car, the tour commenced. Kevin showed the boys the hotels and motels within their price range, but with each one, the fellows looked more and more disappointed.

Finally Ziggy said, "Fuck, it doesn't matter, one's as good as another. Drop us here; this one'll do. Listen Kevin, thanks for everything. You've really been nice."

"My honored pleasure, Zig."

"I guess this is it, then," Josh said. "Kevin, it was nice to meet you. Jeez, we really got to know each other in a short time, didn't we?"

Kevin didn't say anything. He looked at Josh and Ziggy, from one to the other.

"Kevin?"

Kevin looked very sad.

"Kev? Are you okay?"

"Boys, I can't let you stay here. You'd end up having a dreadful weekend, and there's no need for it. I have a spare bedroom, a guest bedroom. You can sleep there. There's no need for you to stay at a hotel. You can stay with me. I'd be happy to have you as guests for the weekend."

"Uh, Kev, we couldn't do that," Ziggy said. "You're inviting strangers into your house. You can't be doing that, bro."

"Oh, nonsense. You're not strangers. And let me assure you there are no strings attached. You'll have complete privacy."

"You haven't known us for three hours, Kevin. Any total jackass jerk can act normal for three hours. You can't be doing that, dude. Sooner or later you get ripped off."

"You don't give me enough credit, Zig. I know you wouldn't do anything to harm me. I've learned that much about you. The same goes for Josh. Three hours is plenty enough time to see a person for who he is, if you know how to look."

"Josh, listen to this dude."

"He sounds like you, Zig. And you know what? He's right. We all trust each other, so why not? I mean, if it feels right . . ."

". . . go with it. I agree," Ziggy said. "Kevin, you are more than generous. We graciously accept your offer. That is, if you're damn sure you want to put up with us."

Chapter 27
PULLED IN

"YEAH KEV, we really like you. So we have to warn you what you're in for," Josh said. "We make it up as we go along. People's lives don't stay the same, for some reason. If you spend time with us, you'll get pulled into it too. One way or another."

"If you're talking about living in the moment, Josh, I will love it. No matter what the outcome. Spontaneity is something I've been lacking lately. So by all means, please do pull me into it."

"Pulled in doesn't describe it," Ziggy said. "That's just how it begins. Twisted is what'll happen to you. I don't understand why, but we seem to affect people that way."

"No Zig. That's not right," Josh said. "We're not twisted."

"Okay then, untwisted."

"That's it. That's your risk, Kevin. You'll get pulled in and you'll get untwisted. So speak now or forever, uh, get on the ride with us until you get dizzy and fall off."

"I got on the ride three hours ago," Kevin said, smiling. "I'm not dizzy yet. Come on, I'll show you where you're living for the next two or three days."

—

"IT'S NOT MUCH DIFFERENT from an apartment," Kevin said.

He was showing them his condominium unit. They walked from the living room out onto the balcony. The ocean was right in front of them, as well as a view up and down the Florida coast.

"Holy shit," Ziggy said.

"It's similar to an apartment, but in a very nice location. And I own it," Kevin said. "A much better situation than renting."

"On the top floor," Josh said, "with a balcony looking out on the ocean and the beach. Kevin, this place is super. We had no idea you lived right on the beach. You must have done good with that company you had."

"Reasonably well. Now, I want you boys to make yourselves at home here. I'll give you my extra pair of keys so you can come and go as you please. Pretend you live here," he said, smiling. "Make it your own home."

Both the boys looked at him in awe. Ziggy said, "Jesus Kev!"

Josh said, "You can trust us, Kevin. We're honest. And we really appreciate this."

"I know you're honest, and it's my pleasure. Would you like to go for a swim?"

"Oh, heck yes. Give us two minutes, we'll be ready to go. Zig, you want to swim don't you?"

"Are you kidding?" Ziggy set his pack down and took off his shoes and socks. "Hell, I'll be ready in *one* minute."

He stood up and pulled his jeans down and half way off before Kevin realized his intentions.

"Zig, you don't have to change out here. You have your own bedroom."

Ziggy was down to his underwear and t-shirt, now. "But I'm almost ready." He pulled his shirt off.

Kevin laughed crazily and grabbed Ziggy's arm like he was a child running wild at the zoo; he held Ziggy's hand away from his briefs so he couldn't take them off.

"Oh, you're so beautiful in those briefs young man. But I want to show you your bedroom."

Ziggy picked up his pack and his shoes and his jeans and followed Kevin, with Josh right behind him.

"Right this way. Across from the kitchen."

The boys followed Kevin into a rather sparsely-decorated bedroom, which contained two separate single beds.

They expected Kevin to say something, but he just stared at the beds.

Finally he shook his head and said, "No, this is not going to work. We'll trade bedrooms. You boys will stay in my bedroom, and I'll sleep in this one. There's a king-size bed in my room for you to enjoy. I'm quite accustomed to this, so it's no trouble."

"Oh no Kev, this'll do us just fine," Ziggy said. He walked in, dropped his shoes on the floor, placed his jeans and t-shirt on top of them, and set his pack on the bed.

"No Ziggy, I insist. This is not acceptable. I won't make you sleep apart from each other."

"Kevin, we won't." Josh sat down on the bed and pulled off his shoes and socks. "We sleep together in a single bed all the time. This will be perfect." He pulled off his shirt.

"Really? Are you sure?"

"Hell yes," Ziggy said. "One of these beds is all we need. That's how we always sleep."

"Well good. That works out well then. So, when you want privacy, you will have this bedroom. I promise I'll stay out. I won't ever intrude in here, you have my word."

"Aw, Kev, don't say that," Ziggy said. "That's crazy. You're welcome in here anytime. You're gonna hang out with us, aren't you? Privacy isn't an issue with us. Especially not with you."

"Oh? And why is that?"

"Why is what? Privacy, or you?"

"Well, both, I suppose."

"Kevin, I grew up in an orphanage. Privacy is something we rarely had. Not when we slept, and if you can picture a dozen kids in one little bathroom getting ready for school all at one time . . ."

"Oh goodness. Yes, I think I can imagine."

"As for me," Josh said, "well, I didn't start out like that, but after living with Ziggy for a year, you tend to lose all shame." Josh grinned.

"And Kevin, the thing is, you're our bro now. That's why it's definitely not an issue in your case."

Josh stood up and took off his jeans. Now they were both wearing only their underwear, but not for long. Ziggy took his swim trunks from his pack and then he pulled his briefs down and took them off, right there in front of Kevin. Kevin took one startled look, and then turned his eyes away.

"Uh, boys, I'll go change too." Kevin quickly left the room and closed the door behind him.

"Jesus." Ziggy tossed his briefs on the bed. "Did we embarrass him?"

"I don't know," Josh said, "but I've never seen anybody get boners so fast in my life." Josh took his underwear off and felt around in his pack for his swim trunks. "As soon as you took off your shoes and socks – boinnng. There it was. And by the time you got down to just your underwear he was so big and stiff I thought it was gonna bust out of his trousers. You must have noticed, Zig. He was hard the whole time he was in here."

"Yeah, I saw it. That's what I was hoping for, that he'd get a hard-on."

"Well, he did. And I was right. It's bigger than mine." Josh smiled.

"You want to play with it, don't you." Ziggy grinned.

"Yeah I do – with you. I know you want to be part of it."

"Thank god it's not as big as Daniel's. Not that anything's necessarily going to happen, but Jesus, Josh. If his boners are any indication, the guy's hornier than we are. I'll bet it wouldn't take much."

"He's definitely, uh, excitable, but still, he might have different . . . sensibilities, Zig. About sex. Or about going naked."

Ziggy sighed. "Yeah, I can see that. He's definitely way more polite. I don't think I've ever run into anyone like him before. I don't know what to expect, to tell the truth."

Josh put on his swim trunks. "Well," he said, "I guess we'll find out."

"That we will," Ziggy said, grinning. "I can't wait to see how he looks in a swimsuit. I'll bet he's ripped." Zig put on his own pair of baggy trunks and then they were ready to go.

They went out into the dining room and sat down. Then Kevin came out of his bedroom, wearing only a short, trim swimsuit, holding some towels in front of it.

"Are we ready, then?" he said, a little red-faced. "Here, I've brought along some beach towels for us."

He still had a boner.

"That suit looks good on you, bro," Ziggy said, smiling. "Jesus, obviously you work out, dude. That's a nice swimmer's build you've got going, there. I'm impressed."

"Oh shush. Compared to you two I'm scrawny." Kevin turned a brighter red.

"Kevin," Josh said. "Do you want us to talk honestly?"

"Yes, of course. I prefer that we all talk freely to each other. Much better than trying to second-guess what might or might not offend."

"Which means honestly, right?"

"Yes, that's right."

"Then there's no need for false modesty. You're not scrawny."

"That's right dude. Let's be straight up, now. You're a handsome guy, Kev, with a sexy, well-defined body. I know you're not the type to brag but hell, be proud of it."

"Alright," Kevin said. "Leave it to you fellows to get the truth out of me. I'm not ashamed of it by any means. But compared to you two . . ."

"Compared to us two, Kev, you rock. Jeez, I hope I can have a body as nice as yours when I'm thirty-five."

"Josh, I'm over forty, I assure you."

"Even better," Ziggy said. "Coulda fooled me bro. Are we gonna swim or not?" He grinned.

—

THEY LEFT THE BUILDING and followed the wooden walkway up over the dunes and down to the beach. As soon as they were on the sand Ziggy stepped out of his borrowed flip-flops and then put them back on immediately. "Jesus H. Christ. That sand is hot."

"Just look at this, Zig." Josh waved his hand around. "We finally made it. We're out on the beach in Florida. We'll be in the ocean in a minute. Kev, it's like having paradise in your own backyard. This is so great."

"I'm glad I can share it with you, Josh."

"We're glad too, believe me. Thanks."

"This deserves a high-five," Ziggy said. "Kevin, put your palm up, dude." Ziggy grinned.

First Ziggy slapped Kevin's palm, then Josh did. Then Josh and Zig high-fived each other.

The boys followed Kevin's lead and spread their towels out on the sand. Kevin announced that he had sunscreen lotion, enough for all of them, but Ziggy wanted to swim first.

"Last one in is a monkey's uncle!" he yelled, and ran for the ocean.

Josh and Kevin immediately looked at each other.

Josh said. "Let's go!"

They took off running, but Ziggy was already splashing into the surf, so it was a race to see who got there next, Josh or Kevin. Kevin turned out to be quite the runner, but he slowed down a bit when Josh started falling behind.

"Jeez Kev, you run good," Josh gasped. Kevin seemed to want Josh to catch up, but he had too much of a lead. Kevin made it to the water first.

Ziggy laughed. "Josh, bro, looks like you're the monkey."

"I ran as fast as I could. I'm not used to running in sand."

"Oh sure, excuses, excuses."

"Yeah, well maybe I *am* out of shape. I need to start working out, like Kevin."

"Everyone should," Kevin said. "You know the saying. If you don't use it . . ."

"Yeah, I know. And I haven't been using it."

"Josh, we walk almost every day. We do lots of walking."

"Yeah, but I used to run in high school. I haven't done any running for, I don't know, four years at least."

"If you want to start, I'll run with you."

"Serious?"

"Sure. Soon as we get back home if you want. It'll do me good too."

"Okay."

Ziggy dove into the water headfirst, and came up ten feet away. "We could swim at the pool two or three times a week too. Hell, even once a week would be fun."

"I'm not all that good at swimming, Zig."

"Don't worry. I'll teach you."

"Cool."

The men stayed in the water for twenty or thirty minutes. Then Kevin said they would get sunburned if they stayed out any longer, so they worked their way back to the beach.

"Fuck, where are all the people, Kev? I've only seen a dozen people max, the whole time we've been out here."

"Oh, there are plenty of people down at the public beach, no doubt, but up this way, well, this is the way it is. It's not at all unusual to be out here alone."

"Really? You think we could get away with swimming naked? That's what I want to do. I wouldn't want to get you in trouble, though."

"I wouldn't risk it during the day, but I don't think anybody would notice if you did it at night."

"Cool. Josh, guess what we're doing tonight."

"Fine with me," Josh said. "I love skinny-dipping."

"You gonna join us, Kev?"

"Well, I don't know."

"Kev, live in the moment, remember?"

"Yes, but the moment's not here yet. Please, do ask me again tonight. Maybe I will. Is anyone hungry?"

"Yeah. And thirsty," Ziggy said.

"Let's take a break then. We can come back out again later. You boys come and go as you please, remember. With sun block next time though. You're already a bit burned. It's best to take this Florida sun in small doses if you're not used to it."

"This is so great," Josh said. "I can't believe our luck in meeting you, Kev. This is the nicest thing anyone's done for us since I can remember."

"The feeling is mutual, Josh. I haven't had the companionship of young friends like you in quite a long time. This weekend will be a time of rejuvenation for me. And I suspect I couldn't have made a better choice. Such wonderful, spirited, honest young men."

—

KEVIN MADE sandwiches. He showed the boys where all the essentials in the kitchen were, in case they wanted to prepare something on their own, later.

While they were eating Josh said, "Kevin, you'll have to let us buy some food or something. And I'll make a nice dinner one night too, if you'll let me."

"Josh is a good cook, Kevin."

"I'd be so pleased, Josh. Make a list of what you need. I'm doing the grocery shopping tomorrow; I'll make sure we have everything."

"Well, what do you want to eat? What do you like?"

"I don't eat a lot of meat," Kevin said. "When I do, it's seafood more often than not. But I'm quite fond of cheese, if that helps any."

"Josh, you ought to make that baked spaghetti and cheese thing you do. I'll bet he would like that."

"Does that sound any good, Kevin?"

"Oh my, yes. Takes me back to my childhood. Baked macaroni and cheese was one of my favorites."

"Yeah, that's what it is basically, except I use spaghetti."

"You don't, uh, by any chance make desserts do you?"

"He's great at pies, Kev. Among other things. He's always trying out something new."

"Oh wonderful. Now I wonder, would a cherry pie be too much to ask? I haven't had homemade cherry pie in so long."

"You got it Kev. Cherry pie and baked spaghetti. And, um, how about a salad?"

"Excellent."

When they finished their snack Kevin said, "I think I'll let you boys go back to the beach without me. I feel as though a nap would do me good."

"Kev," Ziggy said, "you keep calling us boys."

"Yes. And I know you're no longer boys – you're young men, most certainly. It's just an affectionate way of addressing you. I hope it doesn't seem as if I'm talking down to you. Does it bother you, Zig?"

"Well, not really, but it makes it sound like you're older than us."

"Which is certainly true."

"But Kev, you don't think old. You have more experience than us of course, and we think that's awesome, but we don't think about your age. We don't think of you like a teacher, or a coach, or a dad. You're like us. We want you to be our buddy, our bro. You *are* our bro. And we want to be *your* buddies too. Not your 'boys.'"

"Ziggy, I am older, certainly, but I can see your point. I myself prefer to think of myself as young at heart."

"You're not just young at heart, Kev," Josh said. "You're young in body too. And Ziggy's right, we want you to be one of our friends. We want to hang out together. Play together. We might even wrestle or tickle each other. Whatever buddies do. Call us bros, or buds, Kevin. Or guys. Not boys."

"Yeah Kev. Or call us dudes." Ziggy grinned. "And if none of those work for you, call us men."

"Alright. Point well taken. I would much prefer to be your buddy than your dad."

"Cool. Bro!" Ziggy grinned.

"Yeah Kev, very cool." Josh was smiling too. "Kevin, our new bro."

"Oh my. I must say I'm pleased. Tickled. You ... dudes – there, I said it – you young men . . . you are a treasure. I do believe I've truly found some new friends."

"Yes!" Josh and Ziggy both said it unison. They high-fived each other and then, one by one, Kevin.

"This weekend won't be the end of it, Kev," Josh said. "We keep in touch with our friends. We'll write to you, maybe even call you. And you're always welcome to stay with us in St. Louis."

"Yeah bro, if you ever come out that way, look us up. You'll have a place to stay."

"I . . . I will."

"You still gonna take a nap?"

"Yes, a short one. I want to have plenty of energy tonight, in case I decide to skinny-dip with you . . . men." He smiled.

Chapter 28
REVEALING

"RIGHT ON, Kevin. Skinny-dipping with us. Hell yeah. Now you're definitely getting into the bro frame of mind."

"Kevin, you don't mind if we go down to the beach while you're napping?"

"Not at all. We had quite a romp out there. You . . . guys may have endless energy reserves but this, uh, this dude needs to recharge. I often take a nap in the afternoon, it's nothing unusual. Here, let me give you a set of keys. You'll need them to get in and out while you're here."

"A nap actually sounds good right about now," Josh said.

"You're tired?" Ziggy asked.

"Yeah, but let's go back down to the ocean. I can nap on the beach."

Kevin loaded Josh and Ziggy up with sun block lotion, towels, keys, and a small cooler filled with soda.

They were ready to go out the door when Ziggy paused and said, "You know, the more I think about it the more I like the idea of a nap. I feel a little sunburned."

"You *are* burned," Kevin said. "Both of you. Not badly, but some rest would do you good."

"Yeah, Zig. If you're tired too, then let's lie down up here for a while. We can go out later."

—

KEVIN TOLD THE YOUNG MEN they had free run of the condo while they were there. Then he cheerfully went to his bedroom and closed the door.

Ziggy followed Josh into their own room, leaving their bedroom door wide open. It didn't occur to them to close it.

Josh pulled off his bathing suit and stood naked beside the bed. Ziggy stripped down, too.

"We should take a shower," Josh said. "Get this sand and salt water off."

"Yeah, check it out, we have our own bathroom, dude. And the shower's big enough for all three of us."

"Yeah, like Kevin's gonna shower with us. Right."

"You never know, Josh. Stranger things have happened. You know he'd enjoy it."

"We all would." Josh grinned.

The boys stepped into the shower together and got wet. Josh began soaping up.

"Can you believe this place?" Ziggy said. "We really lucked out meeting Kev. Isn't he the greatest?"

"Yeah, he is."

"I'm still not used to how polite he is. And he's so nice to let us stay here."

"A real Southern gentleman, Zig. There's still a few around."

"I really like him. It's all I could do not to hug him when he left for his bedroom."

"You should have."

"I think I will, next time."

"He's a real sweetheart, for sure. I want to hug him, too."

Ziggy sighed. "It's too late to jump on him like I wanted to at the restaurant. It would definitely be rude, now."

"Yeah, he's so polite, and generous. It would be all wrong to jump his bones like that without giving him any warning."

"That's what I'm talking about."

"I still want to have sex with him, though. More than ever. Real sex, Zig, not just a quickie in a bathroom. Don't you?"

"Quickie sex is real sex, Josh. It's . . . well, it's quick, but it's as real as any. The quickies we've had were excellent. I remember each one by heart, bro. As if they happened yesterday."

"Yeah, I know. It's so hot when we do that. But they're always unplanned. That's part of why they're hot."

Ziggy took the soap and washed Josh's back. "I guess that's what I'm getting at. We can't plan an unplanned quickie with Kevin, obviously, and he's too polite for it to ever happen on a moment's notice. Not when we're still being so, um, cordial with each other. I guess that's what etiquette is all about. Fuck, I never thought I'd be wanting to be polite, but then again I've never met anyone like Kevin before, either."

"So you still want to have sex with him?"

"Oh yeah. Definitely. It gives me a hard-on to think about it, Josh. We don't even know what he likes to do, but whatever it is, I want to do it. I want to make him feel good. I want to make him come."

Josh laughed. "I don't know who's more of a sweetheart, him or you. Well, I already know you are. But I'm like you; I want to make him come too. Play with him first; lick him all over, rub our dicks together, stuff like that. That's what I want to do. The three of us."

"Josh, that sounds so hot."

"Yeah, wouldn't it be?"

They switched positions and Zig started soaping himself up. He sighed. "But how? How do we get there from here?"

"We have to get him used to seeing us naked first, I think. And I doubt that he'll skinny-dip with us tonight. I don't think that's gonna happen. He'd be too embarrassed about getting a boner. Plus he'll probably worry about the neighbors."

"He ran like a scalded dog when I took off my underwear. Maybe he doesn't *want* to see us naked?"

"No, that's not it, he's only being polite. He got a hard-on just from seeing you take your shoes and socks off. Of course he'd like to see us naked. Being the gentleman he is, though, he doesn't want to do so, uh, uninvited."

"Okay, so how do we invite him? We can't just say, 'Kevin, let's get naked and look at each other."

Josh laughed. "You're so funny, Zig."

"Seriously though."

"Well, we already told him privacy is not an issue for us. Maybe we need to demonstrate. Show him how much it's not an issue." Josh took the soap and washed Ziggy's back.

"Oh, okay, now we're getting somewhere. Yeah, I like that. Fuck, all we need to do is what we always do. He said to treat this place like home while we're here. All we have to do is take him at his word."

"Well, 'what we always do' is get naked as soon as we walk in the front door, but if we do that in front of Kevin without any warning he might take off running."

"Yeah. We have to prepare him for it, somehow."

"We can start by going naked in our bedroom. With the door open. He's bound to see us when he walks by."

"Dude'll close it."

"Maybe not. Not if he thinks closing it would be more impolite than leaving it open."

"Oh, Jesus. How in the hell do we do that?"

"Easy, Zig. We just think up some reason to tell him why we prefer to leave it open."

"Yeah, like what?"

"Uh, tell him it makes us feel too isolated, too closed off."

"Claustrophobic?"

"No, not that extreme, just . . . a preference. A matter of comfort. Tell him we're used to leaving the doors open at home. Or we could tell him we don't want to be closed off from him; that might be enough."

"Hell, that's the truth. I *don't* want to be closed off from him. We're gonna be here short enough time as it is. I want to get as much of that dude as I can."

"Same here. Well, that's what we could tell him. That we want him to walk in here anytime he feels like it, no warning needed, because we want to see as much of him as possible."

"I like that, bro."

"The next time he closes the door we'll tell him."

"Yeah. Excellent." They took turns rinsing off.

"Then we go naked like we always do. He's bound to see us. If he says anything we'll just tell him the truth – we always go naked at home."

"We're only gonna do it inside the bedroom?"

"Well, at first, I guess, but as soon as he gets used to that we can bring it out into the rest of the place. It'll work. He'll be too polite to tell us not to."

"Cool."

"Plus you know he'll get off on watching us. Then we'll figure out some way to get sex involved." Josh grinned. "We always do."

"Excellent, excellent. You're so smart, Josh."

"Well, if it works."

"It will."

"In the meantime we can leave the door open and make sure he can see us while we're napping."

"Naked?"

"Yeah, definitely. Naked, uncovered. It's not cold in here. Even if it was, we'd keep each other warm. Yeah, let him see us sleeping naked, without any covers over us at all. He'll love it."

"He'll close the door."

"Um, maybe not. If we put one of our backpacks against the door."

"Oh, good thinking, bro. Cool. Okay, we got us a plan." Ziggy grinned. Then he licked Josh's face.

—

THEY FINISHED SHOWERING and dried off in the bedroom. Ziggy put his backpack against the open door. Josh pulled the covers back on the bed.

They lay down naked together on the single bed, front to back like spoons, uncovered and unashamed.

"Josh, what are we gonna do about sex? We can't do it in front of him until we get him used to seeing us naked."

"You can wait until tonight can't you?"

"Yeah, I guess. Of course."

"We'll figure something out."

"Okay. Fuck, I think I'm nodding out, bro."

"Yeah. Nap time."

—

AN HOUR OR SO LATER, Kevin emerged from his bedroom, refreshed by his rest. The fellows were apparently still in their bedroom, because the towels and lotion and keys were still by the front door where they'd left them earlier.

Kevin quietly walked into the kitchen, carefully put some ice into a glass, and then poured some Cherry Coke over it. He didn't want to wake them. Let them sleep as long as they wanted. It was a comfort simply to know that they were enjoying his hospitality. Such an honor it was, to host two beautiful, kind young men who were so much in love.

He saw that their bedroom door was open. Apparently it was true: they didn't feel any need for privacy. And it was so very nice of them to say he was their 'bro' now. Ziggy had said it as if he meant it, too. Such an honor. Kevin was determined to be the best 'bro' possible to these two angels.

He quietly walked over to their bedroom door and gasped. They were sound asleep, Ziggy had his arm around Josh, and they were totally naked and totally uncovered. Kevin got an erection immediately. So much skin; both of them bare all the way from their heads down to their adorable toes. So erotic. And Ziggy's beautiful naked buttocks were exposed, quite viewable from the doorway. Kevin thought for a moment he should walk away, and yet they obviously didn't object to being seen by him like this.

And they were asleep. They wouldn't know how long he lingered watching them; they wouldn't even care. Kevin stood at the doorway for at least five minutes, looking. He felt like a voyeur at first, but he soon convinced himself that this is what his . . . bros . . . wanted. They wanted to share this intimacy with him. Kevin would willingly accept whatever they offered.

It was all he could do to stand his ground, though, when they stirred a little and rolled over to spoon in the other direction. Still asleep, as it turned out, but their penises were erect. Josh's beautiful shaft soon disappeared snugly between Ziggy's buttocks, but Ziggy's impressive hard penis was now right out there in plain view. So inviting. Kevin's face turned red with embarrassment, but he couldn't take his eyes away. He knew this was part and parcel with their gift of intimacy. So lucky, though, to catch a glimpse.

Kevin stood at the door for another five minutes, watching. Then it was time to leave them alone. He thought of closing their door, but there was something in the way. One of their packs. Then he realized it would be rude of him to close the door when they quite evidently wanted it open. He took one more look, and then he walked into the living room and sat down to read.

Chapter 29
EXHIBITION

ZIGGY AND JOSH slept soundly for another hour, and then they woke up, one by one. Josh thought he was the first to awake. He could feel, resting snug within the crevice of his asscrack, Ziggy's stiff, hard cock. *Another one of his sex dreams,* Josh thought. He moved his butt slightly and then he realized Ziggy's dick was wet and slippery with pre-cum.

Josh reached back, held Ziggy's shaft, and heard him moan softly. He held it by the head and slid his fingers around in the slippery stuff, and then stroked it once.

"Unnnnhh!" Ziggy's cock suddenly started launching slimy, thick ropes of cum into Josh's palm. Ziggy gave out a long moan as his balls emptied, spurt by spurt. "Ahhhhhhhhhhh!"

Josh positioned his hand to catch as much of Ziggy's cumload as he could, while Ziggy whimpered in his ecstasy. When he seemed to be finished, Josh held his hand to his mouth to lick up what cum he had. Then he turned around and licked up the rest of the cum off Ziggy's crotch and belly.

When Josh's tongue reached his belly, Ziggy started giggling.

"You goofball. You were awake the whole time?"

"Yeah, I guess. Half asleep, half awake. I was trying not to wake you up. Josh, I wanted to fuck you so bad, bro. I couldn't stop thinking about putting my dick up your sweet ass. And everything kept getting slippier and slippier. I knew I couldn't fuck you though, unless I got up to get a condom. We left them all in our backpacks. I was close to coming, just from sliding up and down against your ass. Then you reached back and . . . you know the rest. Jesus, Josh, I came really good. So good."

"Well, cool." Josh smiled. "I'm glad I could help."

"Now it's your turn, pal. Your dick is so hard I know it wants to shoot its load. And I'm the one to make it happen."

Then they both heard it: Kevin cleared his throat, somewhere in the distance, perhaps the living room.

Ziggy whispered, "Fuck! He's up. You think he heard all that?"

"I don't know," Josh whispered back. "He must have heard some of it. You were moaning pretty loud."

They lay still for a couple of minutes, waiting for something to happen, but there was only silence. Josh's dick was still stiff. Throbbing now, in fact.

Ziggy watched it pulse for a minute and then whispered, "You're getting off on this aren't you?" He grinned.

Josh smiled sheepishly. "Yeah. Thinking about what Kev probably heard. Thinking about his boner."

"And?"

"And how good it would feel for you to suck me off. And about what if he walked by while you were doing it. Maybe he stops and watches the whole thing. He's watching when I shoot my load into your mouth. Or maybe I come all over your dick. He sees my hard dick shooting cum after watching you suck it."

"Dude, you are such an exhibitionist." Ziggy whispered. He grinned.

"Yeah, well it takes one to know one, Zig." Josh smiled.

"Truer words were never spoken. I'll be the first to admit it. So look, the dick-sucking part, I can make that happen. Right now." Zig gently took hold of Josh's cock, so stiff and full it looked as if it was ready to explode, and put it in his mouth.

"Unnh. Fuck, Zig," Josh whispered, "Kevin's gonna hear every-thing. I can't believe we're gonna do this."

"Yeah. We are. Who knows, he might even watch." Ziggy put his mouth back on Josh's cock, wrapped his tongue around the shaft, and then he began sucking gently.

"Unnnh. Zig, ahhh fuck, gonna come in about two seconds if you don't stop. I'm gonna come. Oh, shit."

Ziggy held his mouth firmly around Josh's cock, with the head of it back against his throat.

Suddenly Josh said, "UNNNNH!" and his cock began to spurt. One squirt right after another, inside Ziggy's mouth. Ziggy pulled back just enough for the cum to land on his tongue. He gulped it down as fast as it came out.

"Ohhhhhh!" Josh groaned and shuddered, filled with ecstasy as his balls emptied. Zig didn't miss a drop. When Josh finally finished spurting, Ziggy moved farther down Josh's shaft and gave it a lip massage while Josh was recovering. Then he moved up and down on it, cleaning it up with his tongue to get any cum that might still remain. Finally he took his mouth away and gave it one last lick.

"Fuck." Josh whispered. "That was so good. Best fucking ever."

"You say that every time sweetheart," Ziggy whispered.

"I know. But I mean it. Every time you suck me it gets better."

Ziggy suddenly put his hand to his ear and said, "Shhhhh." They were both silent, listening.

It could have been anything, or even nothing at all. But what it sounded like most was Kevin, quietly tiptoeing back to the living room from somewhere closer.

"I think he was listening," Josh whispered. "From up close. Oh fuck. I'll bet he heard us."

"Okay by me, Josh."

"Well, me too I guess. Why not. By the way Mr. Z, I think you're getting even better than me at sucking."

"How would you know?" he said. "I mean, seriously."

"Yeah, good point."

Ziggy grinned. "I'm glad you like it. I've been doing my best. I'm gonna deep throat you one of these days, see if I don't. I know I can do it if I keep trying."

"Aw, Zig, you don't have to do that. It already feels super."

"I love it when you do it to me. I want to give back, bro. You keep getting better, too, though. You'll always be the best."

—

THE GUYS PUT ON SOME JEANS and came out of the bedroom. Kevin was in the living room, reading.

"Hi Kev," Josh said.

"Well hello there, men." He smiled. "Did you have a good nap? I must say you certainly looked sound asleep and peaceful when I glanced in."

Josh looked at Ziggy and then said, "Yeah, we slept great."

"You looked as though you were resting in an enchanted place, sleeping with the innocence of angels. So peaceful and beautiful."

"Aw, Kev, that's how we always sleep. I never slept so good in my life until I met Zig."

"Josh is my teddy bear," Ziggy said.

"We take turns being the teddy bear, Kevin. The most peaceful sleep I've ever had."

"Peaceful until you wake up, that is. I have to confess I heard what seemed to be a bit of excitement there at the end of your nap."

Josh started to blush, but Ziggy laughed.

"Kev, you should have joined us. We wouldn't have minded. We would have loved it."

"I assume you don't really mean that."

"Sure I do."

"I don't see how in the world the two of you don't fall out of that little bed. There couldn't be room for a third."

"It's easy, bro. We hold on to each other. But you're right; I don't think the three of us could fit. Not for sleeping at least." Ziggy grinned. "For other things, now that may be a different story."

"I don't believe three people could do anything on that bed without falling off. But in any case, there's no chance, Ziggy. I promised I would stay out of your room and I meant it. I'm a man of my word."

"But Kevin, why? We want you to come into our room. Anytime. You don't even have to knock – we don't have anything to hide. Jeez, why would you want to stay out when we want you to come in?"

"Because I want to make it quite clear that I had no ulterior motive for inviting you here. I'm gay, as of course you know, and that made it even more essential for you to know there were no obligations associated with my invitation."

"Oh fuck, we knew that a long time ago. But we're buddies, bro. Buddies hang out with each other. You've already made your point. We're past that now. Anytime we're in our bedroom you're welcome to join us. We want you to wherever we are. We're gonna be here too short a time as it is. We want to spend as much time with you as possible."

"Well, I must say, you have a wonderful way of making me feel wanted."

"You *are* wanted."

"You have no idea how heartwarming your sincerity is," he said. "But I couldn't initiate such an event." He sighed. "My goodness though. Seeing you two cuddled up together like that looked so adorable. It reminded me of how long it's been since I've had someone to cuddle with. I'll never find anyone quite like Drew of course. I wouldn't want to. But I know he wouldn't want me to go without that sort of intimacy indefinitely. Six years is quite long enough don't you think? Too long."

"Josh," Ziggy said, grinning. "Listen to him. Tell me he's not getting pulled in."

"I'm getting untwisted." Kevin smiled. "You chose a good term for it."

—

THEY ATE SUPPER out on the balcony. There was a nice breeze, and Kevin's young guests still considered the view to be amazing.

After the meal, they washed dishes and then sat outside again. They told each other stories about Memphis, St. Louis, and Nashville, as the sky began to darken.

Eventually Kevin asked, "Josh, is Memphis where you were raised?"

"No, I only lived there a couple of years. I grew up outside of Washington, D.C."

"Oh, that must have been a unique experience. The nation's capital."

"Yeah it was cool, definitely. Lots of museums, art galleries, monuments. The Jefferson Memorial was my favorite."

"What was your favorite museum?"

"The Museum of Natural History. But they were all cool. Space and Flight, even the Army Medical Museum."

"You went to the Medical Museum?" Ziggy asked.

"Yeah, I went to all of them."

"Uh, is it true they have, uh, John Dillinger's dick on display? I heard it was the longest dick ever."

Josh laughed. "I heard that story too, Zig. But if it was there we sure didn't find it. We looked."

"Probably an urban myth," Kevin said. "Possibly based on some grain of truth – perhaps he did have a long penis – but I can't imagine a national museum would display something like that. Or even possess it."

"Well, they had plenty of other stuff, some of it pretty gross, so who knows."

"What caused you to move to Memphis?"

"Well, my mother died, my father was already dead, and I guess I just wanted a change. I had a cousin who was assigned to the Millington Naval Air Station and he said I could stay with him in Memphis until I figured out what I wanted to do. So I took him up on it."

"Millington?"

"It's just a thirty-minute drive. He lived in Memphis when he wasn't on a ship."

"And then you met your beastmaster friend."

"Yeah, unfortunately."

"Josh, he was a bastard," Ziggy said, "but you and I might not have ever met if you hadn't met him first."

"Oh, is that right?" Kevin said.

"Sure. Everything's like that, Kevin," Ziggy said. "The littlest things can change the whole direction of your life. The only reason Josh was in St. Louis was because his ex and some friends of theirs wanted to get out of Memphis for a weekend. That's when we met. We went to the same club one night."

"Okay, I get it. You're saying Josh wouldn't have been in St. Louis that weekend if he hadn't known . . . the other fellow."

"Fred. Right, that's what I'm talking about."

"That certainly sounds reasonable. But even *with* Fred, still, it was probably pure chance that you met, correct? If it had been the week before or the week after, you might have been somewhere else. Or you might have stayed home."

"Well, yeah," Josh said. "That makes it even more amazing. The fact is, thousands of things had to come together just so. And Ziggy's right, everything is like that. If my mother hadn't died when she did, if my cousin wasn't in the Navy, if Ziggy hadn't gone out that night, or if he'd gone to a different club . . . it's amazing when you think about it. Our whole lives are like that. If even one little thing had happened differently, you might be in a whole different world. With different friends, in a different city – there's no telling what would be different, but everything happens partly because of what happened before. Little things can make as big a difference as big things."

"I would think there must be some sort of lesson to be learned from that," Kevin said.

"If there is, I don't know what it is," Josh said. "It just makes me feel lucky, that's all. Very lucky."

"Me too," Ziggy said.

The men continued talking, out on the balcony, until the sky was dark. Then Kevin yawned.

"You're not already tired are you, Kevin?"

"Yes, a bit sleepy. I think perhaps I should go to bed. But don't let that keep you two from staying up." Kevin smiled. "Take advantage of your youth."

"But Kevin. You were gonna go skinny-dipping with us."

"Oh goodness, I'd love to, but . . ."

"But what?"

"Well, I was thinking the neighbors might recognize me, for one thing."

"Aw, Kev, you said they probably wouldn't even notice. And anyway, even if they do, they won't be able to tell who it is."

"Yes, quite right I suppose."

"Jeez, people must go skinny-dipping all the time here. Wouldn't you think? It couldn't be much of a shock, especially at night."

"I'll admit I have occasionally seen, from my balcony, people below swimming naked. If there were any objections I was never told of them."

"See? It's no big deal, Kev."

"But there's another matter as well."

"What's that?"

"Well, it's a bit embarrassing actually, but I have no doubt I would at some point, um, get an erection."

"So?"

"It would embarrass me. Endlessly. As well as embarrass you I'm sure."

"No Kev, no. Jesus, first of all, we'd love to see you get an erection." Ziggy grinned. "But besides that, it's only natural. Guys get boners all the time. I know Josh and I do. We wouldn't be embarrassed at all. Chances are we'll get hard-ons, too, while we're down there. It's just part of being a guy."

"Well, you might be used to it but I'd be terribly self-conscious about it, myself."

"All the more reason to do it and get over it, Kev," Josh said. "It's liberating. A hard-on is nothing to be ashamed of. Ever. It's what happens when you're a guy. If you try to control it, it screws up your head. It's fun to get a boner. And it's fun to let other people see it, too. As long as they're not offended by it, and you can count on us not to be offended."

"But what if someone walks by?"

"That's easy. We'll be in the water most of the time anyway. You can let the water hide it."

"Unless the person walking by is naked and has a boner too," Ziggy said. "They'd probably want to see yours in that case."

Kevin let out a short hysterical laugh. "Wouldn't that be something!"

"Stranger things have happened."

"I'm sure they have, but perhaps not in Jensen Beach. This is a small town, fellows. And a bit conservative, certainly."

"Aw, Kevin, we're not gonna have sex out there. We're only going swimming. It's not a big deal. Come on."

"Well, I'll go swimming with you, but I won't promise to take my suit off."

"Cool. Let's go then. Josh, are you ready?"

"Ready as ever."

"Ah, give me a minute," Kevin said. "Let me change into my bathing suit."

Chapter 30
SKINNY-DIP

THE SKY WAS COMPLETELY DARK, except for the stars, which seemed to multiply in number the farther one looked out above the ocean.

They spread their towels out on the sand and then Ziggy and Josh immediately stripped off their jeans. They stood there in their white briefs, waiting to see what Kevin would do.

Kevin said, "Shall we get in the water, then?"

Ziggy and Josh looked at each other. Josh whispered to Ziggy, "Let's not push it." Ziggy nodded his head.

The two boys stripped off their briefs and tossed them on top of their jeans. Totally naked now, their cocks still semi-soft but big and full, they waited for some indication from Kevin.

Kevin looked them over as if he was memorizing every detail. His dick had hardened up the moment the boys pulled off their jeans. The white briefs stood out in the dark, so beautiful, so beautiful. Such perfect bodies the boys had, and their snug underwear held the promise of even more perfection. The anticipation alone was enough to make Kevin's cock wet.

Then they had pulled the briefs off. Shockingly sexual in their nakedness, yet also the image of innocence. Oh, to be so unashamed, so alive. And why not? He should be so himself. Of that he was fully aware, but how to give up his self-consciousness? How to part with his shame?

"Kevin, we're gonna jump in the water," Ziggy said. "If you want to leave your suit on it's okay. If you want to take it off and be naked and free like us that's okay too. Whatever makes you more comfortable, bro. We're just glad to be here and to be with you, our new buddy, our new friend."

The boys started walking toward the surf, and then Josh turned around and said, "Kevin, you're turning me on with that hard dick of yours."

"Oh," Kevin said. "Er, you could tell it's erect, then?"

"Jeez yes, Kevin. You have a big one, and it's making me hard." Josh turned all the way around to face Kevin. "See? Look what you've done to me." Josh smiled and looked down. His dick was fully hard and pointing straight out, curved downward slightly, throbbing with each heartbeat.

"Jesus Josh," Ziggy said. "You too?" Zig turned toward Kevin and said, "See, Kevin? We're both hard as we can be. Feels good too." Ziggy's cock was hard and stiff and curving upward. He turned again and walked out into the water, hard dick bouncing a little with each step.

Josh said, "Come on Kev. Leave your suit on if you want, it doesn't matter." And then Josh followed Zig out into the ocean.

Seeing the young men erect like that aroused Kevin even more. He was getting a wet spot in his swimsuit from leaking pre-cum. "Drat," he said. Then he thought of Drew, his beautiful, smiling Drew. He could imagine Drew standing right in front of him, saying, *Go ahead, Kev. Do it. What's stopping you? Let go, sugar. Let it all go.*

"I think I will," Kevin said. "Yes. Damn it, I will." The boys were out in the water and probably couldn't see him clearly, and there certainly wasn't anyone else around. Kevin pulled his suit down and stepped out of it. His erection stood straight out from his body, hard, stiff, throbbing, wet. Free at last.

Kevin tossed his swimsuit down and stood naked. "It's perfectly natural," he said. Was Drew listening? "Drew," Kevin said, "I love you so much. Thank you." He could even imagine Drew answering. *Thank you, Kevin. I knew you could do it. I'm naked too. Naked and hard and with you at every step. Here whenever you want me to be.*

Kevin waded out toward the boys, hard cock bouncing up and down a little but mostly stiff and horizontal, still leaking pre-cum. Soon he would be waist-deep in the water and not so obvious, and yet part of him *wanted* the boys to see it. And that seemed perfectly natural, too.

Josh and Ziggy were out in waves a little higher than their waist. They splashed water at each other, laughing, having fun. Then they saw Kevin, who was now only a dozen feet away from them.

"Yeah! It's Kevin." Ziggy said. "Here's our new bro."

Kevin grinned. Did they know he was naked? Maybe not.

"Feels good doesn't it, Kev?" Josh said. "Naked or not, this is awesome."

"Yes," Kevin said. "It is. Awesome. It feels wonderful."

"So much warmer than the ocean in Maryland."

"Very comfortable. And wonderfully liberating."

"Kevin," Ziggy said, "I found something out here you might find interesting."

"Oh? And what might that be?"

"Come here, let me show you."

Kevin walked closer to Ziggy, wondering what sort of seashell or other odd object he had found.

"Put your hand out," Ziggy said, "I want you to feel this."

Kevin reached out. Ziggy grasped his wrist and pulled his hand down into the water.

Kevin felt something fleshy and hard. "Oh!" he said, instantly pulling his hand away. "You're still hard, Zig! Oh, my." He couldn't help grinning.

Ziggy grabbed Kevin's wrist again and pulled him closer. "You hardly touched it. Here, feel it again. Put your hand around it. Hold it. I want you to, Kev."

Kevin allowed his hand to be pulled up against Ziggy's cock again, and this time Kevin did as Ziggy had suggested. Mesmerized, he grasped Ziggy's stiff, hard cock. Felt it. Felt the shape of it.

It was harder and bigger than what he had seen when the boys were sleeping. He moved his hand slightly, to the root of it, felt Ziggy's balls without intending to.

"Oh yeah," Ziggy said. "Now you're talking."

Kevin didn't want to let go. He was ecstatic, hypnotized, filled with strange but familiar sensations. He cautiously stroked Ziggy's dick once.

"Oh Jesus, yes Kev. Please. Don't stop."

Kevin stroked it again. Living in the moment.

Ziggy moaned. Kevin felt a hand bump against his own hard cock, and then the hand grasped him there, held him.

Kevin groaned. "Ahh, Zig."

They slowly, gently, almost mindlessly stroked each other, lost to sensation.

Josh was right there, too. Kevin felt his other hand being grasped and pulled. When he felt it bump into Josh's hard dick he automatically wrapped his hand around it.

"Yeah Kev. You don't know how good that feels," Josh said.

"Yes I do. Ziggy's doing it to me."

Josh reached out to Ziggy and gently felt his balls.

"Oh Jesus, guys, yes. Don't stop," Ziggy said.

The three of them moved closer together and soon each one of them had one guy's balls gently in one hand and the other hand stroking the other guy's hard cock.

No one spoke for a few minutes. No one wanted this to end.

Then Kevin moved his hand from Ziggy's balls to his cock, and his other hand from Josh's cock to his balls, and everybody automatically switched the same way.

"Kevin. Bro," Ziggy said.

"Yes?"

"I'm pretty close, are you?"

"Oh yes."

"Me too," Josh said.

"Well then," Kevin said.

He stroked Ziggy a little faster. Ziggy moaned and picked up his speed on Josh. Josh said, "Ahhh." He held Kevin's cock a little tighter and continued stroking.

"Ohhh," Kevin said. "Oh yes, ohhh, yes."

Kevin moaned louder and then suddenly shouted, "Coming!" He groaned louder, leaned forward, and rested his head against Ziggy's as his body started shaking and the feeling took over. All while he stroked Ziggy faster, wanting him to come, too.

Ziggy moaned. "Unnnnnh. Oh shit, I'm gonna come too."

"Yeah, fuck yeah," Josh said. "Ohhhh." Josh leaned forward, too, and rested his head against Ziggy and Kevin. All three men had their foreheads pressed together as the feeling overtook each one of them.

Then suddenly they were spurting, moaning, pumping each other's hard cocks, tugging at balls, shooting unseen into the water below, groaning. Three men in ecstasy, three stiff cocks pumping cum out into the water around them, spurt after spurt, coming, coming, coming.

It was hard to tell when it was over. It seemed to go on forever, and then gradually subsided, each man stroking slower, each one loosening his grip a little but still gently holding a cock and a set of balls.

No one wanted it to end, but they finally lifted their heads and let go of each other. Ziggy moved closer and put one arm around Kevin and the other around Josh, and the other men did the same. A three-way hug, a good and long one, with their spent cocks floating in the middle and bumping into each other.

"Oh my goodness," Kevin finally said. "I never expected that."

Chapter 31
OPEN TONIGHT

AFTER A LONG HUG the men moved slowly through the water back to the beach. They shook the sand off their towels and dried themselves off. Then they stood there, naked, and looked at each other.

"You see, Kev? You can't have a hard-on all the time. You're already getting used to going naked, bro."

"Oh, shush. You'll make me get that way again, talking about it."

"That would be okay too." Josh grinned. "Hard dicks are always okay."

"You two are so shamelessly sexual. It's simply wonderful."

"Yeah, sex is a good thing."

"Do you fellows go naked like this very often?"

"Every chance we get," Ziggy said.

Kevin laughed.

"I'm serious. At home we strip naked as soon as we get inside the door, and we don't put anything back on until we're about to leave."

"Oh my goodness, you *are* nudists."

"Yeah." Ziggy grinned. "Mother nature all the way."

"Well. I suppose you must feel rather unduly restricted then, wearing clothing in my condo. Does it bother you?"

"To be honest Kev, it is a bit annoying. But it's okay, we're used to wearing clothes when we go out, so no big deal. We wouldn't want to impose our habits on you, that wouldn't be right. We're guests."

"Well, I'm not used to seeing anyone go naked on an ongoing basis, but that is correct, you *are* my guests, and as such you deserve to be allowed your comfort. I don't see why I should require you wear clothing when no one can see you but me. It wouldn't bother me if you were to go naked inside the condo, if that is your preference." Kevin smiled. "It wouldn't bother me in any negative way, certainly."

"Seriously? Jeez, we were afraid to ask you outright, but that would be excellent."

"Yeah," Ziggy said, "It would be awesome. Except we would feel really awkward going naked if you were still wearing your clothes. You have to go naked too, dude, otherwise we'll feel weird."

"Oh my."

"But if you don't want to go naked, we're okay with wearing clothes," Josh said.

"No, I'm willing to give it a try. After skinny-dipping together and everything which that led to, we've certainly broken the ice, so to speak."

They stood there together on the beach, still naked.

Then the moon peeked over the eastern horizon.

Josh saw it first. "Oh wow, look, guys."

It slowly but steadily rose while they watched. Before long, it was completely above the horizon.

"Beautiful," Josh said.

"That looks like it's on its way to a full moon," Ziggy said.

Kevin said, "Four days ago I believe. Yes, it's beautiful."

"So really," Josh said, "we're really gonna be naked like this the whole time we're inside?" He grinned. "Awesome."

"Well, I can't promise I won't ever get an erection. I'm certain I will in fact. But I'll try my best not to be embarrassed by it."

"That's all we can ask for," Ziggy said, smiling.

The men shook their clothes free of sand and put them on. Then they took them off again once they were inside the condo.

Ziggy started stripping immediately, Josh joined him, and Kevin hesitatingly followed their example. Kevin had a hard-on again.

"Dude. You recover fast," Ziggy said.

"Well, when faced with such an abundance of stimulation I don't have much control over it," Kevin was blushing a little.

"That's completely okay Kev," Josh said. "Don't even try to control it. Hard dicks are one of Mother Nature's gifts to man. The more often you get one the better."

"Yeah, as long as you're okay with the fact that they tend to be contagious," Ziggy said. His cock was already filling out and starting to rise. "You have a really nice one, Kevin. Sexy as hell."

"Now you guys are making me horny," Josh said. His dick was growing, too.

"Oh dear. I'm sorry."

Ziggy laughed. "For what, making us all feel good?"

"Well, if you're going to put it that way, no, I'm not sorry at all. As long as you don't mind me staring."

Ziggy and Josh looked at each other, smiling.

"Kevin, you're getting more untwisted by the minute, bro."

—

THEY HAD A SHORT SNACK, still naked, of course. Nudity was to be the norm from now on. Kevin wished them sweet dreams, and then he went inside his bedroom.

Josh and Ziggy left their bedroom door open, as always. They took a shower together and prepared for bed.

Josh went out and checked, one last time, to make sure the lights were out in the living room and kitchen, and that the front door was locked.

He came back to the bedroom and said softly, "Zig."

Ziggy was in bed already. He opened his eyes and said, "Yeah?"

"Kevin's door is open. Wide open."

"Really."

"Yeah. What's up with that?"

"Um, I dunno. Maybe he wants us to peep in and look at him. Like we wanted *him* to do last night."

"I thought of that, but Zig, he's not an exhibitionist like we are. Anyway, his bed is around the corner. You can't even see him unless you go a few feet in."

"That wouldn't necessarily stop me," Ziggy said. "Maybe that's what he wants, is for us to go all the way in."

"I did go in, part way. I knocked first. Not loud, but loud enough for him to hear me if he was awake. He was in bed, under the covers, sound asleep. He has some kind of night light on; it's not so dark you can't see in there."

"So, what'd you do?"

"I tip-toed out of there. I felt like I was trespassing."

"Hmmm. He closed the door last night. Tonight it's open."

"It means something," Josh said, "but I don't know what."

"Maybe we convinced him not to worry about privacy."

"Yeah, maybe."

"Or maybe he wants to hear us fuck," Ziggy said.

Chapter 32
TEDDY BEARS

JOSH AND ZIGGY CURLED UP naked together in bed. They left the door open and themselves uncovered again, hoping Kevin might wake up and see them, and this time maybe change his mind about coming in to join them. There was bound to be something exquisitely pleasurable the three of them could do together, something Kevin especially enjoyed.

They slept for almost an hour, and then Josh suddenly sat up in bed. That woke Ziggy up, and he slowly sat up, too. They stared at each other, Josh wide-eyed, Ziggy sleepy but curious.

"What's up?" Ziggy asked. "Bad dream?"

"No, weird dream."

"I was dreaming too, but then I woke up."

"Sorry. But Zig," Josh whispered, "I figured it out."

"Figured what out?"

"Why Kevin left his door open tonight."

"Is that what your dream was about?"

"That's what made me realize. He wants us in bed with him. It's so obvious. He said it himself but we both missed it."

"I don't remember that."

"In my dream some guy woke me up and pushed me out into the kitchen. And there we were, in the living room. You, me, and Kevin, talking. I watched us. Listened. Kevin was saying he looked in on us and saw us naked and liked it. And then he said that he heard us having sex, too. Remember? This is stuff he really did say. And then you told him he should've joined us. That he was welcome to join us anytime, anywhere. Remember what he said then?"

"He said he couldn't do that."

"No. That's what I thought I heard, too, but that's not what he said. He said he couldn't *initiate* such an event. He didn't say someone else couldn't initiate it."

"Meaning . . . what, us?"

"I'm sure of it. And remember, then he said six years was long enough to go without the intimacy of cuddling. Too long, he said. Zig, that has to be what he wants. He wants *us* to go in *there* and cuddle with him. I know he does. He just couldn't say it. He won't come into our room, and it would be rude to ask us to come to his. That's what he thinks, anyway. So instead he told us as politely as he could that he'd be up for it."

"Oh, okay. So, we get to be the rude ones? I can handle that." Ziggy smiled.

"No, we shouldn't be rude, either. There's a way. We could tip-toe in there and gently wake him up and tell him we had scary dreams and ask him if it would be alright if we sleep with him."

"Oh, so he gets to play daddy after all."

"Oh no, uh, shit. Okay, we could tell him he's like a brother to us. That's closer to the truth, anyway."

"He won't be able to refuse. Cool. So what's your bad dream about?"

"Oh, I don't think he'll ask."

"Yes he will."

"I don't know. What about you, what if he asks you?"

"My dream was a good one. Some red-haired dude came in here and led us over there by the hand and all three of us got into bed with Kevin."

"The guy in my dream had red hair too."

"Well, there you go. We tell him it was spooky because the same guy was in both our dreams at once."

"Okay. Jeez, we've done enough talking. We need to get over there. Come on, let's climb into bed with him."

"Josh, are you sure we're dressed right for this?"

"What are you talking about? Yes, we're dressed perfectly for this; we're naked. Hopefully he's naked, too."

"Just joking, Josh."

"Oh. Okay. Duh."

"Fuck, I can't wait to get up next to him."

"Looks like you might get to jump his bones after all." Josh smiled.

"No Josh, I don't want to jump his bones, I want to cuddle with him. Him and you. And I want to be in the middle, can I be in the middle?"

"Zig, you are so sweet. But I want to cuddle with him, too."

"Oops. Sorry. I wasn't thinking. We'll put Kevin in the middle then. And let him call the shots; if he wants any of his bones jumped he'll find a way to let us know. All I care about right now is cuddling up next to him."

"Sounds good."

"This is so cool. Kevin's gonna have two teddy bears."

"Let's try not to wake him up, okay? We probably will, though. If he asks questions, we'll just make it up as we go. Or else tell him the truth."

"I vote for truth, bro."

"Okay."

—

THE BOYS QUIETLY ENTERED Kevin's room. He was still sound asleep. Ziggy crept around the bed to the far side of Kevin, and Josh stayed on Kevin's near side.

They both lifted the covers at the same time and gently scooted in, watching Kevin the whole time. Would he wake up? Maybe he did, maybe not. He didn't say anything. He turned on his side and put his arm around Ziggy, and Josh put his arm around Kevin. They pulled themselves snug up against each other and went back to sleep.

Saturday

IT WAS BRIGHT AND SUNNY outside when Josh woke up. Kevin was already awake, as it turned out, and so was Ziggy. But all three of them were still snuggled up against each other in bed.

When Josh moved, Kevin turned and said "Well, hello."

"Hi," Josh said, slightly embarrassed.

"Now that we're all awake, maybe one of you two can satisfy my curiosity," Kevin said. "How did we all end up this way? I'm not complaining, mind you. I'm quite thrilled actually."

"Josh had a dream and said you wanted us in here, Kev, so here we are."

"Ziggy had a dream too. He dreamed some guy walked into our bedroom and led us by the hand over here and into your bed."

"That's right. The same dude that was in Josh's dream."

"Well, we don't know that, Zig. Just because they had the same color hair doesn't mean it was the same guy."

"So," Kevin said. "Am I to understand you're saying that the fellow in your dreams made you do it? I haven't heard that one before." Kevin smiled.

"Naw, Kev. We already wanted to get in bed with you. The dreams just gave us an excuse, bro."

"You *wanted* us to come in here didn't you, Kev?"

"I did, as a matter of fact. Or at least I was hoping for such a delightful event. That's why I left the door open. But it would have been perfectly acceptable if you had stayed to yourselves. Privacy and comfort, that's what my offer was to you, and it still is."

"Dude, the comfort part turned out to be awesome. Privacy we don't need, but we'll take all the comfort we can get if it means sleeping with you."

Kevin laughed. "You men are more than welcome in my bed, whenever you want." Kevin looked truly happy. "I haven't been this tickled for years."

Ziggy and Josh quickly looked at each.

"Josh." Ziggy grinned. "You thinking what I'm thinking?"

Josh got up on his knees, smiling. "I believe we're on the same wavelength, Zig."

Kevin said, "I haven't slept so well in years, either. It was like old times in a way."

"Well Kev," Josh said, "sleeping well is one of the best parts of cuddling, but now we want to show you one of the ways we wake up."

"Oh, is that right? What does it involve, some sort of yoga torture or something?"

"Not yoga," Ziggy said, "but you got the torture part right." He got up on his knees and looked at Josh. Josh nodded his head. "Kev, we're gonna wake you up really good now with one of our favorite things . . . TICKLE TORTURE!"

Chapter 33
SPIRIT

BOTH BOYS POUNCED on Kevin and started tickling him everywhere. Armpits, belly, feet, behind the ears, and everything they could put their hands on. Kevin reacted instantly.

"No! How'd you know I'm so ticklish! Oh, no, no, stop!" Kevin curled up in a ball, trying to avoid the boys' relentless poking and stroking, but to no avail.

"Kev, you gotta fight back dude, it's the only way. We're not gonna stop until we're worn out, or until you out-tickle us. And we don't wear out easy."

Kevin laughed hysterically. "Fight . . . heehee! . . . back?"

"Yeah Kev," Josh said. "We're ticklish too. It's a battle to the finish. You're not gonna give up that easy are you?"

"You want me to . . . no, not there! . . . okay, that's it, you asked for it." Kevin started tickling back, and that's when things really got nuts.

It would have been hard to say who was the most ticklish. All three were laughing like hyenas. Nobody could stop; nobody wanted to. Ziggy and Josh started tickling each other as well, so it quickly became a free-for-all, each man for himself.

They wrestled and squirmed on the bed, and of course they were naked as ever. Each one was trying to find the most ticklish places on the others. Everyone had his hands all over the other two. They laughed so hard, someone listening would have thought they were crazy.

They were still laughing, even after they all had stiff erections. They were squirming and tickling with constant feels of each other's stiff boners.

Ziggy got a good hold on Kevin's hard dick; Kevin gasped. He suddenly felt it coming on and he was beyond stopping it. "Unnh! Oh god, I'm coming! Ohhhhh!" A big rope of cum spurt out of his cock, and then another.

Ziggy said, "Yeah Kev. Yeah! Shoot your load." He pressed his hard dick against Kevin's shoulder, rubbed up and down, and then Ziggy was shooting thick spurts of cum too, all over the side of Kevin's face and in his hair. "Unnnnh! Ahhhhhh!" Cum was flying everywhere.

Josh was on the edge too. Kevin's hand was on Josh's shaft, and when Kevin was in the throes of ecstasy he squeezed Josh's dick tighter. That's all it took; Josh moaned. "Unnnhh, coming, fuck! Unnnnnhh! Ahhhhhh!" and big spurts of jizz began shooting out of his cock.

They held on to each other, moaning, while their balls emptied, hips jerking in spasms, everyone getting splashed with cum.

Minutes later they lay in each other's arms, exhausted.

Kevin was the first one to speak. "Tickle torture. Exquisite. In all my days with Drew, I don't think it ever occurred to us to, uh, take tickling to such extremes."

"Oh well," Ziggy said, "you probably would have done it sooner or later. You just didn't get the chance."

"All too true," Kevin said. "I dreamed of him last night, you know. That's not unusual of course. I dreamed we were snuggling, just like old times. He got into bed and I put my arm around him. We even talked to each other. But then when I woke up this morning, it was Ziggy who was in my arms."

"Were you disappointed?"

"Oh, perhaps very briefly. Not disappointed it was Ziggy, of course; I was thrilled about that. And thrilled as well to have Josh snuggling up behind me."

"We were thrilled too, Kev," Josh said. "Still are."

They lay there relaxed for a few minutes, enjoying the feeling of contentment. Ziggy closed his eyes.

Josh said, "What are we gonna do next?"

"Let's go back to sleep," Ziggy said. "I want to snuggle some more."

"Okay by me," Kevin said. "You fellows wore me out."

"Josh, can I be in the middle? I want to be in the middle, just for an hour or two. Can I? Please?"

"Okay, sure Zig. Sounds nice, actually. Maybe I can get a turn next time?"

"Deal!" Ziggy climbed over Kevin, who scooted over to make room. Zig nestled in snugly between his two buddies. It wasn't long before they were snoozing again.

They slept a half hour or more but soon, one by one, they awoke again. And then a little clean up seemed advisable.

"Sorry to disturb anyone's reverie," Kevin said, "but I think I'd like a shower. And then we have all of Saturday ahead of us, gentlemen."

"Shower with us, Kevin," Josh said.

"Yeah dude, there's plenty of room for all three of us in our shower. It'll be fun."

"That sounds wonderful. But my shower is even larger. Would you care to join me in here?"

"Hell yes." Ziggy grinned. "Lead the way."

They got out of bed and followed Kevin to his bathroom. On the way, they passed a framed photo of a younger Kevin and some other young man.

Ziggy and Josh both stopped to stare.

Kevin went on into the bathroom before he realized he was alone. He came back out again and said, "Find something interesting?"

"Kevin," Ziggy said, "I know that's you. You look young enough to be in high school, bro, but that's obviously you. But who's the red-haired dude standing next to you?"

"That's Drew. That was taken not long after we first met. We were in college at the time."

All three of them stared at the picture.

Finally Josh said, "I know this sounds stupid, but that's the guy who was in my dream. Except he was a little older."

"Jesus," Ziggy said. "I was going to say exactly the same thing about the dude in my dream. Same smile and everything."

Kevin looked at the boys for a minute without saying anything.

Josh said, "Maybe he's looking out for you, Kevin. He knew you wanted us in here so he made it happen. He must love you so much. He's still doing things to make you happy."

Kevin was silent. Thinking.

"Kev, bro, you okay?"

"Yes, I'm okay." He sighed. "Sorry to have any reservations, but are you men sure you're not jumping to conclusions? Simply having red hair, that's not enough . . ."

"Kevin, that's him," Ziggy said.

Josh agreed. "He was in my dream, Kevin. Not just someone who looked like him; it was him."

Tears came to Kevin's eyes. "Drew," he said, "thank you. For being so sweet. You've always been so good to me."

They stared at the photo for several minutes in silence. Kevin wiped the tears from his eyes.

"So he gets in your dreams, Kev? Like he did ours?"

"Yes, I suppose so. Not every night, but quite often. I assumed I was inventing it all. That's what dreams seem to be, you know, for the most part. Wishful thinking. But if he was in both of your dreams . . ."

"People live on, Kev. We're all spirits, that's the way Ziggy and I see it. Living from one life to the next, along with whatever happens in between. There's no reason why one spirit couldn't visit another spirit once in a while. Dreams would be an easy way to do it."

"It verges on the incredible. Believing in theory is one thing; having evidence of it . . . well, it's amazing," Kevin said.

"Changes everything, doesn't it?"

"Josh, you talk as if you . . . have experienced something yourself, previously."

"Yeah, I have. Ziggy knows what I'm talking about."

"Kev, he'll tell you about it sometime. It's not real easy for Josh to talk about. One of his brothers."

"All things come to those who wait. Come on men, let's take a shower."

—

THEY FOLLOWED KEVIN into his bathroom and Kevin slid back the glass door. It wasn't just a bathtub with a shower; it was a large Jacuzzi, with a showerhead at each end.

"Jesus, Kev. As if a condo on the beach wasn't enough. Dude, you know how to live, I'll have to say that."

Kevin turned on one of the showers and got the temperature right. "Go ahead, Zig," he said, "let's get both of them going. There's plenty of hot water."

The men stepped in, Kevin at one end, Ziggy at the other. They rinsed off the dried cum and sweat while Josh waited patiently.

"Your turn, Josh," Ziggy said. Once they were all wet they passed the bar of soap around and took turns sudsing up. "Kevin, will you do my back?"

"Ah, it will by my pleasure, Zig." Kevin gently moved his hand back and forth across Ziggy's back, soaping and massaging all the way from Ziggy's neck down to the globes of his beautiful ass. "I presume you don't mind if I touch you down there?"

"Not at all, Kev. Absolutely, touch me all you want, anywhere, bro."

"You young men, both of you have such perfect bodies. Lean, with just enough muscle to be strong and wonderfully fit looking. Much preferable to the muscle-bound look, in my opinion."

"Thanks, Kev."

"Josh, would you care for me to wash your back?"

"Oh yeah, Kev, would you?"

"My pleasure." Kevin soaped up Josh and lovingly stroked everything from the back of his head to the bottom of his ass. He even reached under and gently fondled Josh's balls.

"Oh yeah, now you're talking," Josh said.

Meanwhile Ziggy did Kevin the same way.

Josh felt something hard and fleshy bump against his butt. He reached back and grasped just what he expected: Kevin's hard cock.

"You like this, huh Kev?" Josh smiled.

"Oh, yes. You have a beautiful body, Josh."

"Josh," Ziggy said, "I've got my hands all over him. Talk about beautiful. Kevin, I'd like to know what your workout routine is. Whatever it is, it suits you perfectly. Fuck, I've got a boner again from touching you, dude."

Josh said, "Join the club. Kevin and I are hard too."

"Nearly impossible to avoid," Kevin said, "and as I'm quickly learning, there's absolutely no reason I'd *want* to avoid it."

"Dude." Ziggy laughed. "Josh, listen to him. Kevin, bro, you are the man. Told you you'd come untwisted. Didn't we?"

"Yes, you warned me." Kevin smiled.

Ziggy laughed again. "Warning: pleasure ahead. Prepare to enjoy."

"Let's get out of the shower so I can admire you young men properly."

"Ooooh, Zig, he has plans for us."

The men rinsed off and stepped out of the tub. Kevin handed Josh and Ziggy each a big fluffy towel to dry off with and used a third one himself. Then they hung the towels up and walked naked into the living room, their cocks still fully engorged.

"Just so that you know, men, it's perfectly fine with me to go naked anywhere inside, even up to the windows, but I wouldn't advise nudity on the balcony until nightfall."

"It's okay to go out there naked?"

"Yes, at night; why not? Just don't turn the balcony lights on of course. It'll be fine."

Josh and Ziggy went up to the window and looked out. "God, this is really a step above our place. Naked-wise I mean. I feel like I'm looking out on the whole world bare-ass naked, and yet they can't see me. Unless they have binoculars."

"Or a telescope. And some of my neighbors do, I know. But if they see anything, they can only blame themselves for taking the effort."

"Even our hard dicks?"

"Especially your hard dicks. Which I must say are very enticing. So nice of you to keep them hard for me."

"Can't help it, bro, from looking at yours. Your hard cock has us both beat in the enticing department. That's definitely one to be proud of."

"Kevin, what kind of stuff do you like to do?" Josh asked. "In the way of sex I mean."

"Yeah Kev, you have anything special you like? Josh and me are pretty flexible. And if it's something we haven't done before, hell, we'll try it. We'll try just about anything twice."

Kevin laughed. "Not just once, but twice?"

"Well, the first time doesn't count, because you're trying something new. You gotta try it at least twice to get a good idea what it can be like."

"Makes sense I suppose."

"Well?"

"What do I like to do?"

"Yeah."

"Well, to be honest, I'm not a big fan of . . . fucking, or getting fucked."

"Kevin, you're not the only one," Josh said. "There's other ways to get off. I think at least fifty percent of gay men just aren't into fucking."

"Well, I do enjoy watching it," Kevin said. "Especially if both men are thoroughly enjoying it."

"That's cool, bro," Ziggy said. "You can watch Josh and me anytime. We like to be watched. But fucking is only one of the things we like. Tell us what *you* like, Kev. And not just what you've done before; tell us your fantasies too. Stuff you've never done but you'd like to try."

"Oh goodness. I'm not sure I feel comfortable putting such things into words. Using one word to describe a complex act – it doesn't capture the richness of the experience. Fucking, for example. The word mainly suggests the physical act of insertion. But just from watching, I know that for those who like it, it involves so much more: feeling, sensation, emotion; so much more than only one word can imply. The same can be said of . . . other things, as well."

"Couldn't agree with you more, dude. Although when I think of fucking I think of all that stuff. Feeling, emotion, sensation – fucking is all that and more. But so are other things."

"Kevin," Josh said, "maybe you could, uh, you know, show us what you like. That would work, wouldn't it?"

Chapter 34
INITIATE

THE MEN STOOD facing each other with fully erect hard-ons. Josh and Ziggy waited for Kevin to respond.

Finally Kevin said, "Just to make sure I understand, you're asking me to demonstrate? That's what you want me to do? Actually . . . initiate something with you?"

"Yeah Kev. Just do it. With us. Show us." Ziggy grinned. "Look, pretend Josh and I are your slaves. Or your callboys or, uh, your birthday gifts from Drew. We're here to do anything your heart desires. Or to have done to us whatever you want to do. Or both. No words required, no permission required. Show us what you like by doing it. That's what we want you to do."

"Oh my." Kevin stood between the two of them, and looked first at Ziggy's hard cock, standing stiff and curved upward. Then he looked at Josh's dick, which stood straight out, slightly curved downward, throbbing. Then he looked at Ziggy's again. Ziggy started leaking pre-cum as Kevin watched.

Kevin groaned. He slowly got down on his knees on the rug and faced Ziggy's stiff cock. He was only inches away from it. He reached out and gently held it.

Ziggy sighed. "Oh yeah."

Kevin gently caressed the smooth skin. He touched it all over. He gathered up what pre-cum he could and put it in his mouth. Then he ran his fingers over it again, gently.

"Feels good Kev," Ziggy whispered. "Careful, I'm already kinda close."

Kevin moved his hand away. He turned and looked at Josh's stiff cock, still throbbing.

Josh gave out a sigh of relief, thinking now it was his turn. He was right. Kevin turned his body around so that he faced Josh, and then he reached out and slowly raised his palm underneath Josh's hard dick, until he had it resting in his hand. He gently lifted it, just enough to feel its full weight.

Josh moaned. His cock started making pre-cum. The clear fluid slowly pooled in Kevin's palm, trickle by trickle, until finally Kevin gently took his hand away and licked up what he had. Then he held a finger up against the bottom of Josh's dickhead and scooped up the newly-leaked pre-cum glistening there. He put the finger to his mouth.

"Jeez, Kevin." Josh shuddered all over. "I almost shot my load. I don't want to come yet. Fuck, do Ziggy again."

Kevin turned around again on his knees to face Ziggy's leaking cock. He held his hand under it as he'd done Josh, gathering pre-cum.

Josh moved so that he had a close-up view of what Kevin was doing to Ziggy. Kevin's hard dick was raised up horizontal, defying gravity, bouncing stiffly each time Kevin moved. It was slightly longer than Josh's, not quite as thick as Ziggy's, circumcised, with a nicely-shaped head, and looked very inviting. Josh got down on his knees to get a closer look.

Kevin gently took his hand away from Ziggy and licked the pre-cum from his hand. Then he raised it again and held Ziggy's shaft.

"Ooooohh, Kev, Careful. I'm so close, bro. Wouldn't take much to set me off."

Josh moved behind Ziggy. "Zig, spread your legs apart a little." Ziggy moved his feet apart. "More than that." He moved his feet again.

Meanwhile Kevin licked Ziggy's balls.

"Ah, Kev, nice."

Josh ducked his head in between Ziggy's legs. The first thing he did was lick Ziggy's feet. First the ankle of one foot, and then the top of it, then the same to the other foot, then back to the first one to get the toes.

"Oh Jesus, Josh. Ahhhhh. Fuck, I swear you could make me come that way, bro."

Josh didn't want Zig to come yet, so he raised his head. Kevin's hard cock was just inches from his face. Josh licked it.

Kevin shuddered. "Oh Josh. Wonderful. But you better not do that again unless you want a mouthful of . . ."

Josh licked it again. He started halfway down and brought his tongue all the way up to the underside of the head.

Kevin groaned in anticipation and quickly put his mouth over Ziggy's cock and sucked. Slid his tongue back and forth against the bottom of the shaft and sucked hard. That's all it took, for Ziggy.

Ziggy cried out, "UNNNH!" His hips spasmed forward, pushing his cock a couple inches deeper into Kevin's mouth. "Coming! Ahhhhhh!" The first glob of cum spurt out of his dick, deep inside Kevin's mouth.

Ziggy drew back a little and the next shot of his warm cum landed directly on the middle of Kevin's tongue, giving him the full taste of it, sweet and salty. Ziggy's cum. Then another spurt, even bigger, and then more. Kevin drank it all down as fast as Ziggy pumped it out, while Ziggy groaned, "Unnnnh! Unnnnh! Unnnnh!"

Josh decided it was high time to make Kevin come. Kevin was extra hard, from sucking Ziggy, and he was right at the edge. Josh gave him a broad lick starting at the balls, up the length of the shaft, and all the way up and over the cockhead. Then he lapped with his tongue at the corona again, underneath the dickhead. And then again. Josh's intent was to continue licking as long as it took to make Kevin shoot his cum.

It only took three licks. The third time Kevin let out a muffled "MMMMMPH!" Ziggy's cock slipped out from his lips. A big spurt of cum shot out of Kevin's dick into Josh's mouth.

Josh, still on all fours, pressed his lips around the dickhead to catch all of Kevin's cum as it spurt out in a rush. Kevin moaned, "Unnnh! Unnnnh! Unnh!" as his balls emptied.

Then Ziggy squat down over Josh and reached his hand underneath, into Josh's crotch. Josh raised up his butt and Ziggy found the treasure he was seeking: Josh's rock-hard cock. He grabbed hold of it and stroked it up and down rapidly until Josh said, "UNNNH!" Zig kept stroking and Josh started spurting.

"Ahhhhhh! Ahhh! Ahhhhhhhhh." Thick squirts of cum spat out of Josh's dick. Ziggy caught it all in the palm of his hand.

Zig was getting Josh off; Josh was joyfully swallowing the last spurts of Kevin's jizz; and Kevin was immersed in wonderful sensation, shooting his load while he could still taste Ziggy's sweet sperm.

It was quite a commotion, but finally they wound down, pulses slowing down as they leaked out the last of their cum. Ziggy, holding his hand level, stepped off to Josh's side.

He was the first to recover, and the first to speak. "Great demonstration, Kev."

"Ah. You enjoyed that, Zig?"

"Oh yeah. Worked for me."

"Loved it," Josh said. He used his finger to wipe the last bit of cum off Kevin's dick and put it to his mouth.

"Seems a bit of a shame," Kevin said, "that Josh's essence went untasted. But we all had a wonderful time; that's the important part."

"Actually," Ziggy said, "you could still taste it."

"I find it tempting, believe me, but no, I guess not. I better clean it up now, before it dries on the carpet."

Josh sat up and looked down at the carpet. Kevin looked, too. There was nothing there.

"What . . .? Didn't you . . ."

Ziggy held out his hand to Kevin – the hand full of Josh's fresh, warm cum.

Kevin's eyes got large. He pulled Ziggy's hand to his mouth and licked up Josh's cumload. It tasted a lot like clean, rich water from the ocean. Warm, salty seawater, mixed with the taste of Ziggy's hand.

A taste of both of these angels at once, Kevin thought, as he lapped it up. He licked his lips and smiled. "You both are so nice. Very thoughtful."

"Naw, Kev, just looking out for ourselves. The better we make you feel, the more we enjoy it ourselves. That's the way it works." Ziggy grinned. "Our motives are purely selfish."

"What a bunch of baloney." Kevin smiled. "You two are the sweetest, most unselfish fellows I've ever met."

Kevin and Josh stood up and the three of them looked at each other, naked, grinning. Kevin moved forward and they had a long, intimate group hug.

After the hug Kevin said, "Do you men have any ideas about what you'd like to do today?"

"Well, we're at your mercy, Kev," Josh said. "But even if we had my car I probably wouldn't want to go anywhere. The coolest thing I can think of would be to stay here with you. Go down to the beach, swim, just hang out with you."

"Same here," Ziggy said. "We've only got today and tomorrow left. Then on Monday we're out of here. If it wouldn't be too much a nuisance we'd like to be with you, Kevin. Whatever you do. Take us along and we'll be happy."

"Well, I'm certainly agreeable to that. I suppose the first errand we should get out of the way is grocery shopping. Josh, take a little time and make a list of what you need to make dinner. Then you men can come with me to shop if you like. Or you can stay here and relax while I run to the store."

"Oh, take us with you, Kev. We'd like that."

—

ON THE WAY to the grocery store, Kevin stopped for wine to go with dinner. He also made an unscheduled stop: he bought a big, soft, washable throw rug for the living room, which theoretically was to make cleanup easier if any spurts of cum went astray.

The boys were skeptical that it would work. Mainly because, outside of bed, it was totally unpredictable when or where a thoroughly enjoyable event and release would occur. Their idea, instead, which they proposed while Kevin looked over the rugs on display, was simply to ensure all cum not spurted inside a condom disappear directly down someone's throat. Straight from the source.

Kevin was quite agreeable to that, but he bought the rug anyway.

Back in the condo, Ziggy and Josh stripped naked as soon as they got inside the door, with Kevin playing catch up a few seconds later. Then with the groceries put away, and the new rug placed in the living room, it was time for a swim in the ocean. On with their swimsuits.

They waited until they reached the beach to put the sun block on, otherwise they might not have made it out the front door. As it was, all three had obvious boners by the time they were through spreading the slick cream over each other.

"Kev," Ziggy said, smiling, "that trim little suit you have on sure doesn't hide anything. Very nice."

Kevin looked down at the outline of his hard dick. "How embarrassing."

"No Kevin; be proud, bro."

"Or at least don't be embarrassed," Josh said. "It's part of being a male. Nothing more natural. It feels good, doesn't it?"

"Yes, of course, but . . . if someone sees it, some stranger, or even worse, a neighbor, I'd feel as though I were exposing myself."

"But why would it matter? Everybody knows guys get hard-ons. Why hide it? Most people probably *like* looking at them anyway. We sure do. Makes ours get harder, and the harder they are the better it feels."

Kevin sighed. "I suppose it's part of being brought up during a more repressive time. It takes a bit of conscious effort to update one's . . . brainwashing, to current values."

"Kevin, that's the thing; who cares what current values are? There's plenty of people, I'm sure, who still think a dick shouldn't be hard in public, but they're not any happier for thinking that way."

"I know, Josh. What you say makes sense. But it's not easy to overcome the taboos one learns in childhood."

Ziggy said, "I didn't learn any taboos in my childhood."

Kevin laughed. "I can almost believe that, Zig. But think about it. You must have learned a few no-no's, growing up."

"He grew up in an orphanage, Kev."

"Nevertheless, there has to be a few, lurking inside that wonderful brain of yours, Ziggy. Otherwise how could you have turned out to be the sweet, honest person you are?"

"Well, if you're talking about stealing other people's stuff, I don't do that because I know how it feels to get your stuff stolen. I'm not gonna do that to people."

"You care about others. You have no idea how much I respect that, Ziggy."

"Well, yeah, I care about others, but they better not tell me how to live my life. They're gonna be disappointed if they think I give a shit what they think about me. Excuse my language."

Kevin looked at Ziggy without saying anything.

"I hope I didn't offend you, Kev."

"Not at all. I was thinking what a wonderful mixture of principles you have. Honor, honesty, compassion, generosity, and above all, a fierce belief in being true to yourself. One couldn't ask for better character. I find myself slightly lacking in comparison."

"Oh god Kevin, get real. You're the dude, bro. Josh and I are amateurs compared to you."

"Amateurs at what?"

"Um, I don't exactly know. That's part of what we're learning. Being around you, Kev, we're learning all kinds of stuff."

"Well, it's mutual then. Because I haven't learned in years as much as I've learned in the last day or two."

Ziggy grinned. "You're getting untwisted."

"And we're growing up," Josh said.

"Oh no, please," Kevin said, "please, don't ever grow up."

"What I mean is, we're growing."

"Yes, by all means, grow. Never stop growing. Please. Don't ever stop."

"That's what's so cool about you, Kev," Ziggy said. "You're, uh . . . you know, more mature than us, but you're still growing. You're still like a kid. You're like us."

"Thank you. Let's all make a resolution, right now. Never grow up. Are you with me, gentlemen?"

"Never grow up," Ziggy said, smiling.

"Never grow up," Josh said. "Never stop growing." He grinned.

"Okay, now that we have that settled," Kevin said, "the ocean is waiting. Who wants to get wet?"

—

AFTER A SWIM and a bit of sunbathing, Josh excused himself to go back to the condo and get a pie put together and into the oven. A half hour later, Kevin and Ziggy returned as well. Josh, of course, had stripped down naked as soon as he got inside; now Zig and Kev did the same.

"I feel as though I'm in the Garden of Eden," Kevin said. "Naked and unashamed."

"The only way to be. Josh, you want any help with that?"

"Nah Zig, I got it covered."

"In that case I think I'm gonna take a nap."

"I think I'll join you, Zig," Kevin said.

"Um, in whose bed?"

"Mine, of course. My bed is now your bed, too, men. If you wish. Whenever you please. From now on."

"Alright!" Ziggy grinned.

—

KEVIN AND ZIG SHOWERED and then snuggled up together. Josh joined them once he had the pie baking and the timer set. Together they looked like three puppies recharging after a fun frolic, arms and legs draped over each other every which way, naked as always.

Dinner was a success: Josh's baked spaghetti and cheese, along with a salad, and the cherry pie for desert. Accompanied by a bottle of red wine from France.

Afterwards Kevin cleared the table and opened a second bottle.

"A toast," he said, "to our ongoing friendship. We can't let this weekend be the end of it, gentlemen. You must return someday. And until then, we shall stay close in touch."

"Yeah!" Ziggy and Josh yelled it out in unison, grinning.

"Kevin, you're the best," Josh said.

"The absolute best," Ziggy said. "Friends, definitely. Better than that: brothers."

They clinked their glasses together and drank.

"What would you fellows like to do now? Jensen Beach does have a gay nightclub, believe it or not, if you're interested in the local nightlife."

"Oh, hell no, Kevin. I mean, no offense. Fuck, if you want to go we'll sure as hell go with you. Uh, do you go there much?"

"No, hardly at all. I just thought I'd mention it as an option."

"Well, I'm fine with staying in," Ziggy said. "Unless you guys want to go. What about you, Josh?"

"I don't care. I want to do whatever Kevin wants to do."

"Same here. We hardly ever go out to bars, Kev. I think we'd rather chill out with you here, where it's quiet, if you're up for that. And maybe take a late-night skinny-dip, later."

"In that case," Kevin said, smiling, "let's have another glass of wine."

"Yeah," Ziggy said. "I'm getting a buzz already from this stuff. You drink wine on a regular basis?"

"No, not really. Mostly on special occasions. It can add a little extra happiness to what is already an enjoyable evening."

"Josh and I have another way of doing that, but wine's cool too."

"Oh? And what might that be?"

"Uh, well, um . . . weed is our usual buzz of choice. But I know not everybody approves of it." Ziggy watched Kevin for his reaction.

Josh did, too. They'd each learned long ago the subject was a delicate one with some people, and they had no desire at this point to raise a point of contention.

Kevin grinned. "Well now. It just so happens I have a little stash tucked away, of Mother Nature's natural high. It's my 'buzz of choice' as well."

"Kev, that is so cool. Fuck, we should have known you'd be up to speed on that, bro."

"I'm not surprised," Josh said. "Kevin's like us, Zig."

"Shall I get it out?"

Ziggy grinned and said, "Why the hell not."

Chapter 35
LIKE US

KEVIN HAD a nice pipe with a screen in it, well used, and a fragrant little collection of cannabis buds. They were soon sitting together in the living room, buzzed on wine and high on pot.

"Good stuff, Kevin."

"I think I'm lucky to have it. The younger people such as yourselves seem to have the best connections. We older guys have to nurture what meager sources we have."

"You are not old, Kevin," Josh said. "So you might as well stop it with that 'old' talk."

"Compared to you I am, but in the greater scheme of things I suppose you're right. I hope to get a lot older."

"Not compared to us either," Ziggy said. "Thirty years from now we'll be fifty-two and you'll be, what, sixty-five? Won't make that much difference. Doesn't now either, as young as you look and think."

"Thirty years from now I'll be seventy-eight."

The boys stared at him in disbelief.

"Not that it's important. I just thought you'd want to know, since we're going to be ongoing friends," Kevin said.

"Uh," Ziggy said.

"Kev," Josh said, "no way."

"It's true. Better you find out now rather than later. In case it makes a difference."

"Dude, it makes no difference whatsoever. Forty-eight, that's young, bro. Anyway, hell, when you're seventy-eight it still won't make any difference. Age isn't what matters; it's how old you think, that's what matters."

"Ziggy's right Kev. You're young inside, that's what matters. I don't care how old or young you are, you're like us, and that's the bottom line."

They stared at Kevin for a minute or two as if he was the eighth wonder of the world. But after that it truly didn't matter anymore. Except that, more than ever, they wanted to be like Kevin. Learn his secrets. Know what he knew.

Kevin was the first to speak. "Want another hit?"

"Fire it up, bro."

"Yeah, me too," Josh said.

"We'll make it up to you, Kev, when we get Josh's car back. We have some hidden away."

"No worries." Kevin filled the bowl and took the first hit, then handed it to Ziggy, and then it went to Josh. Then they were set for a while.

"Do either of you ever think back to the days when you first started smoking?" Kevin asked. "I do. Those were the days."

"Tell us about it, Kev."

"Well, in my case, we were quite the rebels in that way. We had to keep it very secret. No one but artists seemed to even know about pot, as a rule. Everyone else seemed to believe it made you crazy, or led to harder drugs, as the propaganda suggested. We knew better. We knew it was harmless. Not the greatest thing for your lungs, of course, but back then people hardly knew that tobacco was dangerous."

"You were an artist?"

"I was studying architecture; that seemed to qualify. We would put towels at the bottom of the door of our dorm room when we smoked, and we had a hose going out the window we'd exhale through. Smoked one hit at a time. Never did get caught. A good thing too. In those days you'd get jail time as likely as not. We were young and brash, thought we could get away with it. And we did."

"Damn, Kev. You guys had balls."

"Yes. That's when I met Drew. He lived across the hall. We used to watch each other take showers. That eventually led to masturbating while watching each other. Very hot. Which then led to other things." Kevin smiled.

"Did you have a roommate? What about him, was he gay?"

"No, but he was an artist, too. He had no inhibitions when it came to sex. The three of us had many, uh, 'circle-jerks.' We passed the pipe between us, then we typically enjoyed getting each other off. Immensely. One need not be gay to prefer someone else's hand to one's own."

"Wow." Ziggy was getting a hard-on. So was Kevin. Josh's cock had been hard since they first lit the pipe.

"That's what I remember most often when thinking back to those days. Sitting on the rug in a circle. Drew's hand on my penis, my hand on Sammy, his on Drew. Then we'd switch. We made it last as long as we could stand it. When we couldn't hold off any longer we did our best to have everyone come at once."

"Were you naked?"

"Yes. It was sexier that way, and easier to clean up as well. Quite enjoyable."

"Where did you shoot, on the rug? Or yourselves?"

"On ourselves. Our bellies. And on our chests. Sometimes all the way up to our faces. A little embarrassing the first time it happened, but we became accustomed to it quickly enough. Then Sammy told us he ate his own cum, and after that we all did."

"Oh god. It sounds so hot."

"It was. Extremely so. Our, uh . . . dicks got very hard. Swollen, purple heads. We ejaculated with such force our, uh, cum, the first shot, often flew up out of sight. Sometimes we would discover it later and laugh."

"Oh jeez, Kev. I'd have loved to have been there."

"Me too," Ziggy said. "Damn, no kidding. Jacking each other off." He looked at Kevin's hard cock, and then at Josh's, and shuddered. Everyone had stiff boners. Ziggy's cock was wet with pre-cum.

"Turns out it's a college tradition somewhat. I found out later we weren't the only ones having circle-jerks. It wasn't a gay thing so much as a guy thing. A horny, college-dorm guy thing. We were all living together under one roof and every one of us was as horny as can be."

"Jesus," Ziggy said. "Fuck, I'm horny as hell, guys. Let's do it. Let's beat off. I need to come."

Chapter 36
CIRCULAR MOTION

JOSH'S DICK WAS WET with pre-cum too. "Zig, are you talking about doing a circle-jerk?"

"Yeah, fuck yeah, Josh. A circle-jerk. Let's jack each other off. It sounds horny as all fuck. Let's do it just like you did, Kev, in college. Switch back and forth from dick to dick and stuff. From hand to hand."

"Oh jeez." Josh said, grinning. "I've never been in a circle-jerk before. I always wanted to."

"Me neither," Ziggy said.

"Really, Ziggy? Not when you were in the orphanage?"

"No, and not when I was in high school, either. We jacked off together all the time, and some of the guys did each other, but George and I only jacked ourselves, not each other. Fuck, it sounds so hot, now. Like, a guy thing."

"Oh my. Well, by all means let's do it. It's going to be like old times," Kevin said. "This was always so hot. Let's get down on the floor, on the new rug."

"Yeah, perfect."

They stood up from their chairs and sat cross-legged in a circle on the soft, fur-like throw rug.

"Is everybody stoned?" Kevin said.

"Yeah, but let's do one more hit," Ziggy said.

So they passed the pipe. Then they were ready.

"Okay," Ziggy said. He looked down at his swollen cock. Then he looked up. "Who wants to go first?"

"That's just it," Kevin said. "We all go first." He reached over and gently held Ziggy's shaft.

"Oh fuck," Ziggy said. He reached over and held Josh's big boner gently.

"Ahhh." Josh put his hand on Kevin's stiff cock.

"Ohhhh." Kevin's hips jerked once in a little spasm, but he didn't come yet. Josh was careful. Kevin started stroking Ziggy and then everyone was stroking. And being stroked.

"Fuck, I'm already about to come," Ziggy said. "I'm so turned on."

"We haven't even switched yet. Let's switch," Kevin said. He took his left hand off Ziggy's cock and reached his right hand out for Josh's hard cock instead. Ziggy took his hand off Josh and wrapped his other hand around Kevin's hard wood.

Josh, at the same time, let go of Kevin and grabbed Ziggy's hard horn of a cock. He wiggled his thumb under the head to gather up some of Zig's pre-cum.

"Oh fuck, Josh!" Ziggy's hips spasmed forward and upward into Josh's fist. "OOHHHHH! FUCK!" That one thrust was all it took; a thick spurt of cum suddenly shot out of Ziggy's dick and landed right splat on Josh's face, "Ahhhhhh!" Another spurt followed, then another. And more. "Unnhhhh."

Ziggy instantly sped up his stroking on Kevin, the idea being for everyone to come at once. Kevin moaned, "OOHHHHHHHH!" One more stroke by Zig and Kevin's sexy cock, hard and swollen, fired off its first spurt of cum. Ziggy had it aimed upward and the cum hit Kevin on his own face. Kevin's remaining spurts landed on his chest and abs; seven or eight salvos.

Kevin, the instant Ziggy sped up his pace, did the same with Josh. He had a good hold on Josh's seven-inch piece of hard flesh and Josh suddenly said, "Coming, fuck, I'm coming! Oohhhhhhhh!" Kevin held Josh's cock so it was aimed straight at himself, and Kevin received just what he had hoped for: a face full of Josh's warm cum. One shot after another. On his forehead, his nose, his mouth, and then a couple more ropes of cum on his neck, Josh the whole time going "Unnnnh! Unnnnh!"

The three of them shooting together. Ziggy moaned until the last of his cum was dripping out. Kevin wound down with two loads splattered all over his front. A few moans and a couple more spurts from Josh and he was drained, too, with most of Ziggy's load on his face.

They all leaned back on their hands, exhausted, catching their breath. Finally Ziggy said, "Fuck."

"Wow," Josh said. "That was good."

"That was excellent," Ziggy said.

—

"KEVIN, WERE YOUR CIRCLE-JERKS at school that good?"

They were in Kevin's shower, rinsing off all the cum.

"Yes," Kevin said, "they were always good. Like ours tonight. Exquisite. And the longer we did it the better we learned how to please each other."

"Did you guys ever do anything, you know, like, oral?" Josh asked. "Did you ever suck each other off?"

"Not when the three of us were together. Sammy was straight. You know how straight boys are about things of that sort. Drew and I did, every chance we had; just the two of us."

"But not with Sammy? Aw, Kev, you guys lived in the same room together. You were already jacking each other off; I'll bet you could have done . . . something."

"Well, actually, I, uh, did suck him off. Quite often. Sammy was always the one to instigate it, but I was quite willing to do my part. Eager, in fact."

"That sounds horny," Ziggy said. "He was straight?"

"Yes."

"Right on to that dude. He heard pleasure knocking and went for it. And he made you happy at the same time."

"Kev, he never sucked you off?"

"No, and I didn't expect him to. Drew was quite good in that department, so I was happy with the arrangement. Besides, we were still having our circle-jerks. Sammy could do some wonderful things with his hands."

They were done showering and turned off the water. The men toweled themselves dry and then made themselves comfortable out on the balcony.

"Did Drew know you were sucking Sammy off?"

"Yes, I told him. It was our little secret. He only wished he could be in my place. Sammy was very hot. Straight-boy hot. And he had a perfect body. We both thought he was incredibly sexy. And underneath his bad-boy act he was a sweetheart."

"So Drew never got a taste."

"Drew was always long gone for the night, back to his room by the time Sammy approached me. It would be late in the evening. Sammy was already naked; he called it 'chilling out' – he'd get stoned and strip down naked to read, do his homework, or simply relax. Now and then he would get aroused. But he always waited until after I'd gone to bed to initiate something."

"Were you asleep?"

"I pretended to be. Every night I lay on my side, held my hand in front of my eyes, and looked out between my fingers. Watching him walk around nude. Sooner or later, inevitably, he got an erection."

"Oh, jeez."

"The longer I watched him the harder it got. He looked at me every so often; perhaps checking to see if I was still asleep. Sooner or later his pre-cum would start flowing. That was when he would go lock the door. Then he would come over and stand beside my bed."

Chapter 37
OPEN UP

"HE DIDN'T SAY A WORD; he just stood there next to me, totally naked, with his hard cock erect and sticking straight out above my face. Gently throbbing, leaking pre-cum."

"He didn't say anything? What happened then?"

"He didn't need to say anything. He stood there, letting his pre-cum drip on me, and waited. He knew I'd eventually wake up and suck him. Either that or do what I did the first time."

"What was that?"

"Pretend to sleep through the whole thing."

"What?"

"Well, the very first night it happened, god knows the last thing I was expecting was for him to walk right up so close to me. His hard dick was only inches from my face. If I 'woke up' I was afraid I might scare him off, and I didn't want to do that. So I licked my lips once and opened my mouth. You know, as people do when their nose is stuffed up."

"Oh, Kevin. Jeez. There's no way anybody could sleep through getting his mouth fucked."

"I know. I wasn't thinking, but it was the first thing that popped into my mind. Open my mouth, and keep it open. So that's what I did."

"What did he do?"

"He started stroking his cock. He stood there right next to me, looking at my mouth, stroking. I watched through the slits between my fingers. Then, when he was finally on the verge of coming, he put his cockhead up to my lips and shot his entire load inside my mouth."

"Oh, Jesus!"

"I drank it down as quickly as I could, still pretending to be asleep. It was . . . tasty. When he was done he whispered, 'Sweet dreams,' and went over and lay down on his own bed. A few minutes later, I heard him chuckling. Then the next night we did it all over again."

"Jeez, Kevin."

"Every night that week. He knew I wanted it. At first I pretended to stay asleep, but when he started putting his dick inside my mouth, I realized he wanted me to wake up. That was fine with me. Awake, I could suck him. Sometimes I came without even touching myself while I sucked him off."

"Jesus Kevin, you're giving me another hard-on, bro."

"Sorry." Kevin grinned.

"No, that's a good thing, always a good thing. Just saying."

"How often did he do this?"

"Oh, five or six times a week."

"Man. On top of your circle-jerks and your private things with Drew. Kevin, you were getting more sex in one day than some people get in a week."

"It's just how things worked out. I didn't go out looking for it, god knows. But I think you know how it is, fellows, at that age."

"Young and full of cum," Ziggy said.

"Yes, we were all that way. I hope you don't think I was too promiscuous. Drew and Sammy were both very special."

"I would have done the same thing," Josh said. "Jeez, if I was in college and had, say, Ziggy for a roommate, there's no telling what might happen."

"Oh fuck, Josh, can you imagine? Dude I'd be at your bed every night." Ziggy grinned. "Dripping pre-cum on you until you got off your lazy ass and took care of me."

Josh laughed.

Kevin smiled. "Between Sammy and Drew, I must say my college years were very enjoyable."

"Fuck, you had a *great* time, sounds like."

Kevin sat up and stretched.

"Gentlemen, it's too early to go skinny-dipping; is anyone up for a board game?"

—

THE REST OF THE EVENING was a relaxed one, with no surprises. They played a popular game, Trivial Pursuit, sitting around the dining room table. Naked, as they always were these days when they were inside the condo. After the game they put on some clothes and took a walk on the beach. They finished their walk with a bare-ass dip in the ocean, but it didn't lead to sex as the previous night's did.

No one was horny enough to need it. That, and the knowledge that there would almost certainly be more, later, left them in an unhurried state of mind. All three of them had big, filled-out dicks, but not stiff ones. It was pleasant to let their penises bob in the ocean waves without the usual hormonal urgency.

They swam and played and hugged each other in the water, followed by similar antics naked on the beach. They felt happy and fortunate to be in each other's company.

The feeling of contentment stayed with them back in the condo. Looking forward to cuddling all night, the threesome went to bed relatively early. By unspoken agreement, no one instigated any sex. The pleasure of snuggling up against each other was paramount. They all got hard, but that in itself was enjoyable to experience all night long.

Sunday

IN THE MORNING they lingered in bed for hours, waking and falling back to sleep, trading positions, caressing each other, lying with arms and legs across each other. Josh had his turn in the middle for an hour or two.

He was in the middle when things finally became a bit lively. After all, the hormones were bound to kick in eventually.

The three of them had been sleeping like spoons, with Ziggy's hard cock snugly resting inside Josh's asscrack and Josh's stiff dick pressing against Kevin's back. Ziggy only got harder as time went on. Harder, and wetter. Josh was roused from his sleep and eventually wiggled his butt a little to get a better feel of the situation.

Jeez, he thought. *It's slicker than snot back there.*

He didn't want to wake Ziggy if he was asleep, so it was a pleasant surprise when Ziggy's hand soon appeared in front of Josh's face, waving a condom. They'd left a few on the night table the day before, just in case. Josh turned and looked, and Ziggy was grinning. He whispered, "Wanna?"

Josh smiled, nodded enthusiastically, and braced himself for what was sure to be a good licking and a good fucking.

—

LICKING WAS THEIR TYPICAL way to get their partner ready to be fucked. Josh and Ziggy both enjoyed doing it, and loved having it done to them.

Zig devoted several minutes to slavering Josh's asshole with his wet tongue. He licked and pushed his tongue against Josh's puckered hole until it began to relax. Once his tongue went in, Ziggy alternated with his fingers: first one, then two, and finally three. After three fingers were in and Josh was relaxed, he was ready for Ziggy's stiff cock.

Ziggy slipped a condom over it and gently pressed the head against Josh's butthole. Josh was accustomed to this and after just a little resistance he relaxed; Ziggy's cock popped inside.

"Ahhhh." The initial entry was a thrill for both of them. A promise of what was to come. "Yeah Zig," Josh whispered. "Work it in slow and then fuck me hard."

Chapter 38
Ocean Beach

KEVIN WAS ASLEEP, but eventually the shaking of the bed woke him up.

He turned to see what in the world was going on. There was Josh, his dick hard as wood, happily getting fucked by Ziggy. Ziggy was fucking Josh gently, deeply, relentlessly. He knew how to make it last. Josh's cock was rigid and leaking pre-cum.

And Kevin knew a good opportunity when he saw one. He moved closer and gently licked the shaft of Josh's dick. Carefully. The way it looked, it wouldn't take much to put Josh over the edge.

"Ahhh fuck. Kevin's licking me." Josh said. "He woke up, Zig, and he's licking my cock."

"Cool. Join in, Kev. We were gonna wake you up. UNNNNH. Josh and me are gonna shoot our loads here in a minute. We'll make you come too."

"Kevin," Josh said, "keep doing that if you want a mouth full of cum. Ahhhhhh. I'm gonna shoot pretty soon if Zig keeps fucking me like this. Bring your cock over here, I want to suck it."

Kevin kept licking and sucking Josh's cock while changing position. He pressed his hard dick up closer to Josh's face.

Josh put his mouth around the head of Kevin's cock; Kevin moaned and gently pushed it in farther. Josh caressed it with his tongue and then swallowed it to the hilt on Ziggy's next thrust. Kevin almost shot his load. "Unnnhh! Oh my god, Josh, how do you do that?"

Josh couldn't answer at the moment, of course; his mouth and throat were occupied.

Kevin was in all the way, with his balls pressed up against Josh's nose. Then Josh flexed his throat by swallowing around the cock that was thrust deep inside it. That was it. Kevin groaned and started shooting deep into Josh's mouth. "Unnhh! Unnnnh!"

Ziggy continued fucking Josh's ass. Josh let Kevin's cockhead slip out of his throat so he could taste the spurting cum.

Kevin had Josh's dick in his mouth and sucked hard.

"Mmmmphhh! Mmmmmph!" That did it; Josh was spurting and Kevin was swallowing his cum as fast as it pumped out.

Ziggy thrust hard into Josh one more time and yelled, "Ahhhhh!" He pressed his cock deep into Josh and held it there while his balls emptied. "Ahhhh! Ahhhh! Ahhhh!"

Ziggy's thrust put Kevin's cock back down Josh's throat, which was okay with both of them. Kevin was still milking Josh's cock for the last of his cum. He moaned when Josh swallowed him again.

Three cocks spurting together. First Kevin, then Josh, then Ziggy.

—

WHEN IT WAS FINALLY OVER, when every dick had sputtered its last spurt, they relaxed. Kevin and Josh let each other's cocks out of their mouths. Ziggy's cock stayed deep inside Josh while Ziggy held him close. Kevin switched positions again and then he wrapped his arm around Josh and Zig.

They held each other close while their hearts stopped racing. Cozy and warm. They might have fallen back to sleep if they hadn't already slept so long.

Kevin was the first to speak. "A good thing I woke up when I did, eh? I almost missed everything."

"Kev, we were gonna wake you up, but one thing led to another. I'm glad you woke up, dude. We would never want to leave you out of things, never."

Kevin laughed. "That's quite alright. I'm honored you feel comfortable fucking right next to me. So very sexy. And all that shaking and moaning served to wake me up in time. Thank you, gentlemen, for letting me join in."

—

IT WAS SUNDAY. Kevin took them on a driving tour of the Jensen Beach area, for what few sights there were to see. And of course they spent some time together on the beach and in the ocean.

No one spoke of what was to come the next day. Josh's car would be repaired, and then it was on to Fort Lauderdale and goodbye to Kevin.

What at first was a great disappointment for the boys, being stranded in Jensen Beach with car troubles, had turned out to be a blessing. But now Fort Lauderdale didn't seem to be the wonderful destination it had been just two days ago.

Like it or not, though, that was the plan. They knew Kevin had been overly generous as it was, putting them up until their car was fixed. The boys couldn't ask for more than that.

As the hours went by, everyone became more and more melancholy.

Kevin would be sad to see them leave – it seemed that this friendship was just getting started – but he couldn't ask them to abandon the plans they'd probably been making all year. Still, he knew he'd never forgive himself if he didn't let them know they were welcome.

"So, my guess is you men are about halfway through this anniversary vacation of yours. How long have you been planning it?"

"For a year," Ziggy said. "We took a trip last year to Memphis, and when it was over we knew we wanted to go somewhere again this year."

"Washington, D.C. for starters?"

"Yeah, where Josh was raised. So he could show me around. You know, where he hung out, went to school, stuff like that."

"And then you drove down to Orlando because you wanted to go to Disneyworld."

"Yeah, but mostly we came to Florida to hang out on an ocean beach; that was the main idea."

"'An ocean beach' such as Fort Lauderdale?"

"Well, it seemed like as good a place as any. I don't expect it'll be any better than Jensen Beach, but we'll find out."

"It's a busier place, you may like that. And no doubt there will be others your own age there to meet."

"We don't care about meeting other people. We already met the coolest guy ever. No one at Fort Lauderdale is gonna be a buddy like you, Kevin. We're just gonna go someplace where nobody knows us and hang out on our own."

"Well, I know you'll enjoy each other's company as much as ever, but I'm curious; why go to Fort Lauderdale if you're going to stay to yourselves? You could do that anywhere."

"It's the plan we came up with, Kev. Josh wanted to go. Josh, you still want to go there?"

"No. Anyplace will do. I don't care."

"Well hell. In that case . . . Kevin, do you know of any little beach towns that might be cheap to stay at? We don't need much, just a clean, cheap room somewhere, and the ocean."

"I can suggest a few places, my friends, but . . . you could stay here, you know."

Chapter 39
CELEBRATE

"IF YOU PREFER to go off and be alone together, I would certainly understand, especially on your anniversary. But you're welcome to stay with me for the remainder of your vacation. I'd enjoy that immensely."

Ziggy and Josh looked at each other.

"Kevin, you're asking us to stay with you? All week?"

"Yes, that's exactly what I had in mind. If you'd like to."

Ziggy and Josh grinned and gave each other a high-five. "Yes!" They were nearly jumping up and down they were so happy.

"Kevin, put your hand up, bro." Ziggy slapped their palms together. "You really want us to? Are you sure?"

"Of course I do. As much fun as we've had, and as fond as I am of both of you, nothing else makes sense. Then it's settled? You're staying?"

"Hell yes!"

—

EVERYONE'S SPIRITS were suddenly high, now that the whole week was ahead of them. Six more days together.

"Fuck, we ought to celebrate." Ziggy said.

"What did you have in mind, Mr. Z?"

"Hell, I don't know; just more of the usual, I guess." Ziggy grinned.

"That sounds fine to me," Kevin said. "The 'usual' has been quite special. But let's go out to dinner tonight. My treat this time, gentlemen. I have a place in mind that I think you'll like. It's only a half mile from the condo; we can walk there. We can have a drink or two at home, first. Or a smoke."

"Or both," Ziggy said.

"Well, why not? We do have a lot to celebrate. Your anniversary, for one."

"And our friendship with you, Kevin. That's the other."

—

DINNER WAS FUN. They got a buzz before they left home: a glass of wine each and a few hits of cannabis. Then it was a short walk to the restaurant, a popular place called Café Coconuts. Florida cuisine again, naturally. Seafood was their choice, along with a couple of cocktails each.

By the time they returned home they were as happy as ever, and a little tipsy. As soon as they were inside the door they raced to strip off all their clothes. Kevin had quickly come to enjoy the nudity as much as Ziggy and Josh did. It wasn't to have sex, although being naked did tend to facilitate that – arousal could be contagious.

Skinny-dipping had also become part of the daily routine, but it wasn't dark enough for that yet.

Kevin suggested a game.

"What kind of game?" Josh asked.

"Anything," Kevin said. "Do you have any suggestions? Board game, cards, anything. Perhaps you men can teach me something new. Some sort of party game."

"Zig knows a really great version of strip poker," Josh said, "but I guess that wouldn't work too well at the moment."

"We'd have to get dressed to play it," Kevin said.

"Yeah, never mind. Um, Spin the Bottle is another one. But I don't know if we have enough people for that. How about Truth or Dare? Have you ever played that, Kev?"

"I've heard of the game, but no, I don't even know the rules, how it works. I'm up for anything though. Let's play."

"Kevin," Ziggy said, smiling, "you should know the rules before you agree to play."

"Alright then. Go ahead, please. Fill me in."

"It goes around from one person to the next. One dude asks the next dude, 'Truth or Dare?' The one who is being asked chooses which, and then the first player asks him a question or dares him to do something. And the guy has to do the dare. Or answer the question truthfully. If he doesn't, or if he doesn't do it right, then he has to do another one that's even worse. Until he gets it right."

"People dream up all kinds of stuff that's crazy or embarrassing," Josh said. "But you want to be careful about asking someone to do something you wouldn't be willing to do yourself."

"Yeah, that can come back at you, big time. Anyway, after the dude completes his task, then he asks the next player, 'Truth or Dare?' And it goes around and around like that."

"Good grief," Kevin said. "And how do you win?"

"Oh, jeez, uh, by sticking it out longer than everyone else, I guess. People drop out sometimes when they're not willing to do one. But eventually everyone agrees to end it. And everybody wins because everyone has a fun time."

"Except the one who has to flash a stranger and gets arrested for indecent exposure."

"Aw, nobody would make you do something like that, Kev. Nothing that would get you in trouble. Well, you do have to be, um, cautious when you do some of the wilder ones. But like Josh said, you can always drop out."

"When Zig played this at the orphanage," Josh said, "they made each other do all sorts of crazy stuff. Run outside naked for starters. And when they were horny there was no telling what they'd dare each other to do."

"We played it in high school a few times, too, Josh. It can be different when you get older. The Truth gets trickier than the Dares, sometimes."

"Oh, goodness. I don't think I'm ready for that. Perhaps some other evening, when I feel more daring."

"Aw, Kev. You know we wouldn't make you do anything we wouldn't do ourselves."

"Knowing you two daredevils, you'd be willing to do just about anything." Kevin sighed. "Perhaps I've not completed the 'untwisting' process yet."

"That's what it is, dude. No problem. You've already gone further than most people would."

"There must be something fun we could play."

"What other kinds of board games do you have, besides that trivia one?"

"Scrabble. And Clue."

"Clue is fun, but Josh always wins."

"Scrabble, then?"

"Yeah, sure. Until it gets dark out."

"Kev, you don't have Twister, do you?"

"No, I don't. Now that would be an unusual game to play while naked, I must say." Kevin smiled.

"Josh, you are fucking brilliant. Let's buy us a Twister game tomorrow so we can play. Want to?" Ziggy grinned.

"Yeah! But, uh, does everyone really want to play? Kevin?"

"Yes, count me in, definitely. I've never played before but with you gentlemen? Naked? It's bound to be a lot of fun."

"I've never played it either," Josh said.

"Me neither," Ziggy said. "But fuck. Naked Twister. Brilliant."

—

WITH TWISTER ON THE AGENDA for later, Scrabble was the game of the moment. They set the game up outside. There was a large portion of the balcony that was secluded from the sight of any neighbors. As long as they kept within that area outside, there was no need to wear clothes. So, even when they were out in the fresh air and sunlight – or moonlight – they could be naked and free. As the week went on it became one of their favorite spots.

After dark that night, they took a break from Scrabble to venture out to the ocean. Once again, for a naked swim. With the usual playful touching and teasing and hugging. Again, without actually having sex. It was more like foreplay; they didn't go skinny-dipping to have sex. Of course, it was always a possibility.

Sex would never be something they planned ahead of time; not between these close friends. When it happened, it occurred spontaneously. Kevin's bed was the most frequent location, often in the middle of the night. They would cuddle up with each other in the evening and happily fall asleep in each other's arms, typically with hard cocks pressed against naked bodies held close.

Later during the night, perhaps while dreaming, or possibly half-awake, little movements here and there would gradually become more insistent until eventually stiff erections found their way into willing mouths or holes or crevices. Or simply rubbed against whatever smooth bare skin was available. Frottage, it is sometimes called. Whether by sucking, fucking, or rubbing, every night without fail the men's bodies moved with dreamy intent toward orgasms.

No discussion was needed. In fact, one didn't need to be fully awake to enjoy the exquisite interaction and the eventual release. Afterwards they would fall back to sleep and do it again a few hours later.

Their days were just as enjoyable. Sex was not as frequent as it was during the night, but never a day went by without at least one ecstatic session of three-way intimacy, whether in the living room, bedroom, or their favorite place on the balcony.

One late night the boys decided they wanted to have sex down on the beach. They tried to talk Kevin into joining them, but sex in plain view on the beach, even that late at night, was a little outside of his comfort zone. He encouraged them to go ahead without him, if they wanted to, and they did.

Kevin gave them a big blanket to take down with them, to keep the sand off.

It was a thrill for both of them, doing it out in the open. They took turns fucking each other, flip-flopping back and forth between top and bottom. They prolonged it as long as possible, but finally Ziggy couldn't hold off any longer and shot his load inside Josh. Then they switched and Josh blew his load fucking Ziggy.

There was a quarter moon that night; it rose from the ocean around midnight and provided a small amount of light. Still, realistically no one could see them, certainly not clearly, unless someone actually walked up on them on the beach. Which didn't happen. After fucking, they played in the sand for a while.

Then Josh remembered something he wanted to tell Ziggy.

"Zig, we're gonna try doing some role-play someday, right? After we get home, I mean."

"Uh, yeah, if you want to, sure."

"Don't you remember, Danny talked about it before we left his house? You liked the idea then. Tying him up and making him suck our cocks until we come in his mouth."

"Oh yeah, right. Yeah, that did sound hot. Sure, we can try something like that sometime."

"And then we talked about it again while the car was being fixed."

"Yeah, I remember."

"So, I was thinking, after we get back home in St. Louis, when we try doing role-play? I want to do that thing Kevin was talking about with his roommate in college. Don't you think that would be hot?"

"Uh, you're talking about Kevin pretending to be asleep, and his roommate Sammy walking around naked?"

"Yeah."

"With a hard on?"

"Yeah."

"Until he was so horny he was dripping pre-cum?"

"Yeah."

"And then locking the door and what he did with Kevin?"

"Yeah, exactly."

"Uh, let me guess: with me being Sammy, and you Kevin?"

"Yes!"

"You got it, bro." Ziggy grinned.

—

SO THEN THEY WERE horny again.

Instead of getting each other off again on the beach, however, they decided to go back to the condo, take a quick shower, and make Kevin suck them off. They knew he'd enjoy it, and they planned to pleasure him as well.

He was asleep, but he woke up quickly, to find two hard dicks playfully slapping him in the face. He gladly serviced them, one after the other. Then they returned the favor, but they wouldn't allow him to come, not until he literally begged them to let him shoot his load. Then, together the boys licked and sucked him until he shot cum all over their faces.

The days and evenings were filled with conversation. Josh and Ziggy found Kevin fascinating. Kevin, in turn, was just as interested in learning all about his new friends. They had breakfasts with tea or coffee out on the balcony, took picnic lunches out to the beach, and cooked dinner meals together, the whole time sharing with each other insights regarding their philosophies, and facts about their lives.

Josh's car was retrieved from the shop on Monday. While they were out they purchased a game of Twister, but it lay unopened and unused in a corner of their bedroom. The days were full as it was, with conversation and trips to the beach. The nights were a treasure – cuddling, and the sex that it often led to.

The week seemed to last forever.

Until Friday approached. Suddenly their time together seemed much too short. The drive to St. Louis was to be a long one, and Saturday morning was when they planned to depart. Friday would be their last full day together.

Friday

THEY AWOKE in each other's arms, as usual, with fresh memories of dreamy fucking, sucking, and frottage. First on the agenda was a shower in Kevin's Jacuzzi: their way of greeting the morning, as well as washing off all the cum.

There seemed to be an unspoken agreement not to let the sadness of parting spoil their last full day together. As Ziggy had said before, every moment is precious, and if you dwell on the past or the future too much, you miss out on those moments.

Kevin made it clear that they should stay with him again the next year, for two weeks if they could manage it. He said he would pay for their airfare, and wouldn't abide any argument otherwise.

They had a late breakfast out on the balcony. Nude, as always.

Everyone did their part to keep the mood cheery. Josh remembered the Twister game and asked if they were still going to play; Twister immediately became part of the plans for the evening. Kevin offered to take them out to dinner again, but the boys insisted they would rather hang out at 'home' and enjoy each other's companionship there.

"So it's going to take you gentlemen three days to get back to St. Louis?"

"Yep. We were gonna do it in two days and have all day Monday to recover," Josh said, "but we decided to stop in Memphis to pick up a friend of ours. He'll put us up on Sunday night and then we'll drive to St. Louis on Monday."

"Actually, he's a friend of *yours*, Josh. I haven't even met him yet. Saw him once from a distance, that's all."

"Yeah, but Zig, you guys are gonna like each other, I know. So he'll be your friend too, in a couple days."

"Well, that's what I figure too. Anyway, I know you'll be glad to see your bro."

"Hell yes. It's been a year."

"So he's a good friend, is he?" Kevin said. "What's his name?"

"Tony. And yeah, Kevin, he's the best friend I have in Memphis. The only real friend I have there, actually."

"Josh and Tony suck each other off sometimes, Kev, that's how good of friends they." Ziggy grinned.

"Aw, Zig, we only did that once."

"Okay, but you said you jacked off together a lot."

"Once or twice a week, I guess."

"See, Kevin? They're jack-off buddies. And dude's gonna sleep with us the whole time he's there. At least a week, maybe two."

"Tony doesn't know it yet, though. He probably thinks he'll be sleeping on the couch. Boy, is he gonna be surprised. I'll bet he tries to get you to fuck him the very first night, Zig."

Ziggy laughed. "Wouldn't take much to talk me into it. Not if he's as cute and funny as I remember him."

"I think maybe I'd like to fuck him too," Josh said. "I mean, if it's alright with you. *That* would surprise the hell out of him. He doesn't know I like fucking now. If you don't want me to, though, I won't."

"I don't mind. You gonna let him fuck you? Or does he do that?"

"He's more of a bottom, but he'll fuck guys sometimes."

"Sounds like anything goes, then."

"But I don't know if I want anybody besides you fucking me, Zig."

"If you fuck him he'll probably want to fuck you too."

"Maybe."

"Oh, goodness," Kevin said. "It sounds as if you two will enjoy your visitor in more ways than one. I'm already envious. But I can't say I haven't had my proper share of you. It's only fair someone else should enjoy your companionship, too."

"Well, the sex would be fun, but mainly I'm just glad we're gonna get to see each other and talk and stuff. If I hadn't met Fred first, Kevin, Tony might have been my boyfriend. I think he wanted to be."

"Is that right?"

"Yeah. But everything turned out perfect. Tony's still a good friend, and I'm with Ziggy, the guy I was meant to be with all along."

"In the cosmic scheme of things?"

"Yeah."

"I have no doubt."

Chapter 40
Lucky

JUST AS ZIGGY AND JOSH HAD REQUESTED, the day went much like the previous days. After breakfast there was a visit to the beach, and then a break from the sun back in the condo. A quick shower, and then more conversation while they relaxed in the living room and on the balcony. Then back to the beach.

Then it was back upstairs; everyone agreed that a short nap sounded good, so after another quick shower they cuddled up together in Kevin's bed and pretended to sleep.

Random rubbing and stroking eventually led to more. One thing led to another and they all ended up shooting their cum. No cleanup required, either: Ziggy sucked Josh's cock, getting closer than ever to swallowing his whole dick. Kevin, in the meantime, did the same to Zig. Then after Kevin got a mouthful of Ziggy's cum and Josh shot his load down Ziggy's throat, Josh finished Kevin off the same way.

When they had their hormones under control again, they did fall asleep, but not for long. They still had part of the afternoon and the whole evening left. Josh and Kevin got going with planning dinner and putting it together, while Ziggy stayed close by and helped when he could.

It was just a normal day, exactly what they wanted on their last full day together. Dinner went well, leaving them with a slight buzz from a bottle of wine.

After dinner it was time for a smoke. Kevin had his reserve to draw from, and now Ziggy and Josh had retrieved their little stash from Josh's car as well, so there was no shortage. They sat in the living room, bare-ass naked as always, getting stoned together.

Ziggy told Kevin the story about when he first started to smoke. Kevin, just as Josh had been a year ago, was amazed.

"And you really are bisexual," Kevin said.

"Yeah, most definitely," Ziggy said. "But you know what? Josh was the first gay dude I ever met who was willing to take me at face value. He liked me for who I am, Kevin. He didn't want me to change."

"Bravo, Josh. That's not always an easy stance to take."

"I wanted to be his friend," Josh said. "That's the only way you can be somebody's friend, is to accept him the way he is. Ziggy was the same with me. He's happy with me just the way I am."

"If someone described you two to me, individually," Kevin said, "I'd probably wonder, you two having such differences, how you manage to get along so well. But being around you, talking to you, seeing the two of you interact, it's so obvious. If there were ever any two people made to be together, it's you. The only miracle is that you found each other."

"Yeah," Ziggy said, "for sure. But it's the same way with every-body, isn't it? When you've got something good, seems like the whole universe had to come together just right to make it happen. You and Drew, for example. What if your dorm rooms had been on two different floors? You might not have even met, let alone become partners."

"Yes, good point. So many variables involved. We're lucky we even attended the same school. But Drew and I had similar interests, and similar outlooks. Once we met it wasn't a surprise for us to get along with each other."

"Josh and I have similar interests. We both like to read, like to go for long walks, don't watch TV, we're nudists at heart; so many things . . . and the sex thing, hell, we're about as compatible as any two people can be. He turns me on, I turn him on, and we have great sex together. You couldn't ask for more. And we love each other, Kev. More than anything."

"I think we're in agreement," Kevin said, smiling. "You two are a perfect match."

"Yeah." Ziggy grinned.

"And I'm honored to be friends with you. This isn't the last we'll see of each other, rest assured. And in the meantime, there's the telephone, and letters."

"Fuck, I hate that we have to leave in the morning."

"Ah, well, we just have to make the best of it, don't we?"

"Yep," Josh said. "Kevin, we're gonna miss you."

"Not any more than I will miss you, Josh. I think we all know how much we care for each other. So, let's enjoy being together while we still can."

"Damn right," Ziggy said. "What do you want to do now, guys?"

"We still have that Twister game to play," Josh said.

"Yes, I'm looking forward to that," Kevin said. "There's another game you mentioned that I would like to try, too. I think we have enough people to play a few rounds, if you're willing."

"What's that?"

"Um, Spin the Bottle." Kevin had a sheepish grin on his face. "I've never in my life played it. It's not too late, is it? There's certainly no one I'd rather play it with."

"Kev, it's never too late," Ziggy said.

"I'll play, Kevin. I'd love to," Josh said. "I've never played it, either. Zig, have you?"

"Yeah, in high school a few times, when we got all the girls to hang out with us. It's fun."

"Did any guys kiss each other when you played it?"

"Nah. We probably should have played it that way, but you know how high school is. Or was. Maybe it's changed by now. Anyway, if Kevin wants to play Spin the Bottle – dudes, I'm up for it. Whatever Kevin wants." Ziggy grinned. "Let's find out who the best kisser is."

"Wonderful." Kevin went into the kitchen and rinsed out an empty wine bottle. "This is all we'll need, isn't it?"

"Yeah, that and our kissers. Well, actually, it wouldn't hurt to do a few more hits first. I kiss better when I'm stoned."

"Ha. You think you do, Zig," Kevin said, "but we'll be the judge of that."

"You're on, buster."

They sat on the living room floor in a circle and passed Kevin's pipe around. The goal being to get in a very nice frame of mind, without overdoing it to the point of being zoned out. They succeeded.

After it had gone around two or three times Ziggy said, "Yeah, perfect. Who's ready to smack lips?"

Kevin said "Ready steady."

Josh nodded his head. "Me too. Uh, is it as simple as I think it is, or are there rules?"

"Only rule is the guy who had the bottle pointed at him on the last turn is the one who spins the bottle this turn. And he has to kiss whoever it points to when it stops."

"How do we decide who spins first?"

"That's easy – you, Kevin. You go first."

"Yeah," Josh said. "Go for it, Kev."

"Okay." They were already sitting in a circle on the floor; Kevin placed the bottle on its side in the middle. He looked at the boys with a sheepish grin again. "This will be a bit ridiculous, I'm afraid. Not nearly enough people playing, are there?"

"Kevin, no, we've got plenty of people. As long as there's more than two, that's random enough to work." Ziggy smiled.

"Well, you're both very kind. Thanks for indulging me." Kevin held the bottle steady and then gave it a good spin. It stopped between Ziggy and Kevin.

"Yes! Dude, get ready for the best kiss of your life." Zig rose up on his knees and shuffled over closer to Kevin.

Kevin giggled. "Oh, my." He got up on his knees and watched Ziggy's face. Ziggy licked his lips once to get them wet, and Kevin did the same. Then they leaned toward each other.

Ziggy tilted his head just a little and gently touched his lips to Kevin's. Kevin closed his eyes; Ziggy put his tongue out and licked Kevin's lips.

Kevin parted his lips and let Ziggy into his mouth. Their tongues played swordfight; they did that for a minute or two, then Ziggy said, "Mmmmmmmm," withdrew his tongue, and kissed Kevin a dozen different places on his face.

Kevin held his eyes shut a few more seconds and then opened them, grinning. "That's all I get?"

"Yeah, bro. For now. Game's not over yet." Ziggy smiled. "Must have been good – your dick is getting hard."

Kevin looked down at his chub. "Another half minute and it would have been standing at attention."

"My turn to spin." Ziggy sat down cross-legged again and spun the bottle.

It twirled around and finally stopped between Josh and Kevin – but unquestionably closer to Kevin.

"Pucker up again, Kev." Ziggy moved up close to him. Kevin's cock was already rising higher. He moved closer to Zig and they kissed again. Even longer, this time. When they were done, Kevin was fully hard and Ziggy was on the rise. "Kevin, you kiss good," Ziggy said.

"Not as good as you, 'dude.' Really Zig, where did you learn to kiss? You have me as hard as I can be."

"George started me out on kissing – we kissed each other all over. He said that's what people do when they fuck. Then later, my punk buddies' girlfriends showed me a bunch of stuff. How to get them off, basically. That always included kissing." Ziggy looked at Josh, and down at his hard dick. "Jesus, Josh, this really has you turned on, huh?"

"I love to kiss," Josh said. "I can't wait till it's my turn."

It was Kevin's spin again. This time the bottle chose Josh.

"Yes!" Josh got up on his knees and scooted over to Kevin. They gently touched their lips together, and both of them closed their eyes. Josh licked Kevin's lips and then drew back an inch or two and opened his eyes.

Kevin waited for more.

Josh put his hands behind Kevin's head while he gently put his tongue inside Kevin's mouth. Kevin did the same to Josh. They kept their mouths together for a couple of minutes, licking and nibbling and tonguing each other. Kevin moaned and started leaking pre-cum when their hard cocks touched.

Finally they let go.

"Wow. That was hot," Kevin said. "I haven't kissed anyone that way for years. Josh, where did you learn to kiss so well?"

"From Zig," Josh said. "After I met him, I relearned every-thing."

"Give yourself credit, Josh. You caught on fast. All this stuff pretty much comes natural to you, sweetheart."

"Maybe from a previous life, then, because I never kissed any-one that way until I met you. Fred didn't even like to kiss."

"His loss, obviously," Kevin said.

"Fred was an ignorant asshole," Ziggy said. "Didn't know something good when it was staring him in the face."

"Good thing, too," Josh said. "I might have stayed with him if he was a little nicer, but if I had, it would have been with the wrong person."

They all looked at each other.

"Josh," Ziggy said, "it's your spin."

"Oh, right." Josh set it turning, and when it stopped, it pointed at Zig.

"Cool. My favorite guy to kiss," Josh said. They moved up to each other and Josh took hold of Ziggy's hands. They held hands while they gently, lovingly kissed.

"You guys," Kevin said. "Oh goodness, you love each other so much. It's wonderful."

Ziggy's cock was fully hard now. "Yeah. And he turns me on like crazy when he kisses me like that. Fuck." All three of them looked at Ziggy's stiff boner. "Kev, have you had enough, or do you want to keep playing?"

"Oh, please, let's play at least a couple more turns. This is too good to stop yet."

"Okay, my turn then." Ziggy spun the bottle and it chose Josh again. "Oh yum." They kissed again. Another long, soulful kiss.

Then it was Josh's spin. The bottle stopped at Kevin. They kissed even longer this time. Kevin was leaking pre-cum again.

"Okay," he said, when they finally let go of each other. "Maybe I should stop now. Another kiss like that and I'll have an orgasm."

"Orgasms are good, Kevin."

"Yes, but I don't want to come yet. It feels wonderful just the way it is. And we still have a game of Twister to play, which promises to be equally exciting."

"In that case," Ziggy said, "Maybe we could take a break? Anyone up for a walk on the beach?"

Chapter 41
TWILIGHT

THE OCEAN was as welcoming as ever. They had thrown some clothes on and followed the now-familiar route down from Kevin's condo, outside and over the dunes to the beach.

There wasn't much talk at first. Ziggy and Josh were trying to soak up the beach atmosphere, as though they could store some away for later. Enjoying what might be their last visit to the beach until the following year. They weren't sad, really; they felt content more than anything else.

"It's been a fulfilling week, hasn't it, gentlemen?"

"Absolutely," Josh said. "It's been incredible."

"Never dreamed we would have *this* great a time in Florida," Ziggy said. "Meeting you was the best part, Kev. And you never did 'fall off the ride,' dude. You hung on and enjoyed every minute. Same as we've been doing."

"It's been a week like no other, my friends. Making the acquaintance of such a wonderful pair of young men was sheer luck, and my good fortune. And you both have been so accommodating. Thank you for being so generous with yourselves."

"You've been the generous one, bro."

"Ah, but I received so much in return. Just your friendship alone, that's been wonderful. And the 'untwisting,' well, suffice it say I'll never be the same. All for the better, of course."

"All to resume next year, same time, same place," Josh said.

"Yes. Indeed."

They sat on the beach and watched the clouds turn pink in the twilight.

—

WHEN THE SUN HAD SET and the sky was getting darker, the three men looked at each other.

"Well," Ziggy said, "we could wait until it's dark enough to swim bare-ass, or we could do something else first and swim later."

"Something else?"

"Yeah, like naked Twister." Ziggy grinned.

"Yeah," Josh said. "Let's play Twister."

"Sounds perfect to me." Kevin smiled.

Once again, as soon as the condo door was closed they raced each other to strip naked. Kevin already had a hard-on. Josh ran into the bedroom and brought the game out.

"Let's smoke again first," Ziggy said. "We should be nice and buzzed for this. You know, all touchy-feely sensitive and stuff. It'll make us hornier too." He smiled.

"If that's possible," Kevin said. "I still have an erection from those wonderful kisses we shared earlier."

They sat in the living room and passed the pipe around. Josh opened the Twister box and pulled out the directions.

"Okay," Josh read, "the spinner is used to determine where the players have to put their hand or foot. It's divided into four sections: right foot, left foot, right hand, and left hand. Each section is divided into the four colors."

Ziggy handed Josh the pipe. Josh took a hit and passed it to Kevin. He blew out his smoke and continued reading.

"After spinning, the combination is called out (example: right hand yellow) and players must move their matching hand or foot to a circle of the correct color. No two people can have a hand or foot on the same circle."

"So, like, we're all gonna have our left hand on the same color but on different circles? And likewise with the other hand, and each foot?"

"Yeah, that's exactly right."

"Fuck, tied up in knots is a good way to put it. And we'll be naked." Ziggy grinned. "Naked knots of flesh."

"I don't see how we'll be able to spin it while we're playing," Kevin said. "Not if we're 'tied up in knots.'"

"Good point," Josh said. "Hold on, I think it says something about that. Okay. Yeah. Optional game without a referee. One player calls the name of the limb to be moved and the next player calls the color of the circle it must be moved to. Players take turns calling the limb and color."

"That ought to work."

"A person is eliminated when they fall or when their elbow or knee touches the mat."

"I got this game licked," Ziggy said, smiling. "One way or another."

Josh said, "Is everybody ready?"

"Hell yeah."

"Yes, quite ready."

"Okay," Josh said.

He unfolded the plastic mat with the brightly-colored circles and spread it out in the middle of the living room.

"We each stand on different sides. Kevin, you could stand in the middle of the red side. Zig, you stand on the end there on Kevin's left and I'll stand here on Kevin's right." Then Ziggy's cock started rising. "Jeez, Zig, you're getting a hard-on, too? You guys are making me horny with your hard dicks."

"This is gonna be kinky," Ziggy said. His cock continued to rise until it was high and hard. "Can you imagine a whole room full of naked people playing this?"

Josh took his place. The three of them faced each other, totally nude, Ziggy and Kevin with boners, and Josh's rising.

"Kevin, you go first, call the hand or the foot, and then Zig, you call the color we have to put it on."

"Alright. Um, left foot."

Ziggy said, "Red."

Kevin already had both feet on red; he moved his left foot one circle to the left, spreading his legs apart.

Ziggy moved toward Kevin, taking his left foot from yellow to the red circle between Kevin's legs. Zig was partially blocking any forward movement from Kevin now.

Ziggy grinned. "Got you boxed in, Kev."

Josh moved his foot from blue to the red circle on Kevin's right.

"So far so good," Ziggy said. "Kevin, you might be in trouble, dude, with me in your way."

"I would imagine things change fast in this game," Kevin said. "As it stands right now, Zig, in case you haven't noticed, we could rub our erections together with very little effort."

"Want to try it?"

"Oh, goodness, no. I'm sure I would ejaculate all over you."

"All the more reason."

"Zig, you call the limb this time," Josh said. "And then I'll call the color."

"Okay, uh, right hand."

"Green."

"Oh shit. Why the hell did I put myself with my back to everything?" Ziggy looked behind him for his options. "Fuck, I'm gonna have to lean backwards for this." He nearly fell over putting his hand on a green circle.

Josh leaned forward and put his right hand on the circle next to Ziggy's hand, and then Kevin put his hand in the one next to Josh's. Kevin's arm was on top of Josh's arm, and the rest of his body leaned over Ziggy's left leg.

"Jesus. We've only had two turns and we're already all over each other. And bent every which way."

"Ready for the next turn?"

"Fuck yes. I can't hold this position forever."

"This time I call the limb," Josh said, "and then Kevin calls the color. I'll call . . . left hand." Everyone still had the left hand free, but not for long.

Kevin said, "Yellow."

"Fuck, thank god," Ziggy said. He put his left hand down on the nearest yellow and steadied himself. He was ass-backwards with his hard dick sticking straight up in the air.

Josh didn't have much choice. He leaned over top of Ziggy's upper torso and put his left hand on the yellow circle beyond Zig.

"Jesus, Josh, why don't you put your dick in my face?"

"I can't help it, Zig!"

"I'm not complaining. Fuck, I think I could actually suck you from here." Ziggy moved his head over a bit and licked Josh's cockhead. Josh got stiff as nails in about two seconds.

"Unnnh. Jesus, Zig. You're gonna make me come."

Kevin put his left hand over and below Ziggy's side to get to the easier of the two yellow circles he could reach. This put him partially over Josh's upper torso, and directly above Ziggy's waist. Kevin and Ziggy looked at each other.

"Ziggy, you look as if you'll collapse any minute."

"I might," he said. "But I'm holding on for now. I'm gonna win this game, damn it." He grinned. "And maybe suck off Josh while I'm at it."

"Speaking of fellatio, Mr. Z, your boner seems to be quite convenient to my mouth," Kevin said.

"Go for it, Kev." Ziggy grinned again.

Chapter 42
SHARING OF WATER

KEVIN ANGLED HIS HEAD toward Zig and licked his shaft.

"Oh fuck! I was just kidding. Oh shit. Unnnnnh."

Kevin went even further: he put Ziggy's hard cock inside his mouth and moved his tongue up and down it.

"Unnnnnh! Fuck, Kev, that's cheating. You're gonna make me fall, dude."

Kevin couldn't talk, he had his mouth full. "Mmmmmph."

"Damn it, I'm gonna suck Josh, then." Ziggy put his mouth back on Josh's hard cock and sucked hard.

"Ohhhhhhh." Josh arched his body further into Ziggy's mouth. "Oh fuck. I'm gonna come, Zig! Coming!"

While Josh moaned and spurt, Kevin sucked harder on Ziggy's cock. Ziggy shivered. "Unnnnnh. Mmmmmmm. MMMM!" He started erupting in Kevin's mouth.

Zig thought for sure he'd fall, but he was still up off the floor, shooting wads of cum into Kevin's sucking mouth while he sucked Josh's balls dry. "Mmmmmph. Mmmmmph!"

Josh was in ecstasy. "Ahhhh! Ahhhh!" His body shook, arching with each spurt of his cum. Suddenly he collapsed on top of Zig.

Ziggy couldn't hold up both himself and Josh. Ziggy collapsed and fell on the floor, with Josh on top of him, and Josh's cock still in his mouth. Ziggy's cock slipped out of Kevin's mouth; Kevin groaned in dismay. Then Kevin gave out and fell on top of Josh and Zig, all of them in one pile.

Ziggy shot a couple more good spurts of cum, which landed on Kevin's face. Meanwhile Josh's cock was pushed deeper into

Ziggy's throat. Josh moaned. Ziggy swallowed; Josh moaned louder.

Kevin saw what was going on and was afraid Ziggy couldn't breathe, so he rolled over to take his weight off Josh and lay flat on his back next to Zig.

Josh knew his dick was jammed down Ziggy's throat and the last thing he wanted to do was hurt Zig, so he lifted himself up and out of Ziggy's mouth.

Ziggy moaned. "Ohhhh fuck," he said. He looked up at Josh's cock and lifted his head to lick it one more time.

"That was totally crazy," Josh said. Then he saw Kevin's hard dick, wet with pre-cum, and grabbed it, pulling it toward his mouth.

"No Josh! Ohhhh fuck, I'm coming!"

Josh quickly swallowed Kevin's spurting dick. "Mmm."

"Oh! Unnnnh! Unnnh!" Kevin bucked up, shooting warm cum into Josh's mouth.

Ziggy laughed, watching Josh suck Kevin's cock and gulp down his load.

When Josh had gotten the last of Kevin's cum, he let loose of Kevin and relaxed, face down, half on Kevin and half on Zig. Kevin and Ziggy both put an arm around Josh and the three of them lay still, catching their breath.

The first one to talk was Ziggy.

"I did it, Josh. Took your cock all the way, bro. Did it feel good?"

"Yeah, it did. But you didn't have much choice. I'm sorry I fell on you. I didn't mean to choke you. Jeez, Zig, that must have hurt."

"Naw, it didn't. That's what I've been trying to do for weeks. Finally did it." He grinned. "Just call me Deep Throat. Only for you, though, little buddy."

"Only if you want to, Zig."

Then Kevin spoke up. "That was most enjoyable. In a frantic sort of way, I mean. Very enjoyable."

"No kidding."

"Short game though."

"We'll have to try it again next year," Ziggy said. "Next time I won't make such a dumb move to start out with."

"I would say any move that leads to orgasms for everyone is a good move, all in all."

"And there isn't even any cum to clean up," Ziggy said.

"Oh yes there is. You came all over my face, young man."

Ziggy raised himself on his elbows and looked at Kevin. "Oh, fuck, did I do that?"

"Yes, and I'd appreciate it if you would do it at least once more before you men leave in the morning." Kevin smiled.

"I'll clean it off," Josh said. He put his mouth to work on Kevin's face and licked up Ziggy's cum.

Kevin giggled. "That tickles."

"Don't get us started on tickling again, Kevin."

"Oh? And why not?"

"Not until after we go skinny-dipping, at least. You guys up for it? Our last nude swim in the ocean this year, Josh."

"Hell yes."

"Wouldn't miss it," Kevin said.

—

THEY THREW ON THE MINIMUM clothes required to walk through the halls, and made their way down to the beach.

"Kev, that's the first time I've heard you swear, the whole time we've been here."

"I swore?"

"Yeah, when you were coming. You said, 'Fuck.'" Josh grinned. "You're getting more and more like us."

"Well, it's not as if I don't know the word. I must confess I do use it, sometimes, when talking to myself, driving. Or, rather, talking to other drivers."

"One of the best times to use it," Ziggy said. "Along with the word, 'asshole.'" They all laughed.

"And you said 'coming.' Not 'ejaculating,' but 'coming.'"

"One says all sorts of things at such times," Kevin said. "One can hope I will have another opportunity to speak so freely before you gentlemen leave in the morning."

It took Ziggy and Josh a few seconds to decipher that.

Then Ziggy laughed. "Oh, fuck yeah. At least one more time. We still have all night together." Ziggy grinned.

—

THERE WAS NO conversation while they prepared to get in the ocean; there was no need to talk. The mood was almost ceremonial. Their last sharing of the water, until next year.

First they removed their clothing and placed it on the sand. They looked at each other's nude bodies as if for the first time. There was something almost sacred about removing all pretense and being stark naked with such close friends.

Then they walked into the embracing waves, the endless repetition of the ocean's caress. Josh reached out and held Ziggy's hand, and then held his other hand out to Kevin.

They walked, hand in hand, further into the water, until it was waist high and the swells splashed as high as their nipples.

Ziggy moved around in front of the other two and dipped his hands into the water. He raised his hands above Josh and let the water fall over Josh's head.

"I hereby anoint thy honored self a member of the Brothers of Nakedity." Then he did the same with Kevin.

"What about you?" Josh said. He dipped his hands in the water and repeated the procedure above Ziggy's head. "There, now all three of us have been properly inducted." He laughed.

"You laugh?" Ziggy said. "Perhaps you do not take the Brothers of Nakedity seriously enough, my brother."

"Oh, but I do," Josh said. "Isn't nakedity something to feel joy over?"

"Yeah, good point."

"We need to think up a sacred sacrament to ingest," Kevin said. "Something to finalize our induction. Any ideas?"

"Well, I can think of something appropriate," Josh said, "but we just shot our loads a half hour ago; it might be too soon to do it again."

"Yeah," Ziggy said, "we can wait till later, there's no hurry."

They spent the next half hour horsing around, touching, splashing, hugging, teasing. And swimming, of course. But eventually they'd had enough of the water and went back upstairs.

They were in Kevin's Jacuzzi, washing off the salt and sand.

"What time do you men plan on leaving?"

"No certain time. Whenever we're ready," Ziggy said. "But fuck, I guess the earlier the better."

"You'll both need to be well-rested. We can't have you falling asleep at the wheel. Perhaps we should call it a night."

"Or at least go to bed," Josh said. "We don't necessarily have to go to sleep yet."

"Ah, quite right, Josh."

—

THEY LAY IN BED and talked for an hour or more. Snuggling, rubbing, switching places, snuggling some more, caressing each other, talking about anything and everything.

Kevin was in the middle, between the boys on the bed, when finally Josh said, "Zig, I think you and I ought to give Kevin a licking he won't forget."

"Something to remember us by, huh?"

"Yeah."

Ziggy looked at Kevin and grinned. "Yeah, okay."

"Wait a minute," Kevin said, "don't I get any say-so in this?"

"No, you don't. Now turn over so we can start on your butt. Ready Zig?"

Chapter 43
WHO'S NEXT

"ARE WE GONNA SPANK HIM, or lick him?"

"Uh, Kevin, do you want your ass licked or spanked?"

"Oh, licked, please. No pain, just pleasure."

"Good thing," Josh said. "I've never spanked anybody before. Not sure I'd know how."

"Not even birthday spankings?"

"Well, I received my fair share of those from my brothers, but I never got the opportunity to give back. I thought it felt kinda good, actually. As long as they didn't spank too hard."

Josh leaned down and licked the soft, smooth skin of one side of Kevin's butt. Ziggy joined him, licking the other ass cheek.

"Ahhh. Wonderful."

The boys licked his soft, firm ass for a few more minutes and then sat up.

"Okay, Kev," Josh said, "your choice. What do you want licked now?"

Kevin turned over on his back and his rigid cock stood straight up in the air, wet with pre-cum.

"Okay," Ziggy said, "you got it."

The boys put their heads down together and licked Kevin's shaft. Josh was on one side, Ziggy on the other, and their tongues frequently met.

"Ahhhh, so good." Kevin shivered.

Ziggy went lower and licked Kevin's balls.

"Unnnh."

Josh kept licking the shaft; he pressed harder now with his tongue.

"Ohhhh yes."

Ziggy put one of Kevin's balls inside his mouth, gently.

"Oh Zig." Kevin looked downward. "My god, I've never felt anything quite like that before."

Ziggy let it slip out of his mouth. "You like it?"

"Yes, it feels good when you're gentle with it that way."

Ziggy put the other ball in his mouth briefly, then let it go. Josh continued licking the shaft.

"You two have me getting close now."

Ziggy put his tongue back on Kevin's dick, opposite from Josh. They licked it, together, from the root almost up to the head.

"Oh yes, I won't last long if you keep that up," Kevin said.

They kept it up. Josh licked higher, touching the cockhead. That set Kevin off.

"Ohhhh. Now you've done it."

Ziggy moved his tongue up to the head of Kevin's cock and now both boys licked it relentlessly.

"Unnnh! Coming!"

Josh and Zig moved their mouths into the line of fire, faces pressed together. They both wanted Kevin's load, or at least their fair share of it.

Josh had his mouth open and the first spurt went directly inside.

"Unnnnnh!" Kevin's cock fired off a series of spurts. "Unnnnh!" Ziggy moved his mouth over and caught the next one, a good healthy rope of cum. The boys continued to lick the head and the shaft.

Kevin kept shooting; his sperm landed splat all over both boys' cheeks, lips, and chins. "Ahhhhhh!" Some of his cum remained on the head and shaft; the boys licked that up as soon as they saw it.

When Kevin was nearly finished, Ziggy put his mouth over Kevin's shaft and cleaned it up.

Josh licked Ziggy's face. Ziggy let the cock slip out of his mouth and positioned his face so Josh could get the cum off both sides of it.

When Josh was finished, he drew back a little. Ziggy licked Josh's face the same way, cleaning up what remained of Kevin's cum.

Kevin had collapsed, smiling. "Ahh, so good, gentlemen. Thank you."

"Our first serving of the sacrament," Josh said. "Two more to go."

"Yes," Kevin said. "Yes." He sat up and said, "Who's next?"

"Me," Ziggy said, grinning.

Chapter 44
BROTHERS

ZIGGY LAY DOWN FLAT on his back with his hard cock up in the air. "Don't make me come right away, okay? I'm close, so be careful."

Kevin leaned in and licked Ziggy's balls.

"Unnh. Yeah, that's good, Kev."

Josh licked the shaft.

"Oh fuck, two tongues at once."

Josh and Kevin gave Ziggy the same treatment Kevin had gotten just a few minutes previously. They tried to draw it out as long as possible, but it didn't take much.

"Jesus guys, get ready for a fuckload of cum."

Kevin and Josh moved their heads so their mouths were directly above the head of Ziggy's cock. They licked at his cockhead.

"Coming! Ohhhhh, fuck! Unnnnh!"

Josh caught the first spurt, right on his upper lip. He licked it into his mouth.

"Unnnnh! Unnnnnh!" Ziggy kept shooting.

Kevin caught most of the next spurt. Swallowed it and was ready for more.

"Ahhhhh!"

They held their heads in the line of fire and got their faces covered with at least a half dozen spurts of Ziggy's jizz.

Ziggy finally slowed down, and then Josh and Kevin took turns licking the cum off each other.

"Yummy," Kevin said.

"Yeah, his cum is sweet, isn't it?"

"Yes," Kevin said. "And I can't think of anyone else's face I'd rather lick it from."

Josh cleaned up the last few drops off of Ziggy's cock.

Ziggy sighed. "Nice. That was nice, guys. You both got some?"

"Oh, yes," Kevin said.

"Cool. Josh, you're turn, bro."

Josh lay down on his back in between Kevin and Ziggy. His dick was as hard as steel.

Kevin and Zig tongued Josh's balls and his cock, as well as each other, with the emphasis on Josh's handsome cock.

"Ahhhh, guys, I'm close. You want me to come? If you keep licking I'm gonna come."

They didn't let up. The licking was rhythmic and relentless.

"Guys I'm gonna . . . Ohhhhh fuck, here goes." Josh's cockhead grew larger and looked as if it was going to explode, and then it did. A thick rope of cum shot out suddenly and landed on Kevin's forehead. "Unnnnh!"

Ziggy wanted the next spurt, and he got it. He put his mouth up to Josh's dick and the cum shot right into it.

"Ahhhhh! Ahhhhh!" Josh kept spurting. Kevin received the next shot square on his lips and licked it in.

"Unnnnh!" Josh launched more ropes of cum, which were received eagerly. Finally his balls were empty and he relaxed. Ziggy and Kevin cleaned him off, and then licked each other to get the rest of what didn't go into their mouths directly.

After everyone was cleaned up, Kevin and Zig collapsed on opposite sides of Josh. No one talked for a few minutes while they recovered.

Finally Ziggy said, "Fuck, that was good. Wasn't it?"

"Hell yes," Josh said.

Kevin said, "Very much so. And now we're officially Brothers. Of, uh, what did you call it? Nakedity."

They lay there for a few minutes more, then Kevin said, "We probably should shower; we'll sleep better."

So they showered and got back into bed.

Saturday

ONCE AGAIN, they slept like played-out puppies, arms and legs draped over each other, random dreams playing out in their heads as they shared their last night together.

In the morning, one by one they woke up, but no one was in a hurry to end this intermingling of warm, familiar bodies. It was the last time in bed together until they visited next year.

Finally, Kevin said, "Well, unfortunately we can't stay in bed all day. We might as well face the music. Anyone hungry?"

Ziggy stretched and yawned. "Yeah, I am," he said. "But I can fix us something if you guys want to stay in bed a little longer."

"No, I've slept enough," Josh said. "Let's get up."

They showered together and then spent the next hour in the kitchen and on the balcony, preparing a hearty breakfast and then eating it in their favorite place for viewing the ocean.

After the meal, they sat naked in the living room together. They were reluctant to put clothes on, but they knew they had to.

Finally Ziggy said, "Well, I hate to do it, but I guess we better get dressed for driving." The boys went to their bedroom naked, and came out dressed. They put their backpacks at the front door.

Kevin also had put on some clothes. "How far do you plan on driving today?"

"To Atlanta."

Kevin wrote down his phone number and his address. "I'll be looking forward to a letter or postcard from you gentlemen once you get home, but call me collect if you have any problems. Perhaps you could call me from Atlanta once you get settled in for the night? Just so I know you made it that far."

"Will do, Kev."

"In fact I want you to call me anytime there is anything I can be of help with. You both are wise beyond your years, but it never hurts to get another opinion when you're in a quandary. I'm here if you need me."

"We'll be calling, count on it," Josh said. "If nothing else just to hear your voice."

"Would you like to take one last walk on the beach before you go?"

"Naw. We already did that last night," Ziggy said. "We'll just get in the car and go, I guess. Time to get on the road."

"Well, if you're leaving I'll walk down with you."

—

THEY SAID THEIR GOODBYES, gave each other good, long hugs, talked about next year, promised to write often or, better yet, call, and then they hugged again. Ziggy's eyes were glossy with tears, but he was full of smiles, as were Josh and Kevin. Parting was difficult – never had so much friendship been packed into one short week.

Car doors were finally closed, waves of farewell exchanged, and the boys in their Mustang finally pulled out onto Florida Route A1A going north.

Nothing was said for a few minutes. Then Ziggy spoke up.

"We had a good time, didn't we?"

"Hell yes," Josh said.

Ziggy sighed. "I hate saying goodbye."

Chapter 45
SMALL WORLD

THEY DROVE NORTH, through Orlando and northern Florida, and then into Georgia. It was uneventful and quiet.

Their second stop for gas was just off the interstate, twenty miles or so north of Valdosta, Georgia. Down at the end of the exit ramp there were two motels, six fast food restaurants, and four gas stations. Beyond those appeared to be a little town – a little patch of civilization that probably grew up about the same time as the Interstate.

Ziggy pulled up at the pumps and got out. He didn't see any sign of anyone, inside or out, but the gas pumps were working, so he started filling the tank. Josh stretched and then started walking off to use the restroom.

An attendant came running out of the store waving his arms and yelling, "Hey! Hey! Hey!" Ziggy didn't know what the trouble was, but it didn't seem promising. He quickly looked around for something he could use to be ready for . . . whatever crisis seemed to be approaching fast.

Josh, likewise, saw possible trouble brewing, although what it was he couldn't imagine. He hoped it didn't involve weapons or robbery. He turned and ran quickly back to Ziggy and the car. He got there about the same time the attendant did.

Ziggy held a windshield washer squeegee ready and wasn't afraid to use it, as a weapon or a shield, in case this yelling guy turned out to be dangerous.

The guy yelled, "Zig! Josh!"

Now, that was a surprise. This fellow knew their names?

"I can't believe it!" The guy said. Then he realized by their looks that they were more scared than anything else. He tore the uniform cap off his head and said, "It's Franklin, don't you recognize me? Franklin!"

Ziggy said, "Jesus. You scared the hell out of me."

"Me too," Josh said. "I thought the place was getting robbed. Franklin? Is it really you? No way!" Josh laughed. "Franklin, oh my god! I thought we'd never see you again."

Franklin grinned, and right there in the middle of his smile was that crooked tooth of his, quirky and cute as always. Josh held his arms out, Franklin tossed his cap into the air, and they gave each other a good, long hug. They held on to each other until their dicks started getting hard. Josh gently patted Franklin on the back and let go.

Ziggy was grinning from ear to ear. "Franklin you dog! This is too good to be true. Hell, we thought we'd lost you forever. Come on over here. Jesus dude, we're so happy to see you."

Ziggy held his arms out, and Franklin was happy to oblige. Franklin had a full woody by this time, but nobody seemed to care. They hugged each other until Ziggy was hard, too, and they still didn't stop. Finally, they let loose. None of them could stop grinning, they were so happy.

Franklin repositioned his boner and said, "Jesus. Is everybody in St. Louis so friendly?"

—

"FRANKLIN, WHAT THE HECK are you doing here?" Josh said.

"I done told you I was goin' to Macon. Well, I ain't too far off now am I? Just overshot it by a hundred miles, that's all. I stopped there first, actually."

"But what are the chances? Jeez. I never thought. God! How are you doing?"

"Aw, Josh, I guess I'm okay. Ain't nothin' to brag about but I'm still alive. Things'll get better one of these days. But it ain't gonna happen till I leave this place."

"That bad?"

"Worse. People here got it in for me and I ain't been nothin' but nice to 'em. A guy can't be hisself in this place. But I don't know how to be anybody else," he said. "Here, let me check your oil and shit."

Franklin raised the hood and followed the usual routine. Ziggy stood by the gas pump waiting for the tank to fill. Josh took the squeegee from Zig and started cleaning windows.

"So, where are you guys drivin' from?"

"Florida."

"I figured that much. I meant what part?"

"Jensen Beach."

"Oh. Never heard of it. But that don't mean shit, I ain't never been to Florida. And I don't plan on goin', neither. Already gone farther south than I wanted to."

"You'd like the ocean beaches, though," Josh said.

"Why didn't you go to Fort Lauderdale? That's where the fun is. From what I hear."

"That's exactly what we were gonna do, but we found another place that was even better."

"Cool." He shut the hood of the car. "I recognized your Mustang right off. You guys are darker now, though. Both of you. You got a good tan I'd say. That's what Florida sun'll do to ya. So, last time I saw you, you was on your way to Washington D.C. Did ya ever get there?"

"Oh sure. That same night. We looked around at the sights for a couple of days and visited with one of Josh's old school buddies we ran into. That's where he grew up, is D.C. After that we headed down to Florida."

"So where y'all headed off to now?"

"Memphis first, and then home to St. Louis." Ziggy checked the gas pump to see if it had stopped yet.

"Durn. I wish you was goin' to Knoxville, I'd ask you for a ride."

"But you just got here didn't you? Where are you staying?"

"I ain't been here two weeks and already I'm sick as shit of these people. I shouldn't of come here at all. I'm ready to quit this town any day now. I swear to god, I'm gonna get up and take off any minute. One way or another."

"To Knoxville? Is that where your home is?"

"Naw, it ain't my home. I never been there before. My cuz is gonna let me stay there with him. He says it's nice up there. Mountains."

"Where's your home then, bro?"

"Well, nowhere in particular. Moved around a lot when I was growin' up. Arkansas, mostly. Then we moved to Illinois when my grandpa died. But that's all over with. You know all about that. Now I'm on my own, doin' the best I can. And this ain't the place to do it."

"Isn't there anyone back there you can stay with?"

"They're all dead or else they ain't got no use for me, so here I am. Or there I go, dependin' on your point of view."

The gas pump clicked off. Ziggy topped it once and put up the hose. "Hang in there, dude. Things'll get better," he said.

"I sure hope so."

"They will."

"That's a long drive y'all got ahead of you, to St. Louis."

"Especially since we're taking the long way," Ziggy said. "We got a friend to pick up in Memphis and then it's back home from there. I'll be glad to get there, too."

"You ain't gettin' home tonight or tomorrow, that's for sure. It'll take you three days to get to St Louis thataway. You goin' through Atlanta?"

"Yeah, we are."

"That'd be a good place to stop for the night."

"Yeah, that's what we're planning on."

"You can get from Atlanta to Memphis in one day. I did it once, hitchhikin'."

"Does anybody stop for hitchhikers much these days?"

"Not much, but yeah, some still do. Truckers sometimes, and regular people too, like you." He smiled. "There's still a few good people out there willin' to help out a poor boy."

"Well, that's good."

"Lonely people pick you up sometimes. Or else they're horny. Makes no difference to me. A ride's a ride."

"Needy people like that don't scare you?"

"Hell, everybody's needy one way or another. That don't change just 'cause they're drivin'. I know all about bein' lonely. And fuck, who doesn't get horny? No, that shit's normal, I can deal with it. I get horny, too, don't you?"

"Sure, of course."

"It's the motherfuckers who live around *here* I'm afraid of. Some of 'em would just as soon as kill you, if you offend their sensibilities."

"Is that right?"

"Yeah. You gotta watch out if you're different. Police don't care neither. They're just as bad. Worse sometimes. Mean. And they know how to get away with it, too. Murder don't bother them. They call it law enforcement."

"You don't look different to me," Ziggy said.

"It ain't got nothin' to do with what I look like. It's what I do that they don't like. Like it's any of their business. Ignorant bastards. And it ain't like they haven't heard talk of it on TV nowadays, but that don't matter, they still think it's weird. Or they say they do.

"But you know what? When there's only one of 'em, it's a different story. When no one else is gonna know, turns out they ain't much different from me. They just pretend to be, when there's other folks around – that's when you gotta watch out. When there's more than one of 'em."

"Dude, what the fuck are you staying here for? There's plenty of places to go where people don't care if you're . . . different. Hell, just about any big city."

"Oh I'm gettin' out, count on it. I've already decided. I'm packed and fuckin' ready to go. Cousin in Knoxville tellin' me to come up and stay for a while. All I need is a way to get there, but it ain't quite that simple because, uh, I got a family member here. My Auntie. She's sick, been sick for a while. Her friends don't want me to leave her while she's that way. I guess that's all I'm waitin' for. But I'll take a ride if it comes first, because she don't want me here anyway. Said so herself."

"Waiting for . . . her to get well?"

"Yeah, or die."

"Jesus."

"People here like to think it could go either way, but it ain't lookin' good right now, not to me. Anyway, one way or the other, I'm out of here. She's got other people takin' care of her, it's not like I need to stay. We was never that close, anyway. Your oil's okay, by the way. Up to the mark, and clean, too."

"Thanks. Oh, here," Ziggy said, "let me pay for the gas before we forget." He handed a twenty dollar bill to Franklin, who ran inside the store and came right back with the change.

"So dude. Maybe Knoxville will do it for you."

"That's what I'm hopin'. My cuz says they got bars there for people like us. And he says people generally leaves 'em alone. That's what my cousin says."

"Is he gay?"

"He says he's trisexual. It's a joke, it means he'll try anything. But yeah, I think he's mostly gay."

"Have you even met him? I thought you said you didn't have any family left."

"I've heard stories about him, but I ain't never met him. I didn't know where he lived, or if he was even still alive. Just found out about him and my auntie both, when I stopped in Macon. My dad told me that he's queer, but Daddy didn't mean nothin' hurtful by that. He said some people just are, that's all. Hell, queer sounds good to me. I guess that's what I am, pretty near."

"Franklin, it's worth a try. You never know. You let us know how it goes, you hear? We want to stay in touch with you this time."

"Why wouldn't it work out? He sounded nice enough over the phone. And he's family – actual blood family. I'm not sure exactly how, but he's some kind of cousin, and like I said, he sounds okay."

"He probably is. It's just that things don't always turn out the way you think they will."

"Well now, ain't that the damn truth. Jesus, don't I know it."

"What I'm saying is, if you get in a fix, Franklin, we'll help you out if we can. Let's get each other's addresses, okay? So we can write. So we can keep in touch. We'll give you our phone number too. Ziggy and I both think you're a decent guy. We want to get to know you better."

"Jesus. When did all this happen? You two ain't even had a chance to talk about it."

"We've had plenty of chance. We talked about it two weeks ago after we dropped you off. We wished we had given you our address or phone number then, so we could keep in touch. We liked you. But we thought we'd lost you."

Tears came to Franklin's eyes. "No way," he said.

"It's the truth."

"But you don't hardly know me."

"Yes we do. Well enough. Sometimes it doesn't take long to know the important stuff. You're a good person, Franklin. There's a lot we don't know about you, but we know that much."

"I can't believe this. You don't know how much I wished I could be your . . . your friend. You two was so nice to me, and you was such good people, and I ended up thinkin' you coulda been the best thing ever happened to me if only . . . if only we had just a little more time to get to know each other, but it didn't work out that way. And now you . . . you're . . ." He couldn't finish. Then he burst into tears.

Josh put his arm around him. "Zig and I need friends too."

"I'll be the best friend you could ever imagine. The best I can be. I promise."

"Aw, you don't need to promise. Just be yourself, Franklin. That's the best way. As for getting you to Knoxville, I wish we could, but we've gotta be in Memphis by tomorrow night. You're not ready to leave yet, anyway, are you?"

"The hell I ain't. I'm packed and ready to go. Just let me ride with you part way, that's all I ask. Which way you goin', Birmingham or Nashville?"

"Nashville."

"Cool, I could ride with you all the way to Chattanooga. If you're willin' that is. I can hitch from there to Knoxville, easy. Fuck, I'm ready. I've been ready. All I gotta do is lock up the station and call my boss. My backpack's here with me in the office, all ready to go."

"Are you serious? Hell. It's okay by me. What about you, Zig?"

"Hell yeah. Of course."

Franklin jumped into the air and yelled, "YES!"

—

"YOU KNOW, IT'S A SMALL world," Franklin said. "And that ain't just what people say, it's the truth. It happens when you ain't expectin' it. In someplace totally different from where you was, you meet somebody you thought you'd never see again."

"We thought we'd missed our chance," Ziggy said. "We were worried about you, Franklin. You were so all alone."

"Hell, give me another hug, then. We must have done something right to get this lucky."

Chapter 46
ONWARD

"I GUESS YOU DIDN'T find yourself a good buddy partner yet, huh?" Ziggy said.

"Not in this shithole. Any guys like us, they leave this place as soon as they can, if they don't shoot their brains out first. You can't have a partner, livin' here. People won't abide by it."

"After you leave then."

"That's what I'm hopin'. I ain't givin' up on it, no sir. Life's too lonely otherwise. Look at you two; you did it. So can I."

Franklin called his boss to tell him he was leaving. The boss had been expecting this, so he wasn't upset, just disappointed.

Franklin brought his backpack out of the office, put a sign on the door, and locked the station up.

"I'm ready to go, friends," he said. "Just let me drop the key and then we can hit the road. Hang on." Franklin walked into the restroom. Ziggy pulled the car around, and a couple of minutes later Franklin came out and got in the back seat.

"Where do we have to go to drop the key?" Ziggy said.

"I already done dropped it. There's a hole in the wall of the bathroom. And a closet in the back of the office, that's what's on the other side of the hole. Standard procedure for when I close up."

Josh and Ziggy looked at each other.

"I didn't see any hole in the wall while I was in there," Josh said.

"Neither did I," Ziggy said.

"You didn't go into the stall, then. It's hard to miss it. If it was any bigger you could put your fist through it."

"Jesus. Who . . . I mean, what's it doing there? Nobody complains about it?"

"Sometimes people stuff toilet paper in it, but I ain't never heard nobody complain about it."

"And your boss knows about it?"

"Hell, I think it was him who put it there. I know for a fact he uses it. When I work the late shift, I drop the key through it after I close up. That's what I was told to do. When I come to work the next day the key's hangin' on a nail in the office."

"That sounds weird."

"Naw, it makes sense. Because I told my boss I might have to leave on short notice. This way he don't have to worry about somebody gettin' ahold of the key."

"But . . . a hole in the wall?"

"Well, it was already there, might as well use it."

"It still sounds weird."

"Not as weird as you think. You don't know my boss."

A few minutes later the three of them were in the Mustang heading up the highway together, going north.

—

THEY TALKED, OF COURSE. Franklin wanted to hear all the details about their trip so far. Josh and Zig told him all about Kevin and their extended stay with him in Jensen Beach. They told Franklin about Washington, D.C., too: the sightseeing, their encounter with Daniel and Trudi in the park, and their visit to his house the following day. Between Daniel and Kevin, Franklin said he thought Josh and Ziggy probably had more fun in two weeks than Franklin ever had in his entire life.

Franklin, in turn, reluctantly covered the basics of his two weeks in Georgia, which weren't anywhere near as enjoyable.

"I did have a little fun, one day," Franklin said, "but it didn't go nowhere."

"Oh, now you're going to have to explain that," Josh said. "What kind of fun? And where didn't it go?"

"Well, I'm a little embarrassed to tell you actually. It has to do with sex. And love, too, leastwise I was hopin' so."

"Embarrassed? Franklin, embarrassed about sex?" Ziggy smiled. "And here I thought you were more untwisted then we are. What was it that could make you embarrassed?"

"Well, it weren't so much what I did. It's just that after I did it, I got to thinkin' how trashy my boss was to be doin' what he does. I thought bad of him, after I done did the same thing myself. But I only did it once. And what I did was, well, uh, see, the thing is, I had better intentions than what he does."

"Uh, okay. So, you're gonna explain all that to us, right?"

"Do I have to?"

Ziggy laughed. "Of course not. You can tell us anything you want, li'l brother. Or not. It's all up to you. Nothing is required."

"And we sure don't want you to feel embarrassed," Josh said. "But you might be surprised. Sometimes you feel better about something after you confide in friends about it. But it's your call; if you don't want us to know about it that's okay."

"Well, I do want to tell you. I ain't never told nobody about this kind of stuff before 'cause there weren't nobody I could tell. I never had no real friends I could tell it to, except for my friend who moved off to Macon."

"But now you do."

"Yeah." Franklin grinned. "So, okay, you already know I sucked guys off before, I told you that two weeks ago, right?"

"Yeah, sure. We have, too, you know. It's part of being gay."

"Well sure, I know you do it to each other, and you told me about you and Kevin and Daniel, and hell, I hope I get my chance someday too. But see, I've done it to strangers. Guys who gave me a ride sometimes, you know? Strangers."

"I've done it to strangers too," Josh said. "Not just any stranger, only guys I was attracted to. Not only that, one of the first times I had sex was in a bathroom, if you can believe that."

"Oh, I can believe it. I can definitely believe it."

"Josh used to suck off strangers through gloryholes, Franklin," Ziggy said, grinning. "Or else they'd suck him off. Or both."

"Jeez, Zig. Franklin, like I said, I didn't do it with just anybody. I was pretty picky. Lots of folks would say I was too picky. And besides, it was the only place to meet guys. I wasn't old enough for the bars."

"I should have let Josh tell it, Franklin, instead of opening my big mouth. He always checked them over first to see if they were guys he'd want to be friends with. Right Josh?"

"Yeah. Not that it worked out that way very often, but I was always hoping."

"Ziggy, you never done that?"

"Yeah, I did. Only with one guy, though. Josh."

"But Franklin, do you even know what a gloryhole is?"

"Yeah, I think so. I'm pretty sure I know what you're talking about. I didn't know they had a name, though. Gloryhole; I guess that's a pretty good name for those things. Good as any."

"Have you ever actually seen one? These days if you find one it's usually in an adult book store, in the walls between the booths."

"The booths back where people pay to watch movies?"

"Yeah."

"Damn. I shoulda known there was somethin' like that goin' on back in there."

"But in the old days they were mostly in public bathrooms, you know, between the stalls. You don't see those much anymore."

"And guys suck each other off through 'em, right? Without even knowin' who it is, sometimes?"

"Yeah, exactly."

"Yeah, I know where one is. Two, I know where two are."

Chapter 47
GLORY

"THERE WAS ONE UP THE ROAD from where I lived in Illinois," Franklin said, "at the mall. See, I used to take my bicycle out and ride every chance I got, and I spent a lot of time at the mall in the summer because it was air-conditioned. I was there so much I probably knew everybody who worked there by sight. They got used to seein' me around so much, nobody paid me no mind after a while.

"It was in a little bathroom back in the corner of one of the department stores. When I first saw it, the hole between the stalls, I didn't know what the hell it was for or how it got there. It was a mystery to me. And it made me a little nervous, the idea somebody might be able to see what I was doin' in there.

"But what I *did* like was the writin' all over the walls. Both of the stalls was full of it. Stuff about suckin' dicks and fuckin' asses and cunts. Most of it looked like it had been there forever. And there was cocks, drawings of cocks, big stiff ones, shootin' cum. It gave me a hard-on, all that stuff did. First time I went in there I ended up beatin' off, lookin' at all that stuff on the wall.

"And I went in there at least once or twice a week after that, just to beat off. Nobody came in there much. Once in a while one of the sales clerks would come in to pee. I could see through the cracks who it was, usually.

"God, I didn't know what I'd do if one of them ever came in and sat down in the other stall. It was scary to think about. I woulda been so embarrassed. Somebody bein' able to see me through that hole, sittin' on the can with my pants down. But it was excitin', too, in a way. I was scared it might happen but also I wanted it to. I did. I wanted somebody to see my hard dick. Nobody'd ever seen it before besides me. I wanted somebody to catch me beatin' off, specially if it was one of clerks I had a crush on.

"And one day somebody did come into the other stall. I heard the outside door open, and then the inside door, and I figured it was somebody come to pee like always, but no, it was this guy who worked at the ice cream store, and he walked right into the other stall and latched the door.

"Quick as a wink I covered up my boner with my hands and leaned back so he wouldn't see my face and I just sat there waitin' to see what he'd do. I heard him unbuckle his belt and unzip and then he dropped his pants and sat down.

"I figured he'd take a shit and leave, but he didn't. He didn't make no noise or move around or nothin'. He just sat there, as quiet and still as I was. I could see his shadow. We both sat there for five or ten minutes, and neither one of us moved an inch.

"Finally I couldn't stand it no longer and I leaned forward just enough so I could look through the hole and see his knees, but not enough for him to see me. He had good-lookin' knees. Bare, healthy, strong knees. I wanted to see more, but I was afraid he'd think I was some kind of pervert if he knew I was lookin' at him.

"So I leaned back, and then his shadow moved. He was leanin' forward just like I'd done. He was lookin' at my knees, sure as shit. Somehow I just knew he was.

"And then I saw his shadow move even further forward. Jesus, from that angle he could probably see my hands coverin' my dick. But the good thing about that was, if me lookin' at him made me a pervert, then so was he.

"Finally he leaned back again, and we sat there for a couple more minutes like we done before. Then I figured if he could look at my crotch then I could damn well look at his – what could he say? He would see my shadow move, like I seen his, but he still wouldn't be able to see my face.

"So I leaned further this time, slowly, thinkin' I was probably gonna see his hands coverin' his crotch, too, or if I was lucky maybe he wasn't coverin' it and I could see what his soft dick looked like.

"Man, was I surprised. He wasn't coverin' it up at all, and not only that, his dick was bone hard. It was huge. Standin' up straight, throbbin', and it had wet stuff on the tip. I could hardly believe it. Lookin' at some stranger's hard cock. Except it weren't no stranger, 'cause I knew who he was.

"I stared at his boner for a minute or two, and then he started strokin' it. He had to know I was lookin', but he stroked it anyway. All of a sudden I felt embarrassed and I leaned back for a minute.

"But there weren't no doubt about it. He was lettin' me watch him play with his cock. So, that's what the hole was for!

"I leaned forward again and he was still strokin'. I couldn't believe my luck. It was better than any dirty magazine I'd ever be able to get ahold of. I watched him stroke for another minute or two, and then I leaned back again.

"My own cock was aching and hurting from me holding it down, and he wasn't lookin' just then, so I let loose of it and my hand just naturally took ahold of it and I started strokin' too. Hell, I was gonna have to beat off, that's all there was to it, and the sooner the better.

"Then he leaned forward again and I thought, holy shit, he's gonna see my hard cock. I thought about tryin' to cover it up but hell, wasn't that what I wanted? For him see it? Hell yeah, show off my hard cock, let him get a good look at it, let him see it throb.

"So I took my hand off it and let it stand there, and boy, did it ever throb. It was like it had a life of its own, and it was sayin', 'Yeah look at me, just look at me.'

"And he looked. He moved so close to the hole I could see the side of his head. If he'd got any closer he could have looked up and seen my face, but he didn't.

"He stared at my cock for the longest time, and the longer he looked, the bigger it tried to get. I thought I might shoot off just from him lookin' at it. I heard him whisper, 'Beautiful.' So he liked my dick! I couldn't stand it any longer, I had to take hold of it again and stroke it.

"He watched me stroke for a minute or two and then he leaned back away from the hole, so I figured okay, now it's my turn. So I leaned forward and got a good look at his hard cock again and him strokin' it. I figured he probably didn't want me to see his face so I was careful not to get that close but I knew he could see part of my face now, my chin or cheek or whatever. Okay by me. We were fellow perverts; we were in this together now.

"He kept strokin' his cock and I kept lookin'. He was wetter than ever with that pre-cum stuff. Then he surprised me and stood up. At first I thought maybe he was gonna pull up his pants and leave, but no, he just stood there in front of the hole, givin' me a better view than ever of him strokin' his cock.

"Now I put my face up much closer to the hole, because at that angle I couldn't see his face and he couldn't see mine neither, except maybe a small part of it.

"Now I was just inches away from his cock. If there weren't no wall between us I could have touched it, but just lookin' at it was enough. I felt like I was gonna shoot off in a minute if I kept strokin', so I let my cock alone and watched him. He took his finger and scooped up some of his pre-cum and lifted it up out of sight. Was he tastin' it? I thought I was the only one who did that.

"Then he did it again. Yeah, he was tastin' it. Awesome. He was just as perverted as I was. Or maybe everybody does that? Then he took ahold of his dick and moved it downward so it was pointin' straight at me. What the hell was he doin'?

"He moved closer and closer to the hole – so close I could actually touch the tip of it. And I did. I put a finger out and touched the head of his dick and I heard him give out a sigh and say, 'Yeah.'

"So I touched it again, and this time I did what he'd done: I scooped up some of his pre-cum onto my finger and then I held it up to my nose and sniffed it. Smelled okay, so I went ahead and licked it off my finger, and it tasted okay, too. Not much taste to it but what there was was pretty much like mine. Jesus, I couldn't believe I'd done that, but it was so sexy I did it again.

"But even after all this, what he did next completely surprised me. He pushed forward and moved his cock through the hole until his entire dick was on my side, right there in front of my face. If I hadn't moved back a little, it would have hit my nose.

"'Go ahead,' he whispered. 'It's all yours.'

"I put my hand around it. It was so stiff, and yet so smooth. And the head, oh my god, it was as perfect as the rest of his dick. It was flared out a little, like a mushroom or a helmet, and it was full, round, and wet. I felt like I was holdin' somethin' magical. I guess it wasn't much different from my own dick, besides bein' circumcised, but to me it was a totally new experience. I stroked it and he moaned.

"Then I did something I had tried a million times to do to my own dick: I licked it. I licked the head of his dick, and he groaned. I licked off the pre-cum, tasted it, swallowed it, and then licked it again. It was almost like lickin' my own dick, except I was really doin' it. Then I stroked it some more.

"'Suck it,' he whispered. I wasn't sure if I heard him right. 'Go ahead,' he said. 'Suck it. Please. Suck it.'

"It wasn't like I'd never thought about suckin' a dick before, I just never thought about suckin' anybody's but my own. But since I couldn't do that, what the hell, I thought, at least I could give someone else the pleasure. Why not? Especially this guy, because he was one of the guys I had a crush on. I wished he would be my big brother, and hold me in his arms and hug me and take care of me.

"So I licked it again, and decided to go all the way. I put my mouth around his cock and sucked it like it was a popsicle.

"'Watch your teeth, okay?' he whispered.

"Oh, Christ, I needed to be careful. Okay, I was up to it. He wouldn't have to tell me twice. I wanted so bad to make him feel good. I wanted him to ask me to do it again, some other time. Later. Again and again. So I did everything I could think of to make it good.

"I used my tongue on it a lot, licked the underside of his cock while I was suckin' it, and I moved my lips up and down it too. That's what I'd want somebody to do to my dick. I figured his dick was probably the same way.

"'Yeah,' he whispered, 'yeah dude you're so good at this.'

"When he said that, I moaned and started strokin' my own dick again. What I wanted was to make him come, but I wanted to come too. And I was close.

"I licked underneath his dickhead, you know, where it feels so good, I figured that would get him if anything did. He said, 'Dude I'm gonna come, I'm gonna come in your mouth, okay?'

"I just moaned and kept suckin'. Hell, I'd ate my own cum before, how bad could it be to eat his? So I kept lickin' and suckin', and he was puttin' out a lot of pre-cum, and I wanted it, I wanted all of it. I wanted to drink his cum right out of his cock. I was ready for it.

"Then he groaned and his dick started spurtin' cum out onto my tongue, big, thick spurts, and it was warm and it tasted good, and I didn't want to waste a drop of it. I jerked myself good when he started shootin' and I then I was comin', too.

"I kept his dick in my mouth even after he was finished shootin' all his cum. I liked it there. And I figured when he wanted it out he'd take it out. He left it in for at least another minute or two, and then he slowly took it out and pulled it back through the hole, to his side of the wall.

"'Dude,' he said. 'That was awesome. Thanks. Did you get off?'

"I said, 'Yeah, I came when you did.'

"He said, 'I owe you one then. Look, I gotta get back to work. Catch you next time, okay?'

"And I said, 'Fuck, I hope so. I liked that.'

"'You and me both,' he said. Then he was out of there.

"I got myself buttoned up and all and then I went down to the ice cream store and bought a double dip from him, but I don't think he recognized me. He was nice, like always, but I don't think he had a clue that it was me in the bathroom.

"I just about almost said something. I should have, I guess. The next time I went to the mall they said he didn't work there no more. I asked for his phone number or address or where he went to, said I had something that was his and I needed to give it to him, but they wouldn't tell me nothin'.

"I almost cried right there on the spot, but there weren't nothin' I could do. I went back to that bathroom every day, lookin' for him, but I never saw him again."

Chapter 48
DREAMS

"Sorry," Franklin said. "I didn't mean to tell such a long story. You guys still awake? You ain't done much talkin' lately."

"We've been listening to every word," Josh said.

"Fuck yeah, that's for sure," Ziggy said. "My dick is so hard I'm about to cream in my jeans. What a story. Jesus. I'm gonna have to stop somewhere and jerk off or else I'll have blue balls."

Franklin laughed. "Yeah, makes me hard just to *think* about it. But tellin' you guys about it, it's got me so hard it hurts. I need to come too. Yeah, we oughta beat off or somethin'."

"You got me horny too," Josh said. "But that's sad if you never saw him again. You had a crush on him, huh?"

"Yeah, him and a couple other clerks at that mall, too. They was so nice to me, and I wanted a big brother so bad, they coulda kidnapped me and I would have been in heaven."

"Aw, Franklin; life hasn't been fair to you, dude."

"That's gonna change, though," Josh said. "You have family now. Not just your cousin; you have us now, too. Friends can be family, don't you think?"

"Yeah, I guess, sure. If we get to be good enough friends. Hell yeah."

"And someday maybe you'll meet Kevin and Daniel. I think they'd both like you. Maybe we can all be family for each other."

Franklin had tears in his eyes, but he was smiling. "You guys know how to make me feel good better'n anybody else ever did. Except for maybe my Daddy and Ma. You're like big brothers. I think I finally found me some big brothers." He grinned.

"And we've got us a little brother," Ziggy said, smiling. "But not really so little. You're only three years younger, right? Anyway, you're big where it counts, bro."

Franklin started getting embarrassed. "Aw, I bet I ain't no bigger than either one of you. But I sure hope to find out."

Josh smiled and said, "You're talking about his feet, right?"

"No, actually, I'm talking about his heart. And his spirit. Look at all the stuff he's been through, and he never gives up hope. We could learn a few things about life from Franklin, no doubt about it."

—

"I'VE BEEN MEANING to ask," Franklin said; "you guys live in St. Louis, right? Do you have a place together?"

"Yeah. We've lived together ever since we met. A year ago," Josh said.

"How'd you meet?"

"Well, I was up from Memphis, visiting St. Louis. We met at a gay bar. But we didn't go there to pick up guys, it wasn't like that. I was there with some friends, and Ziggy was on the lookout for a foxy lady that first night, right Zig?"

"Yeah, that first night I was."

"At a gay bar?"

"Well, after-hours it's a mixed bar, straight and gay. It's in East St. Louis, on the other side of the river, and the liquor laws are different. People come there from all over after the other bars close."

"And everybody gets along? So many different kinds of people?"

"Yeah. They do. I like it. It's a fun place."

"I like it too," Ziggy said. "The women there are more relaxed, more natural. Same with the guys. Getting along there means accepting people who are different from you. So it's okay to be different. I like that type of place. You can just be yourself."

"Josh, you wasn't lookin' to hook up with a guy neither?"

"No, I had a boyfriend. Granted it wasn't . . . a good relationship. He wasn't very nice. But I was still being faithful to him."

"Jesus. So neither one of you was lookin' to hook up with another guy, and Josh, you didn't even live there yet, but you two ended up together anyway. There's gotta be a story behind that."

"Yeah, there is. We'll tell you about it sometime."

"Okay, yeah, I'd like to hear about it."

"Sure."

"So okay, you guys been livin' together for a year now. I'll bet you got a nice apartment, right? Or do you live in a house?"

"An apartment. It's nothing special," Ziggy said, "but it's home. A studio apartment, basically just one room, but it's nice enough. Hell, we think it's great. It's our little nest."

"One room? That don't give two people much space."

"It's all we need. We're happy there."

"What kind of work do you do? You know, to pay your rent and all?"

"I'm an automotive mechanic, and Josh works at temp jobs, mostly clerk stuff, you know, typing, whatever. That works well for him, and I like what I do, too."

"Did you have to go to school for that?"

"Yeah, I did. I started out helping my friends work on their cars, but I learned a lot more in school. I probably wouldn't have got hired if I hadn't taken the automotive program."

"I took one typing class in high school," Josh said. "Oh, and a bookkeeping class, too. Everything else I learned from the jobs I worked at."

"I been thinkin' about school. I believe I oughta learn some kind of trade."

"Pick one you like and go for it, dude. That's what I did."

"Cool. So, you guys got any plans in the works? You know, like, someplace different to live? Movin' somewhere you like better?"

"Haven't thought about it much. I'm pretty happy where I am so far. What about you, Josh?"

"St. Louis is fine with me. It feels like home now. If we ever find someplace we like better, I guess I could be talked into it, but I'm not going anywhere unless Zig wants to go."

"How about goals? Like goin' to college, joining the Peace Corp, workin' on fishing boats, you guys got anything exotic like that in mind?"

"We're pretty happy doing what we're doing, bro. Who knows what's in the future – but we're good for now."

Josh said, "My goal is to finish the novel I'm writing. I write almost every day, like for an hour or two. When I finish it, well, then I guess I'll start another one. I have a few ideas already."

"Oh, man. You're a writer?"

"Well, yeah, but that doesn't mean I'm good at it. We'll have to wait and see about that. But I'm trying."

"I'll bet it'll be great. What about you, Zig? Do you write, too?"

"Nah. I read a lot, we both do. We love to read. But Josh is the writer dude, not me."

"We talk sometimes about going back to school. But we wouldn't have to leave St. Louis to do that. I'd study writing, and Zig would probably study psychology. He'd be good at it. He's already good at it, actually, whether he knows it or not."

"Wow."

"Yeah."

"Do you guys have lots of friends you hang out with?"

"No. Really, we don't. We need more friends. We don't get out enough. We've talked about that. That's why we were so glad to meet Daniel and Kevin. And you. All of us are short on family, so who knows. Maybe we could be our own family for each other. We all basically live far apart from each other, but still, it could happen."

"Franklin, what about you, bro? You have any plans? You know, goals? Dreams? You've been shuffled around a lot these last few weeks."

"Yeah, I know. Fuck, I'm short on family and friends both. And I've been thinkin' a lot about it, since my stepparents kicked me out. I never thought much about the future until then, but now it's just about all I can think about. Specially after I met you guys."

"So what have you come up with?"

"Well, one thing I know is, I want some friends. I want to be friends with some guys like you. I been knowin' that ever since I met you hitchhikin'. Life's too lonely without havin' some friends. Specially if they's good people like you. So, uh, yeah, I got dreams. I got plans."

"Cool. What do you have planned? Or is it a secret?"

"It ain't a secret. But you're the first ones I'm tellin' it to. So, uh, what it is, is, I got these ideas in my head about how it would be if, um, well, if I lived in St. Louis. Near you guys. And if I was friends with you. If we was real good friends."

"Oh, yeah?"

"Yeah."

"Hell, why not?" Ziggy said.

"'Why not?' You really mean that?"

"Yeah, I mean it. Why not, if that's what you want?"

"So how do you imagine it, Franklin?" Josh said. "Tell us about it. What have you got in mind?"

"Oh, well, it's . . . a dream, you know. It's just me dreamin'. I think I'd be embarrassed to tell you, like, the details."

"Aw, why?"

"I don't know. I mean, it all might seem like too much. I can dream anything I want, but what if you don't like it? What if it don't sound as good to you as it does to me? What if that's all it's ever gonna be, is a dream? I think I oughta watch out about sayin' too much. Hell, I might jinx it by talkin' about it."

"But Franklin, there's nothing wrong with dreaming. That's how you make things happen. You have to believe, first. It won't happen unless you believe it can happen."

"Oh hell, I know that. It don't always work, but you can't get nowhere if you don't believe in it first. Tellin' other people about it ahead of time, though, that's not always such a good idea."

"Okay, well, just tell us the basics, then. If we're gonna be part of your dream, then it might help if we know at least some of it."

"Yeah, we might even be able to help you with it."

"Well, you guys was so nice to me. Fuck, I'll tell you what, I never met such awesome guys like you before. I want to be friends with you. And anyway, I need to settle down somewhere. So I can *have* friends. Life-long friends. I think about what it would be like if we was real close friends. I could learn a lot from you guys. And maybe I could be your awesome friend, too. Don't laugh."

"We're not laughing. You're already our awesome friend."

"Well, I'd want to be. I'd do anything for you guys. I'd help you out if you need it, like you helped me out, and, well, you know. I think about what it would be like if we was so close we loved each other. Friends can love each other, can't they?"

"Sure, of course they can."

"That's what I want. That's what I want us to be. That's why I want to move to St. Louis."

"You're serious about this?"

"Yes. I am. Oh, I don't mean right away – first I gotta get ready. But yeah, why not? Everybody's gotta be somewhere. I don't plan on stayin' with my cousin forever. So first I get a job, and then, after I save up some money, I'm gonna get my own place. Why not in St. Louis? You guys like it there; I'll bet I would, too. Fuck, if you're there, I know I would."

"Hell yeah. Do it. That would be awesome, dude."

"Have you ever been to St. Louis?"

"No, not really. My family drove by there on our way to Illinois, but we didn't stop. You guys like it, though; that's good enough for me. Look, we know each other now. I want to keep you guys as friends. We can write all the letters we want, and call each other, too, but that ain't enough. That long distance stuff, that's how people lose touch with one another. I want to be able to see you guys. Visit each other. Spend some time together. That's the only way to be friends – good friends, anyway."

Josh and Ziggy looked at each other without saying anything.

"Look, if you guys don't want me there, just say so. I can handle it." Franklin's eyes were shiny with tears. "But that's what my dream is. To have some good friends like you. To be *your* friend. To see you, and talk to you. For us to touch each other, and do stuff together. Not every day, it don't have to be every day, but hell, enough so we can keep up on each other. Enough to be a part of each other's lives." Franklin looked out the window. "Shit, there I go again. Talkin' too much. I cain't ever learn to shut up. I should have kept my mouth shut tight. I probably done scared you off, now. I wouldn't be a burden, though, I promise."

"Franklin," Josh said, "that would be awesome if you move to St. Louis. You heard what Ziggy said: he's all for it, and so am I. We like you a lot and we'd love to have you living nearby."

"You really mean that?"

"Of course. But Franklin, what if you find out you don't like it there? Then what?"

"I ain't worried about that. I don't really care where I live, as long as I got some good friends. Hangin' out together, wouldn't that be cool? I don't mean all the time, only when we want to. I wouldn't be a pest, I promise. I know you guys got your own life to live. With each other. And I wouldn't want you to feel responsible for me, neither. I can look out for myself."

"We know you can. But we're gonna be looking out for you no matter where you are. That's what friends do."

"I just don't want to lose touch with you guys. You're the best friends I got now. I want to know you better, really get to know each other. That don't work long distance."

Josh and Ziggy looked at each other again. Then they looked back at Franklin.

"Dude," Ziggy said, "if that's your dream, then go for it."

"Yeah," Josh said. "If that's what you want, we'll be there for you."

"Our apartment's not big enough for all three of us, not on a permanent basis, but we could put you up temporarily. While you look for a job and a place of your own. Hell, do it, Franklin. It would be cool to have you living nearby, dropping in on us. And we could visit you at your place, too."

"Then you like the idea?"

"Yeah. It's a great idea. Do what you gotta do in Knoxville, stay in touch with us, and when you're ready to move to St. Louis, let us know. We'll be behind you all the way. Maybe we can even help you find a place. Or a job."

"Jesus. You guys. Wow. I wasn't sure if you'd go for it. That's awesome. Now I really got somethin' to work for." Franklin grinned.

Chapter 49
INTERVIEW

AS THEY APPROACHED the next rest stop they were still horny from hearing Franklin's gloryhole story. And thinking about a future together somehow made their dicks even harder, so everyone wanted to stop and get a load off. They went in and lined up next to each other at three urinals and watched each other jerk out three good loads into the porcelain.

Franklin said it was a shame to let all that good cum go down the drain, and Josh said he basically felt the same way, but they needed to get off, had no better place to do it, and besides, it was sexy to watch each other come.

Franklin was especially thrilled about it. It was his first look ever at Ziggy's and Josh's cocks. He hoped it wouldn't be the last. He studied both of them long enough to permanently etch their images into his brain.

—

AFTER THEY GOT BACK on the road Josh told Franklin the story about what happened to him in the bathroom during college orientation. Franklin reacted the same way Ziggy had – he said he wished it would happen to him sometime.

And then Ziggy said, "Franklin, you said you knew of *two* gloryholes. Do you have any stories about the other one?"

"And you still haven't told us about the fun you had last week, either," Josh said.

"I can tell you about 'em both at the same time."

"What do you mean?"

"Well, the other suck hole was in the bathroom of the gas station I worked at."

"Really? You actually worked where the gloryhole was? That must have been interesting."

"Yeah, I guess."

"When did you work there?"

"I just quit there this afternoon."

"There was a gloryhole at THAT gas station? Fuck!"

"Yeah. That hole in the wall I told you about inside the restroom."

Josh and Ziggy both were speechless. They just looked at Franklin in surprise.

Finally Josh said, "But Franklin, you told us that wall had the office on the other side of it. How could people suck each other off that way?"

"Easy, if one of them was my boss."

Ziggy and Josh, like a duet, said, "Ooooohhh."

They drove on in silence for a couple of minutes, with Franklin blushing, not sure what to say next. Ziggy and Josh, on the other hand, had so many questions they didn't know what to ask first.

Josh was the first to speak.

"But Franklin," he said, "how would he know . . . I mean, he didn't wait in the office closet all day long for somebody to come into the bathroom, did he? That wouldn't work. He had a business to run. Didn't he?"

"Sure he did. Don't ask me. I don't know how he got things rolling, but by the time I started working there, he had, like, regulars. Guys would buy gas there, and when they came in to pay for it, they'd tell him they was gonna use the bathroom if it was okay. He'd say, 'Sure, no problem, go right ahead.' Then they'd move their car away from the pumps and he'd tell the guy workin' the day shift to watch things while he took care of the books. He'd go inside his office and lock the door.. And he didn't come out again until the guy came back out of the bathroom."

"Jesus. But how do you know . . ."

"That he was suckin' them off?"

"Yeah."

"Well, I don't know that he did it every time. Not for sure. Maybe some of them really had to pee and they didn't know about the hole. But I worked the day shift that first week and I watched what was going on. And most of the time, the guys would come out of the bathroom grinnin'. Half the time their dicks were still hard and they had wet spots at their crotch. When they saw me lookin' they'd get embarrassed. It was pretty obvious really. Plus they bought gas, like, three or four times a week, and they'd always use the bathroom afterwards. Buy a dollar's worth of gas, go in and pay my boss, and then use the bathroom."

"Wow."

"Some of the guys, the mean ones, when they came out and saw me lookin', they'd say something like, 'what are you lookin' at, faggot?'"

"Aw, now that's not right. That *is* mean."

"Yeah, but it also told me what they'd been doin'. Another way I knew was, a couple of times, when my boss came out of his office he had cum on his shirt. One time he even had cum on his face."

"Jesus."

"Well, he didn't have nowhere to wash up and he ain't got a mirror in his office. I guess it was bound to happen."

"That was pretty bold of him," Josh said. "I mean, those guys must have known it was him blowing them, right?"

"Yeah. They must have. But it didn't hurt his business, not as far as I could tell."

"Okay, so that's the first part of the story. But that's not the embarrassing part is it? There must be more."

"No, you're right, it ain't. There's actually two embarrassing parts. The first time I ever went to that place was one of 'em. I'd just got into town the day before and I was lookin' for work, so I stopped in there and asked. There was this scruffy guy outside, hot and sexy as he could be, pumpin' gas. Not any older than me – maybe younger. I coulda talked to him all day and never got tired of lookin' at him. Anyway, he said go in and ask the boss. So I did, and the boss told me to come into his office and sit down. He gave me a big bottle of Coke and asked me a bunch of questions that didn't have nothin' to do with anything.

"When I finished the Coke he asked me if I wanted another one. I said no, and if he didn't have no more questions for me I had to go pee. So he said go right ahead, the restroom's outside. He told me, come back tomorrow and maybe he'd hire me; he had to think on it first."

"Oh, no," Josh said. "Jeez, I think I see where this is going."

"Yeah, you probably do," Franklin said. "Smart as you are."

"Aw, let him finish, Josh. I want to hear this." Ziggy grinned. "I got a boner already and he hasn't even gotten to the good part yet."

"Yeah, Franklin, go ahead. Sorry, I didn't mean to interrupt."

"Okay, so, he shook my hand and opened the door and let me go. I figured since he didn't offer me a job on the spot I probably fucked up somehow, but that weren't nothin' new. I passed by the scruffy kid, Joey, on my way out and he said, 'Did he hire you?' I said, 'Don't know. Told me to come back tomorrow.'

"So I went around the side of the building and I found the bathroom. All I wanted to do was pee, but ever since that bathroom in Illinois, I check out the stalls to see if there's any sexy stuff on the walls, so I went into the stall to pee.

"There was some writing, but not a whole lot. What got my attention was the hole in the wall. It was the same size as the one in Illinois, and it was down at the same level, but the one in Illinois made sense. This one didn't. What good is a hole in the wall if somebody can't be on the other side of it?

"I finished up peein' and I was shakin' my dick when I heard, through the hole, a door open. There was a little flicker of light but by the time I looked straight at it the hole was dark again and the door was shut.

"Whoever it was in there, did he even know there was a hole? Was he lookin' at me through it? The whole thing kind of weirded me out a little but my dick was beginnin' to get hard just the same. I bent over and looked into the hole and, sure as shit, there was a nose and an eye looking out at me. I said 'Jesus' and I stood up. I didn't know what to do – stay or get the fuck out of there. But my dick was gettin' *real* hard now.

"Then I heard somebody whisper through the hole, 'Let me see it.' So I held my dick up close to the hole and showed it to him. He said, 'No, let me suck it. Put it through, I'll suck it for you.'

"*Who the hell is this?* I thought. Who was on the other side of that wall? Was it Joey, that scruffy gas jockey? When I thought about him on my dick, my cock was ready to go. If it was Joey who wanted my cum, he could have all he wanted. I hadn't jacked off since you guys picked me up hitchhikin' in the rain that day. Whoever it was I was ready to give him a big load. I had more cum in my nuts than I knew what to do with.

"I looked down at that mouth and I got this picture of me bein' on the other side of that wall, and over on this here side is that ice-cream-store guy I had such a crush on. And if that kid wanted my cock, he could have it. He could suck all the cum he wanted out of my hard dick, it was alright with me.

"So I put my dick through the hole and I got the best blowjob I've ever had in my life. He fuckin' drained me. I almost fell over when I came, I was so dizzy.

"When he was done, when I was steady on my feet again, I leaned down and told him, 'Thanks.' He whispered back, 'You bet.'

"I didn't even think about returnin' the favor 'cause by that time the whole thing was weirdin' me out again. I zipped myself up and got the hell out of there. I walked around the front of the station and the boss was standin' there at the door, and Joey was standin' right next to him.

"The boss said, 'Come back tomorrow, I'll let you know.' And the kid winks at me.

"I knew it must have been one of them two who done it, but I didn't have a clue which one.

"Anyway, I came back the next day and the boss hired me. I told him I didn't know how long I could stay, but he said, 'Don't worry about it. Give me an honest day's work while you're here, and don't steal nothing, and we'll be alright.'

"And then, after a couple days of workin' there and watchin' how things went, I figured it out. It wasn't Joey who sucked me off, it was the boss. I guess I shoulda figured it wasn't Joey. That woulda been too good to be true. But hell, I sure did want it to be."

Chapter 50
GET A GRIP

ZIGGY SAID, "You don't think it could have been both of them? Like, maybe they took turns or something?"

"Naw. I never did see Joey go inside that office. It was always the boss. Sometimes when we saw one of the regulars goin' into the restroom and the boss goin' to do his 'books' Joey would say, 'There he goes again. Doin' what he does best.' And we'd laugh. One time I asked him, 'You ever do it?' He said, 'What, let him suck me off?' That wasn't what I meant, but I said, 'Yeah.' He said, 'Once. Before I started working here. I didn't know who was back there, and I didn't care. That was before me and my girlfriend started doing it.'

"So I said to Joey, 'Yeah, same here.' He said, 'When, that first day you showed up here?' I said, 'Yeah.' He laughed and said, 'I thought so. He sucks a mean dick, doesn't he?' I said, 'I didn't know who it was. I was hopin' it was you.' He said, 'Dude. I don't suck cock.' I said, 'I wasn't sayin' you do. I'm just sayin' you're a hell of a lot better lookin' than he is.'"

Ziggy said, "Did he get pissed off at you?"

"Naw. He laughed and said, 'Thanks.'"

"Well, that's good," Josh said. "But I don't see anything to be embarrassed about. Did you ever let your boss do it again?"

"No! He was suckin' at least a half a dozen dicks a day, and different ones from one day to the next, and I didn't want to be any part of that. I mean, who knows where some of them dicks have been? There really ain't no telling what these people around here do. I seen it before, in Arkansas and Illinois. Some of these guys call you a faggot one day, go to church the next day, and fuck a sheep the day after that. Half of 'em that calls you a faggot hope you really are one, 'cause lord knows their wives probably got sick and tired of the selfish pricks long ago. No, my boss can do what he wants, but I didn't want no part of it. That's too much sex anyway. Ain't good to think about sex all the time like that."

"Did he ever *try* to suck you off again?"

"I didn't give him a chance. Maybe he wanted to, maybe he didn't. Who knows? Pretty soon he asked me to work the late shift and that was fine with me."

"And what about the other embarrassing part?"

Franklin winced. "Ain't you guys tired yet of hearin' about gloryholes? I know you think they're hot, but so's a lot of stuff. Suckholes ain't a big part of my life. I'd rather know the guy I'm suckin' off. You can't hardly do that with a gloryhole, not unless you go out afterwards and chat with one another."

"You make a good point there," Josh said. "And we've heard plenty already. And you're right, lots of things are hot."

"Josh and I did it through a gloryhole once," Ziggy said. "We pretended we were strangers. That was extra hot, because we could pretend it was just animal sex through a hole in the wall, but at the same time we knew who it was and, well, you know. We're crazy about each other, so it was good. First time I ever sucked a dick."

Franklin sighed. "I wish I was crazy about somebody. And he was crazy about me. That's what I keep wishin' for. But that's what almost got me in trouble this week."

"How do you mean?"

"Wishful thinkin'. Sometimes when I'm fallin' for somebody I forget to stop and get a grip. Because I know it don't work unless it goes both ways."

"What happened?"

Franklin sighed. "Oh, okay, I guess I'll tell it after all. Here goes. It happened when I started workin' night shift and had the whole place to myself."

"Uh oh. Including the office?"

"That's right, includin' the office."

"Franklin, you didn't."

"Almost, I did. There was this one guy who was always so nice to me. Good-lookin' guy. Treated me like he wanted to be friends. When he stopped by to get gas, he talked to me about stuff. Asked me how I was doin', where I was from, stuff like that. Like he really wanted to know me, you know? A couple years older than me, but so what? And I asked him about hisself, too. Then one day he told me he needed to use the bathroom, and I said, 'Go ahead, it's all yours.' And he said, 'Okay then.'

"And he walked over there to it, and he looked back at me with this goofy grin on his face, like he was lookin' to see what I was gonna do. Then he went on into the bathroom and I thought, *He knows about the hole.* And then I thought, *Hell, why not? We got bell-ringer hoses for when a car drives up, and a beeper on the door when someone comes inside, and the cash is locked up. I could go back there to the office and if anybody does come up, I'd hear it.*

"And I thought, *but then he'd know I'm a cocksucker.* Which was okay with me, if he's one, too, but what if he wasn't? And what if he told somebody else? And I thought about it, and thought about it, and I didn't know what to do.

"Then I thought, wait a minute, this ain't no stranger we're talkin' about, this is a guy I want to be friends with. If I ever suck him it ain't gonna be through some damn hole in the wall. It's gonna be in bed or someplace where we can make love to each other. And the more I thought about it the more pissed off I got. What did he think I was, some kind of cock-crazy slut like my boss who hides in a closet and services any dick that comes through?

"Finally I guess he got tired of waitin'. He came back out again. I'd missed my chance and that was fine with me.

"He came over and said, 'Well, I guess I'll be leavin' now. Maybe I'll need some more gas tomorrow, you gonna be here?'

And I said, 'Yeah, I'll definitely be here.' And he said, 'Cool. You ever give your customers full service?'

"I nearly lost it when he said that. I was so mad I could hardly talk. I couldn't believe he said that. Finally I said, 'No. I don't, and I sure as hell don't suck dicks through a hole in the wall, so if that's all you want, come back when the boss is here, 'cause people say he ain't too particular. I don't know if it's true, but they say he'll suck off just about anybody. Maybe even you.'

"He got all embarrassed and he said, "Aw, don't be like that. See you tomorrow, okay?' And he smiled at me like he had a chance in hell."

"Aw, Franklin," Ziggy said. "He sounds like a jerk."

"Yeah, well, I sure thought so."

"Did he come back?"

"He came back. He came back the next night like he said he was gonna do. And he got some gas and he talked to me and then he said, 'I gotta use the bathroom again, you still up for that full service?'

"I said, 'No, and I never was. Not through some damned hole in the wall. Forget it.'

"And then he says he's gotta pee. I started wonderin' didn't I make myself clear. He winks his eye and walks over towards the bathroom. And I said, 'You really need to pee?' And he said, 'What do you think?' I said, 'I think maybe you're hard of hearin'.'

"He don't say nothin' else, he just heads for the bathroom. So I went into the front of the station, where the store part is, and waited for him. Things wasn't all completely ruined yet. I still woulda been up for makin' out with him if he came to his senses. I thought maybe he'd pee and come back inside with me. We could have even used the office.

"He must have stayed in that bathroom for ten or fifteen minutes. A car pulled up outside. Tourists, leavin' Florida. They filled up with gas, washed the bugs off their windshield, came in and paid, and then they were gone.

"I waited some more. Finally he comes out of the bathroom lookin' pissed off, and asks me where was I? I said, 'Right here, waitin' on you.'

"He said, 'I thought you were gonna give me some of what your boss gives out.'

"I told him, 'That's funny, 'cause I got confused too. I thought you heard me when I said I ain't doin' nothin' through no damn hole in the wall. You want to be friends, we can be friends. You want to have sex, we can go somewhere where we can do it right. Touch one another, and hold each other, and kiss and make love. Do it right.'

"He said 'whoa, wait a minute, I don't do that kind of stuff. I just like getting my dick sucked.' So I told him, 'Fine, come by during the day shift if a mouth is all you're lookin' for. Leave me out of it.'

"He said, 'maybe I will, then, since you ain't interested.' I said, 'You got that right, I ain't.' So he didn't say another word, he just got in his car and drove off. That was it."

"You didn't see him again after that?"

"I saw him one more time. He was riding with a carload of assholes who stopped in for gas. He was sittin' in the car and I went out to talk to him, but he pretended like he didn't know me."

"What? Aw, man, that's cold."

"Yeah, no kiddin'. The way it started out, I thought we could be friends. But around them other guys he was ashamed to even know me. Either that or he was afraid of what I might say. So fuck him. And if he don't know how much that hurt, him thinkin' that's all I'm good for, then there's something wrong with him anyway, so to hell with him."

That was the end of their talk for a while; they just drove on. Finally Ziggy said, "Franklin, you tried. You took a chance. You did what you could. The fact that he didn't have the balls to follow through doesn't reflect on you. You're the one who has heart. It only makes me want to respect you more."

"I did try," Franklin said. "I just tried with the wrong guy, I guess."

"Keep trying, bro. You deserve the best. And one of these days you'll find him. Someone who'll treat you like the special guy you are."

—

THEIR DESTINATION that day was Atlanta. That was the original plan, and there was no reason to change it. More than eight hours on the road was enough driving for one day. Even if they went straight through to Chattanooga, there was no way they would leave Franklin out on the highway that late. They wanted plenty of daylight hours available for him to do his hitchhiking to Knoxville.

So when they reached the outskirts of Atlanta, it was time to look for a hotel. It didn't take them long. Ziggy pulled up in front of the hotel office and turned off the engine. He said, "You guys wait here; I'll get us a room."

"Hey, don't worry about me," Franklin said. "I can . . . I'll . . . I'll sleep in the car."

Chapter 51
SHOWERS

"DUDE," ZIGGY SAID, "you're not sleeping in the car."

"I don't want you guys spendin' any extra money on me. And besides, I'd be messin' up your privacy together."

"Franklin," Josh said, "we get all the privacy we want. We don't need to be alone together every chance we get. We want you with us."

"Anyway," Ziggy said, "most likely we'll have two beds in our room. If you slept in the car, then one of them would go to waste. No, you're gonna stay in our room with us and sleep in a nice, comfy bed tonight. You're gonna be our guest and keep us company. Because we're friends."

—

ZIGGY CAME OUT of the hotel office and got back in the car.

"No problem," he said. "We got a room for the night. I picked us a good one." He started the engine and they drove around to the side of the building and parked. They pulled their backpacks out of the trunk and found their room.

When they walked in, Franklin said, "There's only one bed."

"Not a problem. Look, it's king size, it's big enough for all of us," Josh said.

"Aw, you don't want . . . look, I can sleep on the floor, I don't mind."

"What's the matter, you don't think the three of us can fit?" Ziggy smiled. "Dude, don't argue. You don't have a vote in this. You're sleeping in the bed with us. We both want you to."

Franklin laughed. "Fine with me. If you're sure you don't mind. You guys are awesome."

"I got dibbs on the middle," Ziggy said.

"Don't you think we should flip for it?" Josh put his pack down. "You're the one who always says, 'fair is fair.'"

"Aw Josh, come on, let me be in the middle. I want to cuddle with both of you guys. You know how much I like that."

"I'm just kidding, Zig. You called it, you got it. Besides, we'll probably end up all over each other, anyway."

"We're gonna cuddle?" Franklin went over and felt the bed. "Oooh, I never done that before."

"Franklin, you gotta be kidding, dude."

"I ain't never had nobody to cuddle with."

"Not even your step-brother?"

"I wish. That woulda been nice. Never had a chance to. He slept in his own bedroom upstairs, and the couch was my bed."

"Aw, come on, you never got to double up with him, like when company visited from out of town?"

"Nobody ever came to visit. Not after my dad remarried."

"And you never, like, had a sleep-over with your best friend?"

"I wasn't allowed to have friends over. I guess I could have stayed over somebody *else's* house if I got my chores done. But I didn't have no friends like that. Nobody ever asked me to."

"Dude."

"I didn't have a lot of friends."

"Why not?"

"Hell, I don't know. I wanted friends. But the popular kids, they didn't want to have much to do with me. And some of the meaner guys, well, you know how that goes. They picked on me sometimes. I didn't know how to deal with it so I stayed clear of 'em as much as I could. If they'd have left me alone, hell, I might have made some friends. Lord knows I needed some."

"Aw, that's fucked up."

"Some folks treated me okay. But you know how school is. If you don't fit in, you're basically screwed."

"Tell you what," Ziggy said, "Let's go get some dinner somewhere; I'm starving."

—

THEY FOUND A RESTAURANT not too far away, sat down at a table, and ordered.

While they were waiting, Josh said, "Sometimes I think we were *all* clueless in school. Including high school. Take me for instance. I was so shy I hardly talked to anybody. Unless they talked to me first. And even then it was difficult. Nobody talked to me except for other nerds like me. I guess they noticed I didn't have many friends. Kindred spirits and all. But I found out later all the others thought I was being snobby! Clueless, all of us. Even the ones who had . . . social skills were too busy being popular to reach out to kids like me and you."

"Sounds familiar," Franklin said.

"And god help the poor kids who were labeled with some sort of reputation in younger grades, because it carries on through right into high school. Schools ought to have classes in how to . . . oh, I don't know, how to get along. With everybody. All those adults, trying to teach us stuff, and they end up neglecting some of the most important things we needed to learn."

"Like how to have thick hides?" Ziggy said.

"Yeah, for one. That would have been a welcome part of it."

"I think I was lucky to grow up in an orphanage," Zig said. "We looked out for each other. At the one I was in, anyway. It wasn't like a jail where the weak get picked on. The younger kids, and the new kids, they all got help from the rest of us. Hell, everyone got help when they needed it. We figured we were all in the same boat, so we helped each other survive. And if we got picked on in school we could laugh it off, because we knew we had friends back at the home."

"Kind of like the way a family is supposed to be," Franklin said.

"Yeah, well," Josh said, "sometimes even when you have a blood family, they're not there for you. So friends have to fill in. Sometimes you have to find your own family."

—

AFTER DINNER, when they returned to their hotel room, Franklin said he needed to shower before they went to bed. He stripped down to his briefs, but then he started to get a boner and got embarrassed about it. He went into the bathroom and closed the door.

Meanwhile Josh and Zig called Kevin and gave him an update, and then they settled in for the evening. Atlanta has plenty of activities of every kind to offer, but all they wanted was to snuggle together in bed – with Franklin, too – and recall some of the highlights of their vacation. The wonderful week with Kevin, of course, and also the pleasurable and surprising afternoon with Daniel before they drove down to Florida.

Josh called Tony to give him an update. In the morning they would drive on to Memphis and link up with him. Tony said he was already packed and ready to go. They called Daniel, too, to cheer him up and remind him about Christmas.

There wasn't much else the boys wanted to do. They stripped down to their underwear, got out the books they were reading, and waited for Franklin to finish his shower.

—

FRANKLIN CAME OUT with a towel wrapped around himself, and an unmistakable hard on. He thought they'd be in bed already, either waiting for him or else already asleep. Or making love. But Ziggy and Josh were sitting in their underwear, reading books.

"Gosh, you guys are still up? So, uh, what, are you gonna take showers too?"

"Yeah, dude, been driving all day."

"Okay, well, whoever's next, I'm done in there." Franklin turned toward the sink in an effort to hide his boner, but seeing the big tent in his towel in the mirror made him get even stiffer.

"We shower together," Ziggy said. He and Josh pulled off their briefs and Franklin, speechless, stared at their semi-hard dicks, their balls, their asses, their bare feet, every part of their naked bodies as they walked past him into the bathroom.

And they left the bathroom door open, too. Franklin didn't know what to think. He purposefully had not beat off while he was in the shower, just in case they all three would do something together in bed, even though he didn't actually expect it. But if those two were in the shower together, most likely they'd have sex in there. How could they not?

Franklin took his towel off in order to free up his boner. Naked and with his cock so stiff it ached, he turned on the TV with the volume turned low, and switched channels until he came to MTV.

He crept over near the bathroom door, his dick hard and throbbing, expecting to jerk off while he listened to Ziggy and Josh fucking in the shower. But from the sound of it, all they were doing was showering. Maybe washing each other's backs, maybe not. Just casually talking.

Franklin didn't know whether to be disappointed or glad.

If they'd been having sex he would have eagerly jacked off while listening to the grunts and groans and moans coming from the other side of the shower curtain.

They obviously hadn't had sex while Franklin was in the shower, so if they weren't fucking or sucking or some such thing now, maybe that meant they'd still be horny when they all went to bed.

Franklin decided to hold off on jerking a load out. Instead, he put on a clean pair of briefs, climbed into bed, and pulled up the covers. *We'll just have to wait and see,* he thought. *If nothin' else maybe they'll fuck, after they think I've fallen asleep. If they do, I can jack off then.*

He heard the shower stop, and the curtain pulled back, and a minute later Josh and Ziggy came out of the bathroom, bare-ass naked, toweling their hair dry while Franklin watched from the bed.

"What's that you've got on the tube, MTV?" Josh said.

"Yeah, I didn't think you'd mind. You can turn it off if you want."

"No, it's okay. When we go to sleep, yeah, but we can leave it on for a while. Do you have the remote control?"

"No, it's on top of the TV."

Josh, still naked, picked up the remote and brought it over to the bedside table. He turned on the lamp next to the bed, and tossed his towel over the chair.

Then Ziggy walked over to Franklin's side of the bed. "Comfortable?" he asked, as he finished drying himself off.

Franklin stared at Ziggy's cock. Were these guys always this casual? "Yeah, this bed's nice."

Josh walked back and turned the bathroom light off. "Are we going to bed now?" he said. "I'll turn off the overhead."

"Yeah," Ziggy said. "Go ahead."

Ziggy walked around to the other side and pulled back the covers. That's when he saw that Franklin was wearing briefs. And had a raging boner, but that was only natural.

"Dude, you sleep in your underwear?"

Franklin started blushing. "Well, not usually, but . . ."

"No, it's okay," Ziggy said. "Sorry. I need to learn to keep my mouth shut. No shame. That's one of our basic principles, no shame. Do whatever makes you feel comfortable, bro." Ziggy slipped into bed, naked, his own dick starting to fill out, and scooted over to the middle of the bed next to Franklin. He lay on his back with his hands behind his head and sighed.

"Jesus," Franklin said. "You're gonna sleep naked all night long?"

Chapter 52
THE CIRCLE TURNS

"YEAH." ZIGGY LAUGHED. "That's the way it usually works. Why, you want me to put my underwear on?"

"NO! I mean, uh, no, please, not on my account, I mean, please, sleep naked if you want. Oh, god, I think I'm gonna go crazy. Jesus."

"Dude, what's the matter?"

"Well, I really do want to take my underwear off."

"Well, go ahead."

"But you don't understand . . . I got a hard on."

"Aw, just take them off bro. Why not, if you want to? We don't care if you have a boner. No, let me rephrase that: we don't *mind* if you have a boner. Not at all. Boner's are a good thing."

"Oh . . . uh . . . fuck, okay." Franklin reached under the covers, awkwardly pulled his briefs off, and then he tossed them on the floor. There was a huge tent where, obviously, his hard-on was standing up nearly vertical. Franklin turned bright red with embarrassment.

Josh came over and climbed into bed next to Ziggy. "This is nice," Josh said. "I'm glad we all get to sleep together."

"And cuddle together," Ziggy said, grinning.

"We're really gonna cuddle?" Franklin said. "Oh, my god."

"Yeah, of course."

"That's . . . that's awesome, I guess. Uh, I was hopin' you weren't kiddin' about that. But holy fuck, I hope I can handle it. I think I'm gonna go nuts."

"Of course we're gonna cuddle. Is that gonna be a problem?"

"Uh, well, that's kind of why I left my underwear on. I'm gonna have a boner all night long, and . . . I didn't want it to be, you know, a . . . a nuisance."

"Dude, like I said, boners are a good thing. How could it be a nuisance?"

"Ah, I don't know, uh, you know. Maybe it would get in the way? It'll keep me awake, that's for sure. It might even go off in the middle of the night. And I, uh, well, I leak a lot of pre-jizz when I'm hard. I don't want to get everybody sticky. Jesus, I sure didn't know you guys slept naked. Is . . . is that all we're gonna do? Is cuddle?"

"Well, we always cuddle, but sometimes that's not all we do. You know how that goes. So, dude, you're saying a hard-on will keep you awake?"

"Uh, yeah. But that's okay."

"No, you need to get some sleep. I think we better do something to take care of it. What do you think, Josh?"

"Heck yeah."

"Got any ideas?"

"I'm horny too," he said. "How about if we have a circle jerk?"

Ziggy grinned. "Now you're talking."

"Oh Jesus, thank god. But what's a circle jerk?"

"Think about it, bro. Take a wild guess."

"Uh, we sit in a circle and jerk off?"

"Yeah, you got it. Basically."

"Fuck yeah! I'd love that," Franklin said. "Jesus, I'm gonna come twice just watchin' you guys shoot your loads. That'll be so hot. You can shoot 'em on me if you want to. I don't mind. God, I need to come so bad. Where do we sit, here on the bed?"

"Yeah, the bed'll work." Ziggy tossed the covers down to the foot of the bed. All three of them had big, hard boners. All three of their dicks were up in the air, stiff, throbbing, and exposed for all to see.

Franklin sat up on the bed and crossed his legs. "Is this how we sit?"

"Yeah," Ziggy said, "that's good." He and Josh moved around so all three of them were sitting next to each other in a circle. They looked around at each other, taking in everybody's equipment and its rigid state of arousal.

"This is gonna be cool," Franklin said. "Watchin' you guys beat off. Is it a race, or do we try to see who can last the longest?"

"It's definitely not a race. The longer it takes, the better. But actually," Josh said, "there's one more part of it we haven't mentioned yet. An important part. A traditional part. If you're willing. Only if you're willing, Franklin. We just learned about all this ourselves, while we were in Florida."

"Oh yeah? Fuck, go ahead, tell me. What is it?"

"Circle jerks go way back in time," Ziggy said. "From what we've heard they've been a tradition in college since the beginning. Especially in all-male dorms. But you don't have to be in college, of course. And it doesn't matter whether you're straight or gay. Either way, guys get horny and need to take care of it. They need to get their rocks off. You know how that is."

"I sure do. Of course I do."

"It gets pretty casual in the dorms. Walking back and forth in just their underwear. Some of them even go naked. And they see each other taking showers, stuff like that. They can't help but get horny. It's only natural. And the more guys there are, the hornier they get."

"I can believe that."

"So of course they all jerk off, most of them two or three times a day."

"I know they do. Fuck, they'd have to. I sure do."

"And it feels great, but sometimes a little change can make all the difference."

"Like what kind of change?"

"Like, somebody else's hand instead of your own."

"Oh god!" Franklin's eyes got big. "You're sayin' they . . ."

"Yeah. In a circle like this it's so easy. Just reach over and stroke the guy next to you. If we all do it then we all get stroked off by a different hand than our own."

"That's fucking brilliant."

"So, Franklin, are you ready?"

"Fuck yeah." Franklin was staring at Ziggy's cock, studying it. Then he looked at Josh's cock and took in every detail, watching it throb. Then he looked up. "Jesus. Uh, which way does it go? Who's cock do I get to jack off?"

"We can switch back and forth," Josh said. "That way we'll all get to do each other."

"Franklin, start with my cock, dude." Ziggy grinned. "Is that okay with you? And Josh, you take hold of his. Josh is good, Franklin, you'll find that out quick."

Josh reached over and wrapped his hand around Franklin's stiff boner.

"Ah." Franklin closed his eyes briefly and held his head back. "Oh, fuck. That feels great." Then he opened his eyes and slowly reached out for Ziggy. He carefully wrapped his fingers around Ziggy's hard shaft. "Fuck, I've been wantin' to do this all day," he said. "Damn Zig, you got a thick one."

Ziggy sighed. "Yeah, that's it, Franklin. Use some spit on it; make it slippery, bro."

Franklin put his hand up to his mouth, spat in it, and then put it back on Ziggy's hard dick. He held it loosely and let his hand slide up and down the soft skin.

"Yeah, like that," Ziggy said. "Perfect. Ahh."

Ziggy reached over and gently took hold of Josh's cock.

"Ahhhh," Josh said. "Yessss."

The talk dwindled as they continued stroking each other, adding spit when they needed to, but it didn't take long for all three of them to start oozing pre-cum, and that worked even better than spit.

"Don't know if I can hold off much longer like this," Franklin said. "I'm startin' to feel tingly all over."

"You want me to slow down?" Josh said. Without waiting for an answer he stopped stroking Franklin, but still kept his hand wrapped loosely around Franklin's leaking cock.

"Ain't you guys close? I'm about ready to pop, but I don't want to come yet," he said. "No need to hurry things. Feels great just doin' this."

"Yeah," Ziggy said, "let's make it last."

"When we *do* come, though, we all ought to come together."

"We can try," Josh said. "But it's no big deal. As long as we all come, that's good enough for me."

"I don't think that's gonna be a problem," Ziggy said, with a shiver. "The hard part's gonna be holding off. I could come in a heartbeat. Franklin, you're good at this."

"I've had lots of practice."

"On other guys?"

"Nope, on myself, duh." He grinned. "But this is much more fun."

"Guys, we ought to switch," Ziggy said. "Josh, you need to feel this. He's good. Plus I want to get my turn jacking his cock."

"Okay. Switch," Josh said. And just like that, they all changed direction.

Ziggy took his hand off Josh's hard dick; Franklin took hold of it instead. For a brief moment or two Franklin had both cocks, one in each hand. But he let go of Ziggy when Josh reached over to stroke Ziggy's balls.

Ziggy wrapped his hand around Franklin's boner and the circle was again complete.

Franklin shivered. "Oh god, Ziggy's holdin' my dick."

"You got a problem with that?" Ziggy grinned. Gently, he started stroking Franklin.

"No, but . . . aw, fuck!" Franklin started trembling. "Sorry, I . . . didn't think . . . I was so close – FUCK!" Franklin's cockhead got a little bigger and a trickle of cum leaked out, and then suddenly a huge spurt of thick, white cum shot out of his dick – "Unghh!" – all the way across and splattered onto Josh's arm.

Followed immediately by another thick rope of cum flying through the air. Ziggy kept stroking. He aimed Franklin directly toward himself, and Franklin, trembling and jerking in little spasms, launched at least a half dozen rapid-fire spurts of cum, most of them landing right on Ziggy's chest.

Franklin briefly stopped stroking Josh, but his hand remained clenched around Josh's cock. When Franklin's orgasm leveled off, he resumed stroking Josh, breathing heavily.

Ziggy held Franklin gently now, thinking his dick was probably too sensitive to keep stroking for the moment. Zig used his other hand to tickle Josh's balls while Franklin continued jacking Josh's dick.

Josh moved his hand briefly and smeared Franklin's cum around on Ziggy's chest, and then he put his hand back on Ziggy's cock, slimy and well-lubed now with fresh cum.

Zig gasped. "Oh fuck that feels good. You're gonna make me come."

"Go ahead and come then," Josh said. "I'm almost there too. I got a hand on my cock and a hand on my balls and I'm ready to come along with you."

"Shoot on me, guys," Franklin shouted.

Chapter 53
CLOSE TO THE EDGE

"JOSH, AIM HIM AT ME," Franklin said. "Please." Meanwhile he had Josh's cock pointed straight at his face. Franklin was going to get two hot loads squirted all over him, if things worked out right.

Ziggy started squirming, he was so close. Josh didn't let up; he quickly scooped up some more of Franklin's cum and kept on stroking Ziggy's cock, hard and slick and building to a climax. Zig went on fondling Josh's balls, moaning "That's it Josh, don't stop, I'm coming bro. Coming!"

Josh kept stroking Ziggy like it was his own cock about to explode, because in fact he was right on the verge himself.

Now that Franklin had shot his own load, he wanted both of them to come at the same time. When he heard Ziggy say, "I'm coming, bro!" Franklin gave it all he had, coaxing out the load he knew Josh had rising. And it worked.

"Coming!" Josh yelled. "Ooooh fuck, I'm coming!" Franklin kept stroking, leaning forward, putting his face directly in the line of fire of Josh's cock. Josh's cockhead expanded and then a great big spurt of cum shot out of it, splattering right on Franklin's forehead. And then another spurt followed, this time flying right into Franklin's open mouth.

Ziggy and Josh were coming together. Ziggy groaned as his first rope of cum shot out toward Franklin and splattered on his belly. Josh and Ziggy launched spurt after spurt of cum, together, all of it landing somewhere on Franklin's bare skin.

The coming seemed to last forever, but all too soon all three of them were exquisitely drained of all the cum they had – for now, at least.

They still sat in the circle, each with a hand on their neighbor's spent cock, breathing heavily and grinning as the last drops of cum dribbled out.

Finally Franklin said, "Jesus. I've never had so much cum on me in my life. Fuck, look at me, I'm covered with it."

Ziggy laughed.

Josh said, "Well, that's what you wanted, right?"

"Yeah. I sure did. That was so awesome." Franklin started licking it up, first what was on his arms, then scooping it off his face and licking that up, and then getting whatever he could off the rest of himself. "Fuck," he said, "you guys taste good. We need to do this again sometime."

"Fine with me," Josh said.

"Same here," Ziggy said. "When you move to St. Louis, dude."

"Cool. You know, you guys are my big bros, now." Franklin grinned. "Little bro is gonna want to learn how to make his big bros happy."

"Oh, that works both ways," Josh said. "We're gonna have to keep our little bro happy too."

—

AFTER THEY TOOK A QUICK shower – all three of them, together – they got into bed, pulled the covers up, turned off the TV, and turned off the lights.

"Now for the best part," Ziggy said, smiling. "Well, one of the best parts at least: cuddling."

"How . . . how does it work? I mean, do we just lie up against each other, or do we hold each other, or what?"

"We usually put our arms around each other."

"Oh god. For real?"

"Yeah, dude, for real. But there aren't any rules. We'll probably move around a bit during the night anyway, in our sleep. How do you want to start out? We usually fit ourselves together like spoons, front to back. The guy behind wraps his arms around the guy in front of him. So, what's your choice, Franklin? You hold me, or I'll hold you. Unless you have a better idea."

"No, that sounds great."

"Josh and I like to pretend one of us is the teddy bear. You know, like we had when we were little. Did you ever have one? A teddy bear you hugged up close when you went to sleep?"

"Yeah, a long time ago . . ."

"Did you cuddle up with him, keep him warm? Did he keep you warm?"

"Yeah. I kept him cozy warm. I loved that bear so much. He was my friend, my best friend in all the world."

"Okay, well, does that give you any ideas?"

"Yeah, but promise you won't laugh?"

"Promise."

"Will you hold me in your arms? Hug me up close, that's what I want. That's how I want to fall asleep. If Josh doesn't mind, that is. Only if Josh doesn't mind."

"Josh won't mind. He's gonna hold me the same way. Turn over on your side, Franklin. Yeah, like that. You're my teddy bear, all cuddly and warm and snug." Ziggy smiled. "I'm gonna hug you all night long. And Josh is gonna hug me close too. But if we turn in the middle of the night, Franklin, then you can hug me too, okay? I'd like that."

They were all side by side. Josh put his arm around Ziggy, and Ziggy wrapped his arm around Franklin. Josh's hand was pressed between Franklin's back and Ziggy's chest, and he gently rubbed both of them at the same time.

"This gonna work for you, Franklin?" Josh said.

"Oh yeah." Franklin sighed. "I'm so happy I think I'm gonna start cryin'. I can't remember the last time anybody held me like this."

"Sweet dreams, guys," Ziggy said.

Before long they were all in dreamland. Franklin was the last to fall asleep. He lay there, cuddled up inside Ziggy's arms for half an hour at least, too excited and happy to fall asleep yet. But finally he, too, relaxed in the comfort of friends who truly loved him.

Sunday

IN THE MORNING, after a good night's sleep, Josh awoke to find that Franklin was already awake. The covers had been pushed down so that all three of them were exposed. Franklin was sitting up, stroking. He was looking at Josh, and Zig, and stroking.

Franklin saw that Josh had woken up, but he didn't say anything. He just nodded his head and gently kept stroking. His cock was wet with pre-cum, and he looked as if he was close to having an orgasm, but doing his best not to come yet. He would stop stroking occasionally, wait a minute, and then start back in again.

Josh sat up, too. His dick quickly hardened from watching Franklin. Josh started stroking, too.

Soon enough, Josh, also, was wet with pre-cum. He was following Franklin's example; he took it to the edge, and then backed off so he wouldn't come yet.

They kept that up for at least ten minutes. Then Ziggy stirred a little, and opened his eyes.

He looked at Josh, stroking his wet cock, and then at Franklin, doing the same, and whispered, "Jesus." His dick filled out and raised up rigid. He sat up, and he started stroking too.

No one said anything. The only noises to be heard were of hands stroking hard, wet, slippery cocks, and an occasional whimper or sigh or moan of pleasure.

Chapter 54
CHATTANOOGA

THE THREE OF THEM SAT in bed next to each other and kept on stroking for at least another half hour or more. Watching each other. No one spoke. No one wanted to break the spell. And no one wanted to come yet. The longer they jacked – the longer they delayed it – the better it felt.

It was difficult, though. Each one of them, more than once, almost took it too far. That would have been fine, of course, but Franklin was doing something neither Ziggy nor Josh had ever seriously tried before.

Bringing themselves close to the edge, and then stopping, until they could start stroking again without coming. They weren't doing this for just a few minutes; they were extending the exquisite feeling longer than Ziggy or Josh had ever thought of trying. Letting the wave of pleasure roll in, and then letting it roll back. And then gently resuming stroking again. Over and over.

Franklin was learning something new, also. He was used to staying completely silent while he jacked off, and silent when he shot his load of hot cum. The first and only time, when living with his stepparents, he had moaned out loud when he came, he got in trouble for it.

His stepmother had banged on the bathroom door and asked him what the fuck he was doing in there.

Ziggy, on the other hand, had always made a lot of noise while he was having sex, and even more when he reached his climax. No one had ever complained. Zig was a natural joy to listen to – his pleasure was contagious.

Josh had picked up on it quickly when he moved in with Zig. Josh grew up in a family where sex was a forbidden subject, so he was used to keeping the volume down, but he gladly let that concern go after the first time he heard Ziggy come.

Now Franklin, while beating off with his two favorite people, was learning to let go. He let out a quiet moan occasionally, or some heavy breathing at first, but it wasn't long before he was moaning and groaning as loud as anyone. And delighted to be doing it.

Just when it was starting to look as if they could edge for hours, suddenly Ziggy yelled out, "Shit! Oh, fuck, I'm coming! Ohhhhhhh, fuck! Unnnghhh! Unnghh!" Franklin and Josh stopped stroking and watched Ziggy shoot a huge load of cum all over himself.

Zig's first spurt flew up and over his head. The second landed smack on the side of his face. And the rest of it, a dozen ropes of cum at least, landed all over his chest, belly, and finally, as he slowed down, on his hand, too. When he was done he let himself fall backward on the bed. "Jesus." He put his arm over his eyes. "Incredible."

Josh didn't want to wait any longer now that Ziggy had launched his load. Josh increased the gentle, tentative careful rubbing of his cock to a higher level. He got a good grip on his dick and stroked it up and down intensely like a piston. "Okay," he said, "here I go. No stopping now." He kept stroking. "Oohhhhhhhh," and then, "Unnngh!" when a huge spurt of cum shot out of his dick straight up in the air and hit the ceiling. The next spurt splattered on his chin, followed by so many shots of cum he thought he would never stop. But he finally calmed down as the flow eventually dwindled to a trickle.

"Dude. Not bad," Franklin said, who had stopped stroking to watch. "Guess it's my turn, huh?" He started stroking his dick again, moaning quietly. "Mmmmm. Oh, this feels good. Nothing . . . in . . . the world . . . like it. Unngh. Oh yeah. Oh fuck, here it comes guys." He stroked a couple more times and then said, "Yeah!" He moved his hands away and leaned back while they watched his cum spurt out of his cock, shot after shot, hands free. Accompanied by his new vocalizations: "Ungh! Unghh! Fuck! Oh, fuck!" His cumshots flew up into the air and landed all over himself from his feet on up to his belly. Finally he calmed down, as his spurts of cum slowed down and finally stopped.

Then they all looked at each other and started laughing.

"Christ," Ziggy said, "I have never in my life come like that before. That was incredible."

"I've never held off anywhere near that long," Josh said. "That was amazing."

"Ain't you guys ever edged before?" Franklin said.

"Is that what you call it? Edging?"

"That's what my stepbrother called it. Good name for it, eh?"

"How long have you been doing that?" Josh said.

"Oh, I dunno. Couple of years or more. Since the first time I got him to show me how to jerk off, basically. He'd been doin' it all along, he said. Before he even started makin' cum."

"Franklin, you're just full of surprises," Ziggy said. "I'm gonna miss you while you're in Knoxville."

"Me too," Josh said. "Not just because of this, either."

"If our apartment was bigger, bro, I might say don't wait, come on to St. Louis now with us. But that place is hardly big enough for two of us, let alone three. We'd need to find a bigger place."

"Aw, no, that's okay. Best I go to Knoxville first anyway. It'll give me a chance to get myself together. But thanks. That's a really nice thought."

"Let's get in the shower, guys. Wash all this cum off, and then we'll get some breakfast somewhere."

—

AFTER BREAKFAST they were back on the road, leaving Atlanta and on their way to Chattanooga.

Sleeping together had raised everyone's spirits. Franklin, especially, seemed more at peace, less worried in general. All three of the boys felt a greater connection than they had before. Franklin was fonder than ever of Ziggy and Josh. It was no surprise, then, if they all felt like part of a family. Zig and Josh saw a wider perspective, too: on this vacation trip they had also welcomed Daniel into their little clan, and then in Florida, Kevin had become another part of the growing family.

Would Josh's friend, Tony, in Memphis, be part of the tribe? Only time would tell. It seemed likely. But all the guys were so far away from each other. Would they actually get to meet each other? And if so, when?

If Josh and Ziggy had anything to do with it, the whole big family would meet together, somehow, and the sooner the better. How and when was still to be determined, but in the meantime, they could all talk to each other on the phone and write to one another – share their selves by chatting, get to know each other that way.

—

THE CLOSER THEY got to Chattanooga, the quieter the boys got. As hopeful as the future seemed, they weren't looking forward to parting so soon. But Franklin had his cousin waiting for him. Knoxville was the first step in a greater plan. And in the other direction, of course, Josh and Ziggy had home and jobs to return to.

The good thing, the hopeful thing, was that they'd taken such a liking to each other they knew they would stay in touch. They knew they would meet again, one way or another, and in the meantime there were letters and phone calls to keep them connected.

There was another thing, though, that didn't sit right about splitting up: turning Franklin out on the road to hitchhike. He would be at the mercy of strangers, the good will of random people driving by. Franklin seemed to be used to it, but they all knew there was a certain amount of danger. Someone might hurt him. And he might have to sleep outside somewhere if no one picked him up. And there was always the chance a cop would arrest him for vagrancy, or even accuse him of something worse.

As they drove into Chattanooga, Josh wondered out loud how much a Greyhound bus would cost to Knoxville. Right away it was an option they wouldn't let go. Franklin tried to discourage the idea. He said he was fine with hitchhiking, and in any case didn't have the money to spare for a bus ticket and didn't want to accept charity from his new friends. But the votes were against him.

So they stopped at the bus station. They checked the bus fare and it was low enough they didn't even need to discuss it. Josh and Ziggy wouldn't take no for an answer – they bought Franklin a bus ticket to Knoxville, and so it was decided. They wanted him to get there safely.

—

THE THREE FRIENDS sat down in the bus terminal's waiting room, chatting one last time before parting. The next bus for Knoxville was due in only half an hour, so Zig and Josh would wait it out.

What they talked about didn't matter so much – they had already said what needed to be said, shared what they wanted to share – their affection for each other, and their plans to meet again.

So they sat and relaxed and shared memories from their childhood. Ziggy and Josh told Franklin a bit about St. Louis and D.C. Franklin, in turn, told them a few stories about his real dad and when they lived in Arkansas.

Then came the announcement that his bus had arrived. "Time to say goodbye," Franklin said. He had tears in his eyes. "This don't seem right, leavin' you guys. It ain't what I want to do. But I have to."

"It's part of the plan," Josh said. "You'll be seeing us again before you know it. And you have our phone number, so call us, Franklin. Collect. Anytime you want."

Ziggy's eyes were just as shiny with tears. "That's right, call us – you damn sight better, or we'll be coming after you. We know where you live – we've got your cousin's address, dude." Ziggy was smiling – or trying to.

"Don't worry," Franklin said. "I'll call you guys tomorrow night, okay? You'll be home by then, right?"

"Should be. We're gonna try to get an early start in the morning, so, yeah."

"I'll give you my cousin's phone number when I call. In case you want to call me sometime."

"Fuck yes. You'll probably be having such a good time out there you'll forget to call us."

"Damn it, now, Zig, you know better than that. If I don't call every single day it'll be because I'm workin' two jobs. Leastwise I hope I will be. The faster I save up some money the sooner I'll be back with you guys. In person. You're my best friends. Shit, I ain't gonna forget to call."

"Aw, I was just kidding bro. I know you will."

"What about school? Will you have time for that?"

"I'll figure somethin' out. Right now I'm thinkin' maybe I'll hold off on that until I get to St. Louis. I gotta look into it. We'll see. I'll let you know what's up. We can talk about it, okay?"

—

AFTER BIG HUGS and a few tears, Franklin boarded his bus. They waved as they watched him drive off.

"I'm glad we talked him into taking the bus," Josh said.

"Damn right," Ziggy said. "Fuck, I'll be worrying enough about him as it is. I'd be chewing my fingernails if we'd let him hitchhike."

"Aw, Zig, I'm worried, too, but I don't know why. Franklin's smart. You know he is. He knows how to take care of himself – probably better than we do."

Ziggy sighed. "Yeah, I know. Backwoods little fucker is smarter than either one of us. He'll be alright."

They walked back to their car.

"You drive this time, Josh, okay?" Ziggy tossed him the keys.

##

If It Feels Good is the second novel about Ziggy and Josh. The young men first meet in *Try Anything Twice*, published in May 2011.

Josh Jango grew up in the Maryland suburbs of Washington, D.C. He moved to Memphis, spent some time in St. Louis, and continued westward to the Pacific Northwest, where he still lives.

Josh Jango
jj@joshjango.com

Chapter Titles

1 Hitchhiker
2 Family
3 Balls
4 Road Trip
5 The Rocks
6 Above the Rocks
7 Don't Stop
8 As in Motion
9 Always Wanted To
10 Too Much
11 Confusion
12 Demonstration
13 Licked
14 Show Me
15 Preparation
16 First Lick
17 No Promises
18 It's a Good Thing
19 Getting Into It
20 Ignition
21 Barely Enough
22 Early Rise
23 Florida
24 Route A1A
25 And Everything
26 Stuck
27 Pulled In

28 Revealing
29 Exhibition
30 Skinny-Dip
31 Open Tonight
32 Teddy Bears
33 Spirit
34 Initiate
35 Like Us
36 Circular Motion
37 Open Up
38 Ocean Beach
39 Celebrate
40 Lucky
41 Twilight
42 Sharing of Water
43 Who's Next
44 Brothers
45 Small World
46 Onward
47 Glory
48 Dreams
49 Interview
50 Get a Grip
51 Showers
52 The Circle Turns
53 Close to the Edge
54 Chattanooga

www.ingramcontent.com/pod-product-compliance
Lightning Source LLC
Chambersburg PA
CBHW050617110726
47899CB00001B/142